After Everything You Did

Stephanie Sowden grew up in Manchester and studied History and Politics at Durham University. After a brief foray into magazine journalism, she retrained in another love of hers – food – and now runs her own catering company. Stephanie took part in Curtis Brown Creative's selective novel writing course, during which she completed her first novel. She lives in South Manchester with her partner, Dave, and their little mad staffy, Butter.

After Everything You Did

STEPHANIE SOWDEN

CANELO
US

San Diego, California

Canelo US
An imprint of Printers Row Publishing Group
9717 Pacific Heights Blvd, San Diego, CA 92121
www.canelobooksus.com

Printers Row Publishing Group is a division of Readerlink Distribution
Services, LLC. Canelo US is a registered trademark of Readerlink
Distribution Services, LLC.

This edition originally published in the United Kingdom in 2022 by
Canelo.

Published in partnership with Canelo.

Correspondence regarding the content of this book should be sent to Canelo
US, Editorial Department, at the above address. Author inquiries should be
sent to Canelo, Unit 9, 5th Floor, Cargo Works, 1–2 Hatfields, London SE1
9PG, United Kingdom, www.canelo.co.

Publisher: Peter Norton • Associate Publisher: Ana Parker
Art Director: Charles McStravick
Senior Developmental Editor: April Graham
Editor: Traci Douglas
Production Team: Beno Chan, Julie Greene

Library of Congress Control Number: 2023942022

ISBN: 978-1-6672-0655-4

Printed in India

28 27 26 25 24   1 2 3 4 5

For Mum & Dad – for everything

Prologue

March 1966

It was a slow amble toward consciousness.

The world gradually brightened – sound crept in down her ear canal, light pried apart her lashes, demanding entrance. Sleep encrusted her eyelids and she felt them crunch as they pulled apart, one eye refusing her effort, her skin weighed down by fatigue. The square grey ceiling tiles blurred into detail.

She didn't recognise them.

But then, she wasn't sure what she would recognise. She turned her head to one side and a soft pain pushed into her from beneath thick bandages. A worn green curtain was pulled around her, the sound of someone clattering about on the other side.

She was in a bed, she realised that now. Outstretched on a thin, firm mattress, her sore head propped up by a flat pillow. In fact, her entire body was sore. Her skin itched and burned, her joints ached, her insides rumbled.

A phantom piece of fluff flittered around her nose. Her face was swaddled heavily in dressings and bandages, but the tip of her nose itched all the same. Instinct moved her hand.

Metal stayed her wrist.

Another attempt. Another rattle of metal against metal.

She was shackled. Handcuffed to the bed.

What the *fuck* had happened?

The sound of the curtain pulling back, light aluminium coils against their rail, the swoosh of cheap fabric. 'Ah, you're awake then,' a voice said. Impassive, professional. Not the sympathetic tone she would expect, considering. A white tunic moved closer and inspected the tubes snaking into her arms, its host marking something down on a clipboard.

'How are you feeling?' the voice demanded.

She opened her mouth but sandpaper scratched against her vocal cords. A dry gurgle scraped out.

'There's water here for you,' the nurse said, picking up a plastic tumbler and holding it against her cracked lips. The water tasted stale and warm. It must have been out since she'd arrived.

When *had* she arrived? That question had no answer that would make sense. Time was immaterial. Days, months, years, were blanks.

What had happened before the hospital? She could conjure a general image of the world – buses, roads, televisions, restaurants, trees, people – but couldn't place herself in it. She understood the concept of the hospital. She knew the nurse was there to help her. She knew that something bad had happened for her to be there. But she didn't know what or why. Or even *who*. It would come back to her. Of course it would.

An entire life didn't just disappear.

The water moistened her throat a little and she found she could just about make a guttural sound moulded into words. 'What happened?' she finally asked after several failed attempts.

The nurse paused for a moment and sighed. 'You were in a car crash on the I-75, heading down to South Florida. I can't really tell you any more than that now.' Her voice was still hard, no words of comfort for the patient lying at her mercy. 'Agents Willow and Stephens have been alerted that you're awake. They'll be here for you soon.'

Agents? Oh yes, the handcuffs. She moved her wrist again just to make sure she remembered those correctly. They rattled obediently.

'Why?' she asked, the single syllable a struggle.

The nurse stopped what she was doing for the first time and looked down at her, a curious frown on her face. After a moment's scrutiny she spoke. 'I'd say you probably already know that.'

After that she fell asleep.

She didn't know how long for – how could she? But she felt more human, more conscious when she awoke again. Her mind was blank but sharp, her body still fractured and agonising. This time there were two suited men occupying her space. One sat in the chair to her left, one pacing at the end of her bed, his tie loosened around his throat so tufts of dark curly hair poked free from his shirt.

'Welcome back, Reeta,' the seated one said. The other stopped pacing and looked at her, an expression of anticipation and relief flooding his features. 'We've been waiting a long time to talk to you.' The one in the chair leaned forward so his dark blue jacket fell open a touch, revealing a holstered weapon and metallic shield.

She didn't speak.

Didn't have anything to say.

'I'm Agent Stephens,' the standing man said and nodded at his seated colleague, 'and this here is Agent

Willow. And like he said, we've been waiting a long time for this.'

'For what?' she croaked.

Stephens chuckled silently, a quick shake of the head. 'For you to wake up. We've been on your trail since Mississippi.'

Willow chimed in, a sinister note of satisfaction etching the outline of his words. 'We've been close to you all the way, building our file, just waiting for this moment' – he stabbed a chubby forefinger at her – 'right here. We knew it would come. No one can run forever, Reeta.'

Reeta. That must be her name.

Reeta.

Reetareetareetareeta.

No matter how many times she rolled the name over, it snagged on nothing. But it must be hers. She clung to it like a buoy in open water. Something must be connected to the ground to stop her from drifting madly.

'Reeta.' She tried it out, the sound new and alien in her mouth. She coughed a little and tried again. 'Reeta.' The two agents looked at each other, suspicion creasing their eyes.

'Yes, that's right. And we'd love a family name if you have one for us?'

'Reeta,' she said again.

'It doesn't matter.' Willow, or was it Stephens? Whichever one was seated. He sat back and adjusted his jacket accordingly. 'We don't think you're registered anyway. It doesn't stop the wheels of justice from turning, Reeta. No name doesn't mean no crime.'

'What crime?' she asked. Was she the victim? The handcuffs suggested otherwise.

Stephens laughed, a surprising, hard sound.

'We'll let you get away with that this time – you've only just woken up.' He put his hands on the metal bar at the end of her bed and leaned forward with all his weight, so her head tipped up ever so slightly. 'But my advice to you is to show some remorse, some *respect* to those girls. There's no getting away now so at least do the decent thing.' His voice swam with vitriol. He *hated* her.

After that they left her, promising to return tomorrow.

She must have slept that first night. But she never recalled the usual settling down to rest as her mind slowly turned over the events of the day until, at last, it fell to peace.

What the agents had said made no sense to her – what girls? Why did she need remorse or respect for them?

What could she have possibly done?

The next day they returned, as promised, and still she had nothing to tell them. Stephens, the dark-haired one with a thick moustache and olive complexion, smacked his entire body weight onto the end of her bed when she told them she didn't know what they were talking about. Her body tensed at the unexpected rough movement and she released a groan into the room. The nurse on the other side of the curtain did nothing.

Days like these followed one after the other, like a trail of kindergarteners being led, confused, across a dangerous highway, with no one there to guide or help them. She only had Stephens' aggression batted against Willow's silent hatred for company.

A week passed before the doctor finally sat down to talk to her. He'd popped in and out to check on her progress, but she'd barely been conscious enough to hold a proper conversation. A plastic cup of orange juice was at her lips when the short, balding man with a halo of white hair had pulled back the curtain to step inside. She was propped up in bed, limbs briefly relinquished from their pain by the morphine drip at her side.

'Ah, Reeta,' he said, double-checking his chart as if he didn't already know exactly who lay in this bed on ward 4a. 'I'm pleased to see you're up. How are you feeling?'

She shrugged, a small movement that caused her to wince. 'Better every day. But still like I've been hit by a truck.'

The doctor permitted himself a small smile. 'Well, you're not far off that.' He let out a sigh. 'Physically, you're recovering well. I should think in another week or so we'll have you out of here. But' – he sat down on the chair Agent Willow favoured for his visits and placed his clipboard sideways across his lap – 'we need to discuss your psychological recovery. I hear from the nurses, and the agents, that you still claim to have no memory of the events that brought you here.'

'No, none.'

'And how about your life before? Anything at all ringing a bell?'

'It's a total blank. I only know my name because one of the agents told me.' Her eyes grew hot with the prickle of tears. 'No – my family haven't come to visit, have they?' She asked the question she'd been holding back, fearful of the answer.

The doctor lowered his eyes for a moment. 'Reeta, I may be speaking out of turn here, but I must warn you that even if you have no recollection, you can, and will, still be charged for your crimes. And if you continue with this charade then you may not even get the chance to defend yourself.'

'What charade?' Anger bubbled into her tears. Why would she fake this? What possible reality could be worse than the total rejection of her entire life? 'I – don't – know – anything.' She hiccupped the words. 'Doctor, please, you have to help me. There has to be something you can do.'

He remained silent for several moments, scrutinising her closely. 'If,' he began, 'I confirm this diagnosis, things will not play out as simply as you may be hoping for. If you recover your memory today, or tomorrow, or next week before you are taken from our care then you may have the chance to explain yourself. I'm sure there are avenues your lawyers can advise you on. But you will lose that opportunity if you continue with this… this… memory loss.' He looped his hand vaguely in the direction of her head.

'It's not my choice,' she said, her voice wailing, pleading, her face sodden. 'I just can't remember anything.'

'Very well, Reeta.' The doctor stood up. 'I'll be back tomorrow to see how you're doing.'

And he was.

And for nine more days until she was deemed fit enough to be discharged, a reluctant diagnosis of retro-grade amnesia finally added to her file.

'She may start recalling memories at any time,' the doctor had told the agents as they unshackled her wrists, trying to avoid looking directly into her face. The nurse had gently handed her a mirror earlier that day, warning that the sight was not an easy one. Yellow bruises smothered her left side and the swelling from her splintered jaw gave an uneven silhouette. But it was the tangled mess of healing flesh on her right that she knew caused the agents to avert their gaze. One eye permanently damaged by a thick, deep gash, her cheek torn and churned from within, thick black stitches tracking their way across her features. Only her blonde hair – now partly shorn – apparently remained a constant feature to the photographs they kept talking about.

They said they had their girl, though.

That was all that mattered.

–

'Get me those girls,' US Attorney Crawley snarled, smacking a tense fist against his thigh. He stared through the one-way glass to the interview room as if sheer will alone could get the answers he needed.

'Better to let her think she's winning,' Willow said, sipping his burnt coffee that tasted too much like the cigarettes he was trying half-heartedly to give up. 'Let her think we've bought this whole "amnesia, injured little girl" act. She'll let her guard down, slowly start slipping up, and that's when we'll get her.'

'We've already got her,' Crawley snapped, nodding through the glass. 'She's ours now, no more running, no more chasing. I have my case, but I want those bodies – I don't want any unanswered questions when I get her on trial.' He turned away from the window and stared at Willow, tension pinched around his eyes, purple bags dragging them down.

'We'll get them,' Stephens said, standing from where he'd been perched against a desk. 'I want to nail the little bitch as much as you.' He glanced at Willow. 'We both do.'

Stephens' anger ricocheted off the walls. His last question languished in the interrogation room, his face looming into hers, fists gripped rigidly on the edge of the table.

'I... I... I don't know,' she spluttered, trying to keep tears from falling down her cheeks. Her whole body shook, her grey smock and trousers doing nothing to keep the air-con from penetrating her goose-fleshed skin. There were no comfy knitted blankets now she was out of hospital, just scratchy old wool that did nothing to keep the night-time draughts at bay but swathed her in humid sweat come dawn. Her limbs shivered constantly.

'Where are they?' Stephens repeated. 'You can't play this game forever, Reeta. You *will* be found guilty no matter what – your life is over. Death penalty case this, textbook. But' – he sat back down in his chair, visibly calming his rage – 'if you show remorse, some semblance of humanity, then we can help. We can get the US Attorney to commute the sentence, seek life instead of death. You're fucked, Reeta. It's up to you by how much.'

'I don't even know who they are. I don't even know who *I* am. I sit in my cell at night and replay all of these... these questions that you ask me that don't make any sense. But I didn't, I didn't do it!'

'With all due respect, Reeta.' Willow leaned forward. 'If you can't remember – how do you know you didn't?'

Reeta inhaled sharply, his question a punch to the throat. Silence swaddled them for a moment.

'I... I guess I don't.'

Part I

Criminal

May 1966

One

The door clanged shut behind him and Barry allowed himself a flinch at the sound. Every time he came here it was the same, but this client *really* freaked him out. He was out of his depth here. The way she sat across from him, staring out from one good eye and another half-hidden by scar tissue, her mangled face twisted into an expression of God-knows-what. Every question was met with a blank stare or 'I don't know'. Occasionally he'd see what he'd think were tears shimmering, but then he'd look back down at his file and know he must be mistaken.

'Reeta,' he said, voice gravelly with the packet of cigarettes he smoked every day. He'd only been out of law school five years, two of those spent at a small firm out in the Tallahassee sticks. When the managing partner died of a stroke, he'd taken the opportunity to move out to the big city and make a name for himself in the public defender's office. It had been a mistake so far – and his mother, friends, even the fiancée he'd left behind had all been right in the end. His big dreams were beyond him, and he had only himself to blame for trying. It had been three years of sticking up for crooks and wife-beaters, finding holes in flimsy stories and exploiting an overworked police force's small errors. He'd seen at least four clients go free who he'd never want to share a street with and bargained down dozens more so they'd be out before their crimes had even had chance to settle on their polluted minds.

But Reeta.

She was something else. Now he knew why no one else in his department had fought him for the case. Four murder charges but only two young, blonde bodies, and surely a case of mistaken arrest. Finally, he'd thought, he'd nabbed an innocent client. For what twenty-year-old girl, with the same long, blonde tresses as her supposed victims, could really be capable of the brutalisation that was evident on the bodies the FBI *did* have? The file in his hands could never match the frightened, once-pretty girl in front of him.

But this girl had something blank behind her eyes. Where the compassion and lightness of youth should shine out, there was nothing. His Catholic mother would say the girl had no soul. And if you had no soul then surely the crimes that packed his brown cardboard file would not be given a second thought.

The agents had briefed him on her amnesia ploy, one Barry had never seen before. He now spent his nights re-reading old law school textbooks, drowning in the complexities of a federal case with a suspect with amnesia. It didn't help that she'd taken it upon herself to waive her right of a grand jury verdict as well as her right to have him present whenever the FBI fancied an interrogation. Not that she really had much to say, but still, he'd rather be in the room than reading their memos after the fact.

'Reeta,' he said again, watching her gaze wander from his face and over to the breeze-block wall behind him. 'Reeta, please, you've got to listen to me. I'm on your side. They want Mandy and Susan – first and foremost, that's their main concern. If we can give them that then things might be looking a lot cleaner for you. We can plea down to life imprisonment, even less, perhaps – twenty, twenty-five years if we get lucky. And that would be close to miraculous for a quadruple federal first-degree murder case, not to mention the kidnapping and attempted murder charges.'

He leaned forward across the table, hoping that a closer proximity might hold her attention. 'They're getting desperate. They want to deliver those daughters back to their families and we can really make that work for us. But we have to use it now.' He jabbed a finger onto the table. 'The longer we hold off, the angrier they'll get, and then they'll forget about ever wanting to make a deal.' He stared intently at her face for several more protracted moments before slamming his body back into his chair, bringing the balls of his palms to press into baggy, blueish eyes. His belly strained against his white shirt, a product of late-night junk food binges while peeling through Reeta's case, hoping for salvation somewhere among the smudged black typewriter ink. He hadn't had a chance to go the barber, and his thick chestnut hair was overgrown, his moustache equally ungroomed above thin, grey lips. This girl was slowly destroying him.

'I can't give you anything,' she said finally, a scratchy whisper in the interview room. 'I won't change my story because I *can't* change it. I don't know where they are. I don't even know them. I don't *know* what happened to any of them.'

'You don't *know*?' Barry lost his cool – felt his composure slide immediately from his frazzled body and crash to the floor in an icy splash. 'I'll goddam tell you what happened!' He stood abruptly, knocking his chair down behind him, and began to flick through the file on the table in front of him with one hand. The other hand punctuated his words with vicious finger-stabs in Reeta's direction. 'Hammer blows to the cranium, fourteen in total. Stab wounds to chest, abdomen and back, *nineteen* in total.' He flicked a few more pages over. 'Strangulation marks, fractured collarbones, broken noses, smashed jaws, fingers…' He stumbled as he got to this one, forefinger paused shakily over the medical examiner's report. '…*torn* off. *Torn*, Reeta.' He faltered, his voice quieting as he fell back and looked at her pleadingly. 'Torn.'

She didn't look up. Her gaze stayed trained on her own fingers on the table in front of her, tapping out an uneven rhythm.

'I didn't do any of that,' she said finally. 'I couldn't.' But her voice wavered.

He pressed on. 'Countless witness statements describe you befriending the victims in the weeks before their disappearances. You were found in the driver's seat while your next victim was locked in the trunk of the car you wrapped around the tree that gave you those injuries.' He gestured up at her face. He'd told her all this before. Maybe one day it would sink in.

Barry left her, as he always did, an hour later as disillusioned and stressed out as he had been when he'd arrived. As usual, she was sending him back to the office, to the team her case had been assigned, with no news. Only that the case would go to trial and she would get the chair, while Mandy and Susan's families watched grieving and dissatisfied from the public gallery.

–

After Barry's grey suit had disappeared through the metal door held open by the guard, another two guards entered in his place. One fitted manacles to her ankles, while the other fixed her handcuffs in place, before taking the chain his colleague passed up from her feet to wind around the handcuffs' links and pass back down to be shackled onto the clips in between her legs. It was the same every time. A bleak ballet performed around her body any time she had to travel to or from her cell. They guided her shuffling and unspeaking down the corridors clanging with the din of confined women, directly to her cell to undo the dance of incarceration. She never gave the guards a problem, never mouthed back, never struggled or started a fight. Not like some of the inmates in there. Reeta Doe was docile and quiet, and apparently exactly the type to have a secret penchant for stacking up young women's bodies. *It's always the quiet ones*, she'd heard the guards knowingly laugh to one another as she passed by at mealtimes.

Supposedly too dangerous to be permitted to share with another felon, Reeta was at least afforded her own cell. But she felt like a primed fluffy mouse compared to the big cats that stalked the other cells on her corridor – unable to believe that her two normal, soft-looking hands could be capable of the things the agents, guards, hell, even her own lawyer told her. She'd grown a fascination with her hands since her time in jail, become obsessed with mentally documenting anything notable about them: any flake of dried skin, any slightly dented nail, any scar that predated her hospital stay – murky reddish-brown against harmless pink skin. And every time she performed this ritual, running her eyes formulaically up and down each finger and thumb, zigzagging across each palm, looping around to the freckled back and swooping down toward each nail bed, she found herself forgetting even more.

These hands told a story, but it was a story she didn't know.

Still no family had shown up for her, and no one had told her anything about herself. Her lack of memory was deemed a sham, and every conversation was a test as they waited for her lies to be rumbled. That was yet to happen, and all that filled her memory up until that moment waking in the hospital was a deep, cold blank.

Today had been hard.

She hated when he read out the descriptions, as if that would jog her memory and suddenly she could give them all what they wanted. She would die at the hands of the government, and the only life she'd ever have lived would be right here in this cell. She kicked off her prison-issue slippers and leaned back against the hard brick wall, her tailbone digging painfully into the wire spools of her thin mattress. Her hand slid underneath the papery pillow and retrieved the folded newspaper clipping one of the big cats had dropped on her breakfast tray two days ago in the dining hall.

'Looks like you're famous, sweetheart,' the inmate had said, her straggly red hair a bird's nest atop crinkled features as she puckered her lips to blow a kiss.

The College Girl Who Slayed Her Own by Carol Joyce.

The headline had smudged a little under the constant touch of Reeta's fingertips, as she ran her oily skin across the ink. She'd never brought herself to read it through in full, the thousand-word article filling a neat square box with two black and white pictures front and centre. The legend beneath the posed school photographs read: *Amanda Silas and Susan O'Donnell, who remain missing.*

Snatches of sentences bounced out at her, meaningless words recounting a monster she didn't know.

'Traumatised friends of Amanda…'
'…hung around us constantly…'
'Bruising consistent with strangulation…'
'Ripped flesh in place of a ring finger…'

Reeta wouldn't allow herself to fully understand this case. She didn't need to know what was done to whom.

Could she really be capable of these things?

Inside she felt hollow. No personality lingered, no feeling of happiness or stress or calm or anger filled the void. She felt only weakness. She tried to access the feelings of hate or fury that would surely drive someone to do these things, but she couldn't. She couldn't find a malevolent fascination with the macabre, or a perverted desire for blood and gore. She rooted deep into her absent character and could come up with nothing but empty space. Was a person really only formed by their experiences in life? Surely there must be something remaining of who she once was.

She closed her eyes and allowed the tears to spill down her cheeks, her grip on the paper relaxing.

Each night she did this exercise in self-reflection. And each night, the person she felt she was – deep down inside – was good.

Two

Agent Willow visited alone this time. She didn't ask where Stephens was. They sat across from each other, the black metal table between them, the usual sounds of prison life boiling the air.

His new tactic was to fill the room with a suffocating absence of questions, a silence so thick she could feel it fill her lungs. When they spoke to her, harassed her, begged for information, she could tune out their words and listen blithely as if they were just telling a story – one of those radio dramas the older inmates insisted on listening to in the rec room. Just a tale to follow along with, not details of her supposed life. But this new strategy gave her nothing but time to think and consider. Willow watched her intently, narrowing his eyes at every sigh, every movement, waiting for her to speak the first word.

It surprised them both when his patience paid off.

Her voice creaked like a door opening for the first time in a hundred years.

'I really don't remember where they are,' she said.

'But you admit that you once did know?'

She sighed with almost a laugh of surrender and looked up at him. Feeling the sting of tears, she opened her arms out wide to the side. 'If you say it, then I guess so.' She pulled her shoulders into a tense shrug and inhaled deeply.

'I have nothing to give you, nothing. But if I did the things you say I did then I guess I do deserve the chair.'

Willow twitched a frown but remained quiet.

'You must see so many killers in your job,' she continued. 'You probably know their minds better than anyone. Was I just *born* with a bad brain? I can't feel it if I was. I *care*, I *feel*, I hate hearing about what happened to those girls.' She spat out the sentence as she gestured to Willow's file. 'I *want* to tell Mandy and Susan's families where they are. I can't imagine the pain of losing someone like that. Even though' – she gave a loud sniff as she attempted control over her sobs – 'I guess I don't have anyone to lose.'

Willow leaned forward onto his elbows. The movement was more than just a casual readjustment. 'What makes you say that?'

'Because nobody's been.' She said it quietly, through a curtain of tears. 'No visitors, no letters.' She felt her chest tighten and her breaths came quicker and faster. 'No... no fucking phone calls!' The curse leaped out of her – it felt good. Something felt off about the word on her tongue; maybe it was the institutionalism of her current situation, but it felt wrong, rebellious, *freeing* to scream it. 'Fuck!' she shouted again, laughing loud. 'Fucckk!'

Willow, to give him his due, didn't respond.

'Where are they?' she asked, her confidence riled. 'Where are my family, my loved ones? Why has no one claimed me? I may not remember them, but I *have* to have someone.' Her tone wilted. 'I have to. Everyone in here does.'

Willow scrutinised her for a moment and sat back so his fair hair shimmered under the white industrial lights.

'You know, you sure are putting on a good show of this memory loss.' He dug his hand into the inside pocket of his suit jacket. It was dark navy, with a flash of a silver lining as he pulled it open. From the pocket he retrieved a small rectangle of thick paper. 'I've been keeping this in here whenever we meet. Waiting for the opportune time. Now, I don't know if I'm playing my hand too soon here' – he pulled the sides of his mouth down in an unknowing gesture – 'but I figure now's a good a time as any if it'll help hurry things along.'

He put the paper down on the table in front of him and spun it around to face her but didn't move it forward. She blinked at him and extended her forearm, placed her middle finger on the centre of what she could now see was a photograph and slid it closer. She looked down into the smiling face of a not-quite middle-aged man with shoulder length blonde hair, murky green eyes, a sandy-reddish beard and baggy denim shirt. He was posing proudly on a high-backed wicker chair, which looked to be on the porch of a plantation-style home. She consumed every grain of the image, memorising it, scanning it, chiselling it into her grey matter. This man was someone to her – her father? She looked up at Willow, eyes pleading, desperate for more.

'Who is it?' she asked, eyebrows furrowed determinedly together. 'Please. You have to tell me.'

–

Willow watched her carefully. Her skinny body hunched forward, swathed in its dark grey tunic, patches of dirty blonde tendrils brushing the table. He'd hoped for a visceral response. A start, a clear sign of recognition. But she'd given him nothing.

Genuinely nothing.

She didn't recognise the photograph in her hand. Surely her act couldn't be so refined that natural instincts of shock could be so easily suppressed. He had taken a leap, one that Stephens would never have sanctioned. But Stephens was off again for his wife's chemotherapy, and Crawley had been turning the screw of pressure to get an answer about where the two missing bodies were. Reeta's first two victims had been found in wooded, rural areas around an hour's drive from their last witness sighting. Uncovered by a dog walker and a maintenance worker, their bodies had remained hidden only long enough for the culprit to get out of town and on toward her next victim. But the landscape was against them – vast and remote – and as she'd driven down into Mississippi and then Alabama, it had become near impossible to locate a reasonable search area. Witnesses of her with the missing victims were thin on the ground; they'd been snatched alone, seemingly out of thin air and there was no clue about any direction she might have taken them. He'd taken a punt on a forest about forty-five minutes away from the Mississippi State College for Women, but the dogs had come up with nothing and he'd frittered away even more of their budget.

Stephens would never have permitted this silent interrogation technique, preferring instead to bluster and bully until he got the answers he wanted. But his way wasn't getting them any answers. So Willow had taken advantage of Stephens' difficult family situation to do things *his* way. Run things subtly, quietly, eke out detail by detail and be grateful for whatever information trickled their way. This was the first step.

Or it was meant to be.

She was meant to start with shock, or freeze with recognition, or even break down and beg for information on where he was. Was he OK? Had he got in touch? But she'd done none of those things. Just desperately soaked in the image and looked beseechingly up, craving another droplet of a clue to her life.

'Who is it?' she repeated and looked down to run her fingers around the outline of the man's face.

'It's Jeb.' Willow tried again, analysing her reaction. Nothing.

'Jeb?' she asked mildly, as if she'd barely heard the name amongst her desperation for the picture.

'I think we'll leave it there for today.' Willow stood abruptly and rested the tips of his fingers on the top of the table.

Reeta's head snapped up. 'What?' she said, her voice short, sharp. 'You can't leave it there. You have to tell me who Jeb is.'

Willow almost smirked, lost in the game of cat and mouse his job required of him. Then he remembered himself and his mouth relaxed.

'Well, now I guess we all want something from one another. You can keep that,' he finished and flicked a gesture at the photograph.

Reeta wailed. Loud, screeching, a banshee from his grandfather's Irish folktales. He struggled to ignore her and forced a casual air into his movements as he reached for his hat and flipped it onto his head.

He could still hear her screams as he walked down the corridor, ignoring the perplexed looks of the guards who entered as he left to take the distressed creature back to her cell. He could still hear her screams as he got into his Buick and roared off. He could still hear her screams when he got back to the Florida field office, poured himself a coffee and sat down with the stacks of papers that had flooded his temporary desk. A realisation had occurred to him on the drive over from the jail. One he didn't know how to back, didn't know how to explain, and one his colleagues wouldn't buy.

She wasn't faking it.

He loosened the thin black tie around his throat and sat far back in his chair, staring up into the fluorescent strips lining the ceiling. Beneath his feet, square ceiling tiles were mirrored by drab grey carpet, peeling and drifting over years of pacing feet and stamping shoes. Some unconscious thought jerked him forward, arms spread across the myriad of folders. His hands were searching before his brain could catch up, rifling through papers, sliding unwanted sheets to the ground, until at last they paused on Reeta's hospital discharge papers.

Doctor C. Reid.

He remembered him from the several times they'd spoken at the hospital. An experienced man with a calm demeanour that somehow discouraged time-wasting while still remaining excessively polite. First, he dialled the number on the header of the discharge papers, underneath the hospital's ornate seal. The wheel of numbers clicked painfully slowly as he waited to be connected. A brisk female voice.

'St. Mary's General Hospital, B Ward, Sister Demmings speaking.'

'Hello there, Sister, it's Agent Willow here from the FBI. I believe we met last month when a charge of ours was in your care. A Ms Reeta Doe?'

He heard an intake of breath. 'I recall Ms Doe, Agent Willow. What is it I can do for you now?'

'I need to speak to the doctor in charge of her case, a Dr Reid, I believe.'

A sigh. 'Dr Reid is unavailable at the moment.'

'It's urgent.'

'I appreciate your job is important, Agent Willow, but I can't help you. Dr Reid is off work today for his daughter's high school graduation.'

'What's his home number?'

'Agent,' the sister snapped, exasperated. 'Even if I was at liberty to divulge that information, which *I am not*, as I already explained Dr Reid is not at home either today. He is at his daughter's graduation.' The last sentence was said with the staccato simplicity of speaking to an inattentive child.

'Which school?'

'Agent Willow, I hardly think that's appro—'

'Sister Demmings,' Willow interrupted, his voice harsher than intended. 'This is an urgent matter concerning an investigation I am undertaking for the Federal Bureau of Investigation. This is not just a matter of seeking justice for four grieving families, but of finding the currently missing remains for two of those families. Now I don't give a shit' – the sister's slight gasp of shock broke through his tirade – 'what *you* think is appropriate. I don't understand the mental health of this girl and I need to speak to the doctor *urgently* before the information we need is lost forever. Now.' He paused for a moment to collect himself. 'Which school is he at?'

The sister remained quiet for a heartbeat, two. She was not used to being spoken to like that. 'Garfield Senior High,' she finally said. 'South Dade.'

'Thank you, Sister,' Willow breathed, scribbling down the name and dropping the phone so it clicked back in its holder. It didn't take long to find Garfield High in the directory and a quick phone call to the frazzled receptionist told him the ceremony was on until four p.m. It was only an hour and a half away; if he left now he could be there in time for them to be letting out.

His dark brown Buick Super 8 Riviera stood out in the parking lot. It stood out in most parking lots, but especially in a building full of federal employees. He was well paid after fifteen years on the job, but only his inherent bachelorhood permitted him to afford the car. No wife to keep in jewellery, no kids to save for college. Just him, his two-bedroomed DC apartment and a cat he hardly saw. Hoover was a stray tabby he'd adopted – or who had adopted him – about three years ago, but now saw more of Mr and Mrs Zimmer in the apartment downstairs who took care of him while Willow was off chasing criminals across the country. He was not usually fazed by his excessive travel for work, the open road and a lead on a case was all he needed for life satisfaction. But lately his Florida motel room was starting to feel empty without the sounds of Stephens banging around next door, and every night he stared at the mint-green phone beside his bed wishing he had someone to call. There was only one person in the last six years who'd made any sort of dent on his emotional capacity, and she was off-limits. It had been a one-time mistake that had turned into a three-year-long mistake ending with a broken heart and trust issues. As all relationships inevitably ended, he supposed.

The ride was smooth along the highway, the window cracked to air out the thick Florida spring. Jim Reeves's deep voice caressed 'He'll Have to Go' from the radio, crackling in and out of frequency as the slow melody told its sad story. The sun was still high as he pulled into the parking lot of Garfield High, the noticeboard on the lawn out front announcing the graduating class in high, black letters. The parking lot was deserted, save for the empty cars, and Willow climbed out of his own, leaned against the hood and lit a cigarette. He was almost at the butt when the doors to the school opened wide and a trickle of families came out. They were soon followed by a few more, and more, until at last the steps down from the double doors were flooded with excited teenagers clad in gowns and hats, hugging each other and laughing. Proud parents took photos and posed with beaming smiles while their kin clutched white paper rolls of diplomas.

Among the hundreds of people milling around, it took a while for Willow to spot his man. Eventually he got lucky with the glinting bald head underneath a tree taking a photograph of a beaming brunette, hair perfectly curled under her graduation cap, arm slung around a dumpy woman in a matching dress and jacket adorned with pastel roses.

'Dr Reid?' Willow asked as he approached, modulating his voice to a light, friendly, social greeting.

The doctor turned around and blinked into the sun, a moment's hesitation before recognition. 'Yes? Ah – hello.' He held his finger out in front, pointing at Willow while he tried to recall both his name and where he knew him from.

'Agent Willow,' he supplied, holding his hand out. 'I'm working on the Reeta Doe case.'

The doctor smiled with polite recognition. 'Ah yes, that's right.' He shook the proffered hand. 'How nice to see you again. Is your child at this school too?' he asked, his tone bright and conversational, as if there could be no other reason for the agent to disturb this happy day.

'Ah, no, I don't have any children, I'm afraid to say,' Willow admitted with a deft bow of his head.

The doctor's face collapsed a little from its previous friendly nature, a tension ever so slightly sneaking into the lines around his mouth. 'Well, what can I do for you then? I assume this isn't a coincidental meeting after all?'

'I need to discuss Reeta with you,' Willow said. 'Her medical condition.'

'Mr Willow, please.' Reid gestured back to his wife and daughter. 'This is a celebration day for me and I don't intend to talk shop. You can make an appointment and see me at the hospital.'

'I can't wait for that,' Willow interrupted before the doctor turned his back fully. 'If there's a chance, even the tiniest, slightest chance that the location of those girls' bodies is somewhere in that messed-up brain of hers, I'm not waiting to get it out before it disappears completely.'

'That's not quite how retrograde amnesia works, Agent,' Dr Reid replied. 'And I thought you and your partner were under the impression of a false diagnosis on my part. Some scheme drummed up by the guilty party.'

'I've still not ruled that out,' Willow admitted. 'But let's say, let's just *say*, it's a real diagnosis. What now?'

The doctor sighed and turned his head over his shoulder, holding up his index finger to his wife. *One minute*, he mouthed and she shook her head in confusion but soon turned to speak to the parents of an approaching girl who was talking excitedly to their daughter.

'How is the girl?' Dr Reid asked. 'In herself? Is she angry, sad, confused, manic, violent?'

'All of those things,' Willow said before correcting himself. 'Not the last two.' He realised at that moment that Reeta had shown nothing but calm, despondent patience with them over the weeks of their interrogations. Pulses of genuine frustration had bubbled up, but there was none of the sinister mania they'd expected from the perpetrator of these crimes – especially given the motive they'd deduced and her background. 'She's sad mainly, frustrated on occasion. She says she feels sorrow for the victims. Guilty if she did it.'

'So,' the doctor said, 'she's not engaging with the emotions and feelings that led her to do these terrible crimes, *if* of course she did them.'

'She did them,' Willow responded quickly. 'No question about that.'

'Well then, we have to ask *why* she did them, and why she cannot connect to those feelings now. If she has no memory of the rage that led her to these attacks, then she cannot remember wanting to commit such violent crime in the first place. Her motive for murder clearly comes from a learned behaviour, not a natural propensity for evil. If you want her to remember, she needs to relearn that behaviour.'

'You want me to unlock the killer inside?'

The doctor raised his eyebrows and pursed his lips just a touch. 'Not quite as reductive as that, Agent. Start from the basics. The first time you came across her, any details you've picked up about her victims – remind her of them. Tell her every detail you know about her crimes. There is no set treatment for amnesia, Agent.' He paused and shrugged. 'I didn't believe it myself at first – I agreed, it was all just too convenient. But she's remained remarkably consistent, and I find it difficult to believe that someone would be capable of such prolonged subterfuge. It is my professional opinion that her memory of events before she landed in our care have gone. And sometimes it comes back, sometimes it doesn't. But stop trying to test her. Give her the information she needs to build the framework of her life, maybe then she'll be able to start filling in the blanks you need her to.'

'Thank you, Doctor,' Willow said, nodding, brain whirling with his next plan of action. 'You've been very helpful. I'll leave you to enjoy your day now.' He gestured back over to his waiting family. 'And congratulations on your daughter's graduation.'

'Thank you, Agent,' Dr Reid said, holding one hand up in farewell. 'Oh.' He caught himself before turning away. 'It'll help if she trusts you. And if she doesn't trust you, find someone who she can.'

Three

How dare he tease her like that. Showing her that picture, tempting details of her father – dangling answers so close she could feel them brushing against her fingertips and then – nothing. She sat alone on her bed; her wailing had ceased hours ago. It had exploded out of her, surprising herself as much as Willow. But now it had subsided, along with the daylight that cast tempting warm orange rays on the runway in front of her cell, replaced instead by the darkened silver of dull moonlight. The photograph in her hands had been lost to the gun-grey shadow long ago, but still she held it inches in front of her face, her eye straining to caress every wave in the man's hair, every dislodged wicker beam on the chair behind him, every fold on his denim shirt. A farmer, she had deduced. Her father must be a farmer.

She wondered where he was now.

Jeb, the agent had said. The name meant as little as her own had the first time she'd heard it in hospital.

Jebjebjebjebjeb

Nothing.

What had been Willow's plan? She adjusted her position as her arm went numb beneath her and scrunched her pillow into a tighter ball against the wall to sit half-up against it. Paper crackled as she did so, and she pulled free the article from where it lived under her thin, flat pillow.

The College Girl Who Slayed Her Own.

Carol Joyce. The name was printed in neat capitals above the first line of text. It occurred to Reeta that Carol must have done some research on her to write this piece. Perhaps *she* could give her some answers on who she was. She must have burrowed down into the life of this criminal, interviewed Reeta's family and friends and learned that Reeta wasn't really the monster everyone thought. Carol filled her mind's eye: a raven-haired heroine who stood tall above the weak agents and their pathetic tricks to make her talk, teasing and prodding her like a penguin at the zoo. Carol would help her. She'd understand – she'd believe her.

She'd tell her about Jeb.

She could even bring him to her.

When the morning siren billowed into her cell, Reeta had only been asleep for a few hours, and it had been a fitful, restless sleep at that. Filled with visions of her father laughing on a porch cut down by her small, child-like hands around his neck.

Reeta had shower time before breakfast, a cold, demeaning experience. She waited patiently in the queue with her thin towel barely long enough to cover her modesty and stepped obediently forward when a stall became available – her feet squelching across the mildew-encrusted tiles, rogue hairs clinging to her soles. She stood under the blast of cold water, her skin alight with goosebumps as she ran her small, hard bar of soap across her body. It was less than thirty seconds before she could no longer bear the cold water and slammed the silver handle into the off position. Her hair hung in limp strands down her back and she didn't bother to cover herself with her towel as she vacated the stall and headed toward the bank of sinks and mirrors, her hand trailing along the wall for guidance as she did. With only one fully working eye, her depth perception was off and she'd been caught out by the small step before, tumbling onto the soiled floor, her naked skin smacking against the cold, hard tiles. Another inmate had taken the opportunity to kick her in the ribs and steal her toothpaste. So now Reeta slunk along the wall, counting her paces until she stepped down at the correct moment and staked her claim at one of the sinks. She rubbed her limbs with the towel, mopping up the icy droplets that clung to her. Throwing the towel over her sink, she examined herself in the mirror. It was never an easy task. The wounds on her face were healing but still red-raw and unbearable to look at.

They said she looked like her victims. It was impossible to tell that now.

She stared hard at the features gazing back at her and wondered, for the first time, if underneath the scars and twisted flesh she had once resembled the man in the photograph. Her father.

Jeb.

Had her cheekbones sat as high as his? Had her jawline relaxed into the same smile? Were her own brown eyes from her mother? Did she share the same blonde hair as a sister?

But she knew it was a wasted fantasy. Whatever secrets her face had once held were lost forever.

She dug into her plastic washbag and cleaned her teeth hurriedly, feeling a dull agony break out across her injured cheek as she did so. She packed her bag back up, wrapped the towel around her still damp body and headed to the communal changing rooms where she was issued a freshly laundered uniform and ushered in to breakfast.

She had a new resolve as she walked into the mess hall that morning and once she'd collected her plastic tray of chunky rehydrated egg, she sought out the redhead who'd gifted her Carol Joyce's words. The woman's thin, aged face turned up from her breakfast in sinister surprise.

'What the fuck do you think you're doing?' she growled at Reeta's unexpected presence at her table.

'Which newspaper was that article from?'

'What article?' The woman's face creased into a disinterested scowl. 'What the fuck you talking about, weirdo?'

'You gave me a newspaper clipping last week. Which newspaper? It doesn't say on the cutting.' Reeta didn't give a shit about this woman's intolerance, her snark. She just wanted to find Carol Joyce.

'Jesus, kid, I don't know, *Washington Post* probably. That's the only national we get in the library here.'

Reeta didn't say thank you but turned on her heel and left to eat alone as she always did. She wasn't permitted to borrow books from the prison library. No illicit erotica smuggled in for her, no dog-eared Fitzgerald to help better herself in her cell at night. Only the standard-issue Bible was permitted in her room. But she was allowed access to legal textbooks and, hopefully, newspapers.

She put in her request with the guard, who came back an hour later with permission granted from the warden. He led her along the gangway toward the metal stairs and took slow, deliberate steps so that each foot on a stair clanged loudly into the cavernous jail. The library was on the ground floor, past more bland corridors littered with inmates mopping or sweeping or pushing laundry carts, and finally through a green door. It was a small rectangular room with a single wooden table in the middle and ancient bookshelves lining the walls, squealing under their age and

35

weight. The newspapers were on a rack to the left and Reeta could see the *Washington Post* glittering from the top.

She went immediately for it and the guard eyed her carefully. Trying not to look too enthusiastic, she casually reached up and plucked the paper from the rack, a long wooden pole gripping its spine.

'Apparently they've been covering my case,' she said non-committally in the direction of the guard. He didn't respond. She sat down at the table and opened out the wide broadsheet, scanning headlines and think-pieces about some nuclear bomb in China and the President's endorsement of someone's senate run for the mid-terms. She lingered for a moment on the photograph of the besuited man talking into a microphone and wondered if she'd liked him before. Had she voted for him? Had her father?

But it was not what she was looking for, so she moved herself determinedly on.

Her eyes swooped over the front-page headlines, directly to the masthead, but there was no form of address or contact to be found. She scanned the pages, half-heartedly taking in news of a world she didn't know, until finally she reached a small story about a missing girl in New York. At the bottom the journalist, Charles Bore, had included a plea for tips – for readers with any information to write directly to him at the office address. She could only presume that Carol worked out of the same office.

There was no way the guard would allow her to tear out this article – the redhead with the bird's nest must have some form of symbiotic relationship with the guards that didn't bear thinking about – but Reeta had been unknowingly training for this. In an effort to revive her long-term memory, she'd taken the advice of the prison doctor, who, on their last check-up, had advised that she could start by flexing her short-term skills. She had diligently begun a programme of memorising parts of the Bible in her cell and reciting them back, testing herself against the answers.

She read and re-read the address ten, eleven times. Repeating it under her breath in a sing-song tone so soon it became a chant, a mantra she could repeat at a moment's notice. Calmly, she put the newspaper back and went in search of a legal textbook, enjoying the feeling of wasting another hour of the guard's time while she uselessly brushed up on supreme court cases from the 1930s.

'I want some paper and a pen,' she told the guard when he returned her to her cell.

His eyes creased suspiciously. 'What for?'

'I'd like to write a letter.'

She stared him out, daring him to refuse, to question her further. She'd never written a letter before, had no one to write to. But now she had a reason, a purpose.

She was going to find out about her life.

And maybe, somewhere in this, she could clear herself. Because one thing had become obvious over her fitful night of ruminations about her father and nightmares about killing him.

She was innocent.

She had to be.

She was a simple farm girl, who had somehow found herself in the wrong place at the wrong time. What possible malice could she have in her heart to kill anyone? Her father was peaceful, kind. He would pull her into

37

his broad arms for a paternal hug when all of this was over. Introduce her mother, a kind lady overflowing with cornbread recipes and love. Maybe even a sibling, younger of course so they looked up to their big sister with eyes of awe. Perhaps a dog to run around with, throw sticks for and feed scraps under the table. Yes, this was her life. She was sure of it.

And Agent Willow had given her the first scrap of clawing it back.

The guard returned and handed her a scratchy ballpoint with hardly any ink, a yellow legal pad and a stack of envelopes. 'You can go to the mailroom after mealtimes,' he told her, voice carefully modulated to remain a constant monotone. She'd seen this guard laugh and joke with other inmates before, but maybe he knew he was never getting a blowjob from her so she wasn't worth the effort.

She sat down on her bed, the guard's footsteps echoing away, and positioned her Bible on her knees as a rest for the paper.

> *Dear Ms Joyce,*
>
> *I am probably the last person you expect to hear from, and you may not even believe it is me. But I assure you, and I assume you will see from the postmark stamp, that I am writing to you from within the Florida Women's Correctional Institute as I await trial for the crimes of which I am accused.*
>
> *They call me Reeta Doe, although I have no affinity with that name. They tell me I'm a killer, and a brutal one at that, although I have no memory of being such a person.*
>
> *You wrote about me a few weeks or so ago, an article I have not been able to read in full. The*

*details are too horrifying for me to understand. But
I am coming to you now with a plea. I know you
will have researched me, dived into the depths of
my life — and I need to understand who I am. I
need to know why they speak of me as they do. The
FBI agents assigned to my case show no interest in
helping me build the walls of my life again from
the rubble that is left.*

Please, come to see me.

Even a phone call.

Even a letter.

*I will put you on my visitor list. You will be
alone on there.*

I await your response eagerly.

Regards,

Apparently Reeta

She read and re-read the letter. Reeta knew what she
was trading for answers. She would trade her privacy, her
relative anonymity, and invite the entire United States into
her strange little world. There would be flashing cameras,
news crews at her inevitable trial, outcry from victims'
parents at the attention she would get. But all of that
would be worth it for just one person on her side.

One person who would learn, alongside her, who she
was.

Four

'So *that's* what you've been doing while I've been caring for my sick wife?' Stephens was angry. 'Talking to some quack doctor about how to make our killer feel more at home? How to hug her and stroke her hair and tell her it'll be all right?'

Willow restrained his eyeroll as the diner waitress put an oversized oval plate of pancakes down in front of him. Stephens had biscuits and grits, but Willow knew he wouldn't eat much. Since his wife's diagnosis he'd shrivelled, seemingly over the course of a few weeks. The waitress refilled their coffee cups and Willow smiled a polite nod of thanks at her before leaning in on his elbows, fork dangling over the top of the flapjack stack.

'What I'm saying is that our current tactic hasn't got us anywhere. Lobbing questions at her about Mandy and Susan has clammed her up. We're at an impasse, right?'

Stephens tipped his head but refrained from a full nod of agreement.

'So, let's just *say* she really can't remember anything – she did have a fucking big whack on the head – then we're never going to get those answers. What's the harm in doing what the doctor says?'

Stephens opened his mouth to reply but Willow ploughed on, stabbing his fork down into his stack and carving off a fluffy blueberry mouthful.

'No, listen – if she *is* faking it then we're not showing our hand – we're just telling her the facts. We've told her enough about *what* she did, so now, let's tell her *how* she did it. We'll tell her about how she first turned up at Texas A&M University, first befriended Sarah-Mae Withers – and then we go from there. If she's faking then none of this is news to her – *she* knows what happens next, so maybe we could lull her into a sense of security, trip her up. Maybe we have a detail wrong and she corrects us instinctively. Or' – he paused and put his forkful into his mouth, swallowing but barely chewing – 'she really has forgotten everything, and we can start to jog her memory – bring everything back.'

Stephens sighed and pushed grits around his plate. 'How far do we go back? Jeb?'

Willow shook his head. 'For now we stick to the circumstances of the crimes. What *we* know. If any of that other stuff is connected, her own brain will have to conjure it up. We don't know enough.'

Stephens looked at him with a long, slow gaze. 'All right,' he said finally 'I'm not saying I believe the lying little psycho but you're right – we have to try something new. So' – he gestured with his empty fork – 'we'll go tomorrow like we're scheduled to, and take our files on Sarah-Mae. Tell the little bitch how she did it.'

Willow shook his head and jabbed his fork back into his breakfast. 'Doc says it helps if it's someone she trusts.'

Stephens inhaled sharply and flinched with his still-empty fork. 'Well, who does she fucking trust?'

This was the bit that Willow had not been looking forward to telling his partner since he'd returned last night. Willow had received a phone call, not even through the bureau office – just direct to his motel, two nights ago.

It was a voice he'd not heard in years, but had dreamed about on occasion.

'Hello, Benny,' she said, oozing memories down the wires that connected her Bloomingdale condo with his scruffy Florida motel room.

'Carol,' he'd replied, voice terse.

'How's Florida treating you?' she asked, and he could picture her sitting in her dark green squashy armchair, the one she set up with a small fold-up table propping her typewriter into a make-shift desk.

'How did you get this number?'

'I have my ways.'

He sighed, tight with barely supressed annoyance. 'Carol.'

'Ginny and I still keep in touch.' She admitted this connection to his department's PA without concern or shame.

'Why are you calling?'

'Can't an old friend just check in?'

'We're not old friends.'

'In a sense.'

'Carol.' His voice exhaled over his tension as he sat back on his bed, gripping the bridge of his nose with his thumb and forefinger.

'OK, OK,' she said conciliatorily, and he could hear her sitting forward to lean on the table in front. 'You're on the College Slayer case.'

'Is that a question?' he asked. It wasn't meant to be common knowledge who was on what case, but Carol, as ever, had her contacts.

'No, I know where you are and why,' she said.

Anger flushed through him. 'Are you really calling me for this? After... after,' he stuttered, trying to settle the flash of emotional rage that had clutched him. 'After *everything.*'

She sighed audibly. 'Ben, I had to take my shot. I didn't do anything wrong.'

'*Didn't do anything wrong?*' he repeated, voice breathy. 'You nearly killed my career!'

'But I didn't,' she replied matter-of-factly. 'You're still working. *You* were the one who fucked up. I just saw my opportunity and took it.'

'What do you want, Carol?' he asked, each word wrung tight.

'I've received a letter from your main suspect,' she answered. Of all the things he thought she'd say, that was not on the list. 'She wants me to get in contact with her. It seems she's read the piece I did on her.'

'Where the hell did she get that?' Willow asked, more of himself than of Carol. He'd seen Carol's article, of course he had. It was inevitable that she'd write one; the tale of missing girls from colleges around the Southern states had been raging for months – daughters had been pulled out of schools, politicians lamenting on TV that surely this proved university was no place for a woman. It had been impossible to hide the crash and the significance of the crumpled station wagon's passengers. Local press had been on the scene, selling pictures and stories to the nationals, so that Carol hadn't even needed to leave her cosy little neighbourhood to file the one thousand perfunctory words Willow had read the day it had come out. There was nothing shocking in the story, apart from the facts of the case, and no details that suggested Carol had any sort of inside knowledge or relationship with the suspect. It had been a run-of-the-mill factual story.

'I don't know,' Carol said dismissively. 'I'm sure they get papers in prison these days. Is that really your biggest question, Detective?'

'I'm an agent,' he corrected out of habit, before remembering the way she'd always teased him with his rank and title. 'All right, fine, what did she want?'

'She seems to think I've researched her in depth and can provide some answers as to who she is. I believe she's suffering from retrograde amnesia?'

'That's what the docs say, yeah,' Willow confirmed, before regretting how easily he'd conceded the detail.

'She wants me to come see her.'

Willow exhaled slowly. 'Jesus Christ,' he whispered.

'She says, and I quote, "The FBI agents assigned to my case show no interest in helping me build the walls of my life again from the rubble that is left."'

Willow didn't reply. He couldn't deny it. All he'd done up to that point was give her a picture and a name, with no explanation.

'So,' Carol continued, 'I'm coming to Florida. I'm booked on a flight on Sunday.'

Willow recounted this conversation for his partner now, omitting the parts about his career woes and Carol's cosy acquaintance with their bureau PA.

'You've got to be fucking kidding me,' Stephens breathed, sitting back against the cheap red vinyl cushioning. He gave up the pretence of eating and dropped his cutlery onto the plate with a delicate clatter.

'She flies in today. Got a visitation at the jail tomorrow,' Willow said with a sigh, not looking at his partner. 'So if we're going to do this, we need to brief her tonight. As soon as she gets off the plane.'

'And what exactly do you propose?'

'She has one visit alone with Reeta, gains her trust, finds out exactly what Reeta wants from her. She offers to help in any way she can, maybe give her a little info, whatever she knows, but just a little taster to make Reeta feel comfortable that Carol's the right person.'

Stephens grunted at the suggestion of making their murderer feel comfortable.

'Then Carol brings me in. I'll supervise all their meetings from then on, but I won't say anything. Hopefully if Carol does the talking then my presence won't put Reeta off too much. Then maybe she'll start slipping or' – he prepared himself for his partner's inevitable snort – 'start remembering.'

The snort came as excepted.

'Look,' Willow said, putting down his fork and looking at his partner. 'I've been over and over this in my head, whether it's a good idea, whether we can trust Carol—'

Stephens raised an eyebrow.

'But it's our only shot. If Reeta's faking it then Carol will wheedle it out of her, and if she's not then maybe Carol'll help her memory come back. And *then* we can find Mandy and Susan.'

'And can we trust Carol? She fucked you last time.'

Willow took a deep breath and echoed the words Carol had spoken on the phone. Words that he'd avoided saying for three long years, terrified what they meant if they were true. 'That was my fault. I shouldn't have told her anything about that case. She sat on that info for months.'

'Until she didn't,' Stephens reminded him, sitting forward so their faces were nearly touching across their uneaten breakfasts. 'And then she nearly fucked your career.'

45

'It was my career or hers,' Willow said sadly. 'She needed a win, so she took her shot. It was a lot easier for me to recover from that than it was for her to rise up through the newsroom.'

'Don't give me that feminist bullshit. She's got a job, hasn't she? What more does she fucking want? She should have stayed *loyal*, been there to support you. What would she have done if you'd have given her that ring you carried around for months? Given up her job to stay at home like she should?'

Willow didn't want to talk about this any more. He could feel his skin itch with tarnished memories, and prickles barbed his throat. 'Well, I didn't give it to her, did I?' he snapped.

'Too fucking right,' Stephens said with what he clearly thought was a supportive nod.

'She's our only hope now, though, Ed.' Willow rarely used his partner's first name. 'I've cleared it with Reeta's lawyer, so you're going to have to get on board with her.'

'You've spoken to her lawyer already?' One of Stephens' eyebrows flickered up in surprise.

Willow nodded. 'At first I thought maybe he could help, but it doesn't seem like they've connected too much.' Willow remembered Barry Prince's hollow laugh down the phone wire at the suggestion he might be able to wrangle Reeta's trust into a memory. 'He's agreed to let Carol come on board seeing as Reeta's reached out to her directly. I think he's hoping if she *does* remember where they are, he might be able to wrestle it into a plea deal.'

Stephens blinked and Willow could see the thoughts darting behind his eyes. After several stiff moments he nodded slowly.

'Fine. For Mandy and Susan.'

Carol's flight landed at six fifteen, but the agents had decided against going to meet her at the airport. Instead they arrived at the Royal Grande promptly at seven thirty and Willow took a seat in the plush hotel bar, while Stephens went to order their drinks. Navy-blue velvet washed the ornate lounge, sparks of dull gold brocade glittering through. It was not exactly the motel the bureau was paying for. Willow picked up the menu of thick, expensive paper from the small table and raised his eyebrows at the price of a beer before glancing up to signal to Stephens not to bother with drinks. But Stephens had already been joined at the bar by another figure, one who was signalling to the barman to bring their order over to Willow's table.

Carol Joyce was tall, and, despite his best efforts, Willow still couldn't consider her as anything other than beautiful. With a Black father and white mother, she'd been forced to pay attention in life to things he never had. He noted with a dart of nostalgia that her hair was still cut into the bob she'd always had, sleek from her weekly ritual straightening, it every Sunday evening with a hot comb. When they were together, if she ever woke up to rain, she'd sigh her deep, breathy sigh and wake Willow to help secure her scarf and rain hood around her head so that not a single strand could be affected by the downpour.

'You gonna melt or something, Wicked Witch of West Hampton?' He'd laughed one morning, eyes still crusty with sleep.

She'd whipped around, rain hood askew across her forehead, and snapped, 'Do you get that this isn't just about my goddam hair, Ben? If one strand of this gets wet when I go into the office, you think my colleagues – my supposed peers – won't fucking notice? Won't make some

47

godawful joke about "Negro curls"? I love my daddy but, my God, I've kept him out of my life here for a reason.'

He'd never complained again, and as he watched her make her way over to him across the upmarket hotel bar with not a hair out of place, he couldn't help but wonder who was assigned the task these rainy mornings.

Carol had been the product of an affair between her mother, Helen, and one of the work crew who'd come to build the extension onto Mr and Mrs Joyce's lavish Hamptons home. It had been an in-depth project and over those summer months of 1930, Mrs Joyce had grown weary of her older husband's philandering and found distraction in the foreman Howell Johnson. She'd discovered her pregnancy just weeks after the crew had left town in search of the next construction job, and when the fair-haired married couple gave birth to a dark-skinned bundle of joy, Brian Joyce had immediately understood. Philandering but not cruel, Brian had allowed Helen and Carol to stay in their home – but kept a polite distance from them both. Carol was brought up officially as a Joyce, her supposed parents rarely speaking beyond agreeing to various social commitments. The whitewashing of her upbringing had allowed her darker hue to go outwardly unacknowledged by most of Hamptons society, although Carol had long since grown used to whispered gossip and narrowed-eyed glares.

Helen had enlisted the help of a black nanny to teach Carol how to groom herself and straighten her hair and, when Carol turned eighteen, as Helen struggled for her final breaths, she had produced nearly two decades' worth of correspondence with the man who had fathered her only child. Mr Joyce was long gone by that point, having left everything to his unfaithful wife for lack of a better cause to bequeath. Howell had welcomed his grown daughter with a tearful bear-hug, his new children watching suspiciously the light-skinned, well-dressed girl who had turned up at their Southside Chicago home.

Carol had confessed to Willow, in those early, heady days of dating when you share your deepest feelings, that she had hoped tracking down her father's side would give her a place, a sense of belonging. But she'd quickly understood that to Howell Johnson's new family she was the white anomaly, as much as she'd been the black anomaly to the Joyces'. She visited them these days only on Christmas or Thanksgiving, sending presents and cards for her younger siblings' birthdays, which were never reciprocated. Willow had never been introduced.

Now thirty-six years old, Carol commanded a room. She had beauty and money and influence within the circles of society that mattered when it came to getting ahead. She sauntered easily through the hotel bar and flopped elegantly down onto the chair opposite her ex-lover, not a flicker of strain evident on her face.

'Carol,' Willow said, unmoving,

'Hello, Ben,' she replied, crossing her legs and placing her neat crocodile-skin bag on the floor next to her. 'It's been a while.'

'I'm not here to reminisce,' Stephens cut in brusquely, taking the final seat 'We've got a job to do.'

Carol pulled a face at Willow and raised her eyebrows in a brief expression of amusement. 'Well, you better fill me in then.'

Five

For the first time Reeta sat in the visitors' room, lined with thick glass partitions, and sectioned off with phone connectors between each side. Her only other visitors had been her lawyer and the agents, and they both warranted their own private interrogation room. But today she was receiving a visitor – a real one, who would sit down in front of her and listen to what *she* had to say. Carol had replied within just a few short days, agreeing to come at once to meet with her. *Of course I will help you fill in any blanks I can, and give you a voice to tell your story whenever you're ready.* The sentence had seemed impossible, written in neat cursive in expensive-looking blue ink. But now the meeting was here, and Carol Joyce was keeping her word. Reeta had barely slept last night, staying up to stare at the image of her father until she could hardly see his kind face in the darkened cell, illuminated only by faint cream moonlight. Today she would get answers.

She'd find him.

Reeta sat in her allotted section with the photograph of her father gripped like a talisman in one hand, the other tapping agitatedly at the counter with her fingernail. A fellow inmate told her to knock it off, but Reeta's blank stare into her murky reflection on the dull glass didn't flinch. They'd been seated for ten minutes before the visitors filed in – looking eagerly around, waiting to catch a glimpse of their friend, family, loved one. It was difficult to believe that some of the women in here could possibly have any loved ones, but visitor days came and went every week and everyone but Reeta Doe was called forth. Her family must believe the horrible crimes of which she was accused, and she knew the only way she could get them back was to prove her innocence. And her one ally in that task had just sat down in front of her.

'Reeta?' the woman said with a deep, breathy voice, the phone cradled elegantly between manicured fingers.

'Carol?' Reeta nodded the greeting and felt a small ball of hot happiness rise up her throat when the woman behind the glass smiled broadly and nodded.

'So,' Carol said calmly. 'I'm here. How can I help?'

Suddenly Reeta felt the hot ball burst and it released a singular, desperate sob. She gasped it back into herself, but the tears still rolled and her hand clenched tighter over the photograph.

'Oh, Reeta.' Carol's voice softened and she held her hand up to the glass, gently resting as if she had the power to penetrate it and soothe the crying girl on the other side. It took a moment for Reeta to remember she was wasting her limited visitation time, and she swallowed her emotion back down into her chest where it belonged.

'I need to understand,' she began, every word an exercise in calming her inner angst, 'who I am, and where I came from. *Why* they say I could be capable of the things I've apparently done.'

'And why do you think I could help you?' Carol asked, her voice professionally steady.

Reeta looked down, thinking carefully. 'I have no one else. Other than the FBI, my lawyer and this place' – she glanced around the grey walls – 'you're the only person who has acknowledged my existence. I don't know who else I could even contact.' She gestured to Carol half-heartedly. 'You're a journalist, right?'

Carol nodded.

'I thought you must have done some research on me, tried to interview my family or – or something...' Her voice trailed off, long and hopeful.

—

Carol thought for a moment. Unsure how to tell this girl that her article was cobbled together from police reports and second-hand witness statements. Her crimes had been the focus, not her.

Reeta began speaking again before she could respond. 'One of the agents, Willow, he gave me this.' She brought her left hand up onto the desk in front and peeled her fingers apart to reveal a small photograph. She held it up against the glass and Carol felt unexpected recognition splay her face open. Instinct moved her head forward to stare more closely at the picture, barely listening to Reeta's voice through the other end of the phone.

'It's my father, isn't it?' she asked, her voice suddenly lighter. 'Did you meet him? Can you pass a message on for me?'

Carol shook her head; she needed to silence her brain – this was something she hadn't come prepared for. Had Ben deliberately deceived her? Suddenly this was all so much more complicated than just the case of a mentally disturbed young woman with a bang on the head.

'Reeta, I have to be honest with you,' Carol said, choosing to take the path of least complexity. 'I *am* working with the FBI in some capacity by being here.'

She held up a delicate hand to pre-emptively silence any complaints from the other side of the glass. 'But I do want to help you.' *In exchange for your story*, was what Carol didn't say. It was hard not to feel sympathy for the shivering ghoul beyond the glass, but that didn't change anything. Carol had seen the reports – this girl was guilty, and any jury would find her so. She was headed for the chair and Carol had her career to think about, a career that Ben had once again unwittingly boosted. 'I'm afraid I don't know anything about your life, other than in the context of the crimes you committed – allegedly committed,' she corrected herself. 'But I *can* help you find out. If you still want me as your ally, I am ready and waiting.'

'You're here for the agents?' Reeta's voice had turned numb and blank.

'Yes, and from now on Agent Willow will be present in our meetings. But that could be a good thing, Reeta – we'd get more time together, not limited by standard visitation.'

'I don't *want* to meet with more agents.' Reeta's voice was a tightening coil, and Carol knew she was fucking it up.

'I'm *not* an agent,' she said quickly, her tone forcibly calm. 'I'm not from the FBI; I'm exactly who you think I am, and I've come down exactly like you've asked me to. But anything I find out from you I do have a duty to inform law enforcement officers. Even if – *especially* if – we discover some evidence that proves your innocence. I'm willing to be on your side, Reeta. And I will tell you whatever I can.'

Reeta sat silently for a moment – her uneven, mangled face unreadable. 'Tell me something, then,' she said quietly. 'You recognised my father, I saw that.'

'I *can* tell you who that man is,' Carol said, slowly nodding at the picture Reeta had now dropped from its perch, 'but I'm not sure if I should. Not just yet. I need to check some things first, make sure I get everything right.'

Reeta snorted, exhaled through her nose. 'So tell me something else.'

'I can tell you the story I do know. The story I briefly gathered from the friends and statements of those affected. From what Agent Willow told me,' she ploughed on, despite Reeta's face hardening at his name, 'they've told you of your crimes but not how they came about. They've not told you how you came to know those girls, what connection you had to any of them. If you'd permit me until tomorrow, I can get it all together for you. Tell you your story and why you ended up here – the best that I can.'

'But next time Willow will be here?'

Carol nodded slowly. 'I won't let him interrupt. I'll be here for *you* again.'

Reeta thought slowly and picked up the photograph she'd dropped onto the table in front of her, running her thumb over the face. 'When can you tell me about my father?'

Carol inhaled. 'As soon as I know I could do it accurately.'

Reeta nodded after a pause. 'OK. First you can tell me about the girls.'

The siren blasted, indicating the end of visiting hours and Carol bade farewell to Reeta, mentally making preparations for their next meeting. She joined the queue of other visitors, back through the metal detectors and gauntlet of guards, until — finally — she was outside in the humid Florida spring. While she waited for the taxi the guard had kindly agreed to call, she sat down on a bench refreshingly shaded by the jail's tall walls.

Brother Jeb. Now that was not a picture she had ever expected the girl to pull out. *That* was an angle not a single other soul sitting at a typewriter in a newsroom would know. Carol knew she had her story now and she would happily put in the time and patience to get it right. And if she helped a mentally bereft young woman while she was at it, then so be it. If Reeta's amnesia was true, and it certainly seemed to be, then this torture of the unknown was surely the worst sentence anyone could be slapped with.

Carol chose to avoid Ben that evening, reading up instead on the notes she'd made for her story, which she'd brought down, along with hefty copies of police reports and witness statements, in a large leather briefcase. She set it up on the pale marble table in the hotel lounge, asked politely if a telephone could possibly be made available for her use and instructed the waiter to keep her Chardonnays coming. She knew the facts of the case. She was familiar with the names of the victims and the circumstances of their demise, but she'd failed to read between the lines before to see what was unsaid to build a picture of the murderous phantom the colleges feared.

She started, as logic would dictate, from the beginning. Sarah-Mae Withers. She read into the night, compiling details and notes, anecdotes and observations. Made phone calls to unwilling loved ones and friends, eked answers out where she could. It was gone two in the morning before she finally allowed the waiter to clear her final wine glass and, head still spinning exhausted trails of college campus murder, she took herself up to her room and collapsed on freshly laundered hotel linen.

Willow picked her up at eight o'clock sharp, straight after breakfast. She'd had just shy of five hours' sleep, but her mind was fizzing with the day ahead. The biggest crime story of the year, and she was entrenched within it. They couldn't pass her over for features editor again, not after this. Marty Cook had effortlessly leapfrogged her own junior editor title at the last round of office reorganisation, despite her more senior years and, to be frank, better quality work. Yet, apparently, a Harvard degree and lifetime membership to the same godforsaken Greek club as the editor-in-chief was worth more than that. But this would be too big to ignore, especially if her hunch about Brother Jeb was right.

'She showed me something yesterday,' Carol said, settling into the hour-and-a-half ride to the jail. They'd done their introductions, polite enquiries into sleep and breakfast, and had soon after allowed the crackling radio to clog the gap between them. Willow's head twitched a fraction in her direction and the very edge of his right eyebrow flickered.

'Anything we can use?'

'I doubt it. She said you gave it to her.'

Willow didn't respond. He surely knew the only thing he'd given her, and he certainly didn't want Carol asking questions about it.

'It's who I think it is, isn't it?'

Willow still didn't respond as he visibly picked over all the possible scenarios and their outcomes.

'What don't I know, Ben?'

'You know everything you need to, to jog her memory on the murders.'

Carol laughed, dry and sarcastic. 'I highly doubt that. *Why* did she do it?'

Willow inhaled. 'I'd say only she could tell us that.'

'That's bullshit and you know it. You and Stephens know something. You know why, and you're sure you know why.'

'I can't divulge that to you at this moment.'

'This isn't the same as last time. I'm here to help *you*. I need to be in the loop.'

Willow barked a harsh, grunting laugh. 'Are you really telling me you're not already writing this story in that pretty little head of yours? Haven't already calculated exactly the promotion or pay rise or whatever it is you want that this could get you? You're helping us, sure, but let's not be green about the exchange that's in play here. You get access to her and *that's* your story. I'm not telling you any more than I think you need to know until I think it might get me *my* answers for Mandy and Susan. Does that make sense to you?'

Carol nodded silently. This was a different Ben to the one who'd left her. The easy-going, sharp-minded intellect had been hardened somewhere in the last three years. It was this case. Or it was the legacy of their failed relationship.

She turned to the window and allowed the sounds of the radio to inflate between them once again.

Six

Carol had never been inside a jail's interrogation room before. Interrogation *cell* was a more apt description. But Willow and Reeta seemed right at home as they patiently waited for the guards to undo their complicated display of shackles and chains that seemed so pointless wrapped around the skinny, scarred body of a young woman.

'Ms Doe,' Willow began, sitting himself down at the table. Reeta followed suit without waiting to be asked. He pushed down two buttons on the tape recorder to his left, a heavy click that indicated they were due to begin. 'You wrote to Ms Joyce here last week, is that right?'

Reeta nodded.

'And when you met yesterday you spoke briefly about how Ms Joyce has agreed to bridge the gap that has appeared between myself, my partner and you. An outside agency who, I hope' – the briefest glance toward Carol – 'can help bring you the answers you seek about why you're here, and in return give me the information I seek about Mandy and Susan. From now on I won't speak during your meetings, but I will be taking notes. Is that acceptable to you? You've previously waived the right to have your lawyer present at past interrogations – would you like him present during these meetings?'

Reeta shook her head.

'Very well.' Willow turned and nodded at Carol, before shifting his chair half a foot away from the table with a screech across the concrete floor.

Unsure where to begin, Carol opened her notebook and looked at Reeta's expectant face. She'd said nothing since coming into this room, communicated nothing shy of a nod of greeting as she'd sat down. 'Um, and how are you today, Reeta?' Carol asked, presuming it the polite thing to do. Reeta blinked in evident surprise.

'I... I'm fine thank you,' she replied after a moment before grasping for something to respond with. 'How are you?'

Carol smiled warmly, a smile that had gotten her many an exclusive quote in the past. 'I'm very well thanks, a little tired, but it was worth it.'

Reeta looked pointedly down at Carol's A4 notebook, which was now spread open across the desk, a mosaic of smaller scraps of paper pinned haphazardly, bulking up the pages. 'This is what you've been doing?'

'Some of it – some of it I already had. I thought...' She looked down at her book with a brief sideways glance at Willow, who was sitting, unmoving, just behind her. His expression was unreadable. 'We should just start with Sarah-Mae Withers. The, ah, well, the first victim.' Last night in the comfort of the hotel bar, swathed in the security of a few glasses of wine, none of this had made her squeamish. In fact, a hard stomach and propensity to deal with uncomfortable situations was one of the things that made her an excellent journalist. But sitting here in cold, blue-lit reality, she suddenly felt nervous. Bizarrely rude, as if she was treading on some private matter between Reeta and Willow. As if it was in insult to name

Sarah-Mae Withers a victim in Reeta's presence. Reeta nodded slowly; she'd heard the name before.

'Sarah-Mae enrolled in Texas A&M University last September. 1965. Originally from nearby Austin, she didn't want to be too far from her family, to whom she was close.' Carol flicked her eyes up to see if anything landed on Reeta's face. It was blank. Maybe she'd heard all this before. Or maybe she lacked remorse like the hardened killer they all said she was. 'Sarah joined the Kappa Delta Pi sorority, and lived in Adams Dormitory, where she shared a room with Callie Jefferson. The girls quickly became close. Sarah-Mae was proficient at math, and hoped for that to become her major. She got good grades.' Carol paused and looked up again at Reeta. She remained as cold and emotionless as before. Carol's book was filled with timelines and facts, black scratches on white paper reducing the last weeks of a life to numbers, grade point averages and addresses. After a moment more taking in the well-compiled and organised notes she'd spent the evening collating, Carol slipped her fingers under the front cover of her book to flip it shut. Reeta's good eye narrowed and intrigue crinkled her forehead. 'I'm going to tell you what Callie told me when I called her yesterday evening. She didn't want to speak, not at first. She's tired of journalists pawing grubby hands through her pain. But I managed to get a bit out of her. I was a college freshman once myself. I understand the dichotomy of excitement, loneliness and nerves it brings – *especially* for a young woman. As a journalist it's my job to bring together many perspectives, weave them through with facts and figures, tell the full story in the most accurate way possible. But I don't think that's what I need here. One person's story might just do the trick.'

Reeta nodded slowly – she understood.

Texas

October was always one of the nicest months in Texas. Gentle breezes without the smothering humidity of summer. Leaves turned a shade warmer, blanketing the campus in a russet quilt. For the freshman girls of Kappa Delta Pi, it symbolised one whole month away from home, one whole month into the world of adulthood, one month into their new sisterhood. Callie and Sarah-Mae were lucky to have both got into the sorority; not many roommates made the cut together.

The new girl turned up one day, just out of the blue. She was hanging around outside the Sycamore Building, kicking at fallen leaves with ratty old sneakers and a linen calf-length blue skirt. It had murky green smears down it, reminiscent of childhood grass stains mothers couldn't wait to launder out. Her hair was a bright honey-blonde and long down to the small of her back, framing a pinched, pretty face with a smattering of freckles clustered up by her hairline. She stopped her kicking as Sarah-Mae and Callie approached, discussing the calculus class they'd just endured.

'Do you two go here?' the new girl had asked, not to them directly, but more aimed in their general direction.

'Yeah,' Sarah-Mae had replied, coming to a stop. 'Of course we do. Don't you?'

The new girl shrugged, and her eyes wandered toward the grand old building behind them, before drifting back. She seemed to be lazily scrutinising the two sorority sisters and Callie noticed her gaze land on the glittering silver cross at Sarah-Mae's neck. Sarah-Mae had told Callie it had been a gift from her father for her eighteenth birthday. 'It once belonged to Grammy Daisy,' she'd said with a proud nod.

'I'm Reeta,' the new girl said suddenly, holding out her hand with a surprisingly disarming smile.

'Sarah-Mae,' Sarah-Mae replied, taking Reeta's hand for a gently passive shake. 'And this is my roommate, Callie.'

Callie grinned up through her over-long brunette fringe. The new girl, Reeta, didn't seem that interested in Callie, but she still smiled politely before looking back to Sarah-Mae.

'Do you live here?'

'Yuh-huh,' Sarah-Mae replied, adjusting the textbooks in her arms. 'We're over in Adams.' She tilted her shoulders in the implied direction of their dormitory. 'How about you?'

'Oh,' Reeta replied vaguely. 'I'm not in Adams. But it was nice to meet you. Maybe I'll see you again?'

'Oh sure,' Sarah-Mae said. 'There's the pep rally tonight, we're going with our sorority sisters. Will you be there?'

Reeta blinked in incomprehension. 'Oh,' she said, taking a moment before deciding on an answer. 'Yes.' She gave a determined nod. 'I'll find it.'

'It'll be at the football ground,' Callie explained with a lilt of curiosity. 'Like they all are.'

'The football ground,' Reeta repeated as if she was memorising the term before bidding them farewell. They watched her leave, unsure how they'd gone from simply passing this girl by to arranging another meeting.

Somehow, during that frenzied pep rally, Reeta had found them with their maroon and white scarves twisted around their necks, cheerleader pom-poms pumping at the ends of excited wrists. The air frothed and swirled with shouts and chants, the smell of hot dogs and stale beer curdling around them, the odd squelch of vomit from a student who couldn't hold their drink or spliff.

Reeta was still dressed the same, and not even a badge proclaiming the school's colours was visible on her loose white T shirt. She clutched at a paper cup, the edges uncurled under the pressure of her bite-marks. She said little and watched the group of sisters more than the cheerleaders' routine or the footballers' posturing. Callie assumed she was a rejected pledge, desperate to end up somehow within their fold. Reeta engaged in Callie's polite conversation, but her eyes always seemed to be seeking out someone else. It was only afterwards that Callie had understood who.

The following week Reeta began joining them in lectures. Not every one, and Callie had never seen her name on a roll call, but at least once a day Reeta's blonde head of straggly hair would sit down next to them and quietly assess the rest of the room. After three weeks of this, the girls had unwittingly become a trio. Orchestrated by neither Callie nor Sarah-Mae, even Reeta appeared mildly perplexed that her relationship with these girls had progressed so successfully.

'She doesn't go to school here, you know,' Callie told Sarah-Mae one night while they lay in their neighbouring single beds.

'I know. I feel sorry for her, to be honest, Cal,' Sarah-Mae replied, rolling over to face her friend in the dull room. 'I'm guessing she's trapped at home, didn't get the chance to come to college like us.' A movement of blanket indicated a shrug. 'I think she's real unhappy. What's the harm in giving her a bit of time?'

'You're right,' Callie said. 'I know you're right.'

'But?'

'You know what "but".'

Sarah-Mae snorted a supressed snigger. 'She is awful weird, huh?'

It was the very next day that Reeta bounded up to the girls outside of class, a manic grin tearing at her features. She clutched a piece of paper in her left hand, a sloping script in black ink rippling across the page. Callie couldn't see what it said; the edges had puckered in towards Reeta's grip.

'Sarah-Mae,' Reeta called. Her voice was light, jubilant, and Callie didn't think she'd ever seen her so relaxed in the short time they'd known her. 'It's time, Sarah-Mae,' Reeta gabbled upon reaching them, grabbing at Sarah-Mae's forearms with long, thin fingers.

'What are you talking about, Reeta?' Sarah-Mae laughed. 'Lunch time? Yeah, we're heading over to Max's Deli now. Wanna come? They have meatball subs on Wednesdays.'

Reeta shook her head. 'No, no, you don't understand. You have to come with me, now.' Her face was alight, dark hazel eyes bright and alive.

'Come where?' Sarah-Mae was still laughing, pulling at the strap of her leather handbag as it slipped off her shoulder.

'I don't have time to explain; I'll tell you in the car. You have to come, please.' Her eyebrows pleated upwards and Sarah-Mae shook her head with a smile.

'Sure thing, Reeta, if you say so. I've never seen you so excitable. We'll come.' She nodded over to Callie, who was equally enjoying Reeta's new display of enthusiasm. Maybe she'd got tickets to something? Rumour had it a Beatles tribute was playing in town this weekend; maybe she wanted them to queue up together. But Reeta was shaking her head.

'No, no. Just you. I can't take Callie. Not yet, not now. Maybe not at all. But not now. First you. It has to start with you; we need to go.'

Callie couldn't pretend that the flagrant favouritism hadn't hurt. In that moment, with that sentence, her chest had clenched and a deep rock gnawed with jagged edges at her stomach.

'What are you talking about, Reeta?' Sarah-Mae had asked. She hadn't seemed too bothered or offended on her friend's behalf.

'I can't tell you now,' Reeta had insisted. 'There isn't time, Sarah-Mae. We have to go, come on.' She'd turned on her heel and started tugging at Sarah-Mae's arm.

'OK, OK,' Sarah-Mae agreed, a chuckle breaking her words. She moved her feet to match Reeta's pace and turned back to Callie. 'I'll meet you after lunch in the library, Cal! When I'll have the answer to the mystery!' And just like that she was gone, off with Reeta, two heads of matching blonde hair glowing white in the autumn sun.

Callie felt tears prick. It had happened. The thing she'd most feared since Reeta had come on the scene. She'd taken her best friend, and Sarah-Mae hadn't even put up a fight. Stupid, wishy, friends-with-everyone Sarah-Mae had bounced so easily from the roots of the life-long friendship Callie had thought they'd been planting, to go off and make memories with any other random girl who'd come along. Roommates, sisters – it meant jack shit.

Two days later when Sarah-Mae still hadn't returned and Callie had been forced to call the police to report her missing, she had convulsed with guilt. The rock of jealousy that had gnawed at her stomach now growled with remorse. And four days after that when Sarah-Mae's butchered remains, resplendent with nineteen stab wounds, had been uncovered by a dog walker at the Sam Houston National Forest, Callie had all but imploded.

Case #0347
United States v. Reeta Doe
Exhibit J

[Exhibit J was uncovered at the crime scene of the murder of Sarah-Mae Withers.]

October 20th 1965

Dear Reeta,

I cannot tell you how it warms my heart to see your letters whenever they arrive. It has been a long few months without the support of my closest disciple. Your continued dedication will be rewarded for eternity.

My patience and trust in you, it seems, has finally paid off. I confess my growing frustration these last months as you've reported nothing but random motel rooms and kerb-side preaching. I am glad to hear you took heed of my advice to follow in Zechariah's footsteps — you must search out those who are worthy, not simply await their arrival at your door.

Sarah-Mae seems a worthy fit for our mission. A girl just like you, so you describe, can only be an asset to humanity's salvation. I implore you to

tell her the Word, and be righteous and firm — you
must not allow yourself defeat.

I eagerly await further news from you and
Sarah-Mae.

Blessings in Christ,
Brother Jeb

–

The knife must have belonged to one of the men for hunting.
She'd found it in the trunk of the station wagon during those
first few days alone. She'd not understood at the time why God
had placed such a weapon in her possession.

Not until Sarah-Mae had started to scream.

The things she'd screamed.

She wouldn't listen.

The stupid girl didn't understand. She didn't know what
a glorious gift Reeta was giving her. She had refused Reeta's
salvation, and it had all been so wrong. The ungrateful bitch
wasn't like Reeta at all. She had been wrong and the screaming
and noise was unbearable. Insolent and sinful — that was all
Sarah-Mae had ever been and Reeta had been a fool to think
otherwise. She'd been taken in, just like she had before.

When she'd found the knife in her hand, no doubt placed
there by God's own intervention, it had not just been Sarah-
Mae's earthly body she had slain. Each puncture of blade to flesh
was for every soul who'd scorned and ignored her while she'd
preached their destiny from doorsteps and sidewalks. It was for
Sarah-Mae, who dared to wail in terror at the salvation Reeta
had brought her.

When Sarah-Mae had stopped moving, Reeta turned her fists
and her knife on herself. Soaked, bloody hands smacked and
punched whatever flesh they could reach. The blade flailed and

68

caught at her skin, dragging itself through muscle with an agony as luscious as she deserved.

She was foolish and she was failing.

But she must continue.

For Jeh.

Seven

Reeta watched as Barry took a sip of coffee and pulled a face. It was the first time she'd seen him since Carol's visit, and although only a couple of weeks had passed, his skin sagged lower on his face, his hair more flecked with grey.

'Cold,' he said with a curl of his top lip. He put the cup down and rested his hands across the notepad in front of him. 'Still no trial date,' he said. 'Crawley wants the final two bodies before finalising the charges. He doesn't need them, there's…' He hesitated awkwardly. 'Well, there's enough evidence without, but he likes to tie up his loose ends.'

'And what if I can never give you them? What if I never remember?'

Barry's eyes flickered up to her and he sighed. 'If I'm honest, Reeta, I don't think it matters much. Like I say, he's got enough evidence without those final two bodies and he's getting impatient. I'd say he's confident enough of a case even without them. But' – he held out a finger toward her and forced a smile – 'if you *do* remember then I believe there might well still be hope of a plea deal.'

She shook her head. 'I won't remember. And I won't plead guilty.'

'You're co-operating with this new journalist who's come on board.' Barry checked his notes. 'Carol Joyce? She's working with Agent Willow, right?'

Reeta nodded.

'So there's still some hope – I believe this *was* the doctor's idea after all. You never know.' Reeta ignored his optimism and he continued. 'As for the plea, Reeta, I really can't press enough how important it is you change your mind.'

'I can't admit to what I don't know.'

Barry had resigned himself to this battle long ago and, with a disappointed sigh, he made a check mark in his file, marking off the number of times he'd asked and been rebutted.

'We have our work cut out for us, Reeta Doc.'

Reeta sighed, grinding the breath out of her into the stifling room. They sat in thick silence for a moment while Reeta watched her lawyer as he fussily arranged his notes, slotting them into various cardboard files and noting down dates and times. As she watched him work, she felt a wave break within her.

'I don't expect you to get me off, you know,' she said. He looked up, eyebrows raised in surprise. 'I know it looks bad – you've told me enough.'

'So why not make things better for yourself?' His voice sounded softer than before.

'Because doing that means admitting to something that I don't know and don't feel. I can't...' She paused to consider her next word. '...lie.'

Barry almost laughed, but he shook his head, evidently choosing not to verbalise what had made him catch the indignant 'Ha' he'd muttered into the air.

'I'll do the best I can for you, Reeta.' He shuffled his file closed and pushed his chair back to stand while he packed his briefcase.

With his baggy eyes and pronounced belly, Reeta could see what her case was doing to him, even in the short few months they'd known each other. She felt an unexpected stirring of guilt. But why she should feel guilt for this man who was simply doing his job, but not for Sarah-Mae or the others, she couldn't say. She had a sudden urge to apologise, to get to know him. Their previous meetings where she'd ignored and rebutted him now came crashing through her, leaving a sickly trail of remorse down her oesophagus.

'Are you married?' The words appeared in the room before she'd even really considered asking them.

Barry stopped packing his briefcase and looked up, a glint of suspicion shimmering his eyes. 'No,' he answered simply before elaborating. 'I was engaged, back in Treville – that's where I'm from. Tiny town. But...' He raised his shoulders. 'She didn't want to come with me when I got my job here, so...' His hands mimed an exploding firework.

Reeta nodded. 'Thank you,' she said, again the words materialising without warning or forethought. 'For everything thing you're doing for me. I know it's not easy.'

'It's not easy for you either, I'm betting,' Barry said carefully, glancing around the grey room.

Reeta didn't respond, but the good side of her mouth stretched to an accepting smile. She looked down while he slid the last of the papers into his briefcase and left with a surprisingly polite 'Goodbye.'

The guards didn't follow him in this time to shackle her up for the move back to her cell – Reeta had a packed schedule today. Carol and Willow were due in in an hour, and the guards had decided that rather than go through the hassle of the move twice in sixty minutes, she could stay put until they arrived. The interrogation room wasn't much different to her cell anyhow.

She waited patiently, slumped back in her chair, head bowed forward so her unruly mane fell forward in a curtain around her face. It wasn't thick hair, and it fell in uneven patches from where it had been shorn off during her time in hospital. She sat like that, not quite peaceful – but still, until the doors clanged open and Carol entered, trailed by Agent Willow. Carol looked good, a mustard-yellow skirt suit over a beige satin shirt, which rippled under the artificial light when she took off her jacket. The yellow suited her, brought out her dark skin, and Reeta almost smirked with the realisation that Willow agreed. As Carol had shrugged off her jacket, Reeta had seen his eyes follow the curve of her body as she twisted round to release it from her left wrist where it had caught on her bracelet. The move had caused her shirt to gape a little, her décolletage exposed for just a moment – a moment Reeta saw Willow clock. Was that useful information to her? Her addled mind couldn't work out how to use it to her advantage; the prospect of discovering more – maybe even about her father – took up most of her broken brain's energy.

She'd spent the last three days turning over Callie's tale, trying to turn it from story to memory. Was there an extra detail she could recall? Where had she come from? Where had she been living? Not on campus, that much had been sure. What had she been so keen to show Sarah-Mae? And why had that ended in her death? But all of those questions remained hanging, turning slowly in the breeze without hope of resolution.

–

'How have you been, Reeta?' Carol asked with a gentle smile. 'Sorry it's been a few days – I've been trying to get the rest of the stories in order for you. And Agent Willow has his own schedule too, obviously.' She nodded politely at the man on her right. The truth was that Willow had been called back to Washington to explain to his superiors exactly why a journalist was now leading the interrogation. He'd obviously done an OK job, and Stephens had generously given them his backing too, for he'd returned the night before and sent word to Carol that they could go to the jail the next day. His absence had meant, though, that Carol hadn't pushed him about the photograph Reeta had pressed against the murky glass on their first visit together. How was *Jeb* involved? After Willow's reaction the first time, she'd not wanted to bring it up again. He didn't trust her, so she needed to play by his rules for a little while and tell Reeta only what she was sanctioned to before probing.

'I'm all right, thank you,' Reeta replied quietly.

Carol smiled at her again, making sure to hold eye contact for a moment longer before she glanced over at Willow for his tacit permission to continue. He gave an almost imperceptible nod, clicked the tape recorder on and moved his chair back, readying his notepad on his bent knee.

Carol waited a beat before she began to speak.

'After your time at Texas A&M it seems you crossed the state border, perhaps spent a bit of time travelling, wandering on your own. We don't know; we have no record or witness reports for the intervening weeks. But around early November you arrived at the University of Arkansas. In fact, it was the fifth of November you first turned up. Bobby DeValle, who was Abigail Lawson's boyfriend at the time of her disappearance, has a British mother and so was hosting a fireworks party on an abandoned field near campus. They apparently have some tradition over there that they celebrate with fireworks and a bonfire, and he had recreated it in his first two years of school. Now a senior, he was trying to impress his new freshman girlfriend, Abi, and it was at this event you first stumbled in.'

Arkansas

Bobby wasn't sure if he'd seen the new girl around campus before. It was a possibility, but he didn't recognise her off the bat. Two messy braids tangled her hair, trailing down over a white crochet dress. She was dressed like a hippie but lacked their lightness and sense of freedom – there was a definite strain taut across her freckled features. It might have something to do with the thick yellow bruises smudged across the fronts of her thighs and the raggedly healing gash down her forearm – the reddish-purple line exposed every time she lifted her arm to drink. She must have only just stumbled into the field because she wasn't yet talking to anyone.

LSD maybe explained her barren gaze.

A firework fizzed behind him and a short burst of smoke darted up his nostrils. He turned to see a group of seniors holding firecrackers dangerously aloft.

'Hey, man, watch that!' Bobby called out in warning, rolling his eyes back to his friends and slinging an arm around Abi's shoulder. The new girl had sidled closer and Bobby saw one of his friends' attention perk up at her presence.

'I'm Charlie,' he said with a winning smile, stepping closer. 'Don't think I've seen you round campus before?'

'Reeta,' she replied with a nod. Charlie hesitated for a moment, giving her the chance to continue, but when he was disappointed, he ploughed on.

'We've got Bobby, Chris, Marcia and that's Abi.' Charlie nodded his introductions at each person.

Reeta's eyes lingered on the girls, settling finally with a smile on Abi. In the cloudy night with only the crackling bonfire to light them, the two girls were remarkably similar. Abi was slighter and a good few inches shorter than Reeta, but their hair flowed indistinguishably in the cool night breeze, their skin pricked with identical gooseflesh in the face of the autumn night. Marcia, who actually embodied the hippie Reeta seemed to be trying to imitate, waved hello by trailing smoke across the night sky with her spliff.

'You want some, honey?' she asked, her mouth relaxed, grinning. Reeta shook her head jerkily. Bobby felt the irk of disappointment. Maybe the new girl wasn't carrying after all. Abi laughed and leaned forward to retrieve the joint from between her friend's fingers and inhaled deeply.

The rest of that night continued as a blur of bangs, laughs, chants, games and sloppy making out with Abi in the damp, dewy grass. Bobby woke the next morning, inexplicably back in his bed, his sweater and jeans covered in muddy smears and cigarette ash. Abi was topless next to him, snoring loudly on her back. He laughed and nuzzled into her neck.

'Morning, baby,' he muttered.

She groaned and pulled her eyes halfway open to look at him. 'I think I'm going to be sick,' she said before rolling over and vomiting on his bedroom floor. When she rolled back, she picked up his abandoned watch from the bedside table and blinked into its face. Suddenly she sat upright in alarm.

'Shit! I was supposed to call my parents hours ago. They'll be worried sick – they'll call the goddam pigs if I don't hurry.'

Bobby, who had grown up with easy parents who were satisfied with a quick call every Sunday, couldn't quite get his head around Abi's dedication to ringing every single day. Whenever he pressed her on it, she'd roll her eyes and tell him he wouldn't understand. It wasn't until after she'd gone missing and he'd had to ring her Evangelical pastor father that he'd understood the confines that bound her at home. Her parents hadn't even known he'd existed.

Abi had told him later that it was that morning, as she'd rushed from his off-campus house back to her dorm room to call her parents, that she'd reconnected with Reeta, who'd been parked nearby. Getting groceries or some-thing, Abi had said. She'd offered to drive her back to campus since she was in such a rush, and some kind of friendship developed over that one act of saving grace.

Reeta was with them pretty much every day after that.

It wasn't so much that there was a deep bond between them, but Reeta was harmless enough. She laughed at the right jokes, contributed little to the conversation, faded into the smiling background of photos and sat silently to one side while the rest of them got drunk and high, experimenting the way they were meant to at college.

He'd been leaving the gym the day it turned ugly.

Abi was there to meet him for a low-key date night to see *The Cincinnati Kid*. He wasn't much fussed by cinema but Abi had dreams of acting, so he happily tagged along to whatever latest release she was angling to go see. She usually waited patiently while he had basketball practice, leaning against the tree in the square, long hair draped over her shoulder while she read a book or script to audition for whatever the drama club was putting on next. But that day when he'd sauntered down toward her, she'd been upright, feet firmly apart in fighting stance.

She was arguing with Reeta.

Reeta, who had been nothing but placid in the three weeks they'd known her. She'd even been devoid of an opinion on some of the harshest discussions that divided their group. Civil rights, Vietnam – she'd apparently been raised in a vacuum that these issues had failed to penetrate. They'd all just assumed she was some military kid. But now she stood less that a yard apart from Abi, her voice tense and raised – not shouting, but firm.

'I can help you,' Reeta was saying, a note of pleading to her tone. '*He* can help you. Save you.'

'I don't need fucking saving, Reeta, I came here to get away from all that.' Abi nearly spat the words. Reeta's hand flicked out like a knife and she grabbed at Abi's forearm, stopping her from turning away.

'It's true, though, please, Abi. Let me, let me, you have to let me help.' Her voice was becoming frenzied, undulating over the words.

Bobby approached slowly; he didn't want to get involved in the girls' fight, but Reeta's grip looked like it must be hurting Abi's arm crescents of white skin peeling away under her fingernails.

'Is everything OK, Ab?' he asked gently, arriving between them.

Abi's shoulders sagged and she glanced up at him.

'Yeah, we're fine, Bob. Reeta just wants to show me something, but I'm done with churches.' She turned back to face her. 'I told you, Reeta, I'm done with churches.'

79

'This isn't a church!' Reeta all but wailed, flailing her free arm, which Bobby now saw gripped a piece of paper filled with elegant lines of neat cursive, finished off with a flourished signature.

'Girls,' Bobby said, forcing his voice calm. 'Maybe you should just take a minute.' He looked at Reeta. 'Reeta, maybe you need to chill out a little. Whatever it is, I don't think Abi wants to go.'

'She will when she sees!' Reeta screeched at him, tears breaking dams, so they flushed surprisingly down her cheeks. She gasped loudly; the tears had startled her as much as they had him.

'Reeta, it's OK,' Abi said, her tone modulated to that of one soothing a hysterical child. 'I know how much it can mean to people. I still love my parents, you know that,' she said, gesturing to her new friend's wet face. 'You don't need to worry about me. I just need to get out from their leash a little, that's all. Work out what's right for me.'

'*This* is right for you,' Reeta replied intently, gesturing with the paper. 'You have to trust me. Please.'

Bobby had felt his heart break for her in that moment. A feeling he hated himself for with the perfection of hindsight. But in that moment he saw a poor military kid who'd never had a real friend, trying desperately to share something from her messed-up, unsettled life. He'd known Abi's parents were religious, so maybe that's why Reeta had latched on. He couldn't see the harm in Abi going along to help the girl with whatever new church group she'd found.

'Abs,' he said and looked pleadingly into his girlfriend's face before finishing the sentence he would come to regret. 'Maybe just go with her for now. We can see the movie another time.'

Abi had stirred to argue; she didn't *want* to get drawn back into the folds of a church she'd already escaped. But Bobby knew that she would agree – Reeta needed it.

Just this once.

It took less than a day for a pipeline maintenance man to find Abi after Bobby had alerted the police to her disappearance the day after the scene in front of the gym.

She was barely recognisable under her blanket of hammer blows. Her ring finger lay disembodied, inches from the tips of her splayed-out hair.

Case #0347
United States v. Reeta Doe
Exhibit K

[Exhibit K was uncovered at the crime scene of the murder of Abigail Lawson.]

November 23rd 1965

Dear Reeta,

It was with a heavy heart to learn of yet another failure on your part – the loss of Sarah-Mae is one that will surely hinder the foundations of our new mission. A delay we can ill afford now that the End Times have begun.

You redeem yourself with news of Abigail; the fact that you have already discussed the Lord and her church is promising work. I fear though for your capability of this role which you have been gifted and I wish you to bring her directly to me. You can then return to your assignment to grow our numbers.

You have struck many blows against your Messiah. I pray you do not permit another.

Blessings in Christ,
Brother Jeb

Abigail was meant to be different to Sarah-Mae. She'd grown up with the Lord, just like Reeta. She'd told Reeta herself of chapel and Bible study, her father's dedication to Jesus Christ and God. Abigail was meant to understand.

The hammer was heavy and solid in her hand, satisfying with the power it wielded. Another tool gifted from above, found in the trunk of the car next to a pair of heavy rusty pliers. She hadn't thought she'd need it so soon. Not on Abigail. But Abigail had been a disappointment just like everyone else.

Just like herself.

The hammer head cracked Abigail's skull and Reeta wished it was her own.

The golden ring Abigail had claimed to have been given for her confirmation taunted Reeta. Abigail had made no promises to Christ. She offered no dedication to the Lord to salvage her soul.

She tore at Abigail's lifeless finger with the pliers, wrenching her frustration and hatred into the one satisfying motion of tearing and crunching bone.

And she wished it was her own.

Eight

Carol had invited Willow to dinner on the way back from the jail. His raised eyebrows had betrayed his surprise but he eventually gave a single nod and muttered, 'Sure. That'd be nice.'

She arrived before him at the casual Italian they'd chosen. Neutral ground, no reminders of her grand accommodation against his musty motel room. It was dim inside as per every classic trattoria in the States, lit only by the soft orange of candlelight. She sat down at the table fresh with white linen and smiled up at the waiter to order a bottle of Pinot Noir. That was Willow's favourite – or at least it had been. Sipping on cool ice water while she waited for both her companion and wine, she fished a small stack of photos from her handbag. The thick feeling of eyes traipsing across the restaurant toward her tugged her head a fraction upright. Three tables of couples were looking at her, two with – what she hoped was – harmless intrigue, but one with a menacing scowl pleating the man's saggy face. It had been an adjustment being down in Florida where her complexion was unnerving to some, unable to tell if she was black or white. Pale enough to pass in Washington without much of a to-do, the scrutiny down here was something else. But she knew there was nothing they could do – for the last two years she had the legal right to eat anywhere she pleased, no matter what

they deduced her skin colour to be. She smiled disarm-
ingly at the angry man on one of the occupied tables
before hanging her expensive handbag over the arm of her
chair. The other two couples seemed to have lost interest,
but Carol watched the wife of the third track her eyes
down Carol's smart mustard suit, hover on her crocodile-
skin pumps and settle on the matching bag. She turned
back to her husband with a small shrug, who slouched a
little, but kept one eye keenly trained.

Carol allowed herself to relax and turned her attention
back to the photos in her hand, flipping slowly through
them, taking in Reeta's blandly smiling face at the corners
of big groups. Willow had grudgingly handed the collection over when he'd got back from Washington, admitting
quietly that she might find them useful. The Texas girls
hadn't had much in the way of photographs, but Bobby
DeValle's group had been big on capturing their college
years. Only in one picture did Reeta take centre stage, a
candid shot of an unexpectant face looking directly into
the lens. Her hair was swept over to one side and she wore
a tight mauve sweater over light denim jeans, a record
sleeve in her hand, which she had evidently been reading
before being called to attention for the photo. It was hard
to marry that peaceful look of gentle surprise with the
contortion that now stared back from the other side of
the interrogation room.

Willow arrived before the wine did, with an awkward
hello and fumble to sit down. His eyes rested on the photos
in Carol's hand for a moment, before looking up at the
waiter who had just arrived tableside.

'The Pinot Noir?' he asked and Carol nodded in
confirmation, gesturing to the two squat, empty wine
glasses in front of them. The waiter poured theatrically,

twisting the bottle elaborately away as if they were at some state dinner.

'Cheers,' Carol said, picking up her glass and tilting it toward Willow.

'Cheers,' Willow replied, his tone not quite matching her lightness.

'So how d'you think it's going?' Carol asked, setting down the photos in front of her.

Willow shrugged. 'It's hard to say. I'm not a doctor.'

'How do you think *I'm* doing?' Carol rephrased.

He sighed. 'You're doing great, she's connecting with you and what you're saying. Even her body language is more open than when we were at the helm. But you know that. You get the story, it's what you're good at.' Carol exhaled in frustration but he didn't let her interrupt. 'We're not here for me to give you an appraisal, Carol. Cut the bullshit. Why did you ask me to dinner?'

Carol looked at him for a lingering moment before sitting back in her chair and taking a large mouthful of wine. 'She has a picture of Brother Jeb. That she claims *you* gave to her, Ben. You can't just brush that under the rug.'

Willow closed his eyes and swallowed. 'And?'

She lowered her chin, staring up at him disbelievingly. 'And?' she repeated. 'And I want to know what the fuck he's got to do with this!'

Before he could respond, the angry couple had risen from their table to leave, their unsubtle whisperings of 'disgusting' and 'just distasteful' darted pointedly in Carol and Willow's direction. Willow cracked his neck toward them, rage rearranging his features. He moved to stand, but Carol put her hand on his, stopping him.

'Leave it, Ben. Leave it.'

He hesitated for a moment before dropping back into his seat. 'I'd forgotten about that.'

She gave an indignant exhale. '*You* get to.'

He swallowed thickly and they hovered without speaking for another moment before she collected herself.

'It's not just you – it's everyone. Now.' She repositioned herself, ready for verbal battle. 'Don't change the subject. Jeb.'

'Shit,' Willow muttered under his breath, clenching his fist and wrinkling the tablecloth under his grasp.

'She was there, wasn't she?'

'We think so,' Willow replied after a moment. 'We don't know exactly what happened. But we have some letters.'

'Letters?'

'Three letters found at the crime scenes, addressed to her, from him.'

He didn't know why he'd told her. Some long-lost urge to impress or show off, maybe. Or perhaps it was simpler than that – he just missed confiding in her, poring over interesting details of his cases, their wits banded together to solve the mystery. But he knew where that led.

He needed to save himself from that mistake again.

Carol sat back in her chair, astounded.

'Jesus Christ,' she whispered. 'This is huge.'

He raised his clenched hand and released his forefinger, pointing directly at her.

'This is not a scoop, Carol. This needs to be handled delicately. We don't know what's going on and the US Attorney wants us to be sure before he even thinks about releasing the existence of those letters to the public. This is why we need her to remember where she left Mandy and

Susan *now*, before that broken brain of hers gets addled even more.'

'Wait.' Carol sat back and blinked. 'You're telling me she has no idea about the letters? Why hasn't her lawyer told her? If there's anything that might hint at a motive, might connect *Jeb* then surely—' She cut herself off, an expression of disappointment falling across her face. She closed her eyes. 'He doesn't know about them either, does he?'

'We're not in a position to be brandishing those letters around, when we're not sure what they mean yet.'

'You'll get this whole case thrown out on a Brady violation!' Carol hissed.

'I thought you'd like that, seeing as you're on her side now.' Willow's voice dripped with sarcasm.

'Don't be petty, Ben. You know I want justice for those girls, *real* justice from a fair fucking trial.' Carol adjusted her back and glanced mindlessly around the room while she collected herself. 'You've seen that girl in there, she doesn't know what's going on. Those letters could help her figure it out – you *have* to give them to her lawyer.'

'He'll get them all right.' Willow sat back with a dismissive wave of his hand. 'We're gonna do things by the book, I'm not dumb enough to get this thrown out on a technicality. But we don't have a trial date yet and we can factor in processing time and that gives us a few weeks, OK? A few weeks I intend to use to focus her on Mandy and Susan. The letters aren't going to help her case anyway. They just put her even more in the shit. When you put them together with the witness statements, the students who are going to identify her in court—'

'Even with her face like that?'

'That doesn't matter.' He held up a palm. 'They'll know it's her. We have the hair comparison analysis and we have her *driving the fucking car with Bonnie in the trunk*. This is a lockdown case, Carol. All those letters do is give her a background that gives a possible motive.'

'Or implicate Jeb,' Carol pointed out.

'Don't start on that, Carol. You might be getting attached to her, but I guarantee you she's guilty.'

'Let *me* show her the letters.'

Willow exhaled. 'Not a chance, Carol. Keep her focused.'

'If anything is going to jog her memory it'll be the reason why she did all this. She's floundering now, Ben, you can see it too. None of what I'm telling her is landing.'

'We keep going.' He lowered his eyes to the laminated menu in front of him and made a show of searching up and down the columns. Carol watched him for a moment before following his lead. Just when she was hovering over the antipasti section, he spoke again. 'Tell her about Mandy and Susan. Let us please just find those girls.'

Once they'd gotten business out of the way, dinner was surprisingly warm. They reminisced lightly, updated one another on their parents, families and other mutual acquaintances who had peppered their once joint life. Willow filled Carol in on Stephens' wife, causing her bottom lip to drop open just a touch in shock, grief, nostalgia. Carol had always liked Norma. She was one of the few other wives who'd always made an effort – and hadn't seemed too perturbed by the ambiguous colour of Carol's skin. They were wholly different people, but Carol would happily smile politely when Norma told her how as soon as Carol got married and pregnant she'd be clamouring to give up work just like Norma had – always said with a marigold smile down at whichever of the Stephens' four-strong brood was hollering for attention.

'That's why he's not around as much,' Willow said with a fractional shrug, twirling artificially red spaghetti around his fork.

'Send them my thoughts next time you see them.'

'I will.' Willow nodded sagely. 'I don't actually know why I told you that,' he confessed after a beat. 'Stephens wouldn't want you to know. We're here for work.' His tone had altered just a touch, back to its former stone.

They finished their pasta and paid the cheque, Willow declining the dessert menu without having to awkwardly glance at Carol to check it was the right decision.

–

Now that Willow was back from Washington, they'd arranged to go to the jail every day. If they could finish off these stories within a week, then maybe by next weekend they'd have daughters to return to two grieving families.

Willow had played his dinner with Carol over and over throughout the night. Nuggets of recollection had stopped him from sleeping, surges of unwanted feelings churning his stomach. Each time he'd looked up from his food he'd seen her wide mouth painted seashell pink stretched into her easy smile, and he was right back in her townhouse, in her bed, in her kitchen – making coffee and pulling Danishes from the oven. But every memory was truncated by a gaping waterfall of betrayal and he'd had to turn away.

He was glad he'd ended dinner where he had. They were in danger of straying too far away from Reeta, and he couldn't allow that to happen. This was a bigger case than last time. Those letters weren't currency to be bartered over red wine and Italian food; they held the key as to why a young woman had brutalised four of her friends and attempted a fifth.

But dinner had allowed him to remember that there *were* good times; there had once been easy laughter and private jokes. Fond memories and shared experiences that imbued him with an unintentional warmth when he picked her up the next morning. A stiffness had left his body. Two cups of takeaway coffee sat in a cardboard holder between them. 'Two Sweet'N Low and a dash of milk.' He nodded down.

'Thanks.' She smiled and picked up her coffee, leaning forward to tune in the radio station. 'Where Did Our Love Go' blared bouncily from the speakers and he saw Carol stifle a laugh as she crooned the opening lines, shimmying her shoulders in his direction. It took a moment for him to make a decision. He rolled his eyes, cracked a smile and joined in.

An hour and a half later they pulled up to Florida Women's Corrections, their shimmering lightness juxtaposed with the looming dark they knew lay inside.

Nine

Something had shifted. Even Reeta could tell that. And she wasn't particularly adept at understanding interpersonal relationships given the entirety of the life she could recall had not afforded her much experience of them. But she could see, as soon as she was escorted into the room, that Carol and Willow were more relaxed. Not in general – they had not forgotten the reason they were there, but with each other. The way he passed her a pen, the way she accepted with a gracious smile.

Reeta didn't know if this was good news or not.

'Reeta, hello, how are you since yesterday?' Carol asked.

'I'm OK,' she mumbled quietly while her chains were removed. She sat down in her usual chair and waited. She never started. What would she say?

'Today is quite important, Reeta,' Carol said gently. 'This is how you met Mandy Silas at Mississippi State College for Women and I'll touch on what we know of Susan O'Donnell at the University of Alabama. So *anything* that rings a bell, or jogs your memory while I'm speaking, is crucial. Even if you just recognise the description of a building or a place. Anything at all you think is familiar let me know and we can explore that further. Does that make sense?'

Reeta nodded, although she knew nothing would. Nothing in anything Carol had told her had seemed even remotely familiar. And none of it was leading to her father. But if she bided her time, waited these stories out, then maybe she would be rewarded. That was all she could hope for as she ran the details Carol had shared over and over each night. None of them caught on anything like a memory; none of them helped paint a picture of *who* she was. They were told from above, tainted with the horror of what had happened next. They weren't reliable portraits of her character. They were useless to her. But just a few more fairy tales and she'd get what she wanted.

Her father.

The man on the porch.

'You arrived in Mississippi before Christmas. News of Sarah-Mae and Abi had been circulated in their towns and states; local papers were fearmongering to get young women to leave college and stay at home. No one had connected the crimes, yet, though. There were no leads on you at all; what Callie and Bobby had told their respective police departments about you being the last person to see them alive hadn't crossed state lines yet – jurisdictional pride can get in the way of even the simplest of policework.' She rolled her eyes. 'Each police force had dismissed the idea that you could be the culprit. They assumed you'd both got caught up in something after you'd left, and perhaps they were even looking for another body. Although no one had reported you missing. It wasn't until Mississippi that a young officer with family in Texas who had heard about Sarah-Mae spotted the similarities when Mandy Silas's disappearance came in. He rooted around and discovered your presence in Arkansas and that's when Agents Willow and Stephens were brought in.'

Reeta nodded slowly.

'But when you arrived in Mississippi, still no one knew who you were. You fitted right in at the College for Women, and most reports suggest that you were seen around campus for a couple of weeks before you approached Mandy.'

Mississippi and Alabama

The Christmas pageant was where they first met Reeta. Nancy, Mandy and Linda had worked on the pageant committee for the last two years and now, as seniors, it was finally their time to run the show. The tacky stock of decorations had been discarded from years past, and Mandy had spearheaded the simple white, blue and silver theme that now draped the school's theatre. Hopeless acts had been ruthlessly cut – after all, this was a show, not a charity contest – and the successful ones had been dragged into more rehearsals than the pageant had ever seen. Any participant overheard complaining was cut. Anyone caught up in behaviour unbecoming of a pageant performer was cut. The recent raid at a local bar had seen their programme diminish considerably, but Mandy had risen to the occasion and doubled up the performances of each act left.

The show had gone without a hitch and had been closed by a perfected harmony of the three organisers singing 'Amazing Grace' followed by a group prayer led by Mandy. Reeta had sat in the back. Nancy vaguely recognised her from around campus, or the 7-Eleven in town, but that night the new girl approached them at the after-show drinks held in the theatre. Bowls of bland punch and eggnog lined the tables around the room, chocolate chip cookies, lemon squares and candy canes stacked high around them.

'The show was very good,' Reeta had told them and all three organisers had gifted her polite, vanilla smiles for the compliment. 'You must have worked very hard on it.'

Mandy had taken the bait. Both Nancy and Linda also had blown-out blonde curls dancing like halos around their heads, and afterwards Nancy wondered if it was a simple act of allowing her friend to speak first that had saved her own life.

'Well, when you work hard at something, it pays off,' Mandy had said with a satisfied smirk.

Nancy and Linda had never seen the girl again, but just four days later Mandy had disappeared for good. Later, the FBI analysis would propose that Reeta was working more quickly, growing more frantic in her bloodlust. It was another two weeks before Mandy's friends even remembered about the girl at the pageant, pushed to the brink of insanity by endless questioning about secret boyfriends and new faces in Mandy's life. Finally, Linda had gasped, 'There was that girl. Nancy, that girl.'

'Shush, Linda, the police don't want to hear about some random girl.'

'What girl?' The officer sat forward with interest, fixing his gaze on Linda.

'There was just some girl who came up to compliment us on the pageant.' Nancy waved a shaking hand, dismissive despite its constant tremor.

'Mandy said she'd seen her again outside the Motel 6. She said she thought she was homeless, and that she felt sorry for her,' Linda cut in.

'We all felt sorry for her, we're only *Christian*,' Nancy elongated the final word, her Mississippi drawl looping over it. 'But I only have space in my heart for Mandy at the moment. I feel for this girl, I do, but if she's gone missing too then let her family and friends worry about it.'

'Did you get her name?' the officer asked.

Both girls shook their heads.

'A description?'

'Long, raggedy, blonde hair, not styled.' Nancy gestured, shimmying her fingertips down to her waist.

'Dark eyes,' Linda cut in. 'Brown or dark green. She was maybe my height? Five foot seven?'

'Skinny.' Nancy took back the mantle. 'I remember her clothes were weird, worn and mismatched.'

'What was she wearing the day you saw her at the pageant?'

'Jeans, they were all frayed at the bottom and mud-stained. I remember thinking, *Couldn't she have made an effort for the show? Put a skirt on or a dress?* And a grey sweater; it looked like a man's. Didn't fit her properly.'

'Anything else you remember about her?'

'Only that she seemed kind of lost. I don't think she went to school here,' Linda finished with a small shrug. 'Do you think she's missing too?'

–

Officer Clarke hadn't answered her question. He thanked them for their time, again, and sent them on their way. When he returned to his desk, he called the Texas PD that had dealt with the case his cousin had told him about, to get the description of the girl who'd left with the victim that day.

'We're still conducting a search for her,' the officer on the other end of the phone told him. 'But without an official missing person's report we can't allocate too many resources it.' He sounded defensive, as if Clarke were suggesting the entire might of the Texas PD should be out looking for this phantom of a girl. 'Such a damn shame. I'm telling you these girls shouldn't be at college. They should stay home with their mommas and learn how to make a good wife. I mean look at us, and Arkansas lost one too.'

'Arkansas?'

'Oh yeah, buddy of mine over there said their papers are full of it as well. Young girl, pretty and blonde, turned up dead. Not quite like ours, but enough to make you think about whether college is a place for your daughter.'

Officer Clarke had called the switchboard immediately to get connected to Washington county, Arkansas. The FBI had not long followed. None of the police departments really believed a young woman capable of these crimes, or even that Sarah-Mae and Abigail were connected. But they weren't getting anywhere, so happily handed over their files. No one liked an open case languishing on their desk. Only a handful of newspapers ran with the news about Reeta, and of those the majority were told in a mocking tone of the FBI who dared believe a young woman capable of this. They called for a real investigation; they called for college students to write in with any leads on suspicious men hanging around campus, some papers floating the idea this surely had to do with the legacy of desegregation. Before 'the blacks' were allowed on campus, they never had a problem like this.

–

News died off over Christmas, students returned home and even into the new year, no one else reportedly went missing or turned up dead. The newspapers moved on; the local PDs moved on.

Willow and Stephens, now on the case, were at an impasse. They had no leads, no firm connections between their cases, and no new crimes. They found themselves in the catch-22 of waiting for another young woman to disappear so that they might progress

It was in rainy February that they got their wish.

Susan O'Donnell. Blonde. Sophomore. Disappeared after the opening baseball game of the season. There was nothing connecting her to the other girls aside from her hair colour and a pretty face. She was a jock, a tomboy, most of her friends said. Grew up on a farm in the middle of the state with three brothers and four sisters and could hold her own in any feat of physicality. She played on the first University of Alabama women's collegiate softball team, and campaigned for access to more leagues, more facilities and more funding for female sport. Kind of a pain in the ass, an administration secretary had gossiped under her breath.

The description of Reeta held nothing with any of Susan's peers or other students. Sure, they'd seen girls matching her description, but they couldn't say for certain it was the girl in the photo. By this time, Willow and Stephens had Bobby's photography collection and had received positive IDs from Callie, Nancy and Linda that this was the girl. In Alabama, though, there was nothing. She must have floated in for one baseball game, found her target and floated out. She'd stopped pretending to make friends.

The agents didn't know what to make of that.

It wasn't until the fifth motel they checked that they got an ID. She'd stayed for five days, paid cash, disappeared early one morning or late one night without even checking out. Just left her key in the door and the room strewn with debris. Debris that was now safely in the evidence lock-up of the FBI field office in Birmingham – a collection of abandoned socks, a hairbrush, a cracked biro, a photograph and a neatly folded letter pressed between the pages of a Bible. The press wouldn't be getting these updates, not yet. It suited Willow and Stephens for now to allow the local police, elected sheriffs and governors to dismiss the notion of a mass murderer stalking the college campuses of the South. Individual victims, girls who couldn't handle the real world, that was the only message everyone was interested in peddling.

Susan O'Donnell's disappearance was barely mentioned in the newspapers; even the college paper only said that she'd most likely returned home to her family farm. Willow and Stephens knew that not to be the case, and the grieving O'Donnell family waited patiently each night for their daughter to wander up the long, dusty driveway cutting between the cattle fields.

They'd got their wish – one more girl disappeared into thin air. But there was not even the wispiest trail of where she'd gone.

[Exhibit L was uncovered in Room 42, Sunrise Lodge Motel, Alabama.]

[Exhibit L was accompanied by Exhibit H, a photograph of Lt. Roger Fry aka Brother Jeb. Exhibit H is currently removed from this file.]

January 31ˢᵗ 1966

Reeta,
Your failures grow wearying. You are not the disciple I believed you to be. You have tricked me — does the devil flow inside your veins?
Brother Jeb

—

Her mistake was to befriend them. To befriend anyone was a weakness like torn stitches on a rag doll — sooner or later they would unravel and rip your chest apart.
Reeta knew who she was looking for now.
She needed girls like her.

Girls like them.

Identical angels sent from Heaven above.

And if she refused to come to her salvation then her punishment was also Reeta's own. That was the beauty of every bloody river tangled up in blonde weeds. Reeta could believe they were her own wounds — her own punishment well deserved.

Ten

Today was the final story, and the last chance to nudge any smothered memory in Reeta's battered head. Willow was due to be hauled back to Washington and told to stand down to let the judicial process take control – Crawley had called last night to say he was setting a trial date. There was no more investigating to be done. The case was tight and they didn't need to keep interrogating her. She wasn't going to give them Mandy and Susan – that much was abundantly clear by now. Barry would be given the letters, and she would read them during her pretrial prep – no doubt with the same expression of bewilderment Willow had been faced with when he'd handed her the photograph. Carol would go back too with a pocketbook full of detailed stories that the wider press didn't have yet, and Willow would get blamed for that again as well.

It had been nearly two weeks since he'd interrupted the doctor's family celebration to ask about retrograde amnesia, and for what? Zero. He tossed the cheap filter coffee of his motel breakfast to the back of his throat and pulled a face at the bitterness. Stephens was absent again. He'd taken the opportunity of Willow and Carol's little interlude in their case to stay at home and tend to Norma. Willow couldn't really blame him. At least he was doing something.

One more day in that pit of a jail and he'd be back home, ready to take his rebuke and start on a fresh case. Put Reeta and her baffling trail of dead girls to bed for the judicial system to unpack. He was done.

As he pulled up outside Carol's hotel, the stiffness in her manner told him that she understood the finality of today too. For her, though, he knew she still hoped it to lead to more information about Brother Jeb. But that was information he would never give her – she'd have to read about it in the trial transcripts like every other journalist. Their dinner had been nice – and the resurrection of their tender easiness had made this a lot more bearable – but there was no future with Carol. They'd return to their respective corners of Washington, DC or she would mine his career for whatever diamonds she could uncover, ignoring the crumbling walls of the quarry.

'Morning.' She smiled, leaning forward to pick up the takeaway coffee he'd collected on his way over. Today he'd added doughnut holes to their travelling breakfast, and she plucked one from the box, white icing sugar dusting down her green sleeve.

'Morning.'

'Sleep OK?' she asked, taking a bite out of the doughnut hole.

Willow looked at her and laughed. 'Who *bites* a doughnut hole?'

Her eyebrows raised and her mouth gaped in mock indignance. 'Oh, shut up.' She swallowed heavily. 'Put the radio on.'

Willow complied and then picked up a doughnut hole, popping it into his mouth all in one.

'Very impressive.' Carol selected another and made a show of biting down hard through the middle.

Willow smiled and shook his head, feeling an unwanted tug of affection. With his free hand he flipped closed the cardboard flap on the box and put the car into drive. He pressed on the gas pedal and pulled out for their final morning car journey, unable to help his eyes from sliding toward Carol as she finished her doughnut hole and opened the file in her lap. She glanced up and gave him a questioning smile, which he batted away by returning his attention to the road ahead. He felt her gaze on him for a beat longer before she returned to the papers containing Bonnie Powell's statement.

Florida I

Bonnie had been nearing the end of her first year at college. She'd chosen the University of Florida to the surprise of her parents. Born and raised in the metropolitan Columbus, to a solicitor and high school English teacher, Bonnie had been expected to shoot for an Ivy League, or at least to remain in the north-east. But her grades hadn't quite come up to scratch and Bonnie had the urge to spread her wings. She'd applied to schools in California, Florida, Oregon and Washington State, but only Florida had taken the bait.

She'd settled in well at the University of Florida. For every Southern belle wannabe in search of a husband, Bonnie had been surprised to find a girl like her – keen to make her own way in the world, fizzing with ambition and promise. Through the Students for a Democratic Society, she'd found purpose with sit-ins and protests against the Vietnam War. Her father's letters brimmed with pride in response to every meeting or action she described, and in her own small way she felt like she was doing something.

It was at one of these demonstrations she met Reeta.

It was the biggest turnout they'd had so far and over two hundred students were scattered across the Lake Alice field, home-made pickets waved aloft, the sing-song chants of '*Hey, hey, LBJ, how many kids did you kill today?*' swimming in the thick, humid air. Bonnie was passing out flyers and fake draft cards to burn later, while keeping her eye out for the reporter Nick Lowenstein had invited from the *Gainesville Gazette*. A girl with a long braid swinging down her back approached, her hand held out for one of the patchy xeroxed handouts Bonnie was flinging at passers-by.

'The government needs to realise this war isn't legal!' Bonnie was adamant in her message. The girl looked down at the flyer Bonnie had designed, a three-dimensional peace sign surrounded by hand-drawn flowers and *PEACE IN VIETNAM* in bubble letters across the top. The bottom had details of the SDS regular weekly meetings. 'The more fuss we make now, along with our brothers and sisters at colleges across the country, the more LBJ will understand what the youth of this country want – and that we're a peaceful generation! We don't want the wars of our parents, we don't want our souls marked with those scars!'

'I agree,' the girl said, her tone surprisingly casual for such a politically heightened environment. Apathy was unusual to encounter at these events – that's what had struck Bonnie. Either people were as passionate as her, or they countered her with venom and rage at her lack of patriotism. She'd been called a bitch and slut, a lesbian and frigid, told to get back in the kitchen, told she was a n——r-lover and a hippy bitch. One man had screamed in detail how he would rape her with his gun barrel to teach her what a true American believes, and the cops had done nothing. If she wanted the right to free speech so much, she could hardly complain when that right was upheld for others too. She wasn't threatening violence, though, she'd explained to deaf ears, before walking home shaking and terrified, clinging to Nick's arm, cricking her neck with constant looks over her shoulder.

But apathy was new. And oddly more disconcerting.

'You'll be here all day?' the girl had asked.

'Yes, the demonstration is on all day. We'll probably get moved along by campus police around five when the gardeners will want to tend to the lawn, but that's OK — we'll reconvene at Big Jerry's.' Big Jerry's was a bar that cared more about dollars in the register than ID on their customers. Every college town had at least one. What Bonnie hadn't told her was that the SDS had found that by five, most of the less ardent demonstrators would get bored and want a drink as the sun dropped and a breeze rolled in. If they moved the action to a bar, they could usually hold their attention for the rest of the night.

Big Jerry's was dark and crowded. Record sleeves were pinned to cork panels across the walls, a mismatch of new hits and old classics. The Byrds' version of 'Mr Tambourine Man' was playing above the sound of indignant arguments, mindless flirting and drunken laughter. Bonnie herself was tipsy; she'd sunk four beers and couldn't usually handle her liquor. The bar was in soft focus but she could see enough to recognise faces and move around, nodding in agreement at the edge of Nick's conversations before wandering silently away to dance with a couple of the girls from her dorm.

A sudden wave of sickly warmth passed through her and she stumbled to one side, catching on Debbie Post's shoulder.

'I need some air,' she muttered and pushed her way through the crowded dance floor, burning her forearm on the end of someone's cigarette. The door to the bar was propped open, a constant stream of students wandering in and out, and the light breeze drifting in already eased Bonnie's oncoming nausea. She sidled through the group who'd chosen to commandeer the doorway for their hangout spot and stepped over the girl who was sitting on the stoop. Bonnie leaned back against the wall just to their left and took three deep inhalations, relishing the goosebumps that sprung up across her exposed back. For the demonstration itself she'd worn a plain white T-shirt over her red corduroy flares, but before the bar she had swung by her dorm to replace it with a brown suede halter. Nick had never looked at her like *that* before, and it had been Debbie who'd suggested it wouldn't hurt to show him a bit more of her womanly assets. It wasn't that Bonnie didn't enjoy dressing up, just that in the context in which she usually saw Nick it wasn't really appropriate to don miniskirts or halter tops. Tonight was the perfect opportunity.

'You said you'd be here,' a disturbingly level voice said. There was no excitement of the night, no drunken slur. Bonnie looked up from where she'd been focusing on her feet to see the girl with the long braid occupying the space in front of her.

'Oh, uh, yeah,' Bonnie replied, taking a moment to collect herself. 'Did you enjoy the demonstration?'

Before she could answer, a drunken cackle echoed from the group at the doorway. 'You two could be twins,' a stoned guy shouted before pealing into hysterics. His friends joined in while the girl on the stoop leaned out and peered dramatically at the two of them.

'Clones,' she whispered, and Bonnie could practically see the darts of marijuana-induced paranoia spark. Bonnie turned back to the girl, her eyes narrowing closely onto her face.

'It's good that you're so passionate about a cause,' the girl said. For a moment Bonnie wondered if she was coming on to her. 'That's something important.'

'Yeah.' Bonnie forced a casual tone. 'Got to try and make a difference. Take a stand for what you believe.'

'Take a stand,' the girl repeated and her eyes drifted off, lost in a memory. Her attention was suddenly back. 'Will you come with me?'

Bonnie had refused the odd request, still thinking it a come-on, and returned to the bar, searching for Nick.

When Bonnie awoke in hospital three days later, she couldn't recall anything further past that moment. Nick had told the police Bonnie had left about midnight to walk home – he'd assumed she was leaving with Debbie or the other girls from her dorm, or else he would have gone with her. The next time anyone saw Bonnie she was being rescued from the trunk of a station wagon twisted furiously around a tree off the I-75, her backpack gripped desperately into her stomach.

Eleven

'Does any of that sound familiar?' Carol had finished telling Bonnie's story gently, and Willow slowly exhaled through his nose as if he'd been holding his breath.

Reeta shook her head, expressionless.

'Bonnie has had a few more recollections since that original statement was taken,' Willow said, pulling his chair forward. This surprised Carol – she hadn't been told of any new details from the witness. And wasn't *she* meant to be the one helping Reeta recover her memory?

'Nothing concrete,' Willow said, shooting Carol a knowing look. 'She recalls talk of commitment and sacrifice. She remembers sitting in the passenger seat, which suggests you didn't immediately put her in the trunk, and both your forearms and wrists show signs of a struggle. Our working theory is that she initially went willingly with you, perhaps thinking she was simply accepting a lift home, but at some point – and for some reason – she decided against it and a fight ensued. You were the victor and succeeded in subduing her enough to get her in the trunk. There were no signs of a struggle from within the trunk itself, suggesting she was unconscious in there.' Carol did know about that part. 'She also remembers' – Willow breathed in deeply, as if preparing to play his ace – 'talk of Cuba.'

Carol jerked her head toward him, her forehead furrowed in a deep frown. Cuba? What the hell was he talking about? She turned back to Reeta and saw that the ace had failed to land.

Her face remained blank.

'Do you remember anything about Cuba, Reeta? Does that ring any bells?' Willow pushed, leaning forward in his seat, but his manner had changed in the week since Carol had been there – he'd lost his hard edge. It was impossible to have watched Carol's stories of brutalised and disappeared girls settle over Reeta – watch her face flicker with horror at the details, slow tears falling in frustration – and not have developed at least a modicum of sympathy for her. Carol had given those girls not only an identity, but a backstory, a life – worried friends and family, dreams never to be realised, each girl an individual. They were no longer just a stream of injuries and names.

Reeta shook her head.

'No Cuba,' she whispered. Her tone was soft, desolate.

'Reeta,' Carol said, inserting herself into the moment between them. 'I do need to return to Washington in the next few days – I have appointments and other work assignments – but I will continue to write to you, and would be happy to come down and visit again.'

Reeta's response was instant; her face hardened and she looked at Carol directly.

'You can't go yet. You haven't told me about my father!' Her desperation leaked out like fetid water squeezed from a rag. 'You promised! I listened to your stories – and they mean nothing to me! I can't even picture these girls. I'm sorry about what happened, and if you say it was all me then I don't even know any more how to defend myself. I'll take my punishment, but I can't help you find Mandy and Susan. I just *can't*. But you *can* help me and you promised you would!' She reached inside her pocket and retrieved the photograph. '*This* is all I care about! My family, my f-f-father.' Her words were breaking now over her gasping breath. There were no tears, but the panic was seeping through her. '*You* gave me this!' She pointed at Willow. 'And *you* promised me answers.' Her finger tracked to Carol. 'You said you'd help. You promised me you'd help.' Her voice flagged over the final words, her finger dropping as she looked down at the photograph.

Guilt rushed Carol's limbs. She *had* agreed to help.

'I'm afraid I can't tell you about the man in the photograph. I just don't know enough, and I'm worried I would do more harm than good. I'm sorry, Reeta, I tried, but only Agent Willow or your lawyer will be able to help you with that.'

Had she really tried? She'd asked Ben about it a couple of times and then given up when he pushed back. What had she expected? A full and detailed round-up of Brother Jeb's involvement? She should have investigated harder, pushed him more. But she was too wrapped up in her past betrayals and the exclusive at her fingertips. She'd figured she could wait a little to break the Brother Jeb angle and focused instead on note-taking every single detail of Reeta's reactions to her crimes. She'd forgotten that this wasn't only about her own article. It wasn't even about finding Mandy Silas and Susan O'Donnell. It was about Reeta, the poor lost girl living her Kafka nightmare with only one photograph to cling on to. A photograph Carol had promised to explain. And now she couldn't.

'You recognised him, though, I saw it on your face. You've met him, haven't you? Interviewed him about me?'

Carol shook her head. 'I've never met that man,' she replied truthfully. 'I can only tell you what I *do* know.' She felt Willow stiffen beside her. 'His name is Jeb – he's known as Brother Jeb. And I thought he was dead.'

Reeta's gaze dropped once again to the photograph. 'Dead?' she repeated slowly. A sudden intake of breath and terror swathed her torn-up features. 'Did I kill him?' She stared horror-stricken at Willow, who closed his eyes and sighed.

'We don't currently have reason to believe that Brother Jeb is dead,' he responded professionally. 'Reeta.' His tone softened. 'You will find out about him, but it's up to your lawyer to explain it. That background will come from him now.'

'What the fuck does that mean?' Carol surprised herself. Somehow she'd been hoping Willow would tell them, and for the first time it wasn't a selfish wish. She wanted the knowledge for Reeta's sake. Anything Carol could tell her would be speculation – and latching on to an unconfirmed truth could hardly help the girl. But Willow had letters; he had *evidence* of Brother Jeb's involvement, of why Reeta had done these things. *He* owed her that explanation after their last week together – forcing her to relive all the horrifying details.

'It means,' he said slowly, re-coiling any previous offerings of friendship, 'that we're done here. Today was our last meeting with you, Reeta. Our experiment has failed and you cannot remember the locations of Mandy and Susan's bodies. We have nothing more to discuss. The trial date will be set – you're in the hands of the legal system now.'

Part II

Pine Ranch

September 1966–August 1972

One

The queue for the courthouse bank of payphones was long and Carol had been slow in joining it. It had taken her longer than expected to scribble down her two-hundred word piece on the opening day of the biggest trial in the country – her pad littered with crossings-outs and discarded descriptions. Her editor had told her to keep it simple.

'Just cover the facts, Carol,' he'd told her warningly before she'd departed from Washington. 'I know you and the girl are close, but readers don't want that. Not right now. They want justice.'

It had been a difficult first day, the courtroom crowded and hot, the journalists angsty for details. Reeta had looked more cowed than Carol had seen her in months – every effort the girl had made to rebuild both her body and psyche had disintegrated in that first moment announcing her name and plea in front of the judge.

Carol had seen her on Saturday, just two days ago.

'Why don't you plead guilty?' she'd asked. 'Cut the torture of trial short. It'll give you more leeway with the judge. There's much less chance you'll get' – she swallowed thickly – 'well, that you'll get death.' Carol had discussed this with Barry several times, with the lawyer finally imploring Carol to ask the question herself. 'See if you can't get any sense out of her,' was the way he'd put it.

'Maybe the death penalty's what I deserve,' Reeta had replied, one finger idly twiddling a strand of hair. 'What I did – don't those girls deserve the full extent of justice they can get?'

'They're getting justice!' Carol slammed her hand to the table in frustration but saw only one wry eyebrow float upwards from the girl on the other side of the glass. She softened her tone. 'They would still be getting justice, Reeta.'

Reeta shook her head and adjusted her position so she leaned forward on her elbows.

'I can't do it, Carol.' She'd spoken calmly. 'I can't stand in front of a judge and confess, wholeheartedly, to crimes I don't remember committing. How am I supposed to show remorse for something I have *no* idea why I did it?'

'You'll fake it.' It had been a simple, quick reply.

Reeta had exhaled and given her a knowing smile that was still crooked under the weight of jagged scar tissue on her right side.

'You know I can't do that. I'll stand trial as I am now and accept the consequences of the actions of the girl I used to be.'

She'd seemed so brave, so ready for the courtroom hell to begin. But today, as she stood up in front of the world in her ill-fitting shirt and cheap slacks, Reeta's voice had cracked, the hands by her sides trembling.

'You waiting for that or not?' An irritated voice interrupted Carol's distraction, and she turned to see a man behind her gesturing to a now vacant payphone.

'Oh, thanks,' she said mildly and stepped forward. She dialled the number for the *Washington Post*'s copy room and read out the article she'd scratched into her notepad. The junior copy editor who'd been made to stay late to take her call was abrupt and keen to get her off the phone so he could type it up and send it to the press.

'All right, got it,' he said dismissively, the line clicking dead just as she was about to ask if he needed clarification on any points.

She stepped away from the phones and made her way toward the exit, thinking of a cold glass of wine in the Royal Grande's bar. She'd made the hotel her base for the duration of the trial, topping up the accommodation allowance the newspaper gave her with her own funds. The thought of three months living in a cheap motel had made her skin crawl. Thousand-count sheets and Egyptian cotton pillowcases were far more her speed. She didn't like to think about the sheets Reeta was forced to lay her head down on every night.

'You coming to Mally's?' Carol heard a familiar voice ask as she passed through the doors and onto the wide stone steps leading down to the forecourt. Photographers and cameramen were packing up for the day, fanning themselves in the early evening sun, joking and laughing about the evening ahead.

'I wasn't planning on,' Carol replied, turning to Tommy Macklin from the *New York Times*. He was stocky with wiry hair and a broad face that Carol had never seen without an undertone of mockery.

'Come oonn.' He flung an arm, uninvited, around her waist and pulled her in close, a yellowish grin bearing down into her mouth. 'You've got to learn to play nice with the boys.'

Carol was the only female crime reporter from the nationals, and she tended to avoid hanging out with her counterparts as much as possible. But it was the start of a three-month-long haul, and Carol knew nobody down in Florida who wasn't incarcerated. She may as well try to make the best of it.

'Fine,' she said with a forced smile. 'I'll come for one.'

Tommy gave an outlandish celebratory whoop and squeezed her tighter toward him, forcing her forward as he began to descend the steps. She wriggled away from his grasp just as a shudder ripped through her, but covered it with a grin and a question about how he'd found the first day.

'Seems pretty clean-cut to me,' he said with a shrug. 'But I tell you what, I wanna get my hands on those letters.' He clenched his fist demonstratively. 'Be the first to break that angle.'

Carol nodded silently. She had seen those letters Tommy wanted so badly and had no desire ever to see them again. But they'd be revealed in trial and she'd be forced to distil them for her readers. Peter Crawley, the prosecutor, had already teased their importance, promising the jury one of the most concrete explanations of motive he'd ever seen in his eighteen-year-long career.

They'd reached the entrance to the Irish bar across the street and Tommy held out an arm to gesture for Carol to descend first into the smoky pit. The stairs were sticky and there was no banister, so she steadied herself against the inexplicably damp wall. Neon lights buzzed at her vision and the swell of body heat hit her quickly. Tommy guided her toward a clump of tables surrounded by men Carol recognised from the nationals or bigger state papers and nodded in polite greeting as Tommy introduced her and pulled out a stool.

'You're the one who's been visiting her,' a middle-aged man Carol thought worked for the *San Francisco Chronicle* said.

She nodded. 'Yeah. I helped the FBI a bit.' She shrugged, trying to feign a casualness to the situation. 'We've kept in touch a little.'

'Really?' Tommy said, sloshing warm beer from a pitcher into an empty glass. 'You got any scoops for us?'

She gave a shallow laugh. 'If I did, don't you think I'd have already done it myself?'

'Does she give you that lost little girl act too?' another reporter chimed in. 'You know – the one she gave today in court, all whimpering and shaking.' He did a high-pitched imitation of Reeta giving her name. 'Or does she let you see the crazy bitch she really is?'

'It's not an act,' Carol couldn't help it – her words had come out defensive and hard.

'Ooooh.' Tommy cackled. 'Looks like we've got a friend of the crazy bitch here.'

'You'd like to be a friend of the crazy bitch too, Tommy,' the guy from the *Chronicle* crowed. 'In't that what you said? Mouth still looks to be in basic working order.' They all collapsed into laughter.

'She'd be fucking grateful, I tell you.' Tommy took a deep swig of beer. 'And she's knocked enough of her teeth out it'll be a smooooth ride.' He pumped his hips theatrically and Carol felt sick.

'Nah, not my speed, that,' the *Chronicle* guy said. 'But Mandy Silas…' He pursed his lips together in approval. 'Oh yeah, she'd do.'

'Nah, too prim and proper, that one. She'd never have gone for the likes of you,' another guy called down from the table, opening a packet of chips. 'Abigail Lawson,

121

though.' He wiggled his eyebrows suggestively. 'She was on easy street if you know what I'm saying.'

'Are you all fucking *joking*?' Carol spat with vitriol and stood up so quickly she knocked over the stool behind her. 'You sick bastards.' She was shaking, unable to control herself. 'Those girls are *dead*.'

'Yeah, because of *your* friend!' Tommy hooted.

'She has more fucking integrity and honesty in one hair on her goddamned head than any of you fuckers will ever know.'

Her parting words were met, as she'd known they would be, with mocking jeers and calls for her to calm down. She pushed their laughter away as she flew back up the stairs, a prickling heat burning down her chest. It was a fifteen-minute walk back to the hotel and she still juddered with rage as she pushed through the revolving glass door. She made her way straight to the bar, where Willow had first laid out exactly what they needed her to do all those months ago. She ordered her wine and fell into a high-backed armchair, nails digging into the expensive fabric. Solitude was far more preferable to *that*.

Carol knew, in her most lucid, logical moments that Reeta Doe was guilty of her crimes, and deserved to be punished for them. But late into the evening, as wine washed a softness through her, she couldn't help but tear through her file, desperate for a saving grace she knew didn't exist. Tonight was one of those evenings, and as she waited for her wine to be delivered she fished out the clump of papers she'd read through countless times before. The thought of this poor, terrified young woman being thrown to the wolves of high security federal prison to sit on death row, awaiting an electric chair or toxic gas chamber was one Carol couldn't contend with.

I

Zechariah's turquoise pickup scooted rusty clouds across the dry fields, billowing smoke signals that they'd finally arrived Shouts and calls flooded across the arable land, lapping at the men tending to the high fences and washing over the women gathered by the main house in swathes. Children downed tools in the front field and chased after the car, jumping to try to get a look at the small, frightened faces peering over the side of the cargo bed. Reeta could see three figures squeezed next to Zechariah in the front cab, their expressions lost behind the dusty smears of the windscreen.

He pulled up outside the wooden porch, scattered with wicker furniture and rudimentary children's toys. Reeta carefully finished hanging the cotton pillowcase over the banister of the wide stairs and took a step down toward them. Everyone who'd been on laundry duty hanging sheets out to dry did the same, their anticipation tangible. New arrivals didn't happen often. The cooks had been preparing a celebratory feast since dawn, a couple of the men even permitted on a non-scheduled trip out to town to buy butcher's scraps. But Reeta didn't approve of this special attention. These people had found salvation and that should be reward enough.

The wider community, however, agreed that today was special – the six new figures now climbing from the pickup brought the number of souls saved at Pine Ranch by Brother Jeb to a total of sixty. And that was worth celebrating. So Abra said, anyhow.

Two children, both about Reeta's age, jumped down from the cargo bed, Black skinny limbs streaked with beige dust trails. The tallest, a boy with a nervous toothy smile and staring wide eyes, reached back to haul out a black holdall that looked to contain more personal possessions than were strictly allowed. Reeta made a note to tell Zechariah to double-check on that. The girl, natural hair escaping from plastic tortoiseshell grips, also leaned back in to retrieve a small boy who appeared to be about four or five years old. They stood at the back of the pickup, bewildered, looking out at the sea of faces who'd silently surrounded them. Their smartly dressed parents – the father with a neat moustache and closely manicured Afro and mother with straightened hair and horn-rimmed glasses – climbed from the passenger side door, followed by an elderly lady with coarse grey curls. Zechariah had abandoned the driver's side, the door wide open, and placed his palms on the top of the car, arms spread across the roof.

'Let us pray!' he called, projecting his voice to the very outskirts of the group. 'Today we bring six more souls for our Lord's salvation, in preparation of the End Times our Brother Jeb has foretold. They have travelled hard and the journey was long, but they are with us now' – he tipped his head, adjusting his gaze to the nervous family who had clumped together during the prayer – 'for eternity!' He finished to shouts of 'Amen!' from the watching crowd.

Abra took the first step toward them, with a bright smile and arms outstretched to the women. She wouldn't touch the man, of course. Her brunette braid bounced around her lower back as she embraced first the mother and then the grandmother. The new arrivals' church-going best glowed gaudy and ostentatious against Abra's simple, long-sleeved smock. Other women flowed away from their chores toward Abra and the new family, while Zechariah steered the father off toward the huddle of men who still held tools and hoes in rough-skinned hands. Firm handshakes and solid nods made him welcome.

'Reeta.' Abra turned to look over her shoulder. 'Come here and help us welcome them.' Her voice flowed like melted butter, cornflower eyes sparkling in the golden afternoon sun. Reeta hesitated, glancing back at the pile of bedsheets that still needed dealing with, but she could never refuse Abra.

Even if she was meant to.

Shoulders hunched in her blue tunic, hair tied in a limp ponytail by the nape of her neck, Reeta stepped down toward them. The children were smiling politely at the group of women, nodding hellos at the other kids. The little boy gripped his sister's hand fiercely, terror bathing his eyes.

'Reeta, will you show little...' Abra hesitated, gesturing to the young boy. 'Well, I hope you'll show him the nursery, where he'll be sleeping.'

'His name is Harrison,' the girl said, her voice confident, steady. 'We call him Harry. And he'll be sleeping with us.' She nodded towards the rest of her family.

A delicate silence swept the gathered group, and Reeta's eyes hardened.

'Well, let's show you around first.' Abra spoke after a charged moment, the smile still in her tone. 'Brother Jeb will want to meet you all.'

'*He'll* tell you what you're called,' Reeta said. She had aimed for helpfulness, but the girl flinched and looked with horrified confusion toward her mother.

'Come on, children,' their mother replied, her accent with the same easy flow of the Caribbean as Zechariah's. 'We must go meet Brother Jeb – we are so fortunate to be here.' Her dark eyes shimmered.

'But, Mama—' The girl's voice was unsteady now, the whine of childhood creeping in.

'Hush now,' her mother interrupted. 'Change is hard, but it is a test. We must prove ourselves to our Lord, prove we are worthy.' She bowed her head toward Abra, who stood aside with an outstretched arm, guiding them up the stairs and into the house.

Zechariah was waiting on the top step, ready to escort them to Brother Jeb.

Reeta's eyes creased in suspicion at the children's reluctant pace as they followed their parents into the house. She knew Jeb was in his workshop, where he toiled his days as a carpenter, building furniture and toys for his people. This would be where he'd greet his new arrivals.

Zechariah was his missionary, travelling the world to spread the Word of the prophet, the One who had finally opened the Seven Seals that foretold the End Times coming. Salvation was offered under his watch, the promise of a Second Coming born only unto him. And when that second son of God arrived in flesh on this Earth, he would guide them all to Heaven above when the Rapture came. Jeb had fathered seven children since the start of Pine Ranch, three of them boys – any one of which might well grow to be the Second Coming they all so waited for. The Rapture was nigh, that much was clear. And the more souls protected under Jeb's watch, the more of God's children would be saved.

Zechariah travelled often to the coasts of America and the old world of Europe, where he and Jeb had first met during the darkest years of God's creation. They had served alongside each other, soldiers of their respective armies, and seen the horrors of Revelations come to fruition in fetid trenches, scarred landscapes and torn-apart comrades. It was here that Jeb had been chosen by the Lord with a message of hope. Not all of their fellow soldiers had been worthy – Jeb's American brothers had laughed and ridiculed his preaching. They told him to focus on the real world, to look around and see that no God was present in that place. Only Zechariah, of the British Army's Caribbean Regiment, had proudly heeded his word and prayed at his feet each night. When peace time came, they took it as a sign – a respite from the Lord to allow them to regroup and build their ark. Only this time the ark was to be a compound spread across ten acres of unwanted prairieland in Texas. But they knew the floods were coming, and it was not only water to fear. Many of their number had seen battle; they knew of the gunfire and explosions that would wreak down upon them. They needed to be prepared.

This was the origin story Zechariah would have told this new family in their cold church room in England. Reeta knew this because the other arrivals from across the sea had spoken of how Zechariah's words had sparked sunshine into their grey and rainy existence. The hope of Brother Jeb, the salvation he promised, was worth their return journey back across the Atlantic.

Reeta recommenced her laundry duties, silently moving away from the still-gathered group discussing the new arrivals. The rest soon dispersed, aware of the chores that still needed completing. Young boys picked up their shovels and meandered back to the front field, where they collapsed down on muddy knees to finish the harvest of the potato crop. It would be a hardy and tough-skinned end of crop yield, but the store would last them well into winter in the cool, dark cellar. The men had long since returned to their stations at the perimeter fence, digging foundations for the new concrete posts to reinforce their home.

Reeta had folded her final bedsheet across the porch railings when her summons came. Abra had already left to show the mother and grandmother to their new quarters, and now Zechariah had come for Reeta.

'Damaris is weary.' Zechariah spoke the girl's new name with pride. 'The move has been hardest on her.'

'The move shouldn't be hard on anyone,' Reeta replied, indignant. 'If she does not want the salvation and protection of Brother Jeb then she can go back home and await the hellfire herself.'

Zechariah laughed, a hydraulic, pumping sound. 'Our Reeta, the first child of Pine Ranch.' He smiled down at her; his dark skin had resisted the cracks and wrinkles of sun damage and age that puckered Brother Jeb's own. His hair was neat and close-cropped, courtesy of regular visits to Eunice with her trimmer, who set up a salon on Sundays in the kitchen. 'You have to understand that not everyone is as lucky as you. You were brought here in your mother's belly – you've grown up knowing your fortune and grace at having Brother Jeb in your life. Imagine if you were told you had to leave here for some new place with some new prophet.'

Reeta's eyes widened; Zechariah verged on blasphemy.

He recognised her look and placed a comforting hand on her shoulder. 'I'm just saying, try to exercise patience with the girl. Be vigilant' – he nodded sharply, reminding her of her job – 'and assess her worth, of course. But give her some time. We've lost children before.' His eyes hardened. 'Let's not allow it to happen again.'

Reeta nodded reluctantly. Patience was a virtue – she knew she must endeavour to be better. But what Brother Jeb offered was nothing to be wary of. If Damaris could not see that, then she didn't deserve her place among them.

Two

Reeta didn't have any court-appropriate clothes of her own and so Barry had had to buy her a cheap white shirt and grey slacks. They fitted awkwardly and made her shoulders look as if they stuck out at perfect right angles, but it was better than her institutional tunic and pants. She'd felt surprisingly liberated when she'd first put them on. For the first time she was wearing clothes that three hundred other women weren't also wearing.

She waited with Barry in a small corridor off to the side of the courtroom, her heavily armed guard a silent sentry by the door. The handcuffs and chains around her waist weighed on her hips, but she knew they'd be removed soon. Over the last three weeks of the trial she'd learned the daily banalities they had to move through in the pursuit of justice. The way the judge would always arrive five minutes earlier than scheduled to keep Reeta and her legal team on their toes. The way Crawley would shoot her meaningful glances as he probed his witnesses for testimony that would surely kill her. The way halfway through the day she'd be chained up again to join Barry in a cramped room for an industrial sandwich made of lunch meat so watery it quenched her thirst.

Today Peter Crawley was calling Agent Willow to the stand.

Reeta knew this was the build-up for him to reveal the letters to the jury. Two found with bodies, one found in her supposed motel room. But Crawley was in no rush to get there. He was wallowing quite comfortably through the witnesses on his list, meandering leisurely through the events of the previous year. Stephens had given him a detailed round up on their involvement in the case, the evidence they'd gathered including the hair found on Abigail Lawson, and their first interviews with Reeta. And now Willow would take the stand to tell the jury that no matter how patient he'd been, and how hard he'd tried to make her remember, she had resolutely failed to return two bodies to their families.

Barry was doing his best on cross-examination, but there wasn't much of a defence for him to mount. He questioned the cataloguing of some evidence, queried the interrogation tactics of the agents, but Reeta could see the jury were not convinced.

They'd known from the start it was useless.

'You ready?' Barry whispered to her now in the draughty hallway, waiting for the bailiff to open the doors to her fate.

She nodded stiffly and, as if on cue, the doors creaked open.

As she always did, Reeta turned to scan the crowd of spectators in the court, her good eye searching out only one face, while her right eye remained as useless and mangled as ever. She spotted Carol and they exchanged a small flicker of a smile before Reeta turned back to the bailiff to have her chains removed. She sat behind the defence table and looked blandly ahead. Barry had instructed her to remain as emotionless as possible throughout the court proceedings – any displays of guilt or pain could be seen as an attempt at pandering to the jury and backfire. Reeta had managed this instruction for the most part, hanging her head to hide her face whenever tears had threatened.

The judge arrived and began proceedings for the day with his hands wrapped around a steaming mug of coffee in blatant disregard for the stuffy humidity of the weather. He nodded for Crawley to begin, who called Agent Benjamin Willow immediately to the stand.

'Agent Willow, thank you for joining us here today.' He began with the smile of a close friend. 'Now let's go back to January of this year.'

–

Carol had last seen Ben the Thursday night before she'd left Washington for the trial. He'd stopped by the house with a plastic bag of cheap Chinese food and the offer to help her pack.

'You got egg rolls in there?' she'd asked with a narrowed-eyed nod toward the bag.

'Double portion,' he confirmed.

'How can a girl resist?' She'd laughed and stepped back from the door to let him in.

The progress made in repairing their relationship over an Italian dinner that lost night in Florida had gone from a shaky Band-Aid to callous stitches, and had finally mellowed at a healed wound – the scar of the past still evident underneath their inside jokes and warm affection. She hadn't seen him since he'd arrived in Florida yesterday, though, and as she'd watched him take the stand that morning, she'd felt an unexpected tug in her stomach. The way he moved his hand to place emphasis on a word, the way he brushed his hair from his forehead. She found herself drifting off from the content of his statement to remember those hands on her, that mouth whispering words to her. They'd arranged to meet in the lobby of the Royal Grande at eight p.m., a reservation at that same Italian restaurant beckoning.

'There you are,' she said, swinging round to greet him as he stepped off the elevator. 'How are you liking your new digs?'

This time around the bureau had splashed out for Ben to stay in the Royal Grande himself, citing security because of the furore surrounding the trial.

'Better than the motel,' he said with a humble shrug. 'I can see why you like it.'

'Always was a woman of taste.'

He laughed gently. 'You always were,' he agreed. 'Shall we go?'

'Yeah.' She nodded with a smile. 'Let's go.'

Half an hour later they were settled in a booth at the Italian restaurant, ordering a Pinot Noir and trying to pretend the awful circumstances of this reunion weren't a reality.

'How's it been down here?' Ben eventually asked, putting a slice of garlic bread on his plate.

Carol shrugged. 'Pretty shitty.'

He nodded sympathetically. 'You still seeing much of her?'

'I go once a week on a Saturday. That's visiting day.'

He paused with the garlic bread halfway to his mouth and looked at her earnestly. 'Do you see anyone else?' he asked and she frowned. 'Ever go home on a weekend? Meet up with *anyone*?'

'Visiting days are Saturdays,' she replied simply. 'If I went home for the weekend, I'd only be able to go for Sunday and what's the point of that?' Ben didn't point out that she didn't *need* to go to the jail every Saturday, and for that she felt a swell of gratitude. 'And the other reporters down here...' She paused, remembering that aborted attempt at friendship in Mally's three weeks ago. 'They're not exactly my kind of people.'

'Try,' he said softly after a moment. 'Try to let her go just sometimes.'

'It's not as easy as—'

'Carol.' He dropped his garlic bread and put a firm hand over hers. 'The stress. I can see it all over you. Please, *try* to step away.'

Carol knew why he was worried. He'd been there to hold her five years ago when her father's wife had been on the other end of the phone reporting the heart attack Howell had fortunately survived. Warning her it was a genetic condition, advising her to get checked. Carol had just never got around to it, and for all her intentions she'd never quite been able to lie to Ben about it.

She nodded sagely and was thankful he didn't press the matter about her getting a doctor's appointment. She moved the conversation on by telling him about her friend Julia, who was pregnant for the second time. He accepted the conversation shift without question, and she felt the space between them press even more closely against her.

But a few hours later, over Manhattans in the hotel bar, he looked deeply at her again and said in a soft voice, 'She's sucking you in.'

Carol exhaled through a dry smile. 'She's *sucked* me in,' she corrected.

Ben watched her carefully. 'I thought you were better than that.'

'So did I.'

'She's guilty, Carol. You can't save her, you know that, right?'

Carol had nodded. 'I know.' A tear escaped from one corner of her eye and she let it fall. 'I don't know what I want to do for her. She's just so – lost, I know what that's like, Ben.' She felt the cocktail slacken her lips and suddenly their shared history cloaked her like a comforter. There was only one person in the world who would understand this of her. He didn't trust her, she wasn't even sure if he liked her any more, but he would understand her. 'I was about her age when my mom died, you know. And I was so alone then too. I had all this money, and all this influence, but I was *wrong* in some way. I wasn't a real Joyce and everyone knew it. I couldn't hide from that – it's plastered all over my skin, for Christ's sake.' Ben was listening intently, his mouth tight with care. 'I can't imagine...' The tears had come faster than she'd expected and she found herself gasping to catch her breath. 'I can't imagine what I'd have done if I hadn't found my dad. If he hadn't accepted me with love. *That's* what pushed me to keep going. To go to Washington, to build this life for myself. Knowing that I did have a foundation after all.' She shook her head. 'We all need roots, Ben. We all need to be grounded by something. And when those roots are wrenched away – who's to say what any of us would do?'

Ben leaned forward across the marble tabletop and clasped her hand in his, squeezing tightly. 'She still has to be held accountable, Carol.'

Carol knew he was right. But she also knew Ben understood she was right too.

He walked her back to her room after the waiter had cleared their empty glasses away and Carol had insisted on putting it on her tab. As her hand settled on the golden door handle, she felt his presence close against her. She turned into his chest and looked up as his lips bent down to meet hers. The kiss was one of comfort, of familiarity, of understanding.

It was not a kiss of anything more.

He said nothing as he walked back to his room and she fell into her own, a rock of regret collapsing her onto the bed.

II

Reeta followed Zechariah through the main hall of the house, the sweeping staircase circling around them. The house had once sat as a proud plantation home above rows and rows of bunny-tail cotton crops. But a violent parting gift of the Yankee troops as they marched back north into the glowing light of Reconstruction had seen the crops razed to the ground and the house ransacked. By the time Jeb and Zechariah had come to purchase it in 1946 there was just a hollow shell of the once-grand home, an island in an ocean of wildflowers and weeds. They had fixed windows, rebuilt walls and tended to the land. The first women among them, Reeta's mother included, sewed curtains and couch covers, filling the derelict building with the smells of cheap grits and barbecued squirrels. These stories were told nostalgically over firelight during dinners, and Reeta longed for those simple beginning days.

The back door opened wide onto a gentle rolling slope down towards rough woodland in the distance, marking the end of their territory. The first structure out of the main house was Jeb's workshop, its door now propped open, a varnished stool drying on his bench out in the sun. To its right was a cluster of vacant chairs and an empty pitcher of iced tea. Voices tumbled out of the shed as Reeta and Zechariah approached, and she could see the shadows of two figures huddled close together looking at the wall of carpentry tools.

'Damaris,' Zechariah called through the open door. 'This here is Reeta, she's going to show you around. You'll be in her dormitory.'

'Ah, Reeta.' The deep, soothing tone of Jeb rolled out in reply and the shadows moved toward them. 'You'll be in good hands with Reeta.' They emerged into the bright sunlight, Jeb's hand placed gently, guiding, between Damaris's shoulder blades. The lanky girl still looked uncertain, but Reeta recognised a slight slackness to her bones — the kind of comfort only alone-time with Jeb could bring. His fair hair radiated angel-like, a golden crown around his head. Nearing his forties, the sun and toil of his mission had taken its toll on his light skin, but his features retained their handsome symmetry. A broad chest in a denim shirt squared out his strong stature, and he stood tall above the girls.

'Brother Jeb,' Reeta breathed, nodding her head. 'I would be honoured to welcome our new family member.'

Jeb smiled at her solemn tone and shot Zechariah a knowing glance. Reeta was Jeb's most dedicated follower, and everyone on the compound knew it. It was a badge she wore with a pride unbecoming of her humble aspirations.

'I'm glad to hear it.' He smiled and gestured for Damaris to follow Reeta, who had already begun moving away toward the dormitories. The girl's feet stumbled to catch up.

'You're leaving again today?' Reeta heard Jeb turn his attention to Zechariah as they walked away — their voices now serious and important.

'I've got a trail up north,' Zechariah's deep voice replied.

'Keep me updated.'

The dormitory buildings had sprung up, sprawled and untidily across the back lawn, over the thirteen years of Pine Ranch. As the number of Jeb's followers had grown it had become apparent that the rooms of the house could only be stretched so far. Now, the house provided shelter to Jeb and Zechariah – the only two with their own rooms – and the other fourteen followers who had arrived within the first year. The house also gave over its vast drawing room for the nursery, dining room and parlour for Bible study classes, while the kitchen and larder remained in use as expected. Breakfast and dinner time saw the grand open hallway lined with mismatched tables and chairs, and lunch was provided in tin boxes to eat during midday Bible study.

Reeta guided Damaris to the second of the connected single-storey dormitory buildings. There were three in total – two for the women and one for men, for men were far fewer in their devotion to Brother Jeb's word. She pushed open the door of the dark, windowless building, made from plywood and corrugated iron, and pulled the cord for the single light bulb that illuminated the room. The dormitory buildings and kitchen were the only areas of the compound with an electrical connection. Each side of the room was taken up by eight bunk beds neatly placed at even intervals across the space, blonde varnished pine sanded and buffed by Jeb's very own hand. Pine was his favourite material to work with. They were sturdy and wide, with hard bedframes to remind them that penance was due each night for their true salvation. A soft down mattress does not fortify one's soul for the End Times.

'These ones are empty,' Reeta said, guiding Damaris to the back of the room where two bunk beds stood unused, anticipating. 'You can have whichever bunk you want. I'll fetch you some clothes and linen from the laundry so you can make it up.' She turned to leave, thinking herself kind for giving Damaris the time to make her own choice, when the girl's voice stopped her.

'Wh—' she asked, throat squeaking at the attempt. 'Where will my family be sleeping?'

Reeta forced a smile. 'All around you. We're your family now.'

'No,' she said again, more forcefully this time, her English accent encircling the word in a solid iron ring. 'My *real* family.'

Reeta felt her smile twitch. 'Your family of the flesh have been shown their own accommodation. You will be separated for a little while until you understand the ways here.'

'But they're my family!' Damaris wailed, eyes pulling wide in disbelieving horror. 'You can't take them away from me!'

'*We* are your family, your one true family under God,' Reeta reiterated. 'Your family of the flesh is not important any more. You cannot prioritise *anyone* over Brother Jeb and his message. You will see them, you will work with them, but you are not a unit above anyone. Not any more.'

'You've done that with your family?' Damaris asked, dubious. 'Abandoned them all, you treat them like anyone else?'

Reeta allowed a smirk of pride to flicker on her face. 'My mother of the flesh is of no more importance to me than you.' She turned on her heel and left the ungrateful new girl startled and alone in the dormitory.

Reeta fetched the clothes and bed linen from the laundry and carried them back across the lawn slowly, stretching out the time for Damaris to take in her new home, to accept her blessed fate. When she finally returned, she found Damaris sitting on the lower bunk of one of the beds she'd been allocated, weeping. Reeta moved uncertainly forward, her sandalled feet catching on the uneven cement ground. Damaris didn't look up. Her shoulders heaved dramatically and puppylike yelps escaped between grasped fingers. Reeta moved to a stop, her shadow from the weak light stretching long across the bed.

Patience. That's what Zechariah had preached.

Reeta leaned across and placed the folded sheets next to Damaris before sinking down to her knees in front of her. The ground pressed painfully into the stretched skin across her kneecaps, but she didn't readjust.

'Damaris,' she said, and the girl opened her mouth to interrupt.

'My name is—'

'Your name,' Reeta continued sternly, 'is Damaris. That is what He has chosen. Do you know her story? Damaris converted after Paul went to Athens. One of the only few to see the light of those gathered. That is *you*. And your family. You have all converted, accepted the Word of Brother Jeb, trusted in his knowledge and message. And *you* will be saved because of that.' Her voice sang like Jeb's own sermons, poetic with conviction and righteousness. 'We live our flesh bodies hard and dedicated so that our souls can spend eternity with Him.'

Damaris stared. Her eyes were drying, but shiny tracks carved her face. Reeta had never before heard anyone question their being here.

'You've been here a long time,' Damaris stated after several long moments. 'What happened to your family?'

Reeta smiled. 'Abra is my mother of the flesh. She came here when I was in her belly – her husband had returned from war evil and sinful and she needed to escape. That's when she met Jeb.'

'Where did she come from?' Damaris asked with a frown.

'Just from town. Down the way there.' Reeta gestured in the general direction of the solitary road that connected the ranch with the small town fifteen miles away. 'She arrived here and I was born four months later. The first child of Pine Ranch.'

'She's from down the road?' Damaris asked. 'Is your father still there?'

Reeta's face twitched. 'My father is the Lord. The one true father.'

The two girls looked at each other, neither speaking, allowing the message to wash over them. Finally, Damaris broke the silence.

'We will really be rewarded with salvation?' Her voice waved with uncertainty.

'The End Times are coming. The Seven Seals have been read and the Second Coming may already have been born. The apocalypse is imminent.'

'He's really the One?' Damaris's voice had dropped to a whisper, barely daring to believe.

Reeta's smile returned. 'You will see.'

Three

Carol had woken with a fuzzy head after the wine and Manhattans of the night before. Shame chewed at the edges of her recollection, but she wasn't sure where it was rightly placed. Ben had seen right through her – he'd seen how attached she was getting to a stone cold killer. The Carol he'd loved would never have softened on the subject of a story. The Carol he'd loved had chosen a story over him after all. She'd seen in his eyes as he kissed her goodbye that he finally understood.

She was doing for Reeta what she'd failed to do for him.

And even Carol didn't know why.

Ben was the first man, the *only* man, she'd ever loved. To this day she still did not understand the split-second decision that had taken her to file her copy on his case. When she'd first begun working on the story of the senator who'd been caught up in a blackmail scam for the mob, she'd considered it practice. As Ben leaked more and more details of the confidential case, she'd told herself she was only forming them into prose to hone her skills, to ready herself for a day when she had a legitimate feature to file.

But then...

Then she didn't know what had happened. Bruised pride, another rebuff from the boys' club that ran her editorial room. And suddenly those explosive sheets of paper had found themselves on her editor's desk.

She declined to remember the details of the fall-out from that, the gut-wrenching sight of the moment Ben learned of her betrayal. The venom they'd spat at each other, the apologies she'd been too defensive to say.

With mascara still smudged under her eyes where she'd forgotten to take it off the night before, Carol reapplied the mask of her make-up, wiping away any blemishes that betrayed her imperfections. She changed into jeans and a short-sleeved shirt and pulled her hair into a tight bun. Her baby hairs were curling up around her hairline from the damp of the humidity, but she couldn't be bothered to straighten them out. It was only jail; there were women of every colour and creed in there – her misbehaving strands were the least of their worries.

She collected her rental car from the hotel's valet and made the journey she'd long since become used to, out toward the rural home of the Florida Women's Correctional Institute. The rigmarole of entry was second nature to her now, and she smiled a familiar hello to the guards and regular visitors, succumbing to searches and questions until she was permitted to take her seat and wait for Reeta.

'How did you find this week?' Carol asked once they'd greeted each other and shared a couple of casual enquires into their wellbeing and lives.

Reeta shrugged. 'I don't know how I'm supposed to be *finding* any of it. They're just saying things I've already heard.'

'That's the boring wheels of justice for you,' Carol agreed with a nod.

'Have you spoken to Agent Willow?'

Carol twisted her mouth a little to one side, unsure of how to respond. 'I saw him last night, actually.'

'Did he say anything?'

Carol shook her head. 'Nothing of importance for his testimony.'

Reeta sat back in her chair. 'I guess there's not much more for him to say.'

'Next week Crawley will cover their investigation again.' Carol rolled her eyes. 'He's already done all that with Stephens but investigator testimony always does well with juries, so he wants to hammer it home.' She raised her fingers into a half-hearted air quote. '"Look at how hard these men worked to meticulously find evidence against the culprit", that sort of thing. He'll probably call the hair analysis expert after Ben. I'd imagine he'd think that a neat segue.'

Reeta nodded.

'But he will ask Ben about the photograph he gave you,' Carol said. 'Which will lead him onto—'

'The letters.'

Carol nodded.

–

Reeta was sick of hearing about those damned letters.

Four months ago, Barry revealed that the US Attorney's office had turned over new evidence. Evidence that had been found with the photograph Agent Willow had given her. The man she had believed to be her father. The photograph she had believed to be her one connection to a world outside of this place, to a family of people who loved her, to a home where she could feel secure. But in one meeting that had all crumbled.

She should have been suspicious when she entered the room for her meeting with Barry to find Carol sitting next to him, a grave look on her face.

'I know you two have grown...' Barry had paused to search for the word. '...close, during Carol's time helping the FBI. So I thought it might well be beneficial for you to have her here today.'

'What's happening today?' Reeta had asked with a naivety she'd never thought she'd envy.

'I'm afraid we've been given some more evidence, Reeta. Evidence that suggests exactly why you might have committed these crimes.'

He handed her a cardboard folder containing three sheets of cheap carbon-copy paper. She ran her chapped fingers across the words, not completely understanding them.

And then Carol had spoken.

She'd told her all she thought she knew about Reeta's home, Pine Ranch. She relayed an emotionless list of facts, sparse information consisting mainly of dates and names, underpinned only by these three letters.

It had all meant nothing to Reeta.

She was as unconnected to this tale as she had been to the stories of her victims.

That disconnect had fostered a misplaced hope over the last few months. In the same way she'd failed to read Carol's first article through in full, Reeta refused to understand the true complexities of everything Carol and Barry told her on that day. There was an enduring shard of hope that lived in her, even after she had discovered the cold, clinical truth about her childhood.

'There must be someone who knew me from there, right?' she said to Carol now.

Carol's shoulders twitched into a shrug but after a moment she nodded. 'Perhaps. There's still so much we don't know.'

'I still carry this,' Reeta said, fishing the little rectangle of card from her pocket. Creases defaced Jeb's smiling expression now, a roughness tearing at the photo's edges. 'It was my first lifeline outside of this place. The first time I had an idea that I *was* someone. I know…' She looked at Carol, almost with an apology. 'I know what it was now. I know what I was doing *for him*. But…' She trailed off, her gaze falling back to the man she now knew had controlled her life for nineteen years. It was a sentence Carol did not probe for her to finish.

'I want you to write about me,' Reeta said after a moment's uneasy silence.

'I am writing about you,' Carol replied with a friendly smile. 'Well, about the trial, anyhow.'

'I want you to write about *me*,' Reeta clarified. 'Like you did before.' She gave a shrug that she hoped looked nonchalant. 'Maybe someone will see it.'

'Who do you want to see it?'

'Anyone who knew me.'

'Reeta, I really don't think—'

'Then let me do it for you.'

'For me?'

'You have a relationship with the most famous girl in the country right now and you've given your paper no exclusives.'

'I didn't think—'

Reeta gave a wan laugh. 'It's OK. I trust you. If anyone will tell my story fairly…' She shrugged behind the scratched glass. 'Then it's you.'

'All right,' Carol said with a single nod. 'I'll pitch it to my editor. I think once the trial's over they'll be more open to a more sympathetic piece.'

'I don't think anyone wants sympathy for me, Carol.'

Later that night Reeta fished out the pencil and scraps of notebook paper she'd traded for a bottle of the good shampoo Carol had sent her. She hid them in her pillow-case so the pencil poked uncomfortably into her scalp as she slept. But ever since Carol had told her about the plantation house that had once been her home, Reeta had felt the inescapable need to see it. She'd started with the porch from the photo, the wicker-back chair she knew had stood on it. Soon her pencil had traced high walls with detailed windows and an intricately tiled roof. She imagined life behind those windows, her childhood pushing out. Tonight, she settled in to fill in flowers and bushes on the front lawn, a cat stretched out in the sun. With every line of graphite to paper she tried to force a memory onto the page.

But whenever she paused to look at the picture, she saw only what she knew it was.

A child's cartoon fantasy.

III

Reeta's stomach rumbled involuntarily as she worked in the kitchen after lunch. Her tin lunchbox had been filled only with watery soup and a lump of stale bread. Funds at Pine Ranch had dwindled with more mouths to feed. The latest arrivals had not brought much in the way of assets, and only Gideon's trade as doctor to the local town kept them with any sort of regular income. Most of what they ate they grew, with surplus crops occasionally sold.

Today they were pickling leftover beet harvest and her hands failed to steady as she peeled and boiled the vegetables. She nicked her fingers on the short knife, so blood ran – red ribbons down her hands indistinguishable from the beetroot juice. Her sliced fingers stung in the salt she added to the pickling liquor and she savoured the pain, her skin crackling and puckering under it.

It was unexpected when, just before four o'clock, the uneven wooden door of the kitchen was pushed open and Jeb took a step inside. The gathered women stalled in breathless uncertainty, eyes wide and hands ready to serve.

'Reeta,' he said, and she felt her heart stop still. 'Can you be spared from your chores this afternoon?' She nodded at once and he broke into a warm smile. 'Excellent, wash your hands and meet me out on the porch. I want to take you to town with me.'

Reeta couldn't stifle her gasped inhale, and felt her eyes instinctively pull wider. She had never left the confines of her home. From the fences out front, to the woods out back, the land of Pine Ranch was the only world she'd ever known. As she hurried to clean herself up, Reeta caught a glimpse of Eunice, who was manning the pot of boiling beetroot. Eunice's brow flickered and she glanced toward Hagar, the youngest of the original fourteen, just seventeen at her arrival. Something flashed in Hagar's eyes, but she adjusted her head down, concentrating on peeling beetroot with shaking hands. Eunice turned silently back to the billowing steam. Reeta watched her a moment, Eunice's forcibly blank expression irking. But she turned away from them and pushed through the kitchen door.

Out on the porch she could see Zechariah's truck parked up front and Jeb waiting for her at the top of the steps. A cloudless sky hung lazily above them, beating down glossy rays of Heaven.

'Let's go,' Jeb said smilingly.

Jeb leaned out from behind her to open the door to the truck and waited as she clambered up onto the cream leather seat. Reeta had never been in the truck before. She'd never been in any car or vehicle, although the compound had two – this pickup and Gideon's old brown station wagon. The engine started with a judder when Jeb turned the key, and Reeta felt a blast of hot air plunge toward her from the radiator.

'That handle,' he said, nodding toward the inside of her door, 'will wind your window down.' He grinned. 'You'll want the breeze once we get going.'

She smiled and placed her hand on the steel wrench, pushing all her weight down and then hauling it back up with both arms. The window lowered a crack. She repeated until it was fully lowered, before she noticed that the front field was moving around them. She hung her head out of the open window, feeling the thick air move across her face, and watched as the tyres disrupted the orange soil beneath them. She glanced back at the house to see Abra come to a stop on the porch, staring out after the retreating truck. Hagar appeared behind her and guided her with soft hands back inside. Reeta swallowed heavily and turned away from the house to see they'd already reached the gate at the bottom of the drive, which Gideon was pulling aside with a hand raised in friendly farewell.

Something lurched in Reeta's chest as she felt the safety and security of Pine Ranch peel away, revealing a cold chill. But Jeb was there; she was still safe. This was a test.

And she was ready.

As they drove, Reeta was torn between the sight of her saviour dedicating this time solely to her, and the visions of green racing by the windows. Eventually the green fell away, replaced by squat buildings and tall pylons connected by drooping wires. Jeb pulled the truck into a parking lot outside a building with black bars across the windows, a neon sign buzzing above the door. The Lucky Swine. He climbed out of the truck and moved around to the front, waiting for just a moment before twitching his head over his shoulder. Reeta swallowed heavily; gooseflesh had sprung up across her thighs, tremors aching down her limbs. In her thirteen years she'd never before felt uncertainty or fear like this. No matter how much she searched or prayed, she couldn't dispel the gnaw of terror in her stomach. She felt sick, but Jeb's face was growing impatient, so she forced all her will into her undernourished legs and climbed from the car. His face relaxed and he held out his arm, curling it around her shoulders and guiding her toward the door.

Inside the building was dank and smelled of proving dough on baking day – yeasty and sour. Murky light streamed in through the barred windows, fairies of dust dancing mindlessly in the rays. There was a horseshoe bar directly in front, a man behind it wiping glasses with a filthy-looking rag.

'Howdy, my man,' he said, his accent the drawl of the Texan natives at the compound. Reeta had never taken it on, choosing instead to emulate Jeb's East Coast articulation.

Jeb nodded back in greeting. 'Howdy,' he mimicked.

'You looking for a drink?'

'Just the usual. Coca-Cola for me.' Jeb looked down at her. 'Reeta, you want a soda?'

Soda was not allowed. Gideon had brought a case back from town one time, a gift from a patient, and Jeb had made it clear that it rotted your teeth and your insides, and you mustn't defile the body God gave you like that.

This was part of the test.

She shook her head.

'You sure?' He leaned in close, whispers licking her ears. 'You're allowed one soda, Reeta. Your body is fine. God won't punish you.' She remained paralysed. She could not make this decision. She could not tell what the test was. Reeta didn't move. She stared straight ahead, untangling the dilemma from the depths of her very soul.

'Is she OK?' the man asked, one eyebrow floating upwards.

'She's fine.' Jeb's voice edged on harshness, a snap to reclaim her. 'She'll have a Coke too.'

The man nodded and bent down below the bar. Jeb guided Reeta to a sticky table, motioning for her to sit.

She obeyed.

The Cokes arrived in glass bottles, condensation dripping slowly downwards. Reeta watched as Jeb took a meaningful slug, swallowing demonstratively. Uncertainly and with a shaking hand she reached forward and grabbed the cold glass, bringing it to her lips. The bubbles felt like burning as they pummelled down her unexpecting throat, the sugar lingering sweet and forbidden on her tongue.

'Good, isn't it?' Jeb asked with a smile.

Reeta nodded.

'Sometimes, Reeta, I get messages to reward my most dedicated followers. Little trips like this – they broaden your horizons, show me if you're ready.'

'I'm ready,' Reeta nodded enthusiastically, still not certain what she was meant to be ready for. But she must be ready. She was a woman now, ever since one terrified evening three months previously. Abra had fetched her clean rags and held her, comforting and softly explaining away her tears. Reeta had savoured Abra's embrace that night, her arms cradling away the tension the young girl carried. But the next day Reeta had repented. She knew she'd been weak and had allowed – just for a moment – a small bud of love for Abra to blossom. But her love for the Lord was meant to be all-encompassing; her love for Jeb was meant to be above all others. She'd dealt with two bloods since then alone and stoically.

She was a woman now.

Jeb laughed, tinkling and delicate like music. He looked around the room, empty save for a few tables of hunched-over men, the odd aging couple.

'This place, right here, is a den of sin,' he said. 'And that's why we come. We pray for the people in here. For even the most sinful can be saved, can't they? If they accept the Lord and His Word.' Jeb surveyed the room again before turning back to her. Reeta nodded and took another dizzying sip of Coke. 'You know that I am the Messiah, that I am chosen to reveal the Seven Seals to the world. And that any child born to me will be sacred.'

Reeta nodded again, more enthusiastically this time. She'd cared for all of Jeb's children across the years, knowing that one of them was destined for the Second Coming. And the Second Coming would marker Judgement Day.

'Reeta,' he said, leaning toward her, his expression earnest, sincere. 'I have asked only six of our number if they would give their wombs to the Lord. Each woman chosen for her worthiness.'

He inhaled.

'Today I ask my seventh.'

Four

There was an unsettling shuffle and thunk as Bonnie made her way down the central aisle of the courtroom – the slow dragging of her feet against the hard click of her cane on wooden floorboards.

The room was full of a silence pulled so taut it squeaked.

Reeta closed her eyes and kept her head facing forward, each *shuffle-thunk-shuffle-thunk* a sucker punch. It seemed to take an age for the girl to make it to the stand. The one they'd all been waiting for.

The sole survivor of Reeta Doe.

Eventually Reeta heard the bailiff speak, his voice monotonous and rolling as Bonnie agreed with whispered assurances to tell the truth, the whole truth and nothing but the truth. The truth in court was a funny concept. It didn't account for its duality.

'Ms Powell,' Crawley began in a voice laced with disingenuous compassion. Reeta opened her eyes to stare dead ahead at the bailiff, who remained unmoving. 'Thank you *so* much for being here today.' Reeta knew he would be fastening a button on his jacket with one hand. He did that at the start of every testimony. She didn't know why.

'I didn't have a choice,' Bonnie replied softly.

'I know how hard it must be for you to come here.' Crawley answered so smoothly, Reeta couldn't help but wonder if this line had been rehearsed. 'But it's nearly over now. In the call of justice, we ask for just this last effort of you and then you can begin to rebuild your life.' There was a pause, long and unnatural, before Crawley spoke again. 'Let's begin slowly, Ms Powell. I don't want to push you beyond the realms of comfort. You enrolled at the University of Florida last September, is that right?'

Reeta didn't hear an answer.

'I'm sorry,' Crawley said. 'But we do need you to verbalise your answers for the court reporter.'

'Oh,' the quiet voice said. 'Yes. That's right.'

Reeta braved a look toward the voices. Crawley was standing feet apart, with a slight lean back so his silhouette created a concave around the jurors behind him. The girl on the stand had her head turned toward him, the scarf across her face hiding her expression from Reeta's perspective.

Crawley cycled through the details of Bonnie's life, simple yes and no questions the girl answered with her delicate gossamer tone. They passed through to the events of the day in question. Friday February 25th 1966. The rally, the bar, the strange girl who offered her a ride home.

'But you never made it home that night, did you?' Crawley pounded inelegantly at the point.

'No,' came the answer.

'Now, Ms Powell.' Crawley slowed his pace, an air of severity spreading theatrically through his words. 'Can you tell us what happened once you accepted a ride from the girl at the bar?'

There was a deep void of a hesitation. 'For the most part she was quiet. My dorm room was only a few blocks away so I didn't think it would take long to drive. But then I saw her turning toward the interstate and asked what she was doing.' The words came out practised and fluent, a script she expelled desperately. 'She told me she was taking me home. When I said that my home was in the other direction, she smiled and said she was taking me to my real home.'

'And what did she mean by that?'

'Objection!' Barry was on his feet. 'Clearly calling for speculation from the witness, who cannot *know* what the defendant may or may not have meant.'

'Sustained,' the judge replied simply but did not admonish Crawley for his pointed question.

'Did you ask her what she meant by that?' he rephrased casually.

'She just repeated it when I asked her.'

'What happened after that?'

'It's all a blur.' Bonnie brought a hand to her forehead, her fingertips resting gently against the headscarf on one side, as if she was physically urging the recollection out of herself. 'She mentioned something about Cuba, told me we'd be safe there. I was trying to keep calm and I told her I *was* safe, and that I wanted her to take me to my dorm.' Reeta noticed her hand tremble slightly, but when she spoke her words remained steady. 'I don't remember exactly what happened then, but I think I told her no. I told her to take me home. I was drunk and I got angry and I told her, firmly, that I wasn't going to Cuba.'

'And then what happened?'

'She got angry and she pulled the car over.'

'Ladies and gentlemen of the jury, I direct you to exhibits T1 through T7, photographs taken around ten miles away from the site of the car crash, clearly showing tyre skid marks off the interstate suggesting an emergency brake off the road. Those are deductions made by the crime scene detectives, their statements are attached to the photographs in your jury packets.' There was a brief rustling of papers as the jury located the photographs and statements. 'Ms Powell.' Crawley gestured for her to continue.

'The car was off the road and we argued. I got out of the car and tried to walk home.'

'And then what happened?'

'That's the last thing I remember. The next thing I know I was waking up in hospital.'

'Thank you, Ms Powell, for your bravery here today. Now, ladies and gentlemen.' Crawley was addressing the jury again. 'We've heard from the FBI agents, as well as statements from the responding police and ambulance crew who were first on the scene, that Ms Powell here was found in the trunk of that car with evidence of a hammer wound to the back of the head, as well as severe damage caused by the crash itself.' He turned back to Bonnie. 'We are grateful for your recovery and that you can sit here today. Now, Ms Powell, I have just one final question of you. The girl whom you met at the bar, and who offered you a ride home leading to a brutal attack and near-fatal car crash — is she in this courtroom today?'

'Yes.'

'And can you please point her out for us?'

Reeta had an absurd beat of hope that the girl's wavering finger would direct toward someone else in the room. But very slowly she turned toward her, arm outstretched.

For the first time the two women locked eyes.

Reeta held her gaze with a stoic nod of apology, but Bonnie flinched quickly away.

Barry softly declined the judge's invitation for cross-examination.

—

Carol watched as Crawley helped Bonnie down from the stand, tenderly handing her the cane he'd place against the jury box. A cunning move, she'd noted – don't let the jury forget about the girl's cane. With the same uneven shuffle that she'd entered with, Bonnie Powell began the slow process of escaping the courtroom. Her bit was done.

She could go home now. Live her life. Move on from it all.

But Carol had the distinct feeling that she'd see the girl there again tomorrow, as she had done every day since the start – her frail, crumpled body cowed into the arm of a man with dark hair and eyes laced with protective hatred.

Carol watched her intently as she made her way back to her seat, even long after the other spectators' attention had been turned back to the legal spectacle at the front. Bonnie's expression was almost impossible to read between her facial injuries and her headscarf. But Carol thought she saw the hint of a smile twitch at her lips as she re-joined her companion.

Carol's pen scratched idly onto her notepad as she watched Bonnie closely, and when she looked down it was with horror that she saw two words she'd etched onto the page. Scribbling furiously, Carol perforated the paper, tearing away any evidence of her subconscious thought.

Smug bitch.

IV

There was a timid knock on the door. A reticent, gentle sound as if the knuckles that beat it were tired and bloody.

Reeta lay on the floor, running her fingers across pale waxy skin stretched across her sunken stomach, tucking her fingertips in the grooves under her ribs. She'd had little weight to lose in the first place, so in a week of only two cups of thin broth a day, her body had begun the process of melting away. That was what she wanted. Her shame was too great.

There was a creak and a scuff of wood against the cold cement floor of the basement, and Damaris stuck her head in through the crack of the door, shouldering it open wider. She held a bundle wrapped in a towel.

'I brought you this,' she said, holding it out. 'I saved it from dinner. It's nearly midnight now, no one knows I'm here.'

Saliva flooded Reeta's mouth and she stared for a moment, imagining devouring her first solid food in a week. She shook her head.

'No. My penance is not done yet. Jeb will tell me when I am forgiven.'

Damaris's face was strained, her jaw clenched hard so it squared off her face. 'Please?' she implored. 'We're worried about you. You'll die here.'

'Then that is my journey!'

When she'd first been chosen to carry the seed of God, euphoria had flooded her veins. It had taken two months for her blood to stop, her legacy and gift to the world now growing inside her previously unremarkable body. At mealtimes she sat beside Jeb, serving him from communal dishes with a connection only they shared. On occasion she'd spy his other wives look over from their demoted spots, the sin of jealousy spiking their stare. This was her destiny, her journey since the day of her own birth – to carry the Second Coming of Christ, to follow in Mary's footsteps. Abra had fussed and tended to her more keenly than she should, more than she had for any of Jeb's wives, and Reeta had been forced to report her to Zechariah. It had not felt as righteous as Reeta had thought to see the fruits of Abra's punishment the next day, six hours of hauling wood from Jeb's workshop to the safety of the basement, to keep the precious stock dry from the oncoming storms. Abra had limped and her back hunched unevenly, her hands rough with splinters from the unkempt wood. But still Abra persisted in lavishing her attention on Reeta – her concern undeterred.

Reeta had endeavoured to avoid pride at her new position and not to fall into the easy comfort of Abra's care, but she had failed. Pride had swept up her weak bones and shone out of her, the sin marking her out for punishment to the Lord.

And last week she had bled again.

She had been hauling the handle of the mangle up and down, up and down, out in the midday sun. Damaris worked to feed the sodden men's work clothes through the slot, tugging them out of the other side as Reeta wound them through the thick rollers. Her arms burned with effort, but it felt good.

The handle in front of her eyes had clouded for a moment, her head suddenly empty, blinking with white lights. She gripped it harder, steadying herself against it. White lights beamed again behind Reeta's eyes and a pulse wracked through her from her lower belly. She folded forward, failing to stifle the grunt of agony as she did. Damaris rushed toward her, grabbing her shoulders, asking something, but Reeta couldn't make out the words. Pain flushed her limbs and another pulse radiated from her womb like a bomb. She felt wet down her legs, sticky and warm that shouldn't be there. Damaris caught her as she toppled backward, lowering her gently to the grass, hollering something over her shoulder. Feet punched the ground all around her. Her dress was lifted up, legs smeared with blood and thick white discharge. Reeta knew at once.

She had awoken on a soft wide bed, a fluffy down comforter wrapped around her. Jeb sat on a wooden rocking chair in the corner, watching her. She met his eye and shame wound its way up her limbs. Snaking up from her toes and fingers, it burned spiral barbed marks into her flesh, meeting in a ball of jagged wire in her now empty womb.

'I thought you were worthy,' he said, disappointment and anger shaking his voice. 'My seed should have flourished in you.'

The next morning Zechariah came for her and she was shown to her new home in the basement.

'You may leave when you feel your penance is done,' he'd told her.

She would never leave.

Five

It was a Monday morning at the end of November when the trial was due to close. It would be the last Monday morning Carol would queue from five a.m. to stake her claim to a press seat in the courtroom, a takeout cup of petroleum-strength coffee clutched in her hand from the cart on the forecourt, which had made a killing by opening early for the desperate press pack. Tahir, who ran it, would rake it in all day from the photographers and journalists not permitted entry, as they swarmed the forecourt, agitatedly waiting for the runners from inside to return and call out any important updates or revelations. Carol hadn't missed one day of this trial and knew the schedule well, so when eight a.m. rolled around and the heavy courtroom doors were pulled wide, she was prepared. Her feet were aching already from having stood for so long in her pinched court shoes, and she shifted her weight between them, itching to reach the front of the queue so she could get inside and sit down. She handed the bailiff her raffle ticket and he guided her through with an outstretched arm. The back four rows were saved for press and Carol squeezed onto the end of the already crowded bench at the front of this section.

'Big day for your friend.' A voice said from behind. She turned to see Tommy Macklin standing over her with a snickering expression.

'Fuck off, Tommy.'

Tommy pulled his top lip upwards, displaying his teeth, and emitted a loud buzzing sound while vibrating his arms comically.

'Fry her, that's what they're gonna do.'

A couple of the reporters around them chuckled softly and Tommy, pleased with his audience response, sidled down toward the end of his row in search of a seat. Carol breathed tightly and looked down at the top blank sheet of her pad. Forcing herself to focus on the ruled lines, she inhaled steadily, running her eyes along the length of one of the lines, and exhaled as she went back the opposite way. She breathed until she felt the panic dissipate from her chest, until the images of Reeta's vibrating, smoking body fluttered back into the crevices of her imagination.

Carol looked back up at the courtroom, everyone ready and waiting. Her eyes tracked, as they had done since her testimony, over to the hunched girl with an injured face covered by a silk scarf, flyaway blonde hair escaping around her throat. Who was the man she was with? Why were her parents relegated to the rows behind her – barely a glance shared between them? The courtroom was full of the grieving families and friends of the other victims – Callie Jefferson, Bobby DeValle, Nancy Lawson and Linda Beaumont had all filed in and out over the last eleven weeks, and were all present today, tense and resolute, awaiting justice for their loved one.

But there were no college friends here for Bonnie.

The door to the side opened, and everyone craned their necks in the direction of the girl they'd all gathered to see fry. Reeta was the silent star of this show. Although Carol understood Barry's reasons for not putting Reeta on the stand, she couldn't help but think that maybe, if

164

the jury heard her gentle voice, the care she put into everything she said, the jokes she cracked at her own expense — then maybe they could reach down inside themselves to grasp at that reasonable doubt. But Carol knew that the Reeta she saw in private was not one anybody else was interested in meeting.

—

Reeta filed in and gave the crowd her usual backward glance, her nerves settling slightly only when she'd shared a brief greeting with Carol. She swallowed thickly and closed her eyes as the handcuffs relieved their pressure and her hips felt lighter without the metal bonds.

The judged entered and Reeta watched like a movie she'd seen a hundred times as he opened proceedings for the day. He told the jury emphatically that they were about to hear the final arguments from both sides, and then they were to retire to make a very grave decision.

US Attorney Peter Crawley stood as the judge gestured for him to begin, making his usual show of fastening one button of his smart blue suit, a look of lament on his face. He walked toward the jury and planted himself in front of them, direct and centre, and Reeta could see the back of his head move as he looked each of the twelve jurors in the eye. He twisted his shoulders away from them and turned to face Reeta, a direct stare, a confrontation. He watched her intently for several agonising moments before sighing and dropping his gaze to the floor. When he looked back up, he was addressing the jury once again.

'A young girl,' he said sadly. 'A pretty, young girl. You wouldn't think anything of her if you passed her on the street. Well.' He paused and turned for a second back to her, a flicker of a hand in her direction. 'Well, not before this.' Reeta felt her still-healing face burn hotter than before, each scar, each healed stitch glaring out in bright technicolour. 'And that is the danger of Reeta Doe.'

'The defence has made much of her current mental state.' He said the last two words as if the defence had claimed a unicorn responsible, one eyebrow floating wryly upwards. 'And although many of you may consider it a *convenient* addition to her brutal injuries, I personally wish her the very best in her recovery. After all' – he raised his hands out the side – 'we still have two girls missing. Two daughters not returned home. And so I *do* – I wish our culprit the speediest of recoveries so we can do what's *right* by those poor girls' remains.' He paused and nodded sadly. 'Because, of course, we must not let ourselves be distracted by what the *defence*' – he turned to shoot a look at Barry – 'wants you to get confused by. That this girl sitting in this courtroom, no matter how frail, no matter how *forgetful* she is of her crimes – is still guilty.' His voice soared powerfully over the final word. 'Guilty of so much pain. Guilty of so much *brutalisation*. Guilty. There is no denying it.

'We have successfully shown you in this very courtroom that this girl' – he turned to point toward her – 'was present on all the college campuses. You've heard testimony from friends and witnesses identifying her as the last to be seen with two of the victims. You've heard powerful' – he stopped and shook his head toward the ceiling as if he was pleading with God himself – 'powerful testimony from her final victim, a girl lucky to have escaped with what little life she did. A girl *found in the trunk* of Reeta's car. A girl who has identified Reeta as the person who abducted her.' He paused again for effect. 'If that wasn't enough, we have shown you physical evidence – experts confirming that the microscopic structure of hair found on the body of the second victim, Abigail Lawson, matches that very same make-up of hair plucked from Reeta Doe's head herself. The defence debunk this science as poppycock' – he gave a small chuckle – 'but I come from a world that trusts our science. That trusts that great institution always searching for answers... no.' He raised a finger, making a show of correcting himself. 'No – always searching for *provable* answers. Answers beyond a doubt, with a *provable* scientific basis that is beyond the spectrum of debate.'

He came to a stop and paced a couple of times in front of the jury box, their eyes glued to his every motion.

'So, we have our witness testimony. We have our scientific basis.'

Reeta's fist clenched around the flesh on the inside of her thigh through her cheap trousers – she knew what was coming next. She pinched down hard on the skin beneath the material, a satisfying clunk of pain to distract her from what he was about to say.

'And if that wasn't enough, we have the letters.' Peter Crawley rested his gaze on Reeta and shook his head, almost in apology.

V

It had been a boom five years for Pine Ranch. Another dormitory had been erected on the backs of the existing three, another twenty-four beds added and filled. Jeb himself had been out on the road with Zechariah, travelling their surrounding states in the pickup truck and returning with new members every few months. One girl had shown up while they were still out on a mission, tumbling out of the cab of a haulage truck and traipsing up the drive – a school backpack slung over one shoulder. She'd heard Brother Jeb speak in Amarillo and had hitchhiked her way to eternal salvation. She was assigned a bunk and chore duty and survived three weeks without a name – referred to only as 'girl', 'outsider' or indistinguishable grunts until Jeb had returned and gifted her Kezia.

Sundays brought six hours of Bible study and worship until midday, when the children, men and whichever women were not on kitchen duty were permitted free time until lunch and afternoon worship. Reeta, Damaris and Kezia, natural allies in age, walked across the rolling prairie, down toward the woodland at the edge of the property. Damaris's burgeoning belly had begun to strain against her smock now, and so the girls had commenced a weekly routine of gentle walks to help ease her tight back and tired limbs.

'Ooof,' Damaris breathed, stopping abruptly on their path.

Reeta's head jerked immediately toward her, paranoia snaking terror through her limbs. Not again. 'Are you OK?' she asked, rushing her hands to Damaris's back.

Damaris smiled and gave a gentle laugh. 'Yes, Reeta. The baby just kicked.'

Reeta's mouth gaped, a smile tugging at its corners until her face broke into genuine, pure joy.

'Can I feel?' she asked excitedly, jerking her hands in the direction of the bump. Damaris nodded, still laughing.

By the time Damaris had been chosen by Jeb, Reeta had become accustomed to her new, lowly place at the ranch. It had taken several hard weeks in her basement cell before Jeb dragged her, emaciated and barely breathing, from it. He'd bathed her, cared for her and fed her. It was not her path to die for this sin; her repentance was done. But she'd shown that she was not destined to carry the Second Coming, and he had never again invited her to his room to plant his seed.

But she was grateful for his forgiveness and her humbleness was true.

When Damaris had been invited into the pickup one afternoon the year before, Reeta knew she was to be chosen, and it was with pride and excitement that she'd greeted her back that evening. Damaris had been uneasy, nervous, confused by the sweet taste of soda on her lips that reminded her of home. But Reeta had soothed her, explained the process, reassured her that it was the Lord's plan. The baby was now flourishing in her belly, and in another few weeks they would have a new blessing to care for.

'Let's keep walking,' Damaris said, twisting her shoulders in alternating circles and straightening up. 'It relieves the pressure.' The trio continued on their way.

'What...' Kezia paused, hesitant. 'What was it like?'

Unwanted memories from years ago doused Reeta all at once. Hands in places they shouldn't be, but for such an honour. The pressure, the pain of his body. It was all a contradiction. How wrong she had felt afterwards. But that couldn't be, she'd told herself. It was right and it was glorious. She swallowed heavily and looked over at Damaris, whose own eyes had fallen in on themselves. No doubt she was reliving those same memories.

'I don't want to talk about it,' Damaris replied, her voice a whisper. 'But I have my baby, so everything was worth it.' She smiled down at her bump.

They reached the edge of the wood, the fresh green grass giving way to rough, unkempt ground twisted with tree roots and brambles. The trees further ahead had begun the turn to murky yellow in their leaves, some early droppers already fallen. Come summer they glowed green with life – the earth cloaked in dark shadow below.

'What's on the other side?' Kezia asked, twisting her neck to follow a path through the densely growing trunks.

Reeta shrugged. 'I guess more prairieland. Maybe another town.'

'Has anyone ever been through?'

Reeta swallowed thickly and stared into the woodland. 'Why would they?' she asked quietly after a beat, her gaze now lost amongst the trees.

'I dunno,' Kezia said. 'Curiosity?'

It took another moment before Reeta collected herself and snapped her head back to Kezia. 'What's there to be curious about?' she said. 'We know everything that's gonna happen and we've got all we need right here.' But there was a waver to her voice, an uncertainty she didn't want to acknowledge. Over the years she'd sometimes tried to peer through the woodland, to wind her sight through the dense thicket and catch a glimpse of the world beyond. She'd see blonde hair bouncing through the trees away from Pine Ranch, a small hand gripped tightly in a mother's. She'd feel Abra next to her, pressing close with love and protection and imagine them running side by side together. But then she'd remember what awaited her out there and she'd correct herself, spooling her curiosity back inside where it belonged.

'You've really never been outside Pine Ranch?' Kezia asked with a mix of wonderment and awe.

'Just once,' Reeta replied softly.

'We best get back,' Damaris said, slipping her hand tenderly into Reeta's. 'Eunice is making her famous squash pie.'

'Well, woe betide us if we're late for that,' Reeta said with a relaxed smile she'd only learned in the last few years.

'Let's pick a bouquet for Jeb on our way back,' Kezia said wistfully, sweeping her gaze across the wildflower-strewn route back home.

As they settled down for dinner, Damaris's position now next to Jeb, the girls presented him with their bundles of flowers tied together with kitchen yarn. A grin stretched across his sun-withered face, his eyes smiling gratitude at each of them.

'A gift of God's own creation,' he said arranging the flowers in a water glass in front of him. His eyes lingered on Reeta a moment longer than the others, a searching look, and he gave her another single nod of thanks.

The labour pains had started in the morning just after breakfast. Damaris had been clearing plates when she'd folded over and dropped the crockery in her hand with a clatter to the floor. Reeta had rushed forward and a splash had wet her legs. She looked up with a nervous grin of excitement. They took Damaris upstairs to Abra's bed and Reeta was dispatched for Gideon, who gave her a routine examination and said it would be a little while yet. Someone should stay with her, fetch her cold water and hot sweet tea to keep her energy up, and let him know when the regular pains grew closer together.

The morning drew on and Damaris panted through the pain when it came, but mostly they spent the morning chatting and waiting, the downtime of labour thoroughly unexpected. Hagar came to check on them around lunch, bringing Reeta her tin box of food and a Bible so they could conduct their own study and prayer without coming down to join the others.

'Does Jeb know?' Damaris asked quietly, biting off a piece of cornbread tentatively between her front teeth.

Hagar nodded. 'He'll see the baby when it's here,' she said soothingly. Reeta had seen Hagar survive three labours with only Abra or Eunice at her side. This was no place for a man, and certainly not Brother Jeb. 'You keep your strength up now,' Hagar finished as she left the room. 'You'll need it.'

It was just before dinnertime that Reeta left to fetch Gideon, finding him on the porch, whittling. 'Every couple of minutes,' she told him breathlessly. 'She's in agony, won't eat or drink.'

Gideon nodded sagely. 'I'll go up now. Will you bring hot water from the kitchen? I think Eunice has some boiling ready to go. And Abra has towels ready too – ask her to bring them up, please.'

Reeta nodded vigorously and headed for the kitchen.

'How is she?' Kezia swung around from her position at the counter kneading bread. Flour coated her smock with a light dusting of grey, and thick strings of sticky dough clung to her fingers.

'She's doing well,' Reeta replied and glanced around, settling her eyes after a moment. 'Abra,' she said earnestly, 'Gideon wants the towels upstairs – it's time.'

Abra flared with excitement and moved close enough to grasp Reeta's forearm with a comforting squeeze.

'It will be hard,' she said in a low voice. 'But Damaris is strong and' – her throat seemed to thicken for a moment and Reeta saw her eyes glisten with tears – 'it'll be the best thing that ever happens to her.'

Reeta knew she should bat Abra away. She knew that what was swelling between them was too much like familial love, but Reeta felt her own tears beckon. She thought of the child she had lost and thought of the mother she would never become. Would she have been strong enough to give up her child the way Jeb needed them to? She liked to think she would, but her dedication had been tested over the years – and she'd seen before how the devil can creep into even the strongest resolve and twist devotion into treachery. They held each other's gaze for a moment more before Abra hurried off to fetch the towels. Reeta blinked away her tears and turned to pick up two cloths to grasp the handles of the steaming pot on the stove.

'We're praying for her!' Eunice declared cheerily, an electric sparkle of festivity buzzing through the air around the working women. Reeta couldn't help looking back to give a departing grin as she navigated the steps with the hot pan.

A loud bang shuddered through the house with her first step out of the kitchen, causing her hands to slip and fumble. Hot water splashed against her wrists, her skin flaring neon red at once.

Another bang.

It came from outside followed by the rumble of deep shouts. The windows out onto the porch were curtained, but Reeta could see the silhouettes of running bodies gathering in a long line. Kezia appeared behind her, drying dough still stuck to her forearms, the heads of the other women peering out around her.

'What's going on?' Kezia asked, an interested frown creasing between her eyebrows.

Reeta shook her head. 'I… I don't know.'

A voice, artificially loud, called into the house as the line of silhouettes thickened with running bodies.

'Sally! Sally Henderson, get out here right now!'

Reeta turned her head slowly toward Kezia who had frozen where she stood, floured arms still held zombie-like out in front, eyes round and horror-struck.

'Sally!' the voice, tingling with the mechanical mega-phone that enhanced it, called again. 'Sally Henderson!'

Reeta moved wordlessly to put the hot water down on the sideboard.

'Kezia,' she said softly, turning to put her arms gently around Kezia's middle back, hands cradling her elbows as if she was guiding an injured patient. Kezia rotated her neck so she stared closely into Reeta's eyes.

'What do I do?' she whispered.

'We're going to go outside and talk to them,' Reeta replied, her voice growing in strength. This was what she knew – to defend the Word, to defend Pine Ranch. She'd been preparing for this her entire life. 'You'll tell them Jeb's message and that you're safe here. That they could be safe here too.' Reeta smiled. 'They could join you.'

Kezia's expression remained stricken and she shook her head slightly. 'That's my daddy. You don't know him.'

They could now hear Jeb's strong tone sermonising, pleading with Kezia's father. The words were too muffled to make out, but his voice gave comfort and security.

'Let him see you,' Reeta said, buoyed by Jeb's presence outside. 'Let him see you're OK, thriving and happy.' She narrowed her eyes for a split second. '*Are* you happy?'

'Yes,' Kezia replied, breathless, even before Reeta had finished her question. 'Yes, more so than ever before.'

'Come on,' Reeta said, guiding Kezia toward the door. She understood now that her path was not the one she had expected today. Today she would help protect Pine Ranch and provide Damaris's miracle child the safest haven of walls he could ever know.

The door creaked as they opened it and stepped out onto the porch to see two cars pulled up onto the driveway. Why the gate had been opened for them, Reeta didn't know.

A broad man in a blue uniform was standing half-out of the front police car. In his right hand he held a gun, pointed directly up into the air, while the left held a megaphone to his lips. Three more figures stood, braced with firearms raised, half-out of the front doors of both cars.

'I don't care 'bout your blasphemin' mumbo jumbo,' the man who Reeta now understood to be Kezia's father said. 'I want my little girl back.'

'She does not want to come back,' Jeb replied calmly. 'She is happy here.'

Neither man had noticed the presence of the girl in question appear on the porch. Reeta guided her forward until they stood pressed up against the banister that looked down on the scene.

'Sally!' her father called, seeing the movement after a few long moments. 'Sally, you stop this tomfoolery right now and come home.'

'My name,' she replied, voice cracked and parched as summer grass. 'My name,' she repeated, stronger, louder, 'is Kezia.'

'Your name is Sally-Jo Henderson and you will answer to that, young lady,' her father responded, taking a step toward her, out behind the safety of his car door.

'My name is Kezia. As gifted to me by our prophet, the new Messiah – Brother Jeb.'

Mr Henderson levelled a toxic gaze on Jeb, eyes narrowed, finger pulsing temptingly on the trigger of his gun. Was this how it ended? Reeta watched in horror. Would the prophet leave their world as the Second Coming was born into it?

But the finger remained still: no trigger was pulled.

'Honey.' He was forcing patience into his voice, struggling to match Jeb's calm. 'This man is no messiah, no prophet. He's a blaspheming con man and n—r-lover.' He stroked his eyes down the line of men, taking in the mismatch of races. His colleagues gave a disgusted jeer. 'Now, you come down these steps right now; I am taking you home.'

'No,' she replied firmly. Her hand slid over Reeta's on the banister, gripping it tightly. 'I'm not leaving.'

'We will not let you take one of our number unwillingly,' Zechariah said. He had raised a shotgun to his shoulder and Reeta noticed with surprise that at least fifteen more of the men were armed. 'Go home and leave us be.'

'I ain't taking instructions from no damned n——r,' Mr Henderson spat while his companions moved their guns to take aim at Zechariah. 'Give me back my daughter.'

'The Lord gifted us all free agency,' Jeb said, interrupting the sour stand-off. 'She has chosen to use hers to stay with us, to seek salvation for the Reckoning. You are welcome to our learnings.' He raised his hands up wide. 'My teachings are for all those who wish to be saved.'

'Your teachings are a crock o' shit and you know it. I don't know what game you're running here but I won't allow you to kidnap my daughter because of it!' He stepped forward again, his gun now directed at Jeb's chest.

Jeb sighed, deeply, powerfully.

'I have tried to reason with you, Captain Henderson. But you continue in your antagonism. We have children, women here. One woman currently in labour.' He gestured up to the house. 'And we are men, here to protect them. To protect our weak as is our godly duty. We are armed and we outnumber you. You are acting out of your jurisdiction – with no warrant. You will leave here now, or we will call in our own police force. I assure you – it will not be us who falls under the scrutiny of the law.'

Reeta could feel the frisson of his words buzz through the gathered people. A man of God and of the world.

'Sally.' Mr Henderson reached out one last time to his daughter, his weapon falling by his side. 'Please. Your mother misses you.'

Kezia gave a stiff shake of her head but said nothing.

Her father's face twisted toward Jeb. 'This isn't over,' he snarled. 'You can't get away with this, you freaks.' He gave a twirled gesture with his megaphone and climbed back into the car, followed hesitantly by his colleagues.

'Isaiah. You were on gate duty.' Jeb turned to the teenage boy as the cars pulled away. 'Why were they permitted entry?'

'Th-they...' Isaiah's words tumbled pathetically from shaking lips. 'They were police.'

'And you recognise their authority over my own?' The question was stone and Isaiah had no response. 'You will wait in my workshop.'

The boy was dismissed and walked on shaking limbs back toward the house. Reeta saw Jeb's hand curl into a tight fist as he whirled to address the gathered group of men.

'Did I not tell you the outside world is dangerous for us?' he screamed, spittle flying from his lips, his usually calm face tinged red with fury. 'Did I not warn you of what happens when my word is questioned?' His voice raised an octave, a screech almost running through his words. 'The outside is Gomorrah – it is dirty and sinful and only within our great compound can the Lord see your worth!' He paused, breathless and panting. 'We have lost angels to the outside before. We will lose no more. Our numbers are full. The Reckoning is imminent.'

He turned and strode into the house, following Isaiah.

The boy's screams were fused only with those of Damaris.

Six

Carol had stopped taking notes. She knew what Peter Crawley was going to say, even before he'd taken his spotlight. Closing arguments were not for new revelations; they were for posturing and summing up. Instead, her pen had scratched deep, shiny, black crevices into her notepad, an unconscious habit as he orated the case against her friend. It was a strong case, unbreakably so, and Carol had known that from the start. She'd never expected to be torn in two for the girl at the centre of it all, never thought her sympathies could take over her cold, professional reason.

She thought of Ben. They'd spoken only twice since their dinner a couple of months ago, after he'd taken the stand. He'd called to check in on her the day after the letters were first presented, and he'd called again last night.

'Whatever happens, Carol,' he'd told her gently, 'don't let it break you.'

She wondered what he'd think of her now, blocking out the attorney's closing statement with harsh doodles, like a child not wanting to listen to its bedtime. Had she broken already?

With Ben's words rattling her back to life, back to the present, she put down her pen and looked up at Crawley. He was gazing toward Reeta like a serpent about to strike. The letters were nothing new by this point, but this was

Crawley's chance to weave the story around them. To build his tale of what they meant.

'We need to take it back,' Crawley said, and Carol forced herself to concentrate. 'For you have all seen the letters.' He gestured casually to the jury. 'You have copies of them in the jury packs, which you will take into deliberation with you today. We've heard from FBI Agents Benjamin Willow and Edward Stephens about the circumstances in which they came across these letters. But we need to know about their origin. What do they mean? You need that vital context to help you understand exactly their significance for justice to be done.' His fist clapped into an open palm. 'Who here is familiar with the story of Pine Ranch?'

There was a soft murmur from the jury as they half-heartedly answered, unsure if the question was rhetorical or not.

'The agents have briefly touched on the context of the religious sect started by Lieutenant Roger Fry, or *Brother Jeb* as he renamed himself. Of course, this religious sect, or the man who started it, is not on trial here. But one of his followers *is*.' He paced up in front of the jury again. 'We have no way of truly knowing what life was like for Reeta Doe inside that compound. We *do* know that her days were built on prayer and labouring the land, which sounds like harmless prairie life.' He smiled again, a soft laugh almost on his words. 'But if that life turned us all into killers, well, our ancestors would never have made it west past Texas. This life *must* have been more than simple, modest existence. Look at what it created! Look at what this girl was prompted to do!' His hand flew out in gesture toward Reeta, whose head was bent low so Carol couldn't see her face. 'Make no mistake, I do not blame her upbringing for her crimes – she is wholly responsible and should be held accountable as such. But a life cut off from normal society, people who reject *our* norms, *our* values to isolate themselves from good American society, well, who's to say what values she was taught to fill that vacuum.' He paused again before recommencing his pacing up and down in front of the jury box. 'We can deduce from these letters that she was sent out to find more followers for Brother Jeb. That she failed time and time again to find him servants as devoted as she. That she disappointed him thoroughly.' He glanced back at Reeta then, as if hoping she would jump up in defence of her master. 'And so she killed those girls that failed her. The innocent students that she blamed for her saviour's disappointment and ire. In lieu of any other character testimony of the accused…' He paused and shrugged. 'I'd say that's pretty damning evidence of motive.'

–

Crawley had come to the end of his speech in a blur of accusatory gestures and claims, his words bouncing off the armour Reeta had built across her skin. At first the accusations launched at her smarted pink and sharp against her body, but over the last eight months, each wound of revelation had healed into a tough callus.

The truth of Pine Ranch was a complicated well of nettles Reeta knew she needed to climb down into. But so far, her moral confusion had been overwhelmed by the acceptance of the crimes that had landed her in that courtroom. She'd had no time or emotional energy to understand the significance of her upbringing. She'd read the articles, listened to the story Carol had told her, but it sounded even more alien – even more farfetched than the

181

other stories she'd been forced to sit through. Those tales of her time on the road now had an abhorrent, familiar snugness, like the wretched scars on her face; they were ugly, but she'd begun to accept them as hers. The tales of Pine Ranch floated above her. Another life full of misery that she just couldn't bring herself to reach for.

Barry was up now, rocking on his haunches, giving his own closing argument. It was not one that was having any sway with the jury supposedly on the search for a reasonable doubt. Twelve faces had looked at her at varying points throughout the last eleven weeks, each face marked with the confidence that they were looking at a brutal killer. Barry's claims of procedural misconduct, of unproven science, were weak in the face of raised shaking fingers from the witness box identifying her as the culprit.

Eventually Barry came to a stop, his speech at least a third of the length of his opponent's. He called for one last reminder that they must only convict if they were convinced *beyond a reasonable doubt*. He reiterated what he considered to be reasonable doubts, and then he sat down with the whole courtroom knowing that he had raised no doubts, whether reasonable or otherwise.

The judge then spoke to the jury for a few moments, more reminders of the graveness of their role, more thanks for their duty, and then – finally – the twelve strangers were dismissed to decide the fate of Reeta Doe's existence.

Barry moved his hand over where hers lay on her thigh and he squeezed it tight. She looked up in surprise; he'd never shown any crumb of affection toward her throughout this entire journey. But it was over now. He'd done his job. She twisted her hand inside his so their palms were facing, and wrapped her fingers around the back of his hand, reciprocating his tight clasp in a gesture she hoped he understood as one of gratitude. The moment lasted barely a second longer before the bailiffs ordered her to her feet, the heavy handcuffs clinking in their hands. She was to await the rest of the day in the courthouse cell, to be transferred back to the jail at five p.m. if the jury hadn't returned a verdict by then. Each day she would be brought back to the courthouse cell to await the jury's verdict. Nobody expected her to have to spend too many days in the agony of waiting.

Open-and-shut case.

That's what Stephens had said.

—

Carol saw Reeta twist around to raise her hand in a small wave as the bailiffs chained her up again, leading her shuffling feet back out of the courtroom. It was nearly lunch time, but Carol's stomach turned at the thought of any sustenance to fill it. Instead she waited patiently while she was bustled down the aisle between the benches, the other journalists talking excitedly to each other, discussing angles, where to go for lunch, how long they reckoned the jury would take to deliberate.

'Definitely not before lunch,' someone chortled behind her. 'They get good food in the jury rooms.'

Carol broke away from the crowd streaming toward the exit and made her way to the restrooms down the linoleum corridor. The sensation of Reeta's trial had brought in more people than the court was equipped for, and so they'd had to close half the other courtrooms and reassign those cases to new dates or locations. But of the half that were still in use, their trials were still in session, and so the end of the corridor that led to the women's bathroom was relatively sparse of people.

Carol pushed open the door with her shoulder and made her way to the bank of sinks, pressing her hands onto the refreshingly cold porcelain and pushing her weight down as she stared into it. Clumps of mould and loose hairs wound their way around the silver plug. Carol flipped the cold tap on and let the water run through her fingers for a moment before pressing them into her face. It would make her mascara run, but she had back-up in her bag. She cupped her fingers over her eyes and pressed down hard before dragging them down her cheeks. When she opened her eyes, blurry with the droplets of water, she saw her reflection staring back with thick black smudges trailing down her face.

She started as the door to the bathroom opened behind her, and the slow figure of Bonnie Powell limped in. Carol heard the knock of the cane against the tiled floor, followed by the dragged shuffle of a foot in an uneven rhythm of progress. Forgetting about her face, Carol stepped forward.

'Can I help?' she asked, making a gesture to Bonnie's free side.

The woman looked up from where she had been concentrating on her feet, her headscarf pulled firmly forward so most of her face was in shadow. But two dark hazel eyes were visible under the satin shroud, and they blinked at Carol for a moment.

'Um,' she said, hesitation shuddering the sound. 'No, I'm fine, thank you.'

Carol nodded and stepped back to her sink and waited while Bonnie slowly limped her way into a cubicle. When she reached the door, she turned back to Carol, a movement that tugged the scarf away from her face just enough for Carol to see the caved remnants of her left temple collapse the entire top of her face.

'I...' Bonnie's voice was soft and startlingly light. 'I know I'm not one to talk,' she said. 'But you appear to have something on your face.'

The cubical door clicked shut behind her and Carol found an unexpected laugh on her lips. She turned back to the mirror and ran her fingers under the water again before scrubbing at the black tracks down her cheeks. She was reapplying her mascara when Bonnie shuffled out of the toilet a few minutes later. She laid her cane carefully against the wall to the right of her sink and turned the hot tap a couple of times. As she rubbed the murky bar of soap over her hands, she looked at Carol in the mirror.

'You've been watching the Reeta Doe trial.' It was not a question.

Carol gave a nod. 'I'm a journalist for the *Washington Post*.' She opted for the simplest answer.

'Then I'll have to be careful what I say.'

Carol stopped with her mascara wand halfway up to her face. 'I would never quote you without permission,' she said. 'Not after...' She looked for the right word and plumped weakly for, 'everything.'

'I've said all that I can, anyway,' Bonnie replied quietly.

Carol struggled with what to say to that. She had an illogical urge to tell the girl that she'd already said enough to kill Reeta. But how could Carol really blame Bonnie?

'It must be very difficult for you to relive everything,' she said finally.

Bonnie didn't respond at first, and before she could answer, the bathroom door burst open, framing a middle-aged woman with wiry grey-blonde hair and an inappropriately thick turtle-neck sweater.

'Bonnie.' The woman breathed her name like a lifeline and Carol realised it was the girl's mother. She'd first recognised her from the unending press coverage, and each morning since had seen Mr and Mrs Powell arriving separately from their daughter. Bonnie's face had frozen in her mirror and she tugged her scarf a fraction further across her face, her free hand searching at once for her cane.

'Oh Bonnie, it's nearly over.' The woman was walking closer now, her arms outstretched and then wrapped around the suddenly stiff girl. 'You've been so brave.'

Sensing her cue to leave, Carol nodded politely to them both and made for an awkward exit back into the corridor.

VI

Reeta's eyes fought the drab evening light, dulled by the thick clouds that had hung low for the last week, straining on the small words of her Bible. The sounds of Zechariah directing another unloading of crates from the back of his truck flittered in through the thin glass window, and she had to force herself to concentrate on Jeb's words. She was losing herself recently; distraction had come for her – the long-taloned grip of the devil scratching painfully across her attention span. The large wooden boxes of ammunition and weaponry had arrived every month or so ever since the day of Solomon's birth. The day Kezia's father had come. The threat from outside pulsed constantly against their walls, invisible and silent.

One day it would detonate.

If they didn't arm themselves now, they would not be prepared for the day of Reckoning, which was inching closer.

'The first horseman wields his sword,' Jeb told the evening class – more than eighty people crammed closely on spindly chairs and tables, shoulders pressed tightly together. Only Zechariah's helpers were exempt. 'Today we know that sword is gunfire, metallic artillery and tanks that crush everything before them. We' – he gestured to the older men at the back of the room – 'have all seen that in Europe. When that horseman comes, we must fight our

187

fight to prove ourselves to the Lord. Prove we are worthy to conquer that first task. He will come in the form of police officers, of agents, of politicians and journalists. He will come in the form of heretics who denounce our truth. The world will burn and our time to take in more lost souls has passed. Now is time to defend this haven, to seal our truth off. It is too late for their salvation.'

Heads nodded around them and Reeta's own bobbed in automatic agreement. This was the time she had been waiting for her entire life. Her nineteen years on the Lord's creation had all directed to this point, waiting for the Reckoning, preparing herself and her soul for the necessary fight that was to come.

But.

Now it was here, her righteous anger had softened. She sat through these sermons, listening to Jeb's word, and found that she was tired – she didn't want to fight. The perfect miracle of Solomon had worn her down and she wanted them to stay in the utopia of Pine Ranch forever.

A wail broke in through Jeb's words, cutting across the banging task of Zechariah's team. Screeching anguish.

Solomon.

Reeta sighed a small smile and made to move. Damaris's head had responded like a whip to the sound of her child's cries and Reeta could see Abra's hand, kind but firm, restraining her movement with a reassuring look. Damaris had showed reluctance to relinquish her parental status of Solomon. She cared overtly more for him than for any of the other children of God on Pine Ranch – and that wasn't the way. Solomon belonged no more to her than to any of them. Jeb had reduced their time together, forbidding her from tending to him or holding him more than a few times a week, and always looking disappointedly down at the wet patches on her smock where her breasts yearned to feed her son. Hagar had told her they would dry up eventually.

Reeta had stepped in and held the soft bundle in her arms most nights, clutching his beating warmth to her chest. She'd fed him, changed him, burped him and played with him, secretly reporting each developmental milestone to Damaris with whispered pride as they lay in their beds. At first she had resisted the fantasy that he was *her* miracle, a covetous sin she could not afford to fall to. But as she'd watched his perfect brown mouth stretch into its first smile, she'd found herself slipping. What could have been and what was blurred into a confused jumble.

Closing her Bible and tucking it under one arm, Reeta straightened herself up, rising to respond to his evening cries.

'Hagar, you will tend to Solomon.' Jeb spoke without lifting his eyes to Reeta, interrupting his own sermon with casual fluidity. He did not continue to preach until he'd heard Reeta reclaim her seat, a thick swallow aching her throat. Hagar shuffled awkwardly out without a look back.

'You love him as your own,' Damaris said that night, her voice a delicate strand through the still air from her low bunk to Reeta's above. It was a statement without emotion and Reeta found she was unable to respond.

The following morning Reeta was taken off nursery rotation, an act that required no explanation. She felt as shameful as when she'd lain for weeks in her basement cell, the agony of her empty womb her only companion. Her sin had been laid bare for all to see. The clawed marks of the devil exposed across her soul.

She worked with Kezia out on the dreary land, tending to the new vegetable patch that had been planted.

Sprawled across the sloped plain in front of them, grass newly lush from the wet winter they'd battled through, were lines of men and boys – troops in training. Thirteen veterans of the British and American armies now taught those too young how to handle the arsenal they had amassed. The puckered sound of gunfire had interrupted the girls' conversation all morning, so that their voices had eventually fallen silent.

Kezia flinched with every shot, nose twisting uncomfortably so her lips gathered in an unintentional snarl to one side.

'They're just doing what's necessary,' Reeta said, her voice low and, she hoped, reassuring.

Kezia nodded. 'I know.' She swallowed and yanked hard at a weed that had bored its roots deep into the soil. 'I just...' She inhaled slowly. 'Did I start this by comin' here? Am I...' She shook her head and examined the weed intently. 'Am I the snake that's gonna ruin our Eden?' When she finally threw the weed to the ground, she looked up at Reeta with wet eyes.

'The End Times were foretold long before you were even born, Kezia. Brother Jeb has been preparing for this for a long time.' As she spoke a familiar ire aroused in Reeta's chest. A rage she hadn't felt in a long time. 'This is bigger than you,' she finished with a snap. The hot dart in her words felt cosy and welcome and she watched with satisfaction at the humiliated husk they reduced Kezia to. Reeta had been too soft on her – the girl needed to learn. Reeta had been too soft on herself, on Damaris. On Abra. The Reckoning was around the corner and she'd allowed them to slip with the rules and discipline that Jeb had laid down – all for what?

For the sake of a friendship, for a child, for laughter.

For love.

Reeta pressed her lower lip, thin and tense, into her mouth and bit down, hard. She needed to reassess her path. She'd known her whole life that Jeb's words were gospel. She needed to refocus on him so she could help save Damaris, Solomon, even Kezia too.

Around late morning the sound of Zechariah's truck rumbled to a stop out front, followed by pounding, heavy feet moving purposefully out to Jeb's workshop on the other side of the back lawn from the vegetable patch.

Strained, muffled voices grunted from within the wooden shed walls.

'Where did they stop you?' Jeb said. Reeta knew she shouldn't eavesdrop, but the voices were too close to ignore.

'Just out near the pickup spot,' she heard Zechariah respond. 'Thanks to the Lord that Terry was late.'

'Do you think they knew?'

'Naw, it was just a regular old stop-and-search. Two Black guys, nice truck.'

'You showed them your papers?'

'Yup, Caleb too.'

Abra came out of the kitchen and down the creaking wooden steps, the mesh door swinging closed behind her. She carried a tray with a pitcher of iced tea and a stack of glasses, the shadow cast by the workshop swallowing her before the walls did.

'What did they say when you told them you were from Pine Ranch?'

'Didn't seem to care. Don't think they knew too much about us, to be honest. But they were just local beat cops. Whatever's going on, they're not gonna know about it.'

'Well, you can't go again, that's for sure. You're too conspicuous, and if they *are* local cops then Terry will hear about it and won't want to deal with us again if you're attracting the law.'

'We have Gideon's station wagon,' Zechariah said. 'They won't be on the lookout for that. Could we risk Gideon doing the pickup?' Reeta knew Gideon was too valuable; Jeb would never put their doctor, and only source of regular income, at risk. 'Even if I drive his car...' Zechariah trailed off, leaving the rest of the sentence unsaid.

'No, stop-and-search is too risky.' Jeb's voice trailed away for a moment and Reeta imagined him accepting a glass of Abra's iced tea. His eyes connecting with hers, an idea forming. 'Cops hardly ever pull over a woman,' he said. 'Not if they're driving just fine.' There was another pause of loaded thought. 'Not you, Abra, you're still remembered in this town. Might get an old boy who sees you driving along and wants to check up on how you *bin doin' these last twenny years.*' He mimicked the hillbilly drawl of most of the locals. The drawl Abra had purposefully lost when she first moved to Pine Ranch. 'But Reeta.' Reeta's soiled hands stilled at the sound of her name. She knew Kezia had heard it too from the way her eyes floated upward underneath her thin lashes. 'No one in town knows her; she's bland and pretty enough to skate right on under their radar.'

'No one more trustworthy or dedicated,' Zechariah agreed.

'No.' Abra's voice was a surprise. '*No,*' she repeated, hardened, when it appeared that they hadn't heard her. 'She's a child.'

'She's nineteen.'

'She's never lived outside! She's a child to the world out there. And you want to send her out to pick up an illegal arms deal!'

'For the salvation of our cause!' Jeb roared. Reeta could see him towering over Abra, not responding when her chest caved in with a cracked sob. 'Now you will go and get her. She has a lot to learn.'

'I won't,' Abra replied. 'I... I... can't let you put her in danger like that.'

Her words were aborted by the sound of a loud smack and a yelp.

Abra exited the workshop and instead of going back to the kitchen, she turned left and headed directly for the vegetable patch.

'Reeta,' she said, her voice coarse. There was a pink splotch across her right cheek, raw and spreading. 'Jeb and Zechariah want to speak to you. They're in the workshop.'

Reeta nodded and clambered to her feet, smacking her hands together to get rid of the loosest soil. Her eyes flicked unconsciously toward Abra's cheek, an unexpected tug of upset.

Abra slipped her hand into Reeta's. She tugged it hard with tight, clammy fingers. 'What they're asking of you,' she said, her voice low and whispered, crevices of worry and stress etched around her eyes and mouth. 'Be careful. If you can decline...' She swallowed. 'Do.'

Seven

Reeta wondered how often the experts were right.

But this time they had been.

They'd all predicted the jury would come back with a verdict at about four p.m. – long enough to have enjoyed the free food of lunch, but quickly enough that they all knew which way they were voting. There would be no anguished deliberations for her trial. There was no nuanced discussion of reasonable doubt. They'd known from the moment Peter Crawley had made his opening arguments that Reeta Doe was as guilty as charged.

The bailiff had come for her at four forty-five.

Perhaps they'd snuck in a leisurely coffee break.

She patiently waited for her handcuffs and chains for the transport up to the courthouse, Barry appearing pantingly by her side just as she was moving out of the cell.

'It's quick,' was all he said and Reeta noticed a damp sweat stain on the back of his grey suit jacket. He'd clearly run from wherever the team had been holed up.

'It's what we thought,' she replied.

He nodded.

They all walked together – Reeta, Barry and the two bailiffs – toward the stairs at the end of the cell block, a winding structure that was always awkward for her chained ankles. She'd still not found a knack for it in the last three months and this afternoon – the last time she would ascend these stairs – was no different.

It took about fifteen minutes for her to make it back to the side entrance of the courtroom and soon enough she was shuffling back inside, trying not to catch the eyes of the jurors who had just sealed her fate. She didn't even turn back to try to catch Carol's eye. This was something she needed to do alone.

She sat down and waited for the judge to arrive.

When he did, she followed suit like everyone else and rose to her feet, although she wasn't sure at this point what would happen if she failed to show this man the respect that he believed was his due. What else could he possibly do to her? But obedience was so ingrained into her very being by this point that she did it without complaint.

He addressed the jury and they began the slow process of roll call, before he spoke directly to the foreman, a young woman who looked to be in her thirties. She had neatly blow-dried auburn hair and wore smart slacks with a navy top and matching shrug jacket. Reeta thought she looked friendly. Perhaps an elementary school teacher.

'Madam Foreman,' the judge said, his voice filling out to reach every crevice of the room. 'Have you agreed on a decision?'

'Yes, Your Honour.'

'And is it a unanimous decision?'

'Yes, Your Honour.'

The judge nodded gravely. 'Very well. And in the matter of the United States v. Ms Reeta Doe, for the charge of first-degree murder against Ms Sarah-Mae Withers, how do you find the defendant?'

'We find the defendant guilty.' Her voice never wavered.

Her answers never changed.

They trawled through each victim, each charge the same, each verdict delivered identical. Every time the question was asked was torture, giving the illusion of a new answer, a new hope that perhaps – for just one charge – they'd shown mercy.

But, of course, she'd shown no mercy to the girls listed in these charges.

Why should she receive it now?

'And finally,' the judge asked again, 'in the matter of the United States v. Ms Reeta Doe for the charge of first-degree kidnapping and attempted murder of Ms Bonnie Powell, how do you find the defendant?'

'We find the defendant guilty.'

–

Carol found herself, along with every other head in the courtroom, turning to the cowed, cloaked head who had just been named by the judge. Carol's heart tapped frantically against her ribs, the parade of guilty verdicts simultaneously expected but still sending shockwaves down her limbs.

The judge was speaking again.

'You have, Madam Foreman, also been asked to provide a verdict on the sentencing in this case. When a case deals with accusations as severe as those as have been levelled at our defendant here, it is only right that we consider very carefully when deciding if the highest punishment in the land might be appropriate. We have heard a great deal about the mental state of the accused, and you have all been provided with the adequate materials to prepare you in making such a decision. Have you reached a verdict regarding applying the death penalty sentence in this case?'

'Yes, Your Honour.'

'And is that a unanimous verdict?'

'Yes, Your Honour.'

'And how do you find in the sentencing of this matter?'

The foreman stalled for the first time in her speaking role. Her previous convictions had rolled seamlessly into the courtroom, the guilty verdicts confident and unquestionable. But now, she closed her eyes for longer than a blink, a deep inhale of breath.

'We find that the death penalty should be rightly applied as sentence in this matter.'

It was as if the courtroom had hit pause. As if the world understood that Carol needed a moment of quiet, a moment of stillness to breathe again. Not since the doctor had told her about the tumours littering her mother's insides had Carol felt her lungs cut off or her stomach boil. Before she was ready, the world began to move again, the judge declaring his final summary, but the press didn't care. They were scribbling notes and tearing sheets to hand to the runners, some scrambling over the backs of the benches to get out and be the first the file the story.

Carol sought Reeta out in the tumult but saw only her back curl over as Barry laid a tender hand on it. Eventually Reeta straightened up and allowed her chains to wind their way around her once again, her face visibly drowned in tears. Carol called out to her, but she either couldn't hear or couldn't respond. And then she was gone, through the side door and down to God-only-knew where, ready for her transportation to federal maximum security prison. The press rows had emptied out by now – the news from within had been shared and the power of the trial now belonged outside, in whoever could break the news first. But Carol moved slowly as she got to her feet, a thickness to her muscles that felt as if she were moving through sand. A dream where she just could not escape the horror closing in.

She saw Bonnie leaning against her companion, who had his arm tight around her shoulder. Carol moved across the aisle toward her, dodging clumsily out of the way of a group of victims' friends sobbing with righteous glee as they pushed their way past.

'Bonnie,' she said, surprising herself with the catch in her throat. 'Bonnie,' she tried again, and this time the man twisted his head toward her, a curious frown creasing his forehead.

Bonnie peered up from beneath his arm, her eyes clear and dry. She blinked at Carol but did not speak. Carol found she didn't know what to say, but after a moment sought out some words.

'I hope you get to live your life.'

Bonnie nodded sagely. 'It's over now.' Her eyes glazed a little and Carol had the feeling that whatever the girl was looking at, she was no longer seeing Carol. 'It's all over.'

Carol considered her for a moment longer, a brief frown plucking her eyebrows together. The Powells appeared behind her, tears gushing down their faces, arms outstretched for an embrace that would not come.

'I'm sorry,' the man said, protectively moving in front of Bonnie like a bodyguard. He spoke to both Carol and her parents. 'Bonnie doesn't want to see you.'

'Bon-bon,' Mr Powell said pleadingly to his daughter, twisting his body to catch sight of her around her new companion. 'Please, it's done now. Let us take care of you – we always have, haven't we?'

Bonnie kept her face firmly down and said nothing.

Grief itched into Carol's curiosity at the scene in front of her as she remembered with a bolt that her friend was going to die. Without thinking, she turned on her heel and pushed too roughly past the mourning Powells, her heels clicking quickly as they carried her out of the courthouse.

VII

Reeta's driving lessons were going well. Zechariah had begun by taking her up and down the drive in the dusty brown station wagon, showing her the pedals and shift stick. Other than the exterior grime from years of little use or attention, the car was in decent shape.

After a week of intense training on their own grounds, Gideon had been dispatched to teach her on the roads that encircled the ranch. A white man with a white girl would attract far less suspicion, and if they were pulled over then it was best to have the man named on the car's papers as owner present to deal with the cops. But they needn't have worried; no one ever gave a second glance as Reeta carefully put her new knowledge into action.

Her first pickup was due for the end of the month, just as spring would steepen into the blistering heat of summer. Zechariah had told her little of what to expect, only that Terry, who owned the Lucky Swine, where she'd had that heady Coke all those years ago, was procuring important items for the security of Pine Ranch for when the Reckoning came.

Her new job and lessons had come as a welcome distraction following the removal of Solomon from her care. She hardly saw Damaris any more, other than meal-times, Bible study and at night when they slept with a new forcefield of discomfort surrounding their bunk. It was an adjustment for the two girls, who had become accustomed to spending every hour that sprawled across the day with one another.

But Reeta had a new focus now.

Damaris, she knew, did not.

Damaris pined for her son and had been caught sneaking into the nursery late at night, or just before Bible study when everyone else was gathered and waiting. Reeta knew it had pained Eunice and Hagar to report her to Jeb — she'd overheard them discussing their shared guilt at dinner that evening. Crickets were chirping into the still air and the murky glow of fireflies hung above them. Caleb had managed to negotiate a good deal on the remains of a flock of chickens that had been partially savaged by a coyote from a nearby farmer. Eunice had worked all day to strip and prepare the birds, cleaning and cutting frantically at their wounds so only the cleanest meat was salvaged. It was this task that had made her late for Bible study, and caught Damaris sneaking out of the nursery, rearranging the neck of her smock to conceal her breast.

'I feel bad for the poor child,' Eunice was saying in hushed tones to Hagar, whose head was bent so low a lump appeared on the back of her neck. 'But it won't get easier if she keeps this up.' Damaris had been sent to the dormitory without dinner, the blows from the wooden paddle that hung in the hall hobbling her legs so her disappearing silhouette stumbled and swayed.

'We did what we had to do,' Hagar said, matching Eunice's low voice. 'I gave up my babies for the good of our ark. It's what He wants. And now' — she glanced briefly down the table to where the children were eating quietly — 'I love them all as my own.'

Reeta saw something flash across Abra's face, but she lowered her eyes and didn't respond. Reeta had seen Abra comforting Damaris during their laundry work. Close whispered conversations while Abra soothed Damaris's tears. 'You have to be strong for your son. Strong for one day, maybe one day things will be different.'

Reeta knew she should have reported Abra. But she'd turned away instead and forced herself to mentally run through the starting rituals for the station wagon.

'You did the right thing.' Reeta cut into Eunice and Hagar's conversation, tearing apart her tough chicken breast with a blunt knife. 'Damaris needs to find her way back to the Word.' She looked pointedly at Abra, who stared back with desolate eyes. 'She lost her way a little, but she'll come back.'

Eunice looked deeply at Reeta for a moment, as if she was about to retort, but she just nodded and leaned over to ask Hagar how she liked the chicken.

When they filed back into the dormitory later that night, their bunkmates quietly and obediently climbing the ladders to their beds and pulling back their meticulously made sheets, only Kezia glanced at the shaking lump on Damaris's bunk. She caught Reeta's eye and gave a sympathetic nod in Damaris's direction. Reeta nodded slowly in return and took the two steps toward the bunk they shared. Crouching low, so her knees clicked loudly, she placed an open palm on her friend's back.

'Damaris,' she said softly. 'Would you like to pray with me?'

Damaris didn't answer at first, but as Reeta opened her mouth to speak her prayer to the Lord, she rolled over. Her face was puffy and tear-soaked. Blood-red veins crept across the whites of her eyes, and shiny tracks snaked the dry skin on her cheeks like slug trails.

'Don't pray for me,' she said, her voice hoarse. 'I'm sick of prayer. I'm sick of the Word. I'm sick of being beaten black and blue for wanting to be a mother.'

Reeta's face froze for an instant, before she arranged a bland smile across it. 'We're all mothers, Damaris.'

'No, you're not,' she snapped. 'Not like me. He's *mine*. *My* son, no one else's.'

'He's the Lord's son.' Reeta struggled to keep her voice steady and could feel the ears of their dormitory-mates tuning in to every whispered word.

'You're insane.' Damaris had dropped the soft tone and anger broke across her words. 'You're brainwashed and damaged this isn't the Lord's word.' She gestured around the room and down to her beaten legs. '*My* Lord preaches love and patience and mothers allowed to cradle their own babies! I won't let my baby grow up here, not if he's going to turn out like *you*.' Her face had mangled into a snarl.

'You can't take him, Damaris,' Reeta replied, forcing her voice to stay calm, the way she'd seen Jeb do in the face of Kezia's father. 'He's Jeb's son, the Lord's son. And where would you go?' She leaned forward so her breath puffed into Damaris's face. 'You belong here. You'll see that soon.' With that she pulled herself back and upright, ascending the ladder to lie down above her friend, silently murmuring a prayer for Damaris to find her way back.

Reeta slept deeply that night.

A sleep she would come to regret.

–

Abra stumbled toward Reeta after breakfast, still hobbling on a swollen knee, sooty black bruises dusted across her cheek. She gathered the stacked plates from Reeta's hands and limped silently back to the kitchen.

Reeta had woken two mornings previously to find the bunk below her empty, but meticulously made. In the bustle of feeding eighty people breakfast and gathering for group prayers, Damaris's disappearance had gone unnoticed until mid-morning, when Dinah had raised the alarm of Solomon's displacement. Each of the chore rotations were searched, each one lacking the girl they sought, and an emergency meeting had been gathered on the front field.

'It seems one of our number has felt the need to flee in the night.' Jeb spoke, his tone sorrowful. 'It is always a burden on my shoulders when I lose a soul for the Lord, one more sinner I have failed in their salvation. We will pray for her, wherever she ends up – be it on the streets of the cities that sprawl across this country, with no choice but to sell her body like so many before her. Spat on and abused, disregarded and disrespected. For that is what awaits you out there. The world is washed in sin; after all' – he paused to look around the group – 'that is why so many of you have come to our sanctuary.' A murmur of agreement whipped around Reeta as she listened to this sermon, craning her neck to the far perimeters of their land. She sent up silent prayers for Damaris to return, arms full of Solomon and wildflowers – a glance of casual concern for the worry she'd unintentionally caused. But there was no sign of her, no matter how desperately Reeta played this fantasy over and over.

She knew that Damaris hadn't just fled Pine Ranch. Hadn't just abandoned the Lord's word and the salvation of her soul. She'd abandoned Reeta. Betrayed her and lied to her, leaving her hollow and foolish.

Again.

'But' – Jeb's voice grew stronger now, his left hand grasping into a fist in mid-air – 'it is not the soul of Damaris we mourn today. It is not the soul of a deceptive sinner our hearts ache for. It is for Solomon. The innocent child she saw fit to remove from our care, to remove from the Lord's blessing. Solomon, who is a Child of God, quite literally, has been ripped from our bosom and our teachings.'

'We must find him!' someone called from the crowd.

'No!' Jeb responded like whiplash. 'We cannot lose more members to the pit of treachery and wickedness that is outside these walls. But we can make sure to prevent another such loss.' He surveyed his followers now, mossy green eyes tracking across each face, jaw clenched with emotion. 'Any information anyone has on Damaris's flight, I want to know it. You can come to me directly. The Lord will thank you for your honesty, your bravery. We are nearing the End Times – I can feel it!' He tipped his head back to the sky, as if allowing the very particles of prophecy to fall on his face. 'We must stand united! For the salvation of humankind.' He brought his head down, speaking directly to his followers once again. 'What if the chickens had fled Noah's ark? We'd have no eggs. What if the bees had flown off for their own will? We'd have no honey, no flowers. The pigs, the cows? No meat. And what if Noah's sons, Noah's family, had escaped the very haven he provided for them?' He looked beseechingly at them, and they knew the answer that was coming. 'No humanity.'

Just in front of Reeta, Hagar and Dinah exchanged worried glances. And that afternoon Abra had been dragged from the laundry to explain herself to Jeb.

Eventually she must have convinced him that Solomon had been present and fine when she'd tended to him in the night, when Hagar and Dinah had heard her get up and creak downstairs for her night-time duty. But Reeta wasn't so sure of her innocence. She'd heard her wish for better times to come.

And Abra knew what was on the other side of the woodland.

Kezia had tried to talk to Reeta in the intervening days – she lamented the loss of Damaris and missed their friend. But Reeta had always known Damaris could never truly be saved, right back on her first day as she sat and sobbed on her bunk. Dared to sob at the gift she had been given. Reeta had allowed herself to soften, to fall into the false belief of an easy and pleasant life. But that could never be the case; their work was too important. She felt her skin harden like a cockroach's shell; neither love nor patience would penetrate it again.

Not until her work was done.

Eight

The lobby at the Royal Grande was deserted. Whatever journalists were staying there had taken their celebratory mood to the Irish bar to bid farewell to the case – and the girl – that had kept them gripped at every turn. Carol fell into an armchair and kicked off her court shoes, bending over to massage her toes back into place beneath the thin nylon of her pantyhose. She glanced up and raised a finger to Mike, the barman, silently ordering her usual.

A few moments later he appeared with a large glass of white wine, condensation gripping relaxingly to its outside, and the heavy white base of the bar telephone. The plastic wire trailed across the brocade carpet, but Mike had never complained about the trip hazard.

Carol sipped the wine and stared at the telephone, not quite ready to make the call yet. Speaking the words aloud would make them more real, the grief more pertinent. Instead she relayed the scene with Bonnie and her parents, questions rolling somersaults over each other. Perhaps they'd simply never been a close family, although that didn't square with what Carol had heard. According to friends, Bonnie had written to her parents weekly from college and they'd visited at least once a semester. Ben had told her they'd paid for an apartment in Florida after she was discharged from hospital and refused to return home to Ohio. At the time Carol had put it down to her physical disabilities, the move up north too much for the girl's still healing injuries. But now it seemed that there was more than just the physical the girl was contending with.

Bonnie had seemed hard-faced and rehearsed on the stand, a gulf away from the authenticity Carol saw in Reeta every week. She'd not shed a tear throughout, dry eyes and a hollowed-out soul. *That* was what had unnerved Carol about Bonnie's testimony; that and the twist of a smile when she was done. Didn't she understand the ramifications of her words?

Carol sipped on her wine and out of habit pulled out her file on the case. It was too late now, of course; there was no saving grace to be found among her notes. Even the prospect of working on her two-thousand-word feature splash filled her with dread. *The Trial and Trials of the College Slayer.* Her editor had jumped at the pitch and wanted it for the Sunday edition now the verdict was in – the *Post*'s exclusive access to America's latest villain.

Flipping through the pages, she scanned the information she knew by rote, quotes and sentences blurred into meaninglessness. She paused to take another mouthful of wine, relishing its tartness as it slid down to the back of her jaw. When she looked back down at the papers on her lap, she found she'd stopped on the photograph of the road showing the skidded tyre marks about ten miles away from the crash site. Where the girls had pulled off the road and fought.

Where Bonnie had ended up in the trunk.

A stiff jerk shot through her as she gazed down at the photo. The sudden urge to call Ben.

She dialled the operator and waited to be connected, her voice croaking out of her dry throat. There were only three rings before he answered, breathy and expectant.

'Carol.' His voice was sharp with concern. 'Are you all right? I've been waiting for you to call. I heard.'

Suddenly everything she wanted to ask him dissolved. The photograph slid into blackness as she shut her eyes and tipped her head back. Her eyes finally creased into the sob she'd been holding inside since the verdict.

'They're going to fucking kill her,' she said.

VIII

Today Reeta had one final run-through of the drive with Gideon, just over a week before she would take the journey alone. Gideon watched with a gently impressed smile as she eased the car down the driveway, waving a thanks at Zechariah, who opened the gate for them. She signalled and pulled onto the road, the transition from rough dirt track to paved concrete relaxing the uncomfortable bounce of the car. The journey took two hours one way. Crumbling water towers poked at the sky from the horizon above dirty blue desert stretches. Bright green yuccas dotted the scrub and torn-up clouds drifted above the road.

A battered green sign, directing them to Bryan, 120 miles away, scooted past the windows and Gideon laughed politely to himself. Reeta dared to avert her gaze from the road for a moment and looked at him quizzically.

'Where I went to college,' he said, nodding back in the direction of the sign they'd left in the distance. 'Nice town, Bryan. Good college, Texas A&M.' He smiled again, his eyes skirted with a dreamy look. 'Aggies.' He smiled again. 'That's what we called ourselves. Too young to do wrong, too young to do right.' Reeta thought she saw a note of sadness flash across his face as he looked at her. 'Not doing anything important like you,' he said after a beat, his voice surprisingly downcast. Reeta didn't speak. She had a thousand questions, but didn't dare give life to any of them lest he take her curiosity as tantamount to longing for the outside. She knew she was on close watch since Damaris had left – their friendship had never gone unnoticed and she'd spotted a hundred narrowed eyes on her and Kezia's movements since that fateful morning. But she would prove herself.

Her foot squeezed the brake pedal as she prepared to turn down the barely identifiable dirt track that took them to their destination – an abandoned military airfield that Terry and his cohorts used to smuggle everything from artillery to cigars from their contacts in Havana. Reeta knew nothing of this place Jeb and Zechariah had referenced. Perhaps they were also preparing for the End Times, and so saw fit to help their brothers and sisters at Pine Ranch.

The airfield was outlined by ratty wire fencing that coyotes had long since torn holes in, and a long red track cleared of brush and scrub stretched out toward the horizon. Reeta brought the car to a halt no more than a hundred yards away, eyes scanning the squat metal shed for signs of life. There was no movement or sound, only soft wisps of displaced soil in the breeze and the sinister rattle of snakes in the distance.

'Are you ready for next week?' Gideon asked, staring straight ahead.

'I'm ready to do my duty,' she replied firmly, fixing her jaw in determined steel. Silent anxiety flared through her extremities at the thought of spending so long outside of Pine Ranch all alone. She was as tied to Pine Ranch as one of Hagar's honeysuckle vines – sown and grown against its very walls, climbing constantly upwards toward the Heavenly skies. Hurricanes one year had torn Hagar's garden apart, and the flowering creepers had been found pulled from their roots – strewn instead as weak as cotton threads, limp across the ground.

Without those walls, how could she survive, even if only for a few hours?

Rain came as she drove back to their sanctuary, thick, fat droplets that pummelled the roof of the car and spat violently across the windshield.

She stopped for gas about halfway back, paying from the hulk of notes that lived in the locked metal box in the trunk of the car. Reeta had never seen dollars and cents before, but Zechariah had shown her, painstakingly counting out the stacks of twenty- and fifty-dollar bills so she'd know how to buy gas without catching attention, or to give Terry's men the right number when the time came at the airstrip. As she handed the money to the station attendant, the full smell of frying bacon hit her nostrils from the diner attached. The grease clawed at the back of her throat and she fled back to the car, a retch thickening.

The tension in her wrists relaxed against the steering wheel as they reached the town that signalled home. Thudding beats echoed from the Lucky Swine as they drove by, the neon sign still flickering as it had done all those years ago. It was hours until dusk, but the day had given in to the rain, dull, crackling skies sapping the light around them. The house would be crowded for dinner tonight. Reeta smiled tenderly at this thought – she liked it when they were forced to huddle together, hunkering down against the elements from outside.

Pine Ranch the sole survivor against the world.

Soon they were at the road that took them home, long and skinny – a straight needle in the direction of salvation.

'Stop,' Gideon said suddenly, his voice unusually forceful.

'What?' she asked, glancing over at him, confused.

'Stop!' he shrieked, eyes trained ahead, peering through the dark sheets of early storm that batted the car. His tone shocked her into action and she plunged her foot to the brake, jerking their bodies painfully forward. She followed his gaze into the distance and saw now what he did.

Out in the distance, no more than a few miles away — blue and red lights throbbed at them through the rain.

'Go back,' Gideon said, his voice tense, strained. 'Go back and take the right instead.'

'But that's not the way—' Reeta's protest collapsed with a sharp look from Gideon. She nodded silently and put the car in drive, looping a U-turn to go back on herself.

'Go right here,' Gideon said and Reeta turned the car and found herself driving down a narrow track running alongside thick, ominous woods. Gideon watched the woods scoot by, face pulled in mental calculations. He waited another twenty, twenty-five, thirty minutes before speaking again. 'OK,' he said, nodding at the shallow ditch on the side of the road. 'I think this should be about right. Pull in here.' She looked at him for confirmation and slowed the car. He nodded again toward the ditch. 'That's it, get it right in there.' She followed his instructions and tried to manoeuvre the car as smoothly as possible into the uneven, bramble-tangled ditch. A wall of dirt rose vertically outside her driver's window, so to get out she was forced to clamber over the central console to follow Gideon from his door.

'I think,' he shouted above the rain and wind, which churned around them out of the protection of the car, 'Pine Ranch is through the wood this way.' He held his arm at a forty-five-degree angle, up the slope of bracken that broke into woodland. 'I delivered a baby for the Wheton farm down the way there' – he moved his arm in the opposite direction, toward the mass of black fields behind them – 'so I've driven this road before. It's my best bet.'

'What'll we find?' Reeta screeched over the wind. It seemed absurd that in the near-hour since they saw the light display, neither had discussed it.

'We'll find what we find,' he replied sagely.

'Is it time?' she asked, pulling her eyes wide while her hair whipped across her face in soaking ropes. The Reckoning she'd waited her whole life for.

Gideon didn't reply but dipped his head before turning toward the wood and scanning for the easiest entry. He pointed about five yards away.

'Up this way,' he said, and set off. She followed him, watching his increasingly sodden plaid shirt sucker to his back, bald head funnelling a waterfall down to his shoulders. She scraped her own hair back behind her ears, feeling the weight of its drenched mass. Her thin smock clung to her with freezing fingers, and every breeze sand-papered roughly against her bare skin. The shivering had started almost immediately and already her bones ached with exhaustion.

Together, Reeta trailing Gideon, they clambered up the slope, bracken scratching Reeta's exposed ankles, mud seeping in between the soles of her sandal and her feet. He made it to the top before her, hooked his arm around a young birch's trunk and reached down to help her up.

Instinct hesitated her for a moment; the only man she'd ever really touched was Jeb. Gideon had touched her only a handful of times for examinations, but never once had she willingly thrown her own hand into another man's. Her feet slid an inch down the slope, so she mustered a solid prayer and flung her hand into his, feeling her weight immediately relinquish. He pulled her to him with ease; years of hard physical labour on Pine Ranch kept all the men, even those in their fifties like Gideon, in good shape.

Unlooping his arm from the tree, he stepped back almost at once, reinstating the distance between their two bodies. He tipped his head forward and they trudged side by side into the slate-grey forest. The dense trees gave some respite from the weather, but occasional gusts still thumped at them and fat showers broke in through the canopy

Dusk was falling now, but dull daylight still half-heartedly lit their way and, as she scanned around for the best place to put her feet, Reeta spotted a jumble of blue knitted wool, sodden and muddy on the churned ground. She reached forward and pulled it free, breaking the twigs that tangled it. She knew what it was before it was even in her hands – Solomon's blanket. Abra had knitted it for him, her stockinette stitches renowned to be the best on the compound. This was the way Damaris had escaped.

Damaris.

She had brought the display of blue and red lights to their door.

Reeta felt this betrayal as a sword against her solid armour – where once chinks might have allowed the blade to slash against her skin, now she rebuffed it with a determined shrug. This had always been coming. This was what they'd been preparing for.

Her soul was ready.

The whines of wind through the trees had accompanied them for most of their journey, but now were punctuated by a new sound. A new sound that stopped Gideon in his tracks before flashing a look at Reeta and hurrying his pace forward.

Put-put-put-put-put.

The staccato sound of gunfire that had torn up their land for so many months in training. Pine Ranch's old military weaponry had a rusty, hollow sound compared to the clean bangs she guessed belonged to the police. She threw Solomon's blanket back to the ground and stepped determinedly on it as she pressed forward – her focus must be on Brother Jeb. She was his dedicated servant.

As they reached the dwindling trees spilling against the rolling back prairie of Pine Ranch, it was difficult to see where the action was. Certainly around the front – the concentration of gunfire echoed up from the front field – but there were odd potholes littering the grass at the back, and uneven bursts of soil flung up every minute or so. Fire came from both sides. The police had pressed in through the abandoned fields circling the compound but were apparently still held back by the fencing the residents meticulously maintained. Shots were also coming from the house itself, the high windows emitting the *put-put-put* to the ground below. A disembodied voice, somewhere around the front – tinny and magnified like Kezia's father's had been – called for surrender, instructed them to stand down.

Reeta knew that would never happen.

Reeta knew that *could* never happen.

For the first time on their trek through the woods, Gideon looked apprehensive. The gauntlet of gunfire had stilled him on the edge of the trees.

There was no hesitation for Reeta. She had to get back; Brother Jeb needed her. And if the Lord selected this moment to end her earthly existence, then that was a choice He made well. She didn't even give Gideon one final look as she tore off across the grass, eyes trained only on the rickety kitchen door.

That was perhaps her one regret when she made it back.

Panting relief vibrated her entire body as she leaned forward against the locked door, pressing her forehead firmly into the comforting wood of home. Her feet were in agony from their steel-like grip against the wet grass and she looked back, awaiting her companion, only to see his slumped figure, sodden, blood-soaked and unmoving a few yards behind her. Perhaps she could have remembered his eyes, the bright kindness they'd often shown her, and told them all how he'd died willingly to guide her back to them.

Reeta's journey was not over yet.

The Lord still had his plans.

The Washington Post, *November 2nd 1971*

Five Years On: Remembering the Case of the College Slayer

Carol Joyce

It has been five years since I sat in a humid courtroom in Florida and listened to a trail of guilty verdicts condemning a young woman to a life cut short by the state. It had been a long and gruelling trial to bring one of America's most notorious killers to justice, in a case that had our nation gripped. The tale of Reeta Doe and how she ravaged five young lives across 1965 and 1966 was shocking in the violence and circumstance at its very core. Not only were her victims innocent young women full of promise, but the perpetrator herself could well be mistaken for the same innocent young woman full of promise. A perpetrator with no memory of her crimes.

With the killer unable to give us any answers, we rooted deep and asked ourselves how a young woman could be capable of such brutality and hatred. Were these crimes a reflection of our broken country? A country divided across lines of race and age – younger generations battling with their parents on every issue from civil rights to patriotic duty. Had these battle lines been turned in on each other, the youth pushed so far to the brink by counterculture extremism that they had begun attacking one another?

The answer was far more simple, yet far more terrible. The life of Reeta Doe had been marred with violence and control – an upbringing in an antisocial Christian sect known as Pine Ranch. Whatever the convoluted decision-making process that led her from Pine Ranch to prison cell, we may never truly know, but of what we can be sure is that the Reeta Doe today awaiting her final justice on death row is not the same woman who so brutally stole four innocent lives, forever tarnishing a fifth.

'I have prayed for the strength to forgive that girl,' Patricia O'Donnell tells me, whose daughter Susan is one of the two still missing victims. 'We planted a willow tree down by Susie's favourite part of the creek. We don't have her body to return to the ground, but we have this memorial. It's where I go to speak to her. The Lord has not blessed me with forgiveness yet.'

I do not ask for forgiveness for Reeta Doe – there is no question of the devastation she brought to those who crossed her path. But I do ask for patience. If you have followed my coverage of this case since the beginning, you will know we have developed a personal friendship. It is not a friendship I take lightly – it is a friendship that has weighed heavy on my soul at times, a friendship that requires constant, unending scrutiny. So, as we look back at the five years since her verdict, we must remember the dichotomy of our very human nature. Do I grieve for the lost lives of her victims? I do. And I will I grieve for Reeta's own lost life when that time comes? I will. Both truths can exist together.

Nine

June 1972

It was not often the inmates of the Balmen United States Penitentiary gathered in such quiet. In the five and a half years since her verdict, Reeta had never experienced such silence. Only the sound of the corrections officers shuffling their tired feet scraped through the still, anticipating cafeteria. Scratchy voices came from a wind-up wireless placed on a centre table, the fuzzy transmission bulging into every corner of the cavernous concrete room, a blister waiting to pop.

Reeta shifted on her sit-bones, the hard metal bench burning into her thin flesh. Gloria lifted her head at the movement and gave a reassuring smile, moved her hand over Reeta's and lowered her chin back down. A string of rosary beads was clutched in her spare first, her thumb slowly popping them round and round, one by one.

'We do, it seems,' the reporter on the radio said after several hours of buffer and filler stories that meant nought to the women sweating in the thick Georgia humidity of Balmen, 'have a verdict in the case of William Henry Furman v. the State of Georgia. By all reports this has been a trying time for the justices of the Burger court – a landmark case. OK, we're going to cross now to the Supreme Court building itself where we have Jack Lovell, roaming reporter with GBCN, on the spot ready for the reading of the verdict.'

All around her, women sat up straighter, tensed their muscles and swallowed thickly. Reeta did not move. The verdict that was about to be read technically affected only three of them in this place, and one of those had been in solitary for longer than Reeta's broken memory could recall. But for anybody, across the country, sitting in a penitentiary or correctional institution, this case was a monument. An official acknowledgement of their humanity.

Jack Lovell had gone silent on the radio and a deep voice rolled out in his place, a shuffling of papers, a long-winded introduction. Reeta's stomach clenched hard as though in iron shackles.

'The court holds,' the voice began and the tension of the mess hall reached its unbearable crescendo, 'that the imposition and carrying out of the death penalty in these cases constitute cruel and unusual punishment in violation of the Eighth and Fourteenth Amendments.' Reeta dared let herself exhale, and looked, wide-eyed and blindsided, up at the radio, not daring to believe the words. 'The judgement in each case is therefore reversed insofar as it leaves undisturbed the death sentence imposed, and the cases are remanded for further proceedings. So ordered.'

She sat, transfixed, staring at the small white rectangle, on generous loan from the warden's office, that had seem-ingly just saved her life. 'What does that mean?' a voice crowed from behind her, a wail of ignorant impatience behind the words.

'It means' – Beatrice raised her voice from her seat opposite Reeta – 'call your fucking lawyer!' Cackles of celebration rang out, and Reeta knew that it was Lil'

Philly, Phyllis Brown, who'd asked the keening question. She could hear the movement of Lil' Philly's supporters leaping to their feet, smothering her with sweaty prison tunics and catcalls of victory. Reeta wanted to hear the end of the broadcast but knew that was not to be. Gloria had clenched Reeta's hand hard in her own, and when Reeta looked over at the middle-aged woman she saw her eyes shone with unshed tears. Beatrice had leaped across the table, folding herself in half at the hips, fingers stretched out to grasp at Reeta's shoulders. She was laughing loudly, whooping along with Lil' Philly's gang, who were now chanting some celebratory refrain.

Reeta still couldn't move.

The death penalty was unconstitutional. So ordered.

She couldn't speak, but felt the sob that had been holding court in her chest crack free, a loud, childish sound. Gloria moved closer and gripped her in a tight, maternal hug, her squashy breasts pressing against the lack of Reeta's own.

The corrections officers afforded them a few minutes of celebration before the batons were drawn and the inmates were shifted back to work duty or cells – spirits still immutably high. As she unfurled her cramped legs from behind the bench, Reeta felt a hand on the small of her back and looked around to see Lil' Philly standing, arms outstretched for a hug only acceptable for this extraordinary moment that now bonded them. Lil' Philly had been on death row for near fifteen years, her case benefitting from the constant pro-bono efforts of the NAACP lawyers. The diminutive, five-foot-one woman had shot and killed the white man attempting to rape her twelve-year-old daughter, and her own life had now been

222

saved thanks to the painfully slow process of the United States appellate courts.

She and Reeta had spoken on no more than three occasions since Reeta was transferred to Balmen following the verdict of her own trial, five and a half years ago. The notoriety of both women's cases were well-known in the prison, but Lil' Philly was the wrongly convicted innocent, while Reeta the insane murderess who probably did deserve the chair if it came down to it. Reeta could see Lil' Philly's cohorts eyeing her darkly as she bent over to hug their hero – as if Reeta might be liable to attack at any moment. Despite over five years of head-down solitude that had allowed her to sink blandly into the background of brutal prison life, the legacy of her case and gossip of Pine Ranch clung to her like putrid sewer gunk.

Beatrice moved into line beside her as Reeta straightened up from the silent hug. Lil' Philly patted her on the arm and said, 'Ain't no one but the Lord got the right to say when another life can end.' Reeta did not know if this was an allusion to Reeta's infamous crimes, or a remark of solidarity on the fate they had both escaped. Reeta smiled politely and watched Lil' Philly head back to her cohorts, who guided her in the direction of the phone bank.

'You gonna call your lawyer?' Beatrice asked, her dark eyes staring inquisitively at Reeta.

'I will,' Reeta replied softly. 'Later.' They joined the queue out of the cafeteria and passed by the watchful eyes of the guards. One gave Reeta a half-smile, a deft nod of congratulations, which she accepted with a placid look of thanks. What Reeta wanted to do, first and foremost, was return to her cell and lie down. She was nearly blinded by the overwhelming realisation that she was going to live.

For as long as she could remember, her life was destined to be terminated.

'Jeeez,' Beatrice said as they plodded along the corridor toward the block that housed them both. 'If I'd have known I could avoid the chair, I'd have made sure to finish the bastards off.' Beatrice had found herself at Balmen for the armed robbery of the Davenport Museum in Arizona, which she and eight of her Quechan brothers and sisters had raided, seizing back at least fourteen items of sacred value that the Davenport family had stolen and displayed in their private collection for over a hundred years. Beatrice had hung back to smack the security guards around with the barrel of her pistol, their bound hands and feet unable to provide any sort of self-defence. It occurred to Reeta that perhaps the security guards were nothing more than men just hired to do a job, and that Beatrice's righteous rage was best directed elsewhere – but as Beatrice was one of Reeta's only two allies in Balmen, she had not raised the point.

They reached their row of cells, Beatrice tucking into hers first. A flash of colour darted through the bars of her door from the bright tapestry hung above her bed, which her mother had sent the previous year. Reeta fell into her own cell just three doors along. She tumbled onto the bed, front first, her nose crunching under the weight of her collapse. She lay like that, unmoving save for her thudding heart against the sharp springs of her mattress, for several minutes before pushing herself upright and forcing herself to consider – for the first time – the potential of her life. Unlike Beatrice's, the breezeblock walls of her cell were adorned with nothing but crumbling dust, her small wooden desk stacked only with a Bible and a tin box of cuttings. Together these items informed her past.

Throughout her trial she had only read Carol's articles, tearing them neatly from the *Washington Post* Barry brought her each morning. They were the only ones she could trust to report the truth. She leaned forward from her bed to reach for the tin box, popping off the rusted lid. On top was the article that had started everything for her, *The College Girl Who Slayed Her Own*, protectively covering the revelations of the cuttings that lay beneath. The beliefs of Pine Ranch, the letters from its leader Brother Jeb, the photograph Agent Willow had given her all those years ago. Reeta still knew nothing of how she had come to be at the compound, or how long she'd lived with the sect. When Barry and Carol had first told her about the letters and of Pine Ranch, the loss of hope that a family still waited somewhere beyond the jail walls had smacked her with the brute force of a tank. It hurt her even more so than the realisation, through weeks and months of testimony and positive identifications, that she had in fact stolen four young lives from the world and attempted to steal a fifth.

In her cell at Balmen she had a small window lined with a thick triple-layered mesh that darkened any sunlight that attempted to creep in. But if she pressed her forehead directly against the netted wire and focused her vision through the mismatched squares, she could see a blurred image of the world outside. She watched as the sun sighed low in the sky, setting on the day that had saved her life, and patiently waited for indifferent stars to prick at her eyes. A cool breeze wafted across her face, and the smell of a nature she had never experienced darted up her nostrils – a fresh, clean scent. She had missed the call for dinner hours ago, and the guard who'd gifted her the sympathetic congratulations hadn't pushed for her to attend. A momentous day indeed.

The lights around her shut off with a loud bang, and the sounds of the prison at night suddenly seemed to rise louder than before. Riotous laughter and calls of celebration still echoed around her cell block, chants for Lil' Philly cutting through concrete walls. She adjusted to the dark quickly, and it was with an unusual feeling of expectance for the days, weeks, months and years ahead, that she crawled into bed and pulled the thin blanket across her limbs.

IX

A truce had been called somewhere around ten the previous night. Reeta had been welcomed back with relieved but fearful faces and Jeb had held his arms wide and embraced her deeply. His most dedicated child returned in the face of apocalypse.

Gideon was not the only casualty.

Caleb had also been caught in the early moments of the firefight; an errant bullet had pummelled directly through his throat, tearing muscle and sinew to come out the other side. Apparently, it was still lodged in the wood of one of the porch posts.

The truce had allowed them to collect both Gideon and Caleb's bodies, who were now laid respectfully on large canvas sheets in the basement cool room. The dormitories had been abandoned, and the gathered residents had bunked down in the hallways, nursery and study rooms, prayers recited louder and more frenzied than ever before. Jeb had retrieved both a wind-up radio and telephone from his room that had caused a jolt of surprise through some of the newer residents who'd had no idea such modern amenities existed at Pine Ranch. Reeta, though, had seen them before. They'd once sat in the main hall — a lifeline for the women to place orders at local shops for the men to pick up, or for Jeb to speak to Zechariah when he was out on the road preaching the Word. The radio had often accompanied mealtimes when Reeta was growing up, the honky-tonk of country folk music streaming from its small speaker. When their numbers had grown, these two creature comforts had been moved upstairs to Jeb's private room without word or explanation. The last time Reeta had heard the radio had been in Jeb's room when her body had been chosen, her womb mistakenly deigned worthy.

Now they listened to the news reports on the situation at Pine Ranch, and Jeb had a direct line both to the police and the media.

'We have nothing but peace in our hearts.' Jeb was talking live on air to the local radio station over lunch. He sat in the hallway speaking into the brown plastic handset, while his followers gathered, cramped and crowded, around the radio in the front two rooms, straining to hear from the reedy speaker. 'Yesterday evening our private property was invaded unlawfully and we took up arms to defend our home.'

'The Locke County police department have confirmed in a press statement this morning that they do have in their possession the appropriate warrants to search your property,' the presenter said. 'What do you say to those reports?'

'I say I don't bow down to the law of man and his so-called warrants. Show me a warrant from God himself and then I will permit them entrance.' A cheer around the radio went up. 'Why won't you listen to the Word of God? Why won't you understand the Book of Revelations is *now*? I alone have access to the Word and the message of the Seven Seals, and we will protect our haven with all the firepower and might that we can.'

'How do you feel about the deaths of the two police officers that resulted from last night's dramatic shootout? Reports suggest you have teenage boys manning your weaponry – how does that square with what the Lord wants for their souls?'

'We lost two men last night too!' Jeb's voice rose in passion. 'Two good men who have completed their mission on Earth and who await us with the Heavenly Father when our mission is complete too. The age of our residents is inconsequential – we are one. We work together as one entity under the eye of the Lord.'

'Early reports are also suggesting that it was one of your number who first alerted the police to your stockpile of illegal weaponry. A young woman who had fled in the night.'

Jeb had not replied for a moment but when he did speak, it was soft. 'We lost a soul. That always weighs heavy with me. But this was always our path; this was always the Lord's plan for the Reckoning.'

'And how do you feel about being associated with known local criminal Terrence Hick?' the reporter asked.

Reeta could hear the smile in Jeb's voice. 'The name of the lumberjack who gave Noah his wood is not remembered in the annals of history.' Jeb hung up the phone.

The presenter blustered for a moment, asking 'Have we lost him?' of an unheard entity in the studio, before re-finding his composure. 'Well, there you have it, an exclusive interview with the man who calls himself Brother Jeb up at the old Jacklowe Plantation, now apparently known as Pine Ranch by the followers of his bizarre Christian sect. Reports from locals say residents are hardly ever seen, despite aerial footage showing accommodation for at least a hundred people.' He gave an impassioned exhale, breathing life into his words. 'We're talking about, of course, the situation that arose overnight in Locke County, near the rural farming town of Mariette. Local police sergeant Gerald Matthews was first alerted to the ongoing situation up at the Jacklowe Plantation by a young Negro girl found on the steps of his office in the early hours of April 5th, claiming to have been forced to escape in the night with her child, and reporting mass weapon stockpiling at the property over the last six months. A joint investigation with Locke County PD led them to local petty criminal and fixer Terrence Hick – also the proprietor of the Lucky Swine bar and saloon in the town – who is currently in custody.'

The group gathered around the radio listened in frozen silence to this story about their lives. Reeta had never known Pine Ranch to have a different name, never known the town that had become her anchor on her driving lessons was called Mariette.

'Mr Hick has so far refused to co-operate with the investigation other than to confirm "They got some fire-power up there".' The presenter chuckled slowly. 'His words, not mine, ladies and gentlemen. Heard that quote myself from our contact over at the police department. The story, though, as I'm sure many of you have seen in the morning papers, turned sour last night when Locke County police attempted to enact a warrant permitting them to search the Jacklowe Plantation property and its outlying land. Those brave men were met with gunfire and conflict, and it is my sad duty to report the loss of two of those brave men – police officers Brian Malpern and James Tanning.' The presenter fell silent for a deep moment before continuing, his voice retaining the steady personable quality. 'A truce was called before midnight, and there is currently a state of active siege at the ranch and, as you all heard just moments ago, no intent of surrender from the leader of those trapped inside.' Another pause, and when he spoke again his voice was upbeat, the tale of woe he'd just told forgotten. 'We'll be discussing this later on in the show with police representative Robert Watson, but for now here's Johnny Cash with "Understand Your Man".' As the plinking guitar opened the song, someone leaned forward and shut the radio off.

As if it had been giving light, Reeta suddenly felt the darkness envelop her. The windows had been boarded up during the firefight and only pinholes of daylight penetrated the room, shot through splintered bullet holes in the thin wood. The touch of the people surrounding her burned her skin and she felt spiders' legs stabbing needles into the back of her neck.

She needed to move.

Shrugging off the people around her, she climbed to her feet, igniting movement in everyone else too. Her knees cricked from their long-bent position and she shook her legs out.

'What do we do now?' she heard Hagar ask in a whispered breath.

'We pray,' Eunice replied and grasped her hand, head lowered.

—

Life during the siege developed a new normal of peace stiffened by persistent, inescapable terror. There had been no more gunfire in the eight days since that first night, but the constant manning of Pine Ranch's weaponry from the top windows of the house – those bedrooms now strewn with empty casings and boxes of fresh bullets – meant that no surrender had been made either. Jeb still refused to allow anyone to leave, although no one would have gone even with permission. This was what they told the police officers and lieutenants each night as a new Pine Ranch resident took the negotiation call that came at six p.m. Reeta had been surprised by the man's gentle tone on the other end of the phone, buoyed for a fight that had not come. He had claimed to be a Christian, to want to allow their commune to continue as long as they liked – all they were asking for was the cache of illegal weaponry. Reeta might have fallen at that point; life in Pine Ranch had certainly been nicer before the crates of guns and ammo had started turning up.

It had been utopian, peaceful, perfect.

But then the man on the phone had added, 'and the perpetrators for those weapons' and Reeta's visions of life returning to those heady days of happiness crumbled. They would take Jeb if they were allowed in – the way Jesus had been taken by the Romans. If Jesus's disciples had had what Pine Ranch had, they would have fought just the same. Reeta had instead repeated what had been said by many voices for many evenings previously: they were there until the end.

The police had not only maintained, but strengthened their cordon during this siege, creeping slightly closer with each night that had passed. Soon – Reeta had heard Zechariah tell the rotation of men currently on watch – the police would lose patience and storm the house, without care or regard for the women and children that were supposedly keeping them at bay.

With the only chores left to do kitchen for the women and gun shifts for the men, the cramped inhabitants of the house had more free time than they'd ever known before. Jeb gave near-constant sermons when he wasn't in meetings with Zechariah, who took over the mantle to lead prayers when Jeb left for solo worship in his room. The communal areas were now near impossible to pass through easily, with blankets and mattresses – fetched over several daring night-time missions to the dormitories – cramped on every available floor space. The stench of makeshift chamber pots and unwashed skin spilled into every corner of the house, the only respite in the rooms upstairs constantly aerated by open windows to make space for the arsenal.

Reeta was adding saltwater to the rationed grits in the pot for dinner, her stomach crunching at the memory of a full meal. They had never been permitted indulgence at Pine Ranch, but meat on occasion and Eunice's Sunday pies seemed a luxury far removed from their new survival on only the small stores in the basement. A mouthful of grits with boiled turnip greens was all they had for tonight. Zechariah interrupted her work. She looked up, along with the other women in the kitchen, thinking that perhaps it would be Abra or Hagar's turn to speak to the negotiator.

'Reeta,' Zechariah said. 'Upstairs – Jeb and I need to speak with you.'

Reeta blinked and turned to Abra, gesturing for her to take over her pot. Abra nodded. Her face sagged more with each day, the weight draining from her, leaving pallid, baggy skin in its place. Reeta had seen her silently sobbing as she moved about her day.

Reeta followed Zechariah through the jumble of improvised beds and huddled groups of people, and up the stairs to the welcome breezes of fresh air. Jeb and Zechariah's rooms were the only ones not manned as parapets, and as Zechariah pushed open the door to Jeb's room it was as dark and boarded-up as downstairs. A lamp in the corner illuminated him, sitting on his bed, his possessions laid out before him, an old military backpack open at his feet.

Ten

Reeta waited patiently while the phone connected, knowing an automated voice was asking for permission to connect from the Balmen United States Penitentiary interspersed with Reeta's soft iteration of her own name. She'd got used to 'Reeta' as her identifier in the last six years, accepted it gently and allowed herself to sit snugly within it.

'Reeta,' the voice answered with an audible smile. 'I've been waiting for your call. I was hoping to speak to you yesterday, but I imagine you were wrapped up with Barry all afternoon. Oh, what news, Reeta – what wonderful, wonderful news.'

'Actually,' Reeta said, face stretching unconsciously into a grin at her friend's gleeful tone, 'you're the first person I've spoken to.'

There was a moment's silence and Reeta heard Carol swallow with emotion. 'Well, I'm very touched,' she said. 'But you really should speak to Barry.'

'I will,' Reeta agreed, her voice light. 'Right after this.'

'I'm so happy for you, Reeta,' Carol said. 'Really I am.'

'This will be a good chapter in the book.'

'The Supreme Court has put itself on the right side of history, that's for sure. I'm hoping I can get an interview with one of the justices – Ray from the legal team at the

Post owes me a favour; he should be able to put me in contact.'

'How's it going up there? At work and everything?' Carol was Reeta's only window into life outside of Balmen, a window she only sometimes felt strong enough to peek through. But today there was hope, and with hope came curiosity.

'Oh, it's fine,' Carol answered airily. 'I've been given a case down in Oklahoma, three girl scouts murdered at camp. Pretty grisly but it's high profile – stuff like that always is. I know Cliff wanted it, but Myron trusts me more, I guess.'

Reeta smiled at this. Carol always stopped short of acknowledging outright that the sensation surrounding the exclusive reports she'd gotten directly from Reeta after her trial now ensured she was always the editor's first call for the biggest cases. Reeta didn't really mind so much that her predicament had at least had some tacit benefit for her friend, but Carol obviously deemed it too tacky to mention.

'Ah, screw Cliff,' Reeta said with a little laugh and Carol barked jovially back.

'That's what Georgette's doing,' Carol replied, settling into the light-hearted gossip. 'You know Myron's secretary? She's only twenty, for Christ's sake. I tried to warn her off at the Christmas party, but you know what twenty-year-olds are like.' Reeta didn't really know what twenty-year-olds were like, but she didn't interrupt. Carol groaned after a moment and continued talking. 'God, is that really all my life has come down to? Gossiping about my colleagues' sex lives. Sorry, wish I had something more interesting to report.'

'Well, you've got a hell of a lot more to report than me,' Reeta said with an audible shrug.

'Not today,' Carol replied, looping the conversation back to the momentous Supreme Court ruling. 'Honestly, you must be overjoyed.'

'I'm still in here.'

'True, but maybe there's a way out now, you know? Somewhere down the line.'

'Yeah, maybe...' Reeta trailed off, her imagination floating away to see herself having lunch with Carol in a restaurant. Or going to the movies. Or just to the grocery store. 'Anyway.' She pulled herself back to reality. 'How's the – ah – well, how are the interviews going?' Reeta ran her finger up and down the metal ridges of the institutional telephone wire.

'Well.' Carol's voice dropped a tone. 'Bonnie still won't have anything to do with me. I've written and called several times, and a few weeks ago I got a call from her husband's office telling me to back off.'

'Will you?'

'It's delicate, but I think it's important her voice is heard in the book. I'll lay off a for a little while now, though. The other interviews are almost done, though – everyone who spoke to me back then has been happy to talk again.'

'Are they...' Reeta gulped and closed her eyes, head leaning forward on the thick metal box of the phone. 'Are they awful?'

Carol exhaled. 'You know what they say, pretty much. The facts remain the same as when they stood on the stand six years ago.'

'But *between* the facts are the lives I destroyed.'

'I'm so sorry, Reeta.' Carol's voice collapsed into guilt. 'Sometimes I feel like I should never have started this book – making you relive everything all these years later.'

'It was my idea,' Reeta reminded her.

'I know, I know,' Carol agreed. 'And I *do* believe it's important, I think I can get to something we've missed…' She trailed off vaguely before exhaling. 'I'll bring you the pages when I've finished them. But *only* if you can take it.'

Reeta nodded thickly before remembering the phone. 'I can take it.'

'I want you to remember that this is a book of two parts, Reeta. The you that was, and the you that is now. Whatever you did, or didn't do, it wasn't *your* fault. You woke up anew in that hospital, a blank slate, with no one there to brainwash or manipulate you – and now you're peaceful, and loving, and *good*. That's what we're going to show here.'

'And, and the *other* interviews?'

There was a pause on the end of the line. 'The PO box those letters came from has garnered me no response; I don't think it's still in use. Other than actually flying to Cuba and trying to track down one man in a whole country, I can't see any other way of getting in touch.'

'We expected as much,' Reeta said with a shrug, not really caring about the progress made with tracking down Jeb. It seemed he'd brought her nothing but trouble in her last life; she didn't see how it would be any better now. 'And?'

'Still nothing, I'm afraid.' The sounds of Carol moving around her kitchen streamed through the phone, a bowl clattering to a countertop, the splashing of milk. Carol was making breakfast as she spoke, just like a normal woman, living her own life. 'I think I've got a new lead, though.'

'Well, that's good. Promising, maybe.'

'Hopefully.'

They spoke for a little while longer, Carol promising to put more money into Reeta's commissary account, despite Reeta's protestations. It was a game they played frequently, but they both knew Reeta would have to relent her pride if she wanted clean hair, flavourful food and underwear free of blood smears once a month.

Reeta called Barry immediately after Carol had hung up and was told that he was already in Georgia, most likely on his way to the prison to see her. The receptionist at his Tallahassee office seemed surprised to receive a call from Barry Prince's most famous client, saying he'd taken off immediately after the verdict yesterday afternoon and was expecting to be in meetings with her for most of the day. Reeta had politely thanked her for her help and headed straight to the chapel. That would be where they'd come to find her when he finally arrived.

Reeta had been reluctant to join the chapel committee at first – terrified at what it might unleash in her after hearing tales of her fanaticism during her trial. But she'd found comfort in memorising the Bible while she'd sat alone in the Florida jail, and the stories had wormed their way into her conscience. She'd thought long and hard about the passages and psalms she'd etched into her brain, listened carefully to the pastor's sermons and, although it had taken her a while, realised she felt an emptiness. The words meant nothing to her. She found she couldn't believe them to be anything other than simple stories. It seemed incredible that she'd once killed for them. But her lack of belief hadn't deterred her from working in the chapel – she liked Gloria and Beatrice, and it filled her days to organise and clean.

She was dusting shelves when a tall guard with salt and pepper hair and long, dark sideburns came for her. 'Lawyer's here,' he said, voice uncharacteristically muffled because of the chapel walls. He always whispered in there, as if he believed God averse to particularly loud noises.

The room in which the inmates met with their lawyers in Balmen was far nicer than the dank cell of the Florida jail, although that was saying little. A window looked out on the exercise yard in the distance, a criss-cross of outside pathways framed with tall wire fences filling in the space between. The walls were painted a dull yellowing white that sprouted brown damp from the corners, and the table and chairs were wooden rather than unrelenting metal. Barry had already made himself at home, papers sprawling out in front of him, when Reeta arrived. He looked up with an expression of such delight she felt a lump of emotion rise. He stood, arms outstretched, and made his way around the table to embrace her for just a moment before the guard coughed meaningfully.

'Oh, Reeta,' Barry said, stepping obediently back and raising his hands to his face so the gold of his wedding band glinted sharply. 'What a day, Reeta, what a day.'

The guard left to stand watch outside, and Reeta shuffled to take her seat as Barry followed suit to retake his own. The five and a half years since her verdict had come through had been good to her lawyer – the notoriety of her case boosting his career enough that he was able to move back home to Tallahassee and set up his own private practice. Hers had been an unwinnable case, so his failure to save her from death row mattered little to the people who had seen his name in the papers. Now he defended mainly small-time white-collar criminals and con men, but had kept on the client who'd made his name, pro-bono at his new firm.

'How's little Woody?' she asked, forcing normality into the meeting.

'Oh, he's fine, he's fine. A little scamp most of the time but Peggy keeps up somehow. I swear, that woman is a superhero.' Talking about his family always relaxed Barry's shoulders from the unconscious tension Reeta noticed him hold. He didn't appear to realise it in himself, but for her it was obvious.

'But,' he said, sitting forward with a grin. 'That's not what we're here to discuss, Reeta Doe. We're here to discuss your future. Now that you have one.'

Reeta couldn't help but smile in return.

'The ruling automatically reduces your sentence to life imprisonment, a bit of work for me to file here and there, but generally the job's been done. That means this petition I've been working on for the Eleventh Circuit is – well, to some extent wasted.' He did not look one bit bothered by the useless hours lost to the papers before him. 'But there's still stuff we can do. We can appeal the life imprisonment, get you the option of parole further down the line. I think we gave a fairly good show of your amnesia at trial and Dr Reid's testimony will be crucial to introduce again. There's growing sympathy for the long-term punishment of the insane' – he glanced up for a brief moment of concern that he'd offended her, but she nodded her understanding – 'and yours is a tricky one because you weren't technically insane at the time of the killings, but your mental state *now* should affect the sentencing. We're not appealing the verdict, after all.' He was rambling and she allowed him to continue. Sometimes she thought she only allowed him to stay on the case for his own needs – she'd long ago made peace with the fact that she was going to die in prison, one way or another.

'We can get experts to testify that amnesia can be classified as a type of insanity – that shouldn't be too difficult to do. There's Thomas v. Tennessee, which gets in the way a little – precedent that amnesia is no defence under the law, but – again – we're not disputing the verdict, just the sentence. Unless you *want* to go after the verdict? There's the hair analysis, of course; a lot of controversy has already been raised by that particular branch of science. More guesswork than science, though, really, that's the problem—'

Reeta raised her hand, silencing him with a smile. 'Barry, please. All those appeals' – she gestured down at his papers – 'all your hard work. They weren't going to change things anyway. You can stop fighting for me now.'

'No,' he said, his face a surprisingly full grin. 'I can't, Reeta. You're a different person to the one who did those things.'

She couldn't help but think back to those early days in jail, a flustered Barry trying desperately to get her to admit to things she didn't know. The trial had thawed their relationship, as Carol's advocacy proved to Barry that defending this girl didn't need to be the moral purgatory he'd assigned to himself. And, neither could deny, he did owe this murderer his career.

'You're being punished for your crimes, but you deserve a chance. A chance for a life you've never had. The odds of reoffending in your case are zero in my opinion, and so you deserve the option of parole. And I will keep fighting until all of our options are exhausted.' He sat back and picked up his pen, smoothing down the front of his yellow legal pad. 'Now, you're still working in the chapel?' Reeta nodded and opened her mouth to speak. Barry continued. 'That's good, good,' he said, almost to himself. 'Could be a bit tricky what with Pine Ranch and the motive the prosecution gave at trial, but I think on balance it's not a bad angle to play. The fact that you've been given those freedoms as a death row inmate should only help. I'm sure we can subpoena the warden to testify on your behaviour since getting here.'

She nodded quietly for the remainder of their meeting, answering his questions here and there, confirming facts and dates she'd confirmed a thousand times before. When he had finally scribbled to the end of his fifth sheet, he looked down at his notes for a moment more before raising his head to meet her eyes.

'I think that should keep me busy enough for the time being. Now.' He flipped his pad shut. 'Peggy made you some cookies; the guards are inspecting them, no doubt chowing down on a few, but you should get at least a couple.' His face turned earnest. 'Keep going, Reeta. We'll get there.'

X

'Reeta,' Jeb said warmly, face splitting with a smile she couldn't decipher.

'Brother Jeb.' She nodded respectfully.

'Sit down.' He gestured at a seat in the corner of his room, a tall, stiff-backed armchair next to the blackened window. When she sat, a straight shard of light dashed her face from behind the wooden boards, a luminescent scar cutting through her eye. 'We haven't really discussed the night of the raid,' he said, setting down the shirt that had been in his hands, and focusing on her. 'The night you returned from your driving lesson with Gideon.'

'He was right behind me – I didn't see what happened. Just when I turned around and he was…' She trailed off, having explained this many times before. She wanted Jeb to know she hadn't *seen* anything. And that she would never tell anyone what she thought she'd heard. Because the truth of that night was that far more of the bullets that fired on them were from the house itself, not the fields at their sides. In that final hailstorm of bullets that took down Gideon, Reeta was sure they had come from above, directly ahead of her. She would keep that secret for them all; the guilt and suspicion from whoever had fired those shots and whoever was grieving Gideon could tear them apart.

'I understand that,' Jeb said kindly, raising his palm to quieten her gently. 'It was very brave of you both to run across that field to get back to us. And you were right to – we need you.'

The muscles around her mouth relaxed just a touch.

'No, I want to ask what happened *before* that. You came back through the woods, isn't that right?'

She nodded. 'Yes, we saw the lights as we approached home and Gideon directed me another way. We left the car in a ditch and walked back.'

'This ditch,' Jeb said with an air of reaching the crux of the matter. 'Can you tell me where it is?'

'Along the road on the other side of the wood,' Reeta said. 'We walked for a while through the trees, came at the house from an angle.'

'Would you recognise the route you took that night?' Zechariah asked, stepping forward from the closed door.

She thought for a moment, considering her answer. 'Yes,' she confirmed, thinking it best to be positive, to be willingly helpful.

Jeb shot Zechariah a look. 'Can you describe it to me?' he asked, turning his face back to her, rearranged into one of a compassionate leader.

'Er...' Reeta darted looks between the two. 'There were trees and brambles, a couple of clearings that we passed too.'

'Jeb, it's the only option for her to guide us,' Zechariah interrupted. 'We could spend hours lost in that wood, waste the whole night.'

Jeb dipped his chin for a moment, thinking. 'Very well,' he said. 'Go and make the necessary arrangements while I explain to Reeta.'

Reeta's mind rushed and skidded; what were they talking about? She knew what day tomorrow was; she'd had it burned into her memory from when she'd first been given her new role.

Tomorrow was the pick-up.

Surely they couldn't be thinking about actually going. About procuring more weapons to refortify the ranch?

Zechariah nodded and muttered under his breath as he left, 'Let's hope Terry keeps his silence for one more night.'

Jeb spoke for close to an hour, explaining with impassioned words exactly what was expected of her that night.

It chilled her bones.

But at every moment, every point she had the instinct to argue, to exclaim and cry out, her life – her nineteen years – rushed through her in a riptide of nostalgic grief. Her only purpose on this Earth was to serve the man in front of her. It was all she had ever known. And if her Lord, her Messiah, wanted this of her then she would obey, as she had countless times before.

She nodded her assent and stood on shaky limbs when he had finished speaking, catching herself on the dresser near the door as he turned to load a collection of ratty papers into his backpack. A neat stack of Caleb's photographs, painstakingly developed in his hand-constructed dark room, were between a Bible and an old, tattered comic book. On the very top was a photograph of Jeb from several years ago, seated in his throne-like wicker-backed chair on the porch, denim shirt draped effortlessly over his brawny physique, green eyes beaming out in serenity. She felt her fingers go to it with blind instinct and slid it into her hand. The top picture now saw a teenage Reeta, limbs tangled with Damaris, wildflowers grazing their knees. Effortless, hopeful grins split their faces and arms grasped each other tight. Her hand spasmed toward it, reaching out, grabbing at it. She knocked the stack to reveal the photos near the bottom, older, the colours faded and blurred.

A young blonde girl stood grinning by Brother Jeb's side, his hand draped proudly onto her shoulder. Reeta remembered that day; she'd been six or seven when Zechariah had first brought Caleb a camera. There were more underneath and childhood memories soared back to her: twirling skirts, golden hair cartwheeling along the prairie.

She grabbed at the photos, crumpling them all into her fist just as the memories turned sour.

Jeb was her future, her past and her present.

No one else was important.

She pushed open his door as he continued his packing, and she slipped the photos into the pocket of her smock.

Eleven

It was a warm summer in DC, suffocated by Watergate. Carol couldn't escape it, whatever *it* was. A break-in at a hotel, a Republican security aide, that was all the story seemed to be at this point, but the town was alight with gossip and rumours. And if Carol knew Washington, the story wouldn't stop there. Carl and Bob were up to something in the office, some new informant they'd found after getting the story last month. Carol had other things on her mind, but the only solace she got from rehashing the same rumours that whirled around town was in her home office, the converted second room of her Bloomingdale home. She'd long since abandoned her fold-up table against the comfy armchair, knowing that her work now required more focus and concentration – she needed to be surrounded by it.

The sun was still out with the pink hue of evening, but Carol had chosen not to follow her colleagues to the bar this Friday night. She pushed open the door of her one-time second bedroom and put her large glass of deep red wine down on the desk, not caring that it would leave a faint burgundy ring on the oak top. The desktop was littered with coffee and wine stains, the odd sticky patch of orange juice – the chaos of her workstation was a running joke for those close to her, for the rest of her home was kept as pristine and poised as her outward appearance. Her neat and professional work dress was now slumped across her bed, and Carol's body was instead cosied up in ancient track pants from her days sprinting on the Georgetown varsity team and a baggy navy T-shirt she had a feeling had once belonged to Ben. She moved to the window on the other side of the room and heaved at the old wooden frame, ignoring how it cracked and splintered as she jimmied it up. An almost imperceptible summer breeze spilled half-heartedly through the gap, and she thought again about Ben's once-constant complaints that she should invest in air conditioning. Apologising silently to him that she still hadn't sorted it out, almost ten years later, she picked up her wine glass and turned to the wall to her right.

Pinpoints of blue cornflowers peeked through from the wallpaper behind, glancing in between the photographs and cards that littered the wall, skewered by thumb tacks pilfered from the *Post*'s supply closet. She'd stopped short of connecting various threads by red string, worried about what conspiracies she might begin to see. The column to the very left she could now ignore. It had photographs and names of all the people who had encircled the victims throughout their lives. The top tier of the column was given over to those who had been around for the killings themselves – those who had known Reeta. Abigail Lawson's friends, the ones most willing to speak – Bobby DeValle, Charlie Edwards and Marcia Ryland – were tacked neatly next to each other. They'd given Carol photographs, anecdotes, analysis, opinions. They were also the only people connected to the victims with what could be described as a nod toward sympathy for Reeta. They remembered the strange girl she was and how they'd seen that something was off with her from the start. Carol's admission, upfront, that she was working closely with the murderer of their friend had jarred, but not discouraged their participation. Things had been more difficult with Callie Jefferson and the alumni of Kappa Delta Pi – they had nothing but hatred and anger for Reeta. But they'd spoken to Carol nonetheless, given interviews full of vitriol, changing stories and twisting memories that had warped over the six years since their first police statements. But between the bitterness Carol had understood their words, and she'd got their story. She'd got all the stories in the end. Families had spoken to her, including grieving pleas from Mandy Silas's and Susan O'Donnell's parents for Reeta to finally betray the last resting places of their daughters.

Yes, the column dedicated to the murders themselves was complete. The pages were being written and her timeline was secure.

It was the other three columns that had drawn her home on this warm Friday evening.

Jeb.

Bonnie.

?

These were the headings, printed in Carol's neat hand on the pink cards atop those three sections. Jeb's column was the thickest with information. It was pinned with most of her own articles on Pine Ranch, some notes on his life in the army, copies of the letters that had been exposed in court, and an unfinished list of her own correspondence to the P.O box those letters had come from. The last letter she'd sent had been six weeks ago and, like the others, it remained ignored or unseen. US relations with Cuba weren't exactly progressing well, so there were no official routes she could try to get to him, and certainly no extradition even if she did. The *Post* had a contact in Havana who she'd asked to investigate for her, but he'd come back with nothing – tracking down insane cult leaders was not exactly on his remit as a political informant.

Bonnie's column had the statement she'd given at the time, her trial testimony and a couple of photographs her family had given up. There were a few sheets of Carol's notes on Bonnie's life since the accident, mainly focusing on her marriage to Henry Chandola in 1970. He worked on Wall Street and it seemed they'd met down in Florida in the run-up to the trial, where they were both living in the same apartment building. She'd moved to New York with him as soon as the trial was done.

'That accident changed her,' Bonnie's mother had tearfully told Carol when she'd visited them at their home in Ohio. 'It was as if all her dreams, all her beliefs, just...' She mimed a silent explosion with shaking hands.

'She could have done so much,' her father had cut in. 'She wanted to follow in my footsteps after college, you know – train as a lawyer. But...' He'd trailed off sadly.

'She doesn't speak to us any more,' Mrs Powell had said after a beat. Carol had seen Bonnie's rejection of her mother during the trial, and it had spawned something in her she'd since been trying to repress.

'How long,' Carol had asked tentatively, 'if you don't mind me asking, how long has it been since you've seen her?'

'Oh,' Mr Powell had exhaled. 'Not properly since she woke up in that hospital. We tried to speak to her at the trial but—' A sudden whimper of a sob from his wife cut him off.

'Since the accident?' Carol couldn't keep the shock from her tone.

'She told us she didn't want us to see her like that,' Mrs Powell had explained through gulps of tears. 'Her face, her pretty face was all…' She'd had to stop at that point to make breath.

'We understood,' Mr Powell said, placing his arm around his wife, 'that she needed time. We – *she* – has been through a lot. But we've got through worse as a family and those things brought us closer in the past.'

'She blamed us. I know she did,' Mrs Powell wailed and her husband soothed her softly. 'But I thought the trial would change everything; I thought she'd see that it was over now. It was all done.' Mrs Powell sniffed loudly. 'She said she didn't want us there, but I *knew* she needed us. And I thought when it was all over…' She broke off again and the awkward scene in the court bathroom flashed as bright in Carol's mind as if it had happened just the day before.

'We thought that soon she'd come back to us – who could understand better than us?' Mr Powell continued. 'And we would be waiting, wherever she needed us to be.' He stopped and looked forlornly down. 'But she never has.'

'How about her marriage to Henry? Do you know him?'

'No.' Mr Powell shook her head. 'She didn't want us visiting her at the apartment in Florida – she refused to move home, you see. I believe he also rented an apartment on that floor when he was in town for work. But we were never introduced. Not properly.'

'You didn't go to the wedding?'

Mr Powell gave a sad snort of a laugh. 'No, no. Of course not.'

Carol's own confusion was impossible to hide. She'd understood Bonnie not wanting to talk to *her*, a journalist, and she could even understand Bonnie's college friends saying they'd not seen or heard from her since the accident. But to have cut off her *parents*?

'Like we said,' Mr Powell had said softly. 'The accident changed her.' He nodded meaningfully at Carol. 'Reeta has a lot to answer for.' His eyes caught on his wife's then and they shared an elongated look. 'Brother Jeb has a lot to answer for,' he added in a near whisper.

The mystery of the changing Bonnie Chandola née Powell was a central theme of Carol's book. How one night, six years ago, changed two women so irrevocably. If she could just figure out a way to talk to Bonnie, maybe she could put the obsessive niggling in the back of her mind down.

She turned her attention to the third column, headed by the big black marker-pen question mark. This was the sparsest of the sections, with only a loose physical description and vague reports of a young woman's movements from one day six years ago. There were no photographs, no interviews to pin up. But Carol had known from the start she needed this girl – that Reeta needed this girl.

Sighing, she turned to her wine and took a thick gulp, wiping away a dribble that escaped her lips. She pulled out her desk chair and sat at her typewriter, at a loss for where to go next. A stack of papers to her right covered everything she already knew, one copy of which was packed into a large manila envelope, the address of Balmen United States Penitentiary written in thick black marker across its front. Now she had to contend with writing the rest of the book on the things she didn't know. She'd held off completing these sections, hoping that soon she might have some firm answers to fill in, some more viewpoints to flesh out her story – but that seemed like an impossible task right now. Perhaps her readers were destined to be as frustrated as she was by the full mystery of Reeta Doe.

Standing up against the wall on her desk was a photograph of her and Reeta taken last year on a random date in October they'd assigned as her birthday. Carol was wearing jeans and a sweater with one arm flung across Reeta, who was tucked grinningly into the embrace, her grey institutional uniform a camouflage against the wall. The picture had been taken in the small room usually reserved for lawyers' visits, but Barry had worked some magic with the warden and Carol had been treated to a break from the usual foreboding glass partitions and crackling phones of the visitation room. Reeta had caused no trouble in her time at Balmen, and Carol had ingratiated herself with the guards well enough that they'd permitted her to bring a small cake and a few carefully wrapped gifts for the occasion.

Reeta's first birthday party.

Carol smiled fondly at it, remembering the look on Reeta's face at her first taste of cheap store-bought frosting.

The shrill ring of the telephone in her bedroom cut through her reminiscence, and she rose without urgency. She meandered across the hallway, the trilling cutting annoyingly into her eardrums.

'Hello?' she answered lazily, resting one knee up on her bed.

'Carol, you're home,' Ben said, uncharacteristic excitement wavering his voice. 'Thank God. I think I've got something.'

She straightened up, gripping the receiver harder. 'What is it?'

'I'm coming over. Leaving the office now, but it just came in.' He hesitated. 'I think I've got her.'

They rung off and Carol waited downstairs, pacing excitedly for the twenty minutes until Ben arrived, sweat stains gripping at the thin material of his white shirt.

'You've got her?' she asked with a grin, opening the door wide to let him in.

'I think so,' he answered with a satisfied nod.

He flopped his briefcase on the stool in the hallway and took himself into the small galley kitchen, helping himself to a glass from the draining rack and upending the bottle of Pinot Noir Carol had left open on the side. He came out and leaned against the doorframe, taking a slug.

Carol widened her eyes, incredulous. 'Well?' she demanded and gave in to a reluctant smile when he laughed.

'Come on,' he said, nodding to the stairs and picking up the briefcase with his spare hand. 'Let's debrief in mission control. Nice shirt, by the way,' he added over his shoulder with a smirk.

Carol rolled her eyes and followed him up the stairs.

When she'd first asked him to help with her book, Willow had been reluctant.

'If you want to write about Reeta,' he'd said with a soft frown, 'then go ahead. But don't go dragging everyone else into it again.' But she'd been adamant. Carol *knew* there was something worth digging it all up again for and somehow by the end of dinner she'd convinced him. He'd at first agreed lightly to help in his spare time but, as she'd known, the pull of the chase had sucked him in. Since that first discussion they'd spent several nights making battle plans and drawing up theories to track down the people they needed, his mind visibly whirring as he noted down new records to check or new informants to call.

'Valerie Jackson,' he said, putting his briefcase down on her desk and rooting around inside it before straightening up to look at the wall of notes. In his hand he had a Xeroxed paper, blurred and patchy from where the original's imperfections had shown up in glaring black splodges. He moved over to the wall and tacked the paper up in the third column, Carol hovering keenly over his shoulder. When he moved out of the way she stepped forward and inspected the sheet – a passenger list from the SS *Calgaric* which had sailed from Liverpool to New Orleans in 1959. Willow pointed to a name halfway down the list, Valerie Parker, buried amongst five other Parker family members.

'This is Valerie Parker – thirteen at the time of her crossing from England to Louisiana. She went back to her original name after she got out.' He gave a small, sad shrug. 'Don't know what she was called in there though.'

They knew from the statement of Captain Henderson, whose daughter Sally-Jo had been at Pine Ranch, that Jeb was in the habit of removing his followers' birth names to give them one of his own.

'She never gave her name to Sergeant Matthews in Mariette,' Willow continued. 'And the small-town fool was too excited by her story he never got a proper statement before she fled.'

Carol tossed her head with frustration. They'd attempted to interview Matthews a couple of times, each time knocked back by his misplaced arrogance that *he'd* uncovered the illegal weapon ring at the ranch. The fate of the girl and her baby who'd told him about it, and the infamous disaster it culminated in, seemed of little importance to the now retired police sergeant. 'Anyway, it seems she hitched a ride with a travelling salesman who took pity on her. I called in a favour and sent a field agent to Mariette to ask around.' He paused and returned to his briefcase, fishing out a sheaf of papers. 'He got this statement from the cashier at the convenience store.' He handed over a crinkled piece of memo paper. 'She worked there back then and remembers that day. Everyone in Mariette remembers the day the girl escaped from the Jacklowe Plantation.'

'And what it led to,' Carol said, raising her eyebrows, scanning the statement in her hands.

'Put the town on the map, that's for sure. You know they get tourists out at the old property, taking photos.' He shook his head in disgust. 'Anyway, she says she saw the girl when she opened up that morning. Not hard to notice an unknown black girl with a baby hanging around – Mariette's not exactly known for its diversity. She said the girl disappeared into the sergeant's office for an hour or so and when she came out the rain had started so she ran across to the shop. Said it was evident early on the girl had no money to buy anything, but she let her browse and shelter from the rain with her baby. Eventually she asked her where she'd come from, who she was et cetera. Girl said her name was Valerie – didn't give a last name. The cashier's husband peddles insurance and cemetery plots all around the county and was due to go out of town again that day. When he came in to say goodbye and pick up snacks for the road, she asked him to take the girl with him and drop her off at a shelter or church in Bryan, where he was headed.'

Carol exhaled and raised her eyebrows. 'She and Reeta both ended up in Bryan.'

'Seems that way. Anyway, he dropped her off at a Christian mission in Bryan and they took her in. The mission has a record of Valerie Parker and her son Harrison.' He tapped the passenger list again, this time with a small frown creasing between his brows. 'Harrison Parker, also listed here, but the ages don't quite match up for him to be her infant son.'

Carol pulled down the edges of her lips in thought. After a beat she nodded at the list. 'How did you get this?'

'The field agent who asked around in Bryan spoke to a volunteer at the mission who remembered her. Said he'd asked about her accent – they don't get many Brits in Texas. She'd said she'd moved over with her family about six years ago, so I called in all the passenger lists of ships from '58, '59 and '60, just to be sure. After the ships I was gonna move on to flight records – but I found her.'

Carol nodded, face twitching now with a smile. 'You have been busy,' she murmured.

Willow rolled his eyes but there was laughter in his tone when he spoke. 'Don't start. Anyway, she stayed in Bryan for a few months before she got on her feet, got a job and moved on.'

'So – Jackson?' Carol asked, looking up from the statement.

'Got married in '69. Took some trawling through paperwork for that, let me tell you. She's done a good job of keeping herself under the radar, has Valerie.'

'Where is she now?' Carol asked, almost breathless. Surely Ben hadn't come over here just to tell her the girl had disappeared again.

He smiled, stretching the blonde roughness of his five o'clock shadow, eyes bright. 'Still in Texas. Husband works in an electricals shop in Houston; she seems to clean houses around being a mom to their two kids – and Harrison, of course.'

'Well,' Carol said with a grin. 'Looks like I'm going to Houston, then.'

'Carol,' Ben said after a beat. His face had fallen from its previous joviality. 'The girl's been through a lot, you know.'

'I know,' she said, annoyance fluttering.

'Be tactful. I don't want this coming back to bite me in the ass.'

'It won't,' Carol replied defensively.

'Don't.' He paused and inhaled deeply. 'Don't – well, just don't ruin what's taken me a year to track down.'

XI

The older kids clung on to the clammy little hands of the youngest, the babies carried awkwardly. Abel, at eleven, was the eldest and led the way, gripping baby Rachel in one arm, a duffel bag of their shared possessions slung over the other. They all trembled and wept, looking beseechingly around the semicircle of adults who watched with their own mournful expressions. Zechariah had announced before dinner that tonight the children would be sent out, and that they should be readied and packed for the journey. The decision had been met with a stunned silence, breaths of discord the only disruption. But no one had complained. How could they? They'd seen what had happened to Caleb and Gideon, and they knew the threat they faced increased with each new morning of this siege.

Jeb had told the negotiator on the six p.m. phone call that he was releasing the children and was assured that they would be well cared for and returned to the custody of their parents as and when this situation was resolved. They ate one final meal together, then at nine o'clock the doors to Pine Ranch opened for the first time in eight days and the children nervously emerged into the spotlights of the police's lamps. Reeta couldn't watch. She moved herself to the back of the crowd, past Abra and Hagar, who gripped each other tightly, tears drowning their cheeks. Every person gathered knew what this meant. They knew that the siege was about to hit a violent peak, one that the children did not need to witness, no matter how much of God's protection shielded them.

It was a sombre mood as they lay down to sleep that evening, the uncertainty of life without the purity and unblemished joy of children the next day weighing heavily on everyone's chests. Even those assigned to the watch were allowed a night off – Jeb had negotiated a night of peace in exchange for the children. The battle for their souls would recommence at dawn.

Reeta did not sleep. She was not permitted rest.

The clock in the entrance hall ticked like crickets throughout the night above where her mattress was laid. Next to her were her meagre possessions of a couple of smocks, skirts, T-shirts, sandals and an old pair of sneakers inherited from one of the boys. She heard the breaths slow of those around her, the gentle cries of dampened anguish eventually fall to snores and reluctant peace. Midnight came and tolled a soft bong inside the clock, but it was not until she heard the creak of footsteps on the landing above her that she pushed herself upright. She gathered her things into her bedsheet, securing it with a looped knot she could push her arm through, hooked on her shoulder as a bag. She remained barefoot, choosing silence over comfort, and padded toward the kitchen. After retrieving what she needed from underneath the stove, she silently pushed open the back door to dump her bag on the dewy grass. Two shadowed figures appeared in the kitchen behind her, and she held the door open for them as Jeb and Zechariah crept by her and out onto the lawn.

'I'll take this,' Jeb said, nodding down at her bag. 'We'll meet you at the wood. You know what to do.'

Zechariah's face was unreadable in the dark, but the jerk of his head toward Jeb betrayed his shock. 'She's not coming?' he hissed.

'She is,' Jeb replied calmly. 'She has one more job to help our mission, though.'

Zechariah made an uneasy noise but Reeta knew he was keen not to delay any further, so didn't push any more. The two men made their way outside, sticking to the shadows and skulking delicately in the protective shadow of the house. The half-moon was bright tonight, now the storm clouds had blown themselves out, and the prairie glittered with silver-blue grass. Their figures would be seen easily by anyone looking for them.

It was Reeta's job to ensure no one was looking for them.

She stole back through the kitchen, across the entrance hall and into the now empty nursery. The doors connecting it to the Bible study room were closed – even those cramped in the other parlour felt it disrespectful to take over the children's accommodation so soon after they'd left. Turning her mind away from fears of hellfire, she forced herself to fall instead into the cooling lagoon of trust in Jeb. She already felt better, the water of Jeb's righteous instructions lapping between her toes as she emptied the canister of lighter fluid across the stripped cots and beds. Even though she couldn't fully understand him, she knew he was the Word of God and she was not meant to. His Word guided her with refreshing fluidity as she struck her match and lit one of the long, thin fire-starters Eunice used to stoke the wood-fired oven. In each spot she hovered her small flame above the iridescent liquid, shimmering pinkish-purple against the wooden floors; it erupted in long lines of blue-rooted orange flames.

The heat licked against her and sweat beaded around the nape of her neck, trickled down from her hairline. She found herself paralysed, watching the dancing flames for a moment too long until an acrid hack punched the back of her neck. She couldn't take a breath, thick smoke stuffing itself down her throat. Bending double and coughing onto the floor, she hurried out of the room, stepping over the unknowing bodies that remained peacefully asleep. She picked her way across them, flung herself into the kitchen and repeated the ritual, not stopping this time to feel the flames on her skin before pushing out of the door into the cool night air.

Her legs pummelled the ground, muscles burning from the effort. The house was constructed of wood; it would burn fast, and from the shocked, desperate calls that rang out from the surrounding police, who suddenly seemed closer than ever, it was clear the front of the house was now fully engulfed in flame.

She flung a glance over her shoulder as she ran, her eyes searching out the second-floor window she knew belonged to Abra's room, sticky vomit rising in her throat as she watched the flames climb higher toward it. She turned away. Abra was a martyr. She would be with the Lord, and that would be her blessing.

By the time she reached the edge of the wood, burnt orange flickering the trees behind them, Jeb and Zechariah were watching transfixed.

'What the fuck did you do?' Zechariah whispered, horror-stricken.

'Brother Jeb's Word,' she replied, breathless and panting.

Zechariah turned to Jeb, his features contorting hideously in the dancing flame-light. '*Why?*'

'They are giving their souls, Zechariah,' Jeb replied, his tone forcibly calm, almost emotionless. 'We will start again—'

'No,' Zechariah barked, his head flying toward the house, which was now completely engulfed in towering flames. 'No. They're innocent people! They are *our family!*'

'They weren't pious enough! They allowed failure and treachery; they brought this hellfire to our door!' Jeb's arm flung out in a gesture at the police. His voice had claimed the high-pitched screech Reeta had heard after Kezia's father had left. His eyes danced with the flames from the house.

But Zechariah was not there to listen to his reply, to his theological reasoning, for he was sprinting back up toward the house – a lone figure silhouetted against the angry red blaze.

'They will be forgiven in Heaven!' Jeb screamed after him.

Reeta saw Zechariah burst back into the kitchen door, followed, a split second later, by a sickening crunch as the top floor crumpled in on itself. Jeb tugged her arm, pulling her away from the sight of her crumbling home.

'They are martyrs,' he said, striding backward into the trees. He let go of her arm and took a step closer, his eyes intent on hers. 'But our mission is not complete. Their mistakes can still be rectified. *We* can rebuild our ark. But this time we need to make sure we get it right.'

They were unseen as they raced through the trees toward the dirt road on the other side of the forest, the raging fire illuminating the sky like a soft dawn. They were unobserved as they traced impatiently down the road until, at last, Reeta found the vehicle. They were ignored when Reeta turned the car into town, the sound of screaming fire engine sirens on the road they left behind leading toward Pine Ranch. And they were unfollowed on their two-hour journey to the abandoned military airfield where a small rickety plane was unloading crates of guns, expecting a hefty payday as they had received several times before. The deal they got instead, Reeta could see, was far more beneficial. Their wage was paid from the lockbox in the back of the station wagon, not in exchange for the boxes they had brought, but instead for a return passage to Havana for the man with the denim shirt and flowing sandy hair.

They were reloading their stock back into the plane when Jeb cupped Reeta's face in his dry, cracked palms.

'Reeta. Always my most loyal follower. I knew you would be with me to the end.' He smiled. 'But this is not the end. Not for us, my darling Reeta.'

'I-I'm coming too?' she asked, voice cracking from the clagging smoke that still clung to her lungs despite driving the whole journey with windows wound right down, inhaling every breath of fresh air as if it was her last.

'Not yet,' Jeb said, his voice almost a whisper. 'We will start again, you and me. But we need more people for the Lord. People like *you*, Reeta.' He stood back, holding her head at arm's length, scrutinising her. He smiled in approval. 'Just like you. Remember my angels of Pine Ranch?'

She nodded, breathless.

'Find me my angels. Angels just like you.'

She was given the car and the remaining money in the lockbox for her mission, with a PO box address in Havana for her to write with her progress.

She stood back, one hip leaning against the station wagon as Jeb hoisted himself into the old airplane. It raced down the runway, blowing rusty desert dust into her eyes. Only when it was indistinguishable from the circling eagles of the Texas sky did Reeta climb back into the car and realise that the final memory she had of her saviour was his old military backpack, forgotten on the back seat.

She inhaled deeply and understood that – for the very first time in her life – she was alone.

Twelve

Carol left her hotel into a dry heat and the smell of burnt grease. Houston bustled around her this Monday morning, the sidewalk outside the fast-food joint next to her hotel piled high with trash bags, busy commuters ignoring the stench. The clerk at the hotel had written directions toward the Hertz rental office on the back of a breakfast menu, the biro-map sprawled across flapjacks, waffles and scrambled eggs. It was not a long walk, and soon she was paying for her little Ford and a map of the Houston suburbs. The Jacksons lived in the Third Ward, about twenty minutes from the city. High-rises and grey concrete shrunk down to squat garages and strip malls, before falling entirely into rows of shotgun houses, small front yards marked off with wire fences. The long, straight homes were so called because you could shoot a bullet at the front door and it would exit through the back, hitting nothing. In practice they allowed for a cool breeze to float throughout the home, a necessity in the stifling Texas summer. She pulled the car into a space at the end of Gainsville Street, deciding it best to approach on foot.

As she exited the car, she was grateful for the laid-back jeans and T-shirt she'd chosen to wear, a canvas backpack containing her tape recorder and notebook over her shoulders. Something had told her that her crocodile-skin handbag would garner her as much attention here as it had from her father's family in Chicago. It was not a scrutiny she relished.

One side of the Jacksons' street saw the narrow wooden homes sit flush against the sidewalk, two steps feeding down onto cracked concrete torn up by weeds. The other side of Gainsville Street – the side the Jacksons lived on, Carol could tell from the numbers hand-painted on trashcans, mailboxes and crooked gates – had a small, narrow strip of grass out front. Some were evidently tended to with pride, flowerbeds and plant-pots radiating with colour, while others were an abandoned patch of dead, dried grass, perhaps with the odd lawn chair and beaten-up cooler. The Jacksons' yard, Carol could see as she approached number 143, lay somewhere between the two. The grass was watered and mown, but that was the limit of their gardening prowess. A swing set stood to one side, and six garden chairs around a rusty white table filled the remainder of the space.

Carol pushed open the squeaking gate, ignoring the raised glance from the suspicious neighbour across the street, and made her way across the yard. She raised her hand to the screen door and knocked on the wooden frame. She could hear what sounded like a kids' TV show from inside, a baby crying and a hollering of 'Ma, Ma, there's someone at the door.' Carol smiled to herself and was not surprised when, a few moments later, the front door was opened by a tall child with skin as ambiguous as Carol's own. It was too light compared to the baby held in his arms, and his mossy green eyes glowed quizzically.

'Can I help you?' he asked, politeness overriding his suspicion when he looked at her properly through the dark blur of the screen door.

'Hello,' Carol said. 'I'm here to see your mother.'

'You a friend of hers?' he asked, shifting the baby from one arm to the other. The baby had stopped crying and was now also looking at the stranger with a curious little frown.

'Well, I…' Carol hesitated, picking her next words carefully. 'I know an old friend of hers.'

'MOM!' The boy cricked his chin over his shoulder toward the back of the house. 'There's a lady here for you.'

At his words a toddler appeared at the doorway in the far end of the front room and waddled toward them, stumbling onto the boy's leg at the very end, gripping him hard as if he couldn't quite have made it any further. A figure followed him out, a dishrag in her hand. Valerie Jackson.

'What did you say, Harry?' she asked, her accent a transatlantic mangle, her voice a weary sigh.

'Some lady to see you,' the boy replied, before heaving his siblings back toward the threadbare couch and the gentle breeze of the fan plugged in behind the television.

Carol waited patiently while Valerie walked toward her. She wore a long paisley skirt with a simple white vest, which had collected the beads of sweat from her décolletage. Her hair was big and natural, kept out of her face by a dark red bandana.

'Don't have that fan on all day, Harry,' she admonished on her way to the door. 'Electricity don't grow on trees, you know.'

The boy grunted reluctantly but did lean forward and turn it off after another extended moment of feeling the breeze against his face.

Valerie reached the door with a reticent, but polite smile. 'Hello,' she said. 'How can I help you?'

269

Carol flashed her most engaging grin, the one that had persuaded people to talk and tell their stories many times over. 'My name is Carol Joyce, and I was hoping to talk to you.'

'Oh yes?' Valerie replied, absentmindedly swinging the dishrag over her shoulder. 'What about?'

'Well, about your life, really.'

Valerie's eyes narrowed.

'And about Reeta Doe.'

For a moment Carol wasn't sure if Valerie had heard her – her entire body had frozen, face blank and unreadable. But then venom surged through her expression, animating her features and she hissed, 'How did you find me?'

'It was difficult,' Carol admitted, maintaining a soft, apologetic tone. 'But I have now, and I think you could be important.'

'I have nothing to say,' Valerie said.

'Please.' Carol allowed a tone of pleading to creep in. 'I know Reeta well – I've been working with her since before her trial. I'm writing a book on her case and I think your involvement is crucial so we can tell this story with the respect and accuracy it deserves. I want people to know the truth about Pine Ranch, to give a voice to those who perished there.'

Valerie's face twisted. 'There's no respect to be given to Pine Ranch.' She shook her head. 'I have nothing to say to you.' She made to close the door, but Carol raised her voice.

'Do you remember Reeta? Can you help her remember why she did what she did?'

This seemed to still Valerie again; her hand paused on the edge of the door instead of slamming it shut. 'The stories are true?' she asked quietly. 'She really has no memory?'

Carol shook her head. 'She remembers nothing.'

Valerie didn't respond, but looked closely at Carol's face, scrutinising her through the thin mesh of the screen door.

'You two are the same age,' Carol continued. 'Were you close?'

Valerie blinked and after a few seconds Carol realised she was crying.

'You knew her,' Carol said, her voice barely a whisper. 'She needs you now.'

Valerie pressed her lips tightly together and forced a tight sigh. 'I have nothing to say,' she repeated, but she didn't move to shut the door again. Carol could see that she was torn by what had happened to her lost friend.

'I think you do. Will you talk to Reeta, even if you won't talk to me?'

Valerie looked over at her children, who were engrossed in the flashing bright colours of the cartoon dashing across their small TV screen. After several more moments of deep thought, she stepped backward, nodding for Carol to pull the screen door open and enter her home.

'Harry, keep an eye on Lulu and Marvin for me,' she said. 'I'll be in the kitchen with Ms Joyce.'

Harry twisted around on the sofa and looked up at Carol for a long, intense moment. 'OK, Mama,' he said, but kept his eye on them as they passed through the living room into the small kitchen at the other end.

Scuffed cream vinyl peeled off the kitchen work surfaces, and Carol could see two more rooms through the door to the back of the kitchen, discarded children's clothes and toys flooding the floor of the closest one. Valerie caught Carol looking, so she quickly averted her gaze and sat in the chair Valerie pointed too.

'You want a drink? We've got iced tea, lemonade – not much else. I wasn't expecting company.'

'Iced tea would be great, thanks.' Carol made an effort with her smile, grateful and encouraging. She dropped her bag between her feet and flipped open the top, reaching in to get out her notepad and pen. Her fingers brushed against the tape recorder but she decided not to push her luck. 'Do you mind if I take notes?'

Valerie gave a tough laugh. 'I thought you'd want to record it.'

Carol felt her face fall to one of a naughty schoolgirl hiding contraband in her backpack.

Turning back with two full glasses of iced tea, Valerie surveyed Carol's expression. 'Do what you must,' she said with a sigh, pulling out a chair with her foot and setting the drinks down on the table. Carol fumbled back into her bag and retrieved the recorder and microphone. It took a few seconds for her to set it up in the middle of the table, Valerie eyeing it with derision as she sipped on her drink.

'So,' Carol said, clicking the two buttons down together on the recorder. 'You knew Reeta at the Jack-lowe Plantation – or as it was known on the inside, Pine Ranch.'

Valerie nodded.

'How close were you?'

'Closer than we were allowed to be,' Valerie responded after a moment of thick recollection. She looked down at her hands, which churned within one another. 'We became like sisters. She helped care for Sol…' Her voice faltered. 'Harrison, when he was first born. We *survived* that place together.'

'What did you need to survive?'

Valerie exhaled loudly, a watery snort. 'Everything. Too much to tell you.'

'There have been rumours of abuse. The father of Sally Henderson—'

'Oh, what does he know?' Valerie interrupted. 'One afternoon he came to Pine Ranch, one afternoon.' She held up a single shaking finger to emphasise her point. 'He only says that now after what happened – where was he then? Where was he so I didn't have to run thirteen miles in bare feet with my baby strapped to my back, just for the hope of freedom? Where were his rumours and suspicions when he had the chance and the resources to come in and actually see what was going on with his own two eyes? You know what I was doing when *Captain Henderson* was arguing with Jeb on the front field? Giving birth to a baby that was forced upon me. A baby I then wasn't allowed to nurse or tend to or play with – in case I loved him more than the precious *Brother Jeb*.' She practically spat the name. 'So that's what I say to Captain Henderson's fucking *rumours* of abuse.'

'Was the abuse widespread?' Carol forced the whisper, her pen yet to meet the page.

'You tell me.' Valerie nodded. 'You've seen how Reeta ended up.'

It was the answer Carol had dreaded, but the answer she hadn't known she couldn't take. In that moment a thick lump rose in her throat and tears burned her eyes like acid. She gasped and clasped a shaking hand over her mouth, lowering her head so Valerie couldn't catch her eye.

'I'm sorry,' she said, voice still shaking. 'I'm sorry, I...
I don't know what came over me.' She looked up and was
surprised to see Valerie's lips pulled into a small smile.

'That,' she said, gesturing to Carol's wet face with an
open palm, 'tells me that some of the Reeta I knew is still
in there.'

'What happened to her?' Carol barely wanted to ask.

'She was born on Pine Ranch,' Valerie said, sitting back
in her chair. 'She never knew anything else. No world
outside and no authority higher than Jeb. As we got older,
she began to question their ways. Not much and never
out loud, but I could see her resolve waver, her curiosity
deepen. She loved me. She loved my son. She loved her
mother. But that wasn't allowed. Jeb snatched her back
into his bosom as soon as he saw any of this in her. His
most dedicated follower, right to the very end.'

'She's not his follower now,' Carol said.

'No,' Valerie said, raising her eyebrows. 'I guess she's
not.'

Carol straightened up in her seat and dropped her pen
to her still clean pad. 'Valerie, will you come and see her?
I think it would help to know about her past.'

Valerie hesitated. 'I think it would be kinder to leave
her in the dark.'

'Please?' Carol found her tone embarrassingly
desperate. 'You're the only person I've met who knew
her back then. You're the only person who can tell her
who she is.'

A crash came from the other room, the cry of a young
baby following soon after. Valerie looked jerkily over her
shoulder and pushed back her seat. 'All right,' she said,
standing up. 'Let me talk to my husband, see if his parents

274

can watch the kids for a few days. If you have a card, leave it.' She nodded at the table. 'I'll call you.'

Thirteen

Oatmeal dripped thickly off her spoon, lumpy mounds in the disturbed breakfast. Reeta couldn't eat this morning. She'd barely eaten last night either, as her stomach gurgled with anxiety. All around her was the buzz of Saturday visits: mothers excitedly preparing to see their children, daughters counting down the minutes to see their parents. Wives awaited husbands, and Reeta whiled away her breakfast hours anticipating a stranger. Beatrice was talking animatedly about her new nephew, just nine months old, who was finally taking his first journey off the reservation to visit his aunt. Her brother had called from the motel last night, and the echo of the child's cries through the phone had brought warm smiles to those in the queue.

Reeta rarely had Saturday visitation; Carol was her only contact in the outside world and she lived north in Washington, DC, travelling the country in between her work responsibilities to track down the threads of Reeta's forgotten life. But this morning Carol was setting off from her favoured hotel in Atlanta with a second visitor for Reeta Doe in her passenger seat. Reeta had also used the phones last night, connecting to the family-run hotel whose reception staff had long since become used to the pre-recorded warning and put her call through to Carol's room without further question. Carol told her that she'd met Valerie at the airport and they'd driven together to the hotel. Reeta hadn't asked who had paid for Valerie's flight and accommodation – the unending financial bill of Carol's friendship was a burden too great to consider.

She queued up to scrape her leftover oatmeal into the trashcan, her back twisted to block the uneaten meal from the guard on duty. Beatrice was still gabbling excitedly, and Reeta threw her the odd smile and nod of encouragement. But Beatrice's words didn't land. The far door into the cafeteria clanged open and a fat custodial officer with a thin smile and quick baton hand called into the air, 'All right, ladies, shut the fuck up!'

Quiet settled across the room; only the sounds of clanging pans from the kitchen at the other end interrupted him. 'I've got roll call for Saturday morning visitation. Your guests are ready and waiting.' He laughed loudly and Reeta felt the slime of its echo sop at her skin. 'Line up when you hear your name!' He recited the list slowly and painfully, waiting for each inmate to make her way fully over to him, winding between the tables, before reading out the next.

'Reeeeeeta Doe!' The call came like a drum-roll. She nodded her goodbye to Beatrice and Gloria then sidled through the obstacles of the dining hall to join her place eleventh in line. The guard patrolled the line steadily, waiting closely by the new addition for a moment too long. When Reeta took her place, he hooked his index finger around a few strands of her loose hair and pulled them up toward him. Running his finger down its full length, he puckered his lips thickly and ran his eyes down her body. Not for the first time, she was relieved the prison uniform swamped her frame – a stick figure in a child's drawing. He moved back to the front of the line and continued his roll call. Beatrice wasn't far after Reeta, and attracted similar attention, but eventually after twenty-five stiff and awkward minutes he put his clipboard to one side and gestured for them to follow him. Six other guards, who had been lingering by the door throughout, fell into position to escort the waiting women.

Arbitrary body searches violated them as they passed through the prison security system, probing fingers and unnecessarily grabbing hands, but eventually they were brought to a door that led to the visitors' room and opened into the middle of two banks of thick glass dividers connected by phones. The women pressed forward, each desperate to get in to find their loved ones. The sound-proof glass made that central bank eerily quiet before the women found their seats and greeted their families, the phantom spectre of life beyond the glass failing to permeate into the world of the prison. Reeta heard a loud cooing from Beatrice and glanced across to see a chubby baby grabbing at his father's long braid, giggling as the hair tickled his face. Reeta allowed a smile and noted the glistening in Beatrice's eyes.

Three sections down from Beatrice, Reeta saw Carol, smiling anxiously, the phone gripped in her hand already. Carol was dressed demurely in a navy shirt with a patterned collar, her straightened hair tucked neatly behind her ears. Next to her was a woman in a purple polo-neck, jangling wooden bangles at her wrists and matching wooden hoops in her ears, a black bandana across the top of her forehead. She gasped when she saw Reeta, her mouth dropping inelegantly open. Reeta sat down and smiled nervously at the woman, noticing the stranger's fingers brace against the tabletop and a thick swallow judder her neck.

Carol nodded at the phone as a prompt, and Reeta fumbled for it. The woman had one on her side too but had yet to pick it up.

'Reeta, how have you been?' Carol asked, as if this were nothing but a simple catch-up. 'I'm sorry it's taken me so long to get down and visit you again.'

'It-it's OK,' Reeta said quietly, glancing at the woman. 'I've been all right. Nothing much to report.' She gave a shallow laugh and Carol smiled kindly in return.

'As you know, one of the people I've been anxious to speak to for my book is, well, Valerie Parker, now Valerie Jackson.' She smiled encouragingly and nodded over at the woman, as if a kindergarten teacher setting up a play date. 'She knew you at the Jacklowe Plantation – at Pine Ranch.'

Reeta nodded and gave a small smile at the woman, who continued to look at her in horror. It was rare for Reeta to meet new people, and the days of her fellow inmates staring in disgust at her twisted face had dwindled after the first year or so. She'd grown used to navigating her altered depth perception from only having sight in one eye and speaking without requiring too much from the right side of her mouth, so she was afforded the sanctuary of forgetting about her disfigurement at times. But now she could see the tight, settled scars and misaligned features reflected at her in Valerie Jackson's own expression. As if realising her gawp, Valerie blinked and gave an almost imperceptible shake of the head. She picked up the phone.

'Hi, Reeta,' she said softly, testing the words out.

'Hello,' Reeta replied. 'Thank you for coming all this way to see me.'

'I… I…' Valerie dropped her face down and shook her head, taking a moment to compose herself. When she looked back up, tears smudged her eyes. 'I can't believe it's really you.'

'I guess this' – Reeta gestured up at her face – 'must be a bit different from what you remember. It's all I've ever known, though.'

Valerie nodded, wide-eyed. 'I don't just mean that,' she said after a beat. 'I never thought I'd see you again. When I read about the fire, they said there were no survivors. I mourned you.' She paused and looked at her intently, a darkness descending somewhere behind her eyes. 'I mourned you as hard as my own family. I'd thought it would all end differently. I was so naïve and foolish.' She gave a thin laugh, mocking her past self. 'I thought you'd be freed, that we could go on together and live a life, have adventures like we were meant to.' Tears escaped now and she dabbed at them delicately with the backs of her middle fingers. 'I lost everyone in that fire. I'd been keeping an eye on the news, waiting to find out how to contact everyone who would be liberated. The mission I was in said they had room for my family if they came. I saved the bunk next to me for you.'

An unexpected and new feeling swept over Reeta. A sadness that for once didn't ache of guilt or regret, but instead throbbed with what might have been. She felt the tickle of a tear trace down her cheek.

'Anyway, it was only a few days and then there was news of the siege. I still kept my hopes up, especially when they sent the kids out. I thought perhaps Harrison, my brother Harrison... I named my son after him eventually,' she explained. 'I thought he'd be released, but then the news said no one older than eleven had come out. He'd have been twelve at that point.' She held her hand up, thumb and forefinger barely touching. 'His life nearly saved by this much.' Her hand dropped to the tabletop with a thud. 'We all know what happened after the children were sent out. I've thought about tracking them down over the years. The eldest would be nearly adults by now. But…' She shrugged and looked off to one side. 'They were all given homes, they're living their own lives. They don't need me dragging up a childhood they'd rather forget.' Suddenly her eyes were back on Reeta, fierce and probing. 'You got the gift of a lifetime for any Pine Ranch survivor.'

Reeta didn't know what to say. She darted a look to Carol, who was watching both women without expression. She settled on 'I don't know what happened there,' unsure if this would frustrate or appease Valerie.

Valerie sat back in the cheap plastic chair and it squeaked loudly in protest.

'You don't need to know.' Her voice was surprisingly kind, unexpectedly gentle.

For the first time in her short six-year life, Reeta felt a twinge of gratefulness for her condition. This woman spoke with the protection of a parent shielding their child from the terrible truth of the world. Reeta found herself trusting Valerie, believing that perhaps she didn't want to understand the details of her past after all. But next to this woman was Carol, unmoving and impassive, who'd spent the last six years fighting for the truth for Reeta. She couldn't turn that away, choose the easy option and give up. Her world was defined by actions she didn't remember, and Valerie might hold the key to that.

'I do,' she said, forcing a strength she didn't feel into her voice. 'I *do* need to know.'

Valerie gave a twisted smile, blowing her lips out with an incredulous sigh. 'You really want to know?' She sat

281

forward, one forearm on the table, the other raised to hold the phone firmly against her face, the mouthpiece pressing hard into her chin. 'We were starved,' she began, eyes daring Reeta to blanch at this first revelation. Reeta held her gaze. 'All the best food was saved for the men. We were worked to the bone, six days a week, hard physical labour interspersed with hours, *fucking hours*' – spittle flew from her lips – 'of Bible study and worship of the man claiming to be our prophet.' She spat her last word. 'But that wasn't just it, Reeta. We weren't allowed relationships, or friendships. I was separated from my family as soon as we arrived, and later from... from...' She paused and visibly collected herself. 'They separated me from my *son*.' She shook her head and looked up at the ceiling, as if bracing herself for what was to come. 'Only a few of us were chosen to carry his seed. It was meant to be an honour, Reeta, and we were so brainwashed we actually believed it was. We were *raped*.' The word landed on Reeta like a kick to the temple. 'You were thirteen when he chose you. Just a child.' Valerie's wet eyes narrowed in on Reeta's face, as if trying to see how much she could take.

Reeta had not moved; she had not reacted to Valerie's words. She had felt herself fuse to her chair, cement snaking up her veins so she might never move again.

'You got pregnant.' At this revelation, Reeta heard Carol's unexpected intake of breath through her previously silent receiver. 'And when you lost the baby, you were put in the basement without food for weeks. We thought you were going to die.' Her voice dropped. 'It's a miracle you didn't.'

Valerie looked between Reeta and Carol, whose cheeks glistened with tears under the strip lighting. 'So that's what made you, Reeta Doe. And frankly I could believe anything of a person who has known nothing but abuse, pain and deception. So now *you* tell *me*.' She jabbed her free finger at the thick glass between them. Her face hardened; her mouth pulled tight. 'Who started that fire? Did *you* kill my family?'

Reeta felt the question like a cannon ball to the gut. It winded her more than when she'd been jumped outside the commissary her first week here. It was an agony deeper than the searing ache of her face when she'd woken up in hospital. And the guilt scorched hotter than she'd ever had to contend with over her trial.

Next to Valerie, the phone slipped out of Carol's hand, her eyes wide with shock and horror. She fumbled to pick it up again, hands visibly trembling.

Reeta stared between the two women on the other side of the glass for what felt like a minute stretched to breaking point. When she spoke, the words blistered her throat.

'I... I don't know. How... how could I know?'

Valerie opened her mouth to speak but paused a moment to swallow back thick tears. 'Because only two people walked away from that fire. And I know one of them doesn't get his own hands dirty.' Valerie slammed the phone down and stood up, striding off toward the exit. Carol watched her leave, then looked back at Reeta with a startled expression mingled with dread.

Fourteen

'How did it go?' Ben sounded tired on the other end of the phone.

It was Sunday night and Carol had flown home after Valerie bid her an icy goodbye at the bus station. 'You shouldn't have asked me to see her,' she'd said through the window of Carol's car. 'I don't know how you found me, but make sure you never do again.'

'It was hard,' Carol answered Ben honestly now.

Ben sighed gruffly and Carol envisaged him running his hands through his hair, which he did when he was stressed.

'Hard for who?' he asked.

'Everyone, I guess.'

'How was Valerie?'

Carol sighed. 'Upset, of course she was – the stuff they went through there.' She shook her head and sat back against her headboard, the bedspread twisted around her legs as she struggled to get comfortable. 'She asked if Reeta set the fire.'

'Carol, you're a fool if you haven't asked yourself that question,' Ben replied, and Carol noted the edge to his voice.

'Well, what does she expect her to say?' Carol snapped. 'She can't fucking remember anything.'

'The world isn't such a blank for everyone else who orbited this girl, you know.'

'And what's that supposed to mean?'

'You know what that means. Maybe it's time you stopped harassing her traumatised victims just because you've got a soft spot for her.'

'You've changed your tune, Ben. You were the one who gave me Valerie, remember?' Carol heard the faint sound of breaking glass through the phone and a soft '*Shit,*' under Ben's breath. 'Everything all right?'

'No, it's fucking not all right.' Ben's voice was tight, stressed. 'I broke my glass.'

'Have you cut yourself?'

'I'll be fine.' He exhaled deeply and loudly. 'Carol, listen, I shouldn't have given you Valerie. You should let her live in peace.'

'I've spoken to her now. I'll leave her alone.'

'Look.' He spoke with an air of finally reaching the thing he'd wanted to say when he'd dialled her number. 'I'm out, I'm done helping you with the book.'

Carol sat up urgently, the phone clammy in her hand. 'But you said you'd get me Bonnie. You know I need to speak to her.' She felt a frantic panic tickle at her insides.

'I'm out,' he repeated. 'Whatever you want from her, forgiveness or a reason to think Reeta's innocent or *whatever* – I can't give it to you.'

'You can't just be out, Ben! We *both* need this. I know you, so don't tell me you don't want answers as much as I do.'

'She made a fucking complaint against me.' Ben's voice was loud and strained as he interrupted, and she knew he hadn't been listening.

285

'Y-you didn't tell me that.' Carol fell back against her headboard, knocking painfully against the wood. She felt her ally slipping away into the tide that also took with it the answers she so desperately wanted.

'I knew you had the big meeting yesterday,' Ben replied matter-of-factly. 'Richard called me into his office on Friday. Asked why I was harassing the wife of a partner at one of the biggest finance firms on Wall Street. I'm already on thin ice, Carol; in fact, I don't know how I've survived this far. But I'm not doing it again. I'm not fucking up my career *again*, for—'

'For me?' Carol asked.

'Yeah,' he admitted with a breath of exasperation. 'Yeah, for you to stomp all over me again.'

'Ben, that's not—' A surge of guilt rose through her.

'Goodbye,' he said. 'If you want my advice, leave them all alone. Write about your friend if you must, but leave the people she devastated out of it.'

Ben clicked off and Carol surprised herself with a thick sob. After all this time, she hadn't wanted to lose Ben again.

–

Valerie had departed the prison impatient and angry, as if she'd expected Reeta's memory to return, a long-lost wanderer just waiting for the path home along the route of tortured reality Valerie had set for it. But her words had navigated nothing inside Reeta; the images she'd conjured as Valerie had spoken were ones of faceless individuals, a rough outline of the compound gleaned from news articles. She still couldn't see the fire, couldn't feel the flames against her skin. Were the deaths of the Pine Ranch residents also sagging on her conscience? It had been proved – unanimously, according to a jury of her peers – that she'd been capable of four brutal murders already. What were another eighty or so souls?

Reeta sat on the hard concrete yard in the late afternoon sun, the mesh wire fence pressing into her spine. The ground in front of her shimmered in the heat, like silky ribbons fallen from a young girl's hair. Desert scrubland surrounded the several layers of fences, the jackrabbits, coyotes and reptiles under the same scrutiny of the armed guards, surveying from their towered posts. A gecko had scurried through the fence, small darting movements exploring this new environment. It froze and sprinted uncertainly, aware that this wasn't its home any more. It took refuge in the shadow of Reeta's elongated legs, settling on the darkened concrete, evidently unaware that the unmoving figure was, in fact, alive. Reeta watched it for a while, their shared ability for stillness matched only in each other amongst the basketball games and constant movement of those in the yard. One living creature on this planet that did not recognise her as a threat. The whistle came to end their designated hour of simulated freedom, and Reeta was loath to bend her legs to clamber up – knowing as soon as she did, her new companion would scarper away, darting and panicking in search of better salvation.

The cool darkness of her cell was welcome after the stuffy humidity of the visitors' room and harsh heat of the exercise yard. She fell onto her bed, not adjusting herself around the broken springs that pierced her body. For the first time that day she allowed Valerie's words to settle. Her fingertips danced across her concave stomach, trying to imagine the feeling of starvation as a child. She ran her thumb across those callused fingertips, trying to remember if the cracked, dry skin predated her prison life, forever marked by hours of physical labour. Her hand stretched flat across her abdomen; had she really been pregnant? Had she really been violated the way Valerie described? Disgust surged through her, but it soared on a feeling of numbness. The words were revolting, but the feeling was absent.

She knew now there was nothing inside to recover. There was no life to salvage inside of Reeta Doe. She had known only abuse, pain and deception, and she had brought nothing but abuse, pain and deception.

Blackness was all she deserved.

The next morning at breakfast her silence was unnoticed among Beatrice and Gloria's bickering over Reeta's uneaten toast. Neither woman cared why she had not wanted it herself, their thoughts on only their own rumbling stomachs. She followed them silently to the chapel after they were dismissed from breakfast and commenced the cleaning duties she'd done a thousand times before. Every inch of that chapel had been buffed by Reeta's hand at one time. Every peeling bit of carpet, every bloom of mould was known to her.

Every splintered pew.

Old wood, barely cared for, kicked repeatedly in the same spot every Sunday, began to peel and split. Shards sprung proud against the floor, nicking at Reeta's arms as she polished patiently around them, trickles of scarlet painting her skin.

Some long-lost instinct from somewhere inside her died as her hand encircled the largest of the splintered stakes, wrenching it free. Her palm pricked with hair-like splinters, pain receptors catching every time they brushed against something. She tucked the stake down the side of her trousers, through the waistband of her underwear. Her tunic top swamped her small body, so any lumps from within her trousers were lost to the fabric.

She relished the pain of it cutting into her thigh as she moved about her chores. There was a satisfaction in the discomfort she knew she deserved as she sat down for dinner, her mouth an unavoidable grimace around the boiled rice that would be her last meal.

Teeth pinned her lips together that night on her bed, her empty pillowcase wrapped around her mouth to muffle any instinctive sound of agony.

The stake tore her skin apart, shredded long gashes down her forearm, the blunt splinters driven into her veins with only the strength of the desperate.

Burgundy drenched her grey nightgown, sticky, warm and wet, pooling down into her bedsheet, spreading like a portal to hell.

White light fuzzed her vision, and she found she could no longer concentrate on the shapes of her cell around her. Her grip slackened; she had no choice but to drop the wood splinter to the floor, her head swimming and rocking into unconsciousness.

Her head met the pillow, a soft, welcome embrace.

And oblivion came once more for Reeta Doe.

Fifteen

New York was not one of Carol's favourite places. Grand Central bustled around her, pressing too close against her body. Impatient men in pinstripe suits and trench coats barged past, while scruffy youngsters attempted to pick their wallets. Carol tightened her hold on her crocodile-skin handbag and steadied herself in navy-blue pumps, preparing to dodge away from sticky fingers at any moment. The train hadn't been long, but she'd been impatient the whole way, toes twitching against the dull, patterned carpet, beating out an uneven rhythm. She'd drunk black coffee in the restaurant car but balked at the cheap breakfast sandwich spilling down the chin of the man in the next booth. Her stomach growled at her now, the smell of pretzel stands and pizza slices awakening her hunger. It wasn't the cosmopolitan frenzy that made her uncomfortable. Washington, DC had its own hectic dance – a similar buzz of power, money, crime and filth that kept the city spinning. But New York was where she'd grown up – a disturbingly bland upbringing where she'd never known the truth of who she was. New York was a passive deceit in place of Washington's outright dishonesty. If you knew you were surrounded with crooks at every turn, nothing was a surprise. But in New York you didn't know where to look, which corner to beware of, who to trust.

Three cabs passed her before one responded to her waving arm, and the memory of her blonde mother having to step forward to hail taxis for her sparked somewhere.

'East 85th and Park,' she said, sliding onto the plastic-covered seat. A portrait of a heavy-eyed Virgin Mary stared out at her through the driver's divide, and a rosary looped around the rear-view mirror jangled as the driver silently pulled back out into traffic. She flipped open her handbag and pulled out the battered notebook stuffed with scraps of paper and notes. Nerves tingled her stomach in a way they so rarely did these days. She'd been a journalist for nearly twenty years now; interviewing an unwilling subject was barely a daunting prospect. But Bonnie was key – she *needed* her voice. Bonnie and Reeta together made this story – victim and perpetrator – and Carol couldn't help but feel she still had only half of it.

It wasn't the way she'd wanted to do it but when Ben had backed out, she'd been left with no choice. For every week obsessed with finding Valerie Jackson, at least two had been dedicated to her musings of Bonnie. The girl who had survived but had nothing to say. The girl who had turned away from those closest to her in her hour of most desperate need, choosing instead to dedicate her life to a man she barely knew. It had bothered Carol back then when she had first seen the girl's rehearsed testimony. Reviewing the transcripts had brought much of it back over the years – Bonnie had answered questions briefly and without emotion, refused to look up at the accused and identified her only with a nervous, half-raised finger. Shell shock, some doctors suggested – new thinking believed it could be triggered from events outside of war and there was no denying it could change a person from within. An event like that at any stage in life, let alone at only nineteen years of age, could force anyone to re-evaluate their very soul.

The address was a penthouse apartment in the Upper East Side, close to the park. Carol had had a colleague call Henry Chandola's firm the day before, claiming to be writing a piece on upcoming traders under thirty to watch out for. Once their credentials had been checked, the secretary was only too happy to provide Mr Chandola's personal contact details to arrange an interview. But today was a workday, and Mr Chandola would not be present at the interview Carol intended to conduct.

Carol knew the street well when the cab pulled up – the Upper East Side was familiar grounding for the supposed daughter of Brian Joyce. She'd not been back in years as there were no long-lost friends to catch up with, no elderly parents to visit with bouquets of flowers. Just another place she knew she didn't belong. As far apart as these streets of pale-bricked townhouses and cherry blossom trees were to her father's Southside Chicago home, they all had that one thing in common.

She had no place in either of them.

The Chandolas' building was tall with blonde brick, a lavish red and gold awning out front with a doorman dressed in formal livery. Carol peered out of the taxi's window, checking the address on the slip of paper with the number and building name on the plaque beside the door. The taxi slowed to a stop, tucking into a vacant space on the other side of the street. Carol paid the man and climbed out, taking a few moments to straighten herself up before approaching.

The doorman greeted Carol with a distracted welcome smile. Waving her business card was enough to get her through the door and up to see the wife of the man she was profiling for her *Washington Post* article. 'I think she's expecting me,' Carol explained with her well-practised easy air of belonging. Her nice clothes and elegant gait were certainly not cause for concern for the building staff trained to keep an eye out for hoodlums and gangs.

The elevator was one of the old style, with a grille she pulled noisily closed, having to shove her entire weight into the side to get it to reach the far end. The penthouse was number 56, and a neat gold plaque with a hand-written note declaring *The Chandolas* told her she was in the right place.

She knocked and after a few moments a short Asian woman answered the door, her face scrunched into perplexity.

'May I help you?' the housekeeper asked suspiciously, her accent strong.

'Hello.' Carol smiled politely. 'I'm here to see Mrs Chandola. Mrs Bonnie Chandola?'

'Mrs C not in,' the housekeeper answered, making to shut the door again.

'Are you sure?' Carol pushed. 'Do you know where she is?'

The housekeeper narrowed her eyes suspiciously. 'Who are you?'

'A friend.' Carol replied, keeping it vague.

'I've never seen you before. Mrs C doesn't have friends.'

'I'm an old friend from her past.' As soon as she said it, she knew it was the wrong thing to have done. The housekeeper grunted loudly and reached to slam the door, her parting words just audible from behind the heavy oak as it shut.

'Nobody from past.'

Carol banged on the door again, loud, desperate pounds with the side of her fist. After a few minutes the door swung open again with an aborted sentence.

'What in hell is going on—?' Bonnie Chandola stopped talking as soon as her eyes found Carol's face and widened in recognition. 'You.'

'Hello, Bonnie,' Carol said, composing herself from her previous racket on the door. Without her headscarf, Bonnie's injuries were far more shocking than Carol had expected. Half of her temple was collapsed in on itself, a concave chunk in place of a forehead. Her chin was split by a heavy scar and one eye drooped dramatically. 'I've been trying to get in touch with you.'

'You've been harassing me.'

'I don't think—'

'And you've been using your friend at the FBI to do it.'

'I think it's important that we speak.' Carol tried to collect herself in the face of Bonnie's deformity. She tried not to be distracted by the evident pain the girl had gone through.

Bonnie blew out a sigh. 'I don't know what you possibly think we could have to speak about.'

'I'm writing a book.'

'So I've heard.'

'I want your story to be in it.'

Bonnie looked at her carefully and made to swing the door shut.

'Please?' Carol said, stepping forward to block the door with her leg. 'I want to get to know you. The way I know Reeta.'

Reeta's name seemed to be the key. At the sound of it, Bonnie inhaled tensely and closed her eyes. She stood like that for a moment before stepping back, holding the door open as she did.

'Thank you,' Carol said quietly and entered the apartment.

'I don't know why I'm letting you in.'

Bonnie led her slowly through the impressive hallway and into the open lounge that was flanked by long French windows, looking out onto a large balcony. Carol could hear the maid fussing about in the kitchen behind a thick closed door.

'I don't imagine you get to talk about that night much these days,' Carol said by way of suggesting an explanation.

Bonnie gestured for Carol to sit, but remained standing herself, arms folded, back to the balcony. Carol sat on the end of the sofa closest to Bonnie and surveyed her again. She stood at an odd angle and still walked with the cane she'd used at the trial, which she leaned on heavily as she stood. Carol took in her chic white shirt that fell in such a way she knew it was expensive.

'All right,' Bonnie said impatiently, interrupting Carol's assessment. 'You've got my attention. What do you want from me?'

'Why don't you speak to your family?' It wasn't the first question Carol had expected to ask but it had come out all the same.

Bonnie looked startled for a moment, as much as her face was able to betray such an emotion.

'I don't see how that's relevant.'

'It's part of your story. Which is what I want to tell.'

'My parents...' Bonnie waved a hand dismissively before bringing it up to tuck her now-bobbed blonde hair behind her ear. 'They don't know me. Not any more.

And…' She stopped to consider for a moment. 'I'm not sure I want them to.'

'You refused to see anyone in hospital.'

'As was my right.'

'You met Henry soon after?'

Bonnie's eyes jerked away. 'He's taken care of me. Promised to look after me – who am I to refuse that?'

Carol nodded and wished she could look in her notebook, but it was in her bag at her feet and she feared that any movement could break the spell of Bonnie's willingness to speak.

'Reeta,' she said after a beat.

Bonnie's head twitched. 'Reeta,' she repeated and the name sounded soft, familiar in her mouth.

'She's not the same person.' Carol hadn't thought she'd come here to defend Reeta. She'd thought she'd come for the story. But Ben, as ever, had known her better than she had known herself, and now, faced with Reeta's final victim – the *only* victim Carol could face – she had only the urge to clear her friend's name.

'I'll bet she's not.'

'What makes you say that?'

'*I'm* not the same person either.' Carol watched her carefully, saw her hackles rise in the way she shifted her weight to another foot and shoved one hand into her jean pocket, the diamond from her engagement ring twinkling as she did. 'Look,' Bonnie said impatiently, 'is this really all you wanted to say?'

Carol got to her feet; her stomach was vibrating as uncertainty coursed through her. 'Could I use your bathroom?' she asked. She needed to cool down and collect herself before she could continue.

Bonnie sighed as she bowed her head before nodding to the door they'd just come through. 'Out there, third door on the left.'

Carol followed her instructions and once she was in the gilded bathroom, she closed the toilet seat and sat down. It took a few well-practised breaths to steady her breathing and push down the rising anxiety. When she stood, she went to the sink and turned the faucet, holding wet fingers against her eyes like she had done in the court bathroom when she'd first met Bonnie six years ago. Feeling steadier, she pulled the door to and made her way back to the living room.

It was now empty, but Carol could hear voices behind the kitchen door.

'Jesus Christ, you've smashed them all.' Bonnie sounded irritated and Carol heard the maid begin to apologise but was cut over by Bonnie's chiding.

While Bonnie dealt with her domestic emergency, Carol paced the room and inspected its polished oak furniture with inlaid mother of pearl and gold leaf details. She ran a hand along the perfectly polished sideboard, taking in the lack of photographs. Not even a wedding photograph or holiday snap. There was a squash trophy bearing Henry's name, and a display of crystal decanters with little silver signs declaring what was inside. Carol's hand found the small golden knob of one of the drawers and tugged it, revealing a collection of shining silver cutlery. She didn't know what she was doing but journal-istic instinct and sheer nosiness could often be confused, so she continued down the sideboard, tugging open the stiff drawers and taking in the contents of old bills and paperwork, a thick stack of placemats, and – in the third one she tried – a small wooden box with a looped clasp keeping it closed. She flipped the clasp down and opened the box, still hearing Bonnie informing her maid how expensive those glasses had been.

Carol looked down and felt her heart shudder to a halt.

She glanced quickly up to the kitchen door and, confident that Bonnie wasn't coming through, picked up the photograph that lay on top of the folded papers inside.

This changed everything.

She scrutinised every detail, desperately trying to fit it into place. But she couldn't. Her mind was blank; she couldn't remember the details she needed to. She flipped shut the box and shoved the drawer closed, the photograph still clutched in her palm. Her insides trembling with the weight of an earthquake, she grabbed her bag and fled the apartment, shoving the contraband into the inside pocket as the door swung shut behind her. She barely said 'Thank you' to the doorman as he guided her out, and she hurried with short, desperate footsteps down the street and away from that godforsaken penthouse.

Carol managed to get the five o'clock commuter train back to Washington, DC, crowded and smelling of sweat, newspapers rustling, pens scratching answers into crossword puzzles. She felt dizzy as she leaned her head against the juddering window, allowing the uncomfortable vibration to jolt her thoughts. Her hands slid into her bag and pulled out the photograph and the Montblanc pen she'd inherited from her stepfather. Mr Joyce had no children of his own and so had gifted the twelve-year-old Carol his pen from his deathbed, knowing that she already showed the aptitude to write. That and the introduction letter he'd left for his old friend and editor of the *Hamptons Messenger* were the kindest things he had ever done for her.

The nib of the pen hit the back of the photo, black ink spilling out the cataloguing her journalistic training had ingrained in her.

Found in Bonnie Chandola's apartment. Sept 14th 1972.

She stared at it a moment longer, and an explanation finally fell into position. The only thing that made sense – the thing Carol had seen from the very beginning but couldn't quite put her finger on. She lowered her pen and added two more words to the back of the picture.

She needed to speak to Ben. Needed to ask him why they'd been so desperate to lock up the poor creature that had been Reeta Doe.

The phone was ringing off the hook when she finally made it home, a frantic, tangled sound as if the phone itself knew of the news on its other end.

'Hello?' she answered, breathless, lifting the receiver in her kitchen. The front door was still falling closed.

'Carol, Jesus, where the hell have you been? I've been ringing you all day.' It was Ben. Agitated and staccato.

'I've been in New York for the day. What's happened?'

'There's been an incident at the prison. She was found this morning.'

The words hit Carol like a truck. As Ben relayed the details from Balmen, Carol thought of the photograph in her bag, and of the life that had been so desperately wasted.

And she felt a shot of agony sear down her left arm. She staggered back and fell against the wall, the phone falling by her side as her hand went to clutch at her chest. Her breath wouldn't come. She battled for another gasp of air, but was met with only tight, suffocating pain.

'Carol?' Ben's tinny voice swung at the end of the abandoned phone cord. 'Carol, are you still there?'

Part III

Freedom

January 1983

One

Reeta was not handed a plastic bag of her belongings. The only known possessions she'd ever owned were the blood-drenched clothes the paramedics had cut off her at the scene of the accident seventeen years ago. The court clothes from Barry were never returned to her and she'd been in institutionalised garb ever since. All the commissary knick-knacks she'd accumulated over her time in Balmen had been donated to the various acquaintances she'd made. Beatrice and Gloria were both gone, replaced over the years by other inmates. There had been periods of solitude, with no friends to speak of, and periods of boom, with a full group to sit with, eat dinner and play cards. Neither period stood out to Reeta – she had long since grown used to the idea that she would outlive all their tenures at Balmen. Even Lil' Philly had walked through the gates that now beckoned Reeta. Lil' Philly had benefited from the full showmanship of her case – the NAACP had invited press and notable politicians to speak out about her, tirelessly campaigning and appealing to get her time in front of the parole board. Times were changing and suddenly keeping a black woman locked up just for protecting her daughter was an embarrassment rather than justice. There was no such circus around Reeta's own parole appeals and perhaps under any other lawyer she would never have made it. But Barry had worked just as hard as Lil' Philly's team – any appeal he could file and any expert he could have assess her was hired. There had been a slow shift in attitude as the Eighties had rolled in, a slightly more liberal parole board with just a little more sympathy for the injuries that blotted her face. The interview itself had been a blur, a false hope she hadn't dared believe in. It had never occurred to her that Barry would come true on his near-two-decade-long promise to get her out.

Her peaceful prison life, including her solid dedication to the chapel, had all stood her in good stead for proof of rehabilitation. Even her suicide attempt was deemed to show remorse, but the fact that it was a solo episode eleven years ago demonstrated a renewed strength of character. She'd seen a couple of headlines about her impending release, each one half-heartedly trying to raise protest and discord. But the truth was that, like Reeta Doe herself, her crimes were basically forgotten. The friends of the victims, those who'd given testimony at court, didn't reappear to once again have their say.

Three others were also being released that day, thick plastic carriers clutched in their hands while they shuffled uncomfortably through processing. The clothes they wore looked wrong on them somehow, as if not one of them was the same person they had been when they'd first entered Balmen. Reeta wore grey sweats with a matching sweatshirt, picked up by a sympathetic guard from a Kmart nearby. The others whispered about the world they were re-entering, what would have changed, what remained a constant. But for Reeta there was no buzz of comparison, only trepidation of the unknown. She had never lived in the outside world before.

A thirty-seven-year-old newborn.

The gates were finally pulled apart and cheers and whoops splashed over the fences of the exercise yard. Her fellow releasees called back excited yells of farewell, promises to write and send commissary payments. Reeta remained quiet, trembling limbs too scared to move forward. Three cars were scattered around the parking lot and two of the no-longer incarcerated women raced forward to greet their families.

'Well, *he* ain't here for me,' the third said, looking to Reeta and jerking her head in the direction of the final car, a sedate black sedan. '*That's* my ride.' She raised her hand in the direction of the decommissioned school bus that provided new releases a free ride into town if they had no one to pick them up.

'He's for me,' Reeta confirmed with a low voice.

The girl looked at her a moment longer, a deep, penetrating gaze. Reeta hadn't come to know her during her time at Balmen, but the girl obviously knew her story. Finally, the girl barked a laugh.

'Good luck,' she said, slapping Reeta on the back. 'You gonna need it.' She swung her bag over her shoulder and made her way toward the bus, climbing on two steps at a time – a schoolchild ready to start the day.

Reeta walked slowly toward the car. Its driver now stood outside the open driver-side door, having spotted her against the imposing backdrop of the prison complex.

'Reeta,' he said with an uncertain smile. Thin lips crooked in a face sagging with age and grief.

'Agent Willow,' Reeta said with a nod, coming to a stop in front of the car.

'Please. Call me Ben.'

Reeta knew she would never call him Ben.

He gave her a once-over and nodded. 'I didn't think you'd have anything. I've got you a few essentials.' He tipped his head toward the car. 'But we can stop off and get you some more.'

She nodded silently.

'Well, er...' He cast about the parking lot, one car pulling out, one former inmate and her family still gripping each other tightly. 'Should we get going?'

Reeta shuffled awkwardly forward, expecting to be stopped at any moment. Called back that there had been a mistake — of course she wouldn't be permitted life in the real world. Seeing her move, he sat back down in the car and pulled his door to, watching her from behind the windscreen. The cold of the door handle against her palm shivered her arm, an electric bolt to her joints. She pulled it open and smelled an unexpected blend of coffee and pine air freshener.

'It's a long drive back north,' he said when she sat down next to him, hands awkwardly pressed between her thighs. 'I've booked us a motel on the border of South Carolina for tonight. And if we get an early start in the morning, we should make it back by tomorrow evening.'

Reeta nodded again, unsure of what she could possibly say.

'Do you mind the radio?' he asked and she could tell he was babbling from nerves of his own. Her silence demanded to be filled. 'I like the country stations down here,' he said, putting the car into drive and pulling out. 'Music with a story, like it used to be. This modern electronic stuff doesn't really do it for me.' He chuckled softly. 'Funny how I used to rage at my father for hating on rock'n'roll. If I had any kids now, they'd be ranting at me that I "just don't understand".' He pulled a face and shrugged toward her, a facsimile of two old friends sharing their observations on ageing. Reeta had no observations on ageing, aside from the lines that had begun to etch into the skin on her face that wasn't already scar tissue. She had no opinion on music then or now. Willow leaned forward to flip the radio on so folksy guitar filled the car. She noticed his shoulders relax – his self-assigned role of filling the silence passed on.

Country music accompanied them for a couple of hours before Willow pulled into the parking lot of a motel with two storeys of red doors, a leaf-drowned pool and a cheap-looking diner attached. Reeta was starving – she'd barely eaten last night and breakfast this morning had seemed an impossible task. Somehow Willow knew this, and he directed her immediately towards the diner, steamed-up windows and the blurred outlines of life inside blinding against the dark evening. Reeta swallowed and took comfort in the breeze of the night air on her face. Willow had gone ahead and was holding open the door, glancing back toward her while he smiled a hello to the server. It had probably not occurred to him that, for the woman in his charge, this was the first time she would ever eat in a restaurant. The first time she would mingle with the general public. The first time she would be permitted to choose what was on her plate. The possibilities were overwhelming and Reeta felt a sudden lurch in her stomach. Burning bile flooded up her throat and she turned back to the car, retching on the ground behind it, one hand steadied on its trunk.

Jogging footsteps grew louder and she felt a hand on her upper back. 'Reeta,' Willow said, concerned. 'Are you OK?'

She wiped her mouth with the back of her hand and straightened up, looking him in the eye properly for the first time. His grey hair shimmered under the street light, the way she remembered his youthful blonde had glistened under industrial strip lighting in the Florida jail.

'I'll be fine.' She looked toward the diner, the concerned waitress peering out through the glass door. 'Come on, let's eat.'

They settled into a booth, the only one that was free. The diner was busy: local families crowded together, single travellers propping up the bar. The scent of stale alcohol, burnt coffee and cooking grease crammed the room, alongside children's shouts, parents' sighs and a sports commentator from the TV on the bar. The plastic-covered menu in front of Reeta was huge, and the photographs of dripping burgers and frothy milkshakes turned her stomach again. She had barely heard of most of the food items, dumbfounded by choice. The waitress returned and asked what they'd like, Reeta still staring at the unending options in panic.

'We'll both have the house burger, ranch dressing, fries, pickles on the side. And two chocolate milkshakes,' Willow replied.

Reeta looked up, an unexpected smile nudging her lips.

'Figured you've never been to a diner before.' He nodded down at the menu. 'Or at least not one you remember. I got us the best stuff on the menu.' He grinned at her, and she found herself reciprocating.

'Thank you.'

-

Willow watched the woman in front of him slurp on her milkshake like a child. Her face had lightened immediately with her first taste, her scars seeming softer all at once. The wounds had settled over the years, shiny skin in place of angry red, but it was still twisted and mangled, her lips not quite in the right place, one eye heavy under the weight of its damage, nose at an angle. He'd watched her pretend not to notice the waitress's reaction as she'd sat them down, pretended not to hear the gawping child's loud questions to his mom behind them.

He was glad he'd agreed to pick her up from Balmen. When the news had come of her release date, he'd known he had no other option. It was what Carol would have wanted and the girl – no, woman – had no one else. She wouldn't survive out here unless he took care of her. Whatever she'd done, she'd paid her dues. The parole board had made their decision and it wasn't for him to disagree. All that was left was to try to rescue whatever remained of the life of Reeta Doe.

The burgers arrived and he saw from Reeta's expression she'd forgotten all about them. His own milkshake was thick and filling, so he'd only had a few mouthfuls. She'd demolished hers within minutes. On a stomach that was used to prison slop, she'd be sick – again.

'Go slowly with that,' he said.

She nodded in agreement and picked up a fry, popping it in her mouth. 'Fuck,' she whispered. 'That's delicious.'

He laughed and reached for the ketchup bottle, squirting out a dollop on the edge of her plate. 'Wait till you try that.' He nodded.

She rolled her eyes. 'I've had ketchup before,' she said. 'And fries. But' – she looked down at her plate – '*fuck* – not like this.'

'Welcome to America. Where everything is deep-fried and covered in sugar.'

She grinned. 'That sounds amazing.'

After they'd eaten, Reeta picking slowly at her burger, visibly stuffing every inch of her stomach, Willow ordered them a couple of beers. The glass bottles were set down and Reeta pulled a face at her first sip. 'I think I preferred the milkshake.'

'What? You didn't try any booze inside?'

'Tracey's rotten-apple hooch wasn't exactly my bag,' Reeta said.

'Well, go slowly with this then. Don't wanna get you drunk.'

A pleasant silence fell over them, both sated and finally relaxing into the strange situation in which they found themselves. Willow had eventually decided his role wasn't to fill every gap in conversation, and it seemed Reeta was happy to just sit for a while, taking in the momentous prospect of her freedom.

It was inevitable, really, that she eventually asked, 'Was she happy, when it happened?'

He shrugged. 'Hard to say. It happened so quickly.' His eyes grew hot as he remembered the aborted call the day Reeta had been found in her cell. He'd heard a strained wheeze after a few moments of terrifying silence and had immediately hung up, called 911 and rushed over to meet the ambulance at her house. But it was too late. Suddenly the *one day* he'd been waiting for to tell her he forgave her, and how he truly felt about her, had been snatched away – and he'd been the one to deliver the news that had caused it.

After he'd stepped back from helping with the book, he'd had to keep his distance. No more cosy Chinese takeaways or long nights of laughter over red wine. When he'd been called into Richard's office back then, his boss's lip had curled up in scorned confusion, an incredulous laugh of 'She really that good in the sack?' after he'd relayed the complaint they'd received from Henry and Bonnie Chandola. Every time Ben found himself wound up with Carol Joyce, somehow she seemed to kick him in the nuts. His male pride had been trampled on time and again, his back still bruised from her stiletto marks.

So he'd never told her how proud he was of her.

How her tenacity, her ambition, her strength were never a burden but an inspiration. How her capacity to feel for Reeta had tugged only a jealous spite that she'd never afforded him the same attention. How many times he'd wanted to snake his arm around her back, to pull her in for a deep kiss, to make her laugh with her bright, wide smile.

It had been Willow who was tasked with sorting her belongings, as the main beneficiary of her will. Carol's mother had died young and so Carol had always had a healthy awareness of her own mortality. And yet she had always failed to take into account her father's genetic heart condition. Willow supposed it was easy to forget a biological link to a man who'd only shown up in your adulthood, easy to forget that the heart beating in your own chest was made of the same weak material as his. She'd had her own will since she was thirty, something Ben would tease her about – a gentle ribbing that barely hid his frustrations of her morbidity. 'None of us are promised tomorrow,' she'd reply with a shrug and, as ever, she'd turned out to be right. Much of her liquid capital had been donated to various causes around the country, some to her half-siblings in Chicago. But her home in Bloomingdale had been left to Willow, and a healthy monthly commissary allowance would continue to be paid into Reeta Doe's account.

It had taken months before he was ready to use the key the lawyer had handed him and enter Carol's home. He'd packed away the clothes the hospital morgue had handed him in a plastic bag with a nod of condolence, and the crocodile-skin handbag he found still abandoned at the foot of the stairs, and then locked the house back up for ten years. He could never quite bring himself to sell it – to profit from Carol's death. That house had been so ingrained in her, such a part of who she was. The place was entrenched in Willow's happy memories with her, so he'd just paid the bills for its upkeep and kept on top of the leaking roof or cracked windowpanes over the years. Only when he got news of Reeta Doe's release did he understand what he'd been saving it for.

It was what Carol would have wanted – to provide Reeta a home when she was free.

He'd never even found out what she'd been doing in New York the day she'd died.

He took a deep slug of beer and pulled his gaze from his shredded beer label to look into Reeta's face: innocent, mournful, curious.

'Yeah,' he said softly. 'I like to think she was happy.'

Two

They returned to the diner for breakfast. Pancakes fluffier than Reeta had ever seen – maple syrup drenching them in deep sweetness – left her overwhelmed by the plate in front of her. It was early, but Reeta had been awake for hours already – her body not yet used to the freedom to sleep as long as it wanted. The bed had been comfortable, too comfortable, and she'd tossed and turned, unsure where to put her limbs in all the space available. At four a.m. she'd given up on any attempt at sleep and taken a long hot shower, the luxury of which she'd never quite realised she'd been missing. Willow had brought her shampoo and conditioner that smelled, apparently, of honeysuckle and wildflowers. She lathered her body with a green gel that tingled with minty freshness, and when she was done she wrapped herself up in a towel that was big enough to cover her entire body. Hair dripping down her back, she got dressed in her grey Kmart tracksuit and went to sit by the clogged pool on a broken plastic chair. The world slowly awoke around her; a tabby cat stalked around one edge of the pool, batting its paw at something below the water's surface. A car pulled into the parking lot and a man climbed out with a travel mug then went to open the motel's office. Another man in a crumpled suit rushed from his room, the sound of his clock radio alarm chasing him out the door to his car, where he raced towards the road.

So this was the outside world.

'Breakfast?' Willow had asked from behind her and she turned and nodded with a close-lipped smile, blinking into the rising red sun.

He'd chosen something she'd never heard of from the menu and two eggs soaked with a thick yellow sauce had turned up, weighing down an English muffin. 'You wanna try?' he asked and she nodded, wiping her fork on her napkin and leaning forward to scoop out a cross-section. It tasted – full. Full was the only way to describe the creamy sauce and rounded egg yolk, a distant hint of acidic tang.

'Good?' he asked, an eyebrow raised, watching her in amusement.

She shrugged. 'I can't tell.'

They both laughed and Reeta dug back into her pancakes, feeling the sweetness reach her bones.

'Are you going to see Barry now you're out?' Willow asked.

Reeta nodded. 'Maybe. He's done a lot for me. But he's free now too. I want to give him a chance to enjoy his freedom first.'

Willow checked them out and paid for their rooms, while Reeta waited in the car.

'Let's stop at the first store and get you some more clothes. You must be sick of wearing something someone else has told you to.'

Until he'd said it, it had never occurred to Reeta that other people chose what to put on their bodies. She'd admired Carol's elegant fashion and had never quite realised it was a form of self-expression she'd never had available to her. But, she had to concede, the prospect of finding a self to express was daunting and bewildering all at once. They drove for a little while before passing through a nearby town and pulling into the parking lot of a strip mall on its outskirts. Willow directed her toward a building with a sign of a large red dot inside a large red circle.

'I'll grab us some sandwiches from next door so we can eat on the road.' He nodded in the direction of a store called Subway and reached one hand into his back pocket. He pulled out a twenty-dollar bill from his wallet and handed it to her. 'Get yourself whatever you want.'

Her chest grew tight as she watched him disappear into the sandwich shop, but she collected her fractured courage and stepped forward. The doors opened automatically, and her feet stumbled at the shock. They closed again. She took another step and they opened again, inviting her in. Tinny music escaped through the open doors – a lively pop song of the kind Willow had complained about. She passed through the doors, half-expecting them to slam shut on her, but flinched with relief when it seemed she'd made it through the threshold unscathed. The choice was overpowering, racks and rails of clothing sprawled out in front of her. The music seemed to grow louder and her heart pounded in her ears to its beat. She had the urge to flee, to escape back to the car, hand Willow back his twenty and say she was happy with her singular tracksuit.

But no.

That wasn't what Barry had worked so hard for, and it wasn't what Carol would have wanted her to do with her freedom. She picked up a red basket and entered the fray.

It must have been an hour later that she finally left the store, buoyant and giddy, already dressed in new clothes. Even the cashier's odd look at Reeta's scarred face hadn't dampened her mood as she leaned forward to scan the various labels hanging off Reeta's body with her red laser gun. Her grey tracksuit was stuffed into a thin plastic carrier bag and Reeta walked back into the parking lot in brightly coloured leggings covered in geometric shapes and an oversized pink sweatshirt. Willow was leaning against his car smoking a cigarette and sipping from a polystyrene takeaway cup. He grinned when he saw her approach.

'Have fun, then?'

She laughed and held her arms out, twirling for him to see. 'Colour!' she exclaimed giddily.

'I can see that,' he said.

She stopped then and dropped her arms, her plastic bag crinkling loudly with the movement. 'Thank you. You didn't have to do this.' She looked down at her new outfit. 'You didn't have to do any of this.'

'Oh,' Willow said, his tone unexpectedly low. 'I did.'

They climbed back into the car and set off on the long journey back to Washington, DC.

–

Willow's neck was aching, and his eyes were dry and tired. He'd splashed some water on his face at the last rest stop but it had done little to revive him after nine hours of near-solid driving. They'd listened to the radio – he'd introduced her to various genres of music, explained news stories, told her about the different sporting results the DJs discussed. It had been a crash course on life in America in 1983. She'd soaked in the information, hanging visibly on his every word, eager for context to the stories she'd read in newspapers over the years. He hoped he'd done a good enough job.

They arrived back at Carol's house, which Willow had opened again about a month ago. He'd hired a team of cleaners, made up the bed with new sheets, and finally started the process of packing Carol's things into boxes. He'd thought Reeta might want some of it, or at least could help him clear his conscience that it was finally the right thing to do to get rid of it. As he'd moved through the house, folding shirts and pants ready for Reeta or Goodwill, he imagined the life that could have been. The two of them moving around each other with an easy, happy pace, the past forgiven, the gentle rhythm of a shared life restored.

He was older now and out on active duty less. He'd been promoted a couple of times over the years and now occupied a nice supervisory position in the white-collar division. Reading through reams of numbers and corrupt bank transfers from his desk appealed to him far more now than the violent homicides of his youth. Stephens had left the bureau in the early Seventies to consult at a private security firm for a fat cheque. Willow didn't begrudge him the role – he had four kids to put through college and a dead wife's medical bills to still pay off. They didn't see each other much any more.

Willow opened the door and they walked into the small hallway, the kitchen off to the right. Reeta clutched her Target bag in one hand, the only luggage she'd ever owned.

'I've made the bed for you,' he said awkwardly, nodding up the stairs. 'I didn't know if you'd be ready to be alone yet, so I've made myself up a bed on the couch. The second bedroom...' He stalled, unsure how to explain that the second bedroom had been left as a shrine to a long-dead woman's work for eleven years now. 'The second bedroom was Carol's office and I haven't quite cleared it out yet.'

Reeta nodded. If anyone would understand, it was her.

'But I can go home if you'd rather have some space.'

Reeta swallowed. 'Some company would be nice,' she said with a small voice. He could see that she was tired too. Nine hours in close proximity with the man who'd put you in prison for seventeen years, no matter how many nice clothes he bought you, would surely have a toll on anyone's emotions.

'The bathroom is up the stairs and to the right,' he said. 'I'll, ah, leave you to it.'

He moved through to the kitchen and listened as she took herself upstairs, while he opened the fridge he'd stocked up a couple of days before. He'd bought ingredients for grilled cheese and set about making the sandwiches as he heard the shower turning on. What Reeta's future would be, he did not know. He'd help her get her GED or find a job – whatever she wanted out of life, he owed it to her to help make the most of the autumn years that had to be her summer. He shook his head, imagining what Stephens would say to see him helping their cold hard killer all these years later. But life had moved on from those frantic days on her trail – Willow had learned the true agony of grief and with it the soft relief of forgiveness. He knew it wasn't his place to forgive Reeta for her crimes, but she'd served her time and he saw no benefit in allowing the girl to rot. It wasn't what Carol would have done.

Reeta came back down the stairs with straggly wet hair trailing damp patches on the sweatshirt she'd put back on after her shower. He handed her the grilled cheese and they ate on opposite sides of the breakfast bar, chewing in silence.

'I might head to bed,' Reeta said when her plate was clear. 'It's been a long day.'

Willow nodded his goodnight and raised a hand. 'I'll just be down here if you need me.'

'Thank you.'

He heard her creak into the bedroom above him and poured himself a glass of the Scotch he'd added to the basket at the grocery store. He sat down heavily on the couch and kicked off his shoes, staring out at the line of boxes on the other side of the room. The handbag he'd found at the foot of the stairs – the one that Carol must have dropped as she'd rushed to answer the phone the day she died – was on the top of one of the boxes. He put down his drink and moved over to kneel by it, picking it up in his hands, feeling the weight of the expensive crocodile skin.

Carol always had had good taste.

He smiled at the memory and flipped it open. It was jarring to see her wallet again after all these years, fifty dollars still tucked into the note-fold. Her Montblanc pen was clipped to her notebook, full of scribbled short-hand research for the book. He ran his fingers along the silk lining, dipping them into the inside pocket, thinking perhaps he'd find a decade-old pack of Altoids. Instead, his hand brushed against something else.

A photograph.

He pulled it out and stared, his brows flickering in confusion. He flipped it over and saw what Carol had written – and his blood ran cold.

Three

When Reeta woke, it took longer than the usual moments of drowsy disorientation to locate herself. Her back was cradled with squashy pillows and soft sunlight drifted in from behind a mesh curtain overlooking a small yard. She sat upright and stared around the room, blinking into its corners, taking in details, clues of where she was. Why she wasn't in her cell.

She was released.

She'd spent a night in a motel. She'd eaten pancakes and drunk beer. She'd bought her own clothes.

Carol's house. It settled on her with a comforting familiarity as she gazed up at the artwork and framed photos of Carol as a young woman with what was presumably her mother. She stretched and felt her back begin to loosen from the comfortable bed, seventeen years of hard, narrow cots finally falling away. She'd slept in the Kmart tracksuit, her new clothes folded neatly on the chair by the dressing table. She rose without changing and as she headed across the landing she noticed the door to the second bedroom – Carol's office – was ajar. She poked her head around and stepped into the empty room, taking in the still-messy desk and back wall littered with cards marked with names and statements in thick black ink. She inhaled the musty scent and caught sight of the photograph from her birthday party, propped up against the wall.

'I made it, Carol,' she whispered down into the glassy-eyed stare of the picture.

She pulled the door to as she left and went downstairs toward the sounds from the kitchen below.

'Good morning,' she said to the turned back of Willow, as he poured himself a cup from the filter coffee jug in his hands. 'I won't say no to one of those,' she added with a smile as he turned at her greeting.

Willow looked dreadful. Eyes ringed red with purple bags sinking down into his cheeks. He still wore his clothes from yesterday, plaid shirt and jeans crumpled and creased from where he'd been sitting in the car for most of the day.

Reeta blinked in surprise. He evidently hadn't slept as well as she.

'Sorry,' she said. 'Was the couch not comfortable?'

His eyes clouded with confusion for a moment before he seemed to understand what she'd said.

'No, no.' He shook his head. 'The couch is fine. It's not that.'

She glanced back to the couch and noticed the coffee table was a mess of photographs.

'What's all that?' she asked, nodding over.

Willow swallowed and put down the coffee jug and mug, steadying himself on the counter in front of him. 'They're the photographs Carol collected. From the friends of the victims.'

'The photographs of me?' Reeta asked, cricking her head over her shoulder to look back to the table. She moved over and sat down on the couch, taking in the assortment of pictures. Her hand went automatically to the one of her holding the record sleeve, staring into the camera with wide, surprised eyes.

'It's funny,' she said softly. 'Even after all these years, this girl is a stranger to me.'

Willow exhaled, a deep, wavering sound.

'Reeta, I need to speak to you,' he said, his hands braced against the countertop, his body at an angle. She looked up at him, her expression open, enquiring. He sighed gruffly again and pushed himself upright, coming around in front of the breakfast bar to perch on one of the stools. 'You were my hardest case you know?'

'I thought it was open and shut?' she asked, raising an eyebrow, a smirk playing on her lips. It had taken almost two decades, but somehow, now it was all over, the terror of her life seemed almost comical.

'Only once we'd got you. It took *such* a long time to track you down. We just had to keep waiting for another victim to show up, and that's not exactly the best way to conduct police work. We were so...' He struggled for the word and gave up. 'When we got the call about the car crash – about the blonde girl driving the car, with another blonde girl in the trunk – we were so *confident*. Certain we'd finally got the culprit we'd been chasing all that time. It just seemed to fit so well.'

Reeta swallowed thickly and felt the hairs underneath her clothes flicker upright in warning.

'I never thought. It never *occurred* to me...' He trailed off again.

Reeta got to her feet and took a step closer. 'What are you trying to say?' she said slowly.

'I don't know,' Willow admitted, bringing both his palms up to his face and dragging them down so his skin tugged with the movement. 'I honestly don't know.' He dropped his head down toward his lap and with his right hand fished a photograph out of his back pocket. 'I found this last night,' he explained, handing it over. 'It was in the pocket of Carol's bag. The bag she'd been using the day she died, the day they found you...' He nodded to Reeta, who knew he was talking about the morning after she'd jammed a wooden stake into her arm. 'All I knew was she'd been in New York for the day. I never found out what she'd been doing.'

Reeta looked down at the picture in her hands but didn't understand what it had to do with Carol being in New York. It was a photograph she'd never seen before, one that had not made it into the case. But it was her as a young girl, about five or six, with long blonde hair, standing grinning next to Brother Jeb. His hand was draped on her shoulder protectively – possessively.

'That's me,' she said, 'at Pine Ranch?'

Willow closed his eyes. 'Turn it over.'

Reeta did and read what Carol had written on the back, confusion clouding her again.

>   *Found in Bonnie Chandola's apartment. Sept 14th
>   1972.*

Her gaze settled on the two words she'd written below the date and location.

>   *Swapped places?*

—

Reeta stared at him, visibly unable to comprehend what he was trying to tell her.

'Bonnie had this?' she asked after several beats. 'And Carol saw her?'

'Apparently so,' Willow said.

'How... how could Bonnie get this picture?'

Willow blew out his cheeks. 'That' – he gestured to her – 'is the million-dollar question. I've been up all night,' he said, nodding at the coffee table, 'going over every picture of you back then. Trying to understand.'

'Tr-trying to understand what?'

The words felt like hot coal in his mouth. 'Trying to understand if we could have made a mistake.'

She gave a small yelp like an injured bird and stepped backward, falling onto the sofa again, staring at the photograph in her hand.

'You know that Bonnie's cut off everyone from her life before the accident? Refuses to speak to her parents, her friends,' Willow said.

Reeta nodded slowly. Willow braced himself before he asked the question that had been pounding at him all night. 'What if she did that because she didn't want to be caught out?'

He had whispered the words, but they razed through the room with brute force. He watched as Reeta gagged and held a hand to her throat, the photograph of Brother Jeb and the young blonde girl falling to the plush green carpet. He felt tears prick at his eyes and guilt bind him. They stayed in choking silence for a few moments before Reeta spoke again.

'How?' she asked, looking to him. The word was hard, furious. 'How could you have made a mistake?'

He shook his head. 'I... I don't know. I don't know if we did. But...' He paused, calculating how to verbalise the explanation he'd spent the night building. 'When the car came off the road,' he said, inhaling deeply, 'there's a chance that Bonnie fought back.'

'What do you mean?' Reeta asked slowly.

'That Bonnie managed to subdue Reeta with the hammer in self-defence. That she put Reeta in the trunk. And she drove away. When the car crashed, it was Bonnie behind the wheel. Not Reeta.'

Reeta was sick then. She leaped to her feet and raced into the kitchen, and Willow turned away as she retched into the sink.

Reeta stood for a few moments, her hands resting on either side of the silver basin. When she turned to him, her body remained still, but her face twisted into sheer rage.

'Are you telling me,' she said slowly, 'that the *only* reason I was initially identified as the culprit is because I was driving the car?'

Willow did not know what to say. The truth was that yes, that was why she'd first been identified as the culprit. It had made sense – it had all made sense. They'd got their girl – caught her in the act.

'It made sense,' he told the woman before him and he knew how weak it sounded. How pathetic a reason it was that they'd stolen her life.

'But her parents.' There was a desperate note to her voice that pained Willow to hear. 'They were in court. If – if they saw me, wouldn't they know?'

He'd thought about this through the long night. 'With the injuries you both have, there's a chance they wouldn't recognise you. She barely saw them after the accident. And as far as I can tell from Carol's notes, Bonnie never contacted them again after the court case ended.' He shook his head, guilt dragging up an unwanted memory from that first Italian dinner with Carol all those years ago. *Even with her face like that?* She'd asked. 'Carol even asked me if the witnesses could be trusted. She'd seen it, even back then – how could any witness identify you beyond a reasonable doubt when you look like-,' he raised a hand limply in her direction, 'well, like that.'

Reeta turned back to the sink and seemed to comprehend what he'd said.

'They found my hair,' she said before shaking her head in correction. 'They found *someone's* hair. They said it was mine.'

Willow closed his eyes and blew out a sigh. 'That science was never as accurate as we thought. We've all but stopped using it now.'

'So there's nothing?' Reeta snapped her head back toward him. 'You're telling me there's *nothing*! There's no case. There was never a case?' Willow couldn't answer, he hung his head low and stared at his knees while Reeta paced the kitchen. 'How can we find out?' she asked after a moment, her tone calmer than before.

'I… I don't know,' Willow admitted.

'There must be something! I need to know!' Reeta raised her voice and slammed her palm down onto the kitchen counter. Willow shook his head, at a loss.

'I need to go to New York,' she said after several thick moments. 'I need to see her.'

Willow nodded, understanding. 'I'll take you.'

Four

Willow didn't balk at the immediacy of her request, nor did he comment on the fact that she hadn't showered or changed since she woke up, or delay for a few minutes so he could finish his coffee. He stood abruptly and reached for his keys, grabbing a brown worker jacket on his way to the door. He knew the Chandolas' address from those days at the bureau when he'd been trying to persuade Bonnie to speak. There was every chance they'd moved, and if they had then Ben would call in whatever favours he needed to track them down.

'Agent Willow.' Reeta's voice stopped him just as they reached the door, and he turned to face her where she'd followed him into the hallway. Her expression had softened and her throat trembled a little as she spoke. 'Thank you,' she whispered. 'For picking me up from jail, for, for letting me stay here.'

'Reeta, I—'

'No.' She held up a hand to stop him speaking. 'Whatever we find out. I just wanted to say' – she straightened her shoulders and looked him firmly in the eye – 'I forgive you.' He felt a lump of emotion in his chest. 'Whether I did them or not, my life has been bettered by people willing to forgive the crimes they believe of me. So, whether you made a mistake or not…' She gave a single nod. 'I'll forgive you.'

Willow gave her a small, appreciative smile. 'I think you're going to do just fine out here.'

He drove confidently up the highway – the journey to New York was one he'd taken many times before, on cases, for conferences, even the odd social weekend away. He only had to stop to consult the map when they reached the city limits because the Chandolas' exact address was in an area he was not familiar with. He pulled up outside the building on the opposite side of the road and turned to Reeta. Or was she Bonnie? No, Reeta – they didn't know anything yet. She looked a state, her frantic eyes heavy with bags hung low beneath them. Flyaway hair she made only worse by constantly running her fingers through it. Her tracksuit overwhelmed her small body and her sneakers were too new and bright white.

'I'll get you in,' he said, patting the inside pocket of his jacket where his FBI ID rested. 'And I'll be waiting out here for whenever you're ready.'

She nodded.

'Are you sure you don't want to get something to eat before you do this? You haven't eaten yet today.'

She shook her head. 'I couldn't eat now.'

He nodded and climbed out of the car. She followed.

It had taken some persuading of the doorman that the unkempt woman in the cheap tracksuit had any sort of FBI business with the glamorous couple in the penthouse. But Willow had been an agent a long time; he knew how to bluff his way past people. When the doorman finally permitted them entry, Willow saw the look of confused dismay when the agent with the ID had turned on his heel to leave the woman unescorted inside. The doorman's mouth gaped a little, and Willow turned back to see the calculation of whether to question what the hell was going on dart across his face. The doorman caught Willow's stern look and opened the door for Reeta in resignation.

Five

The building was grander inside than anything Reeta had experienced before. She'd had to get the concierge on duty to show her how to pull the grille across the elevator, and to press the correct button for her. She saw him glance over his shoulder at the doorman, silently questioning how on earth this woman had been let in.

The carpet was gold and plush and she could feel the spring against her sneakers as she made her way down the hallway to number 56. The Chandolas.

Would this have been her life? No, she figured, probably not.

She stood and stared at the front door for at least a minute, unmoving, unblinking, allowing the dark varnished wood to swim in and out of focus. Why was she there, really? Nothing would change. She would still be free, and her years of incarceration could never be undone. Bonnie – the real Reeta, she was now sure – would never pay for her crimes. How could they prove anything?

But *she* would know.

She would know that the false memories planted in her mind over the last two decades were never hers. She'd know that the goodness she'd always felt course through her was real, not just a reaction to her guilt.

She would know who she was, finally.

She raised a hand and knocked on the door.

Six

The car was too stuffy, despite the cold New York winter, and Willow chose instead to stand outside, leaning on its hood in the chilly air. The sky was grey and the weatherman had predicted snow across the north-east coast next week. Reeta would never have seen snow before, he thought with an ache. He could take her to Meridian Hill Park, show her the children building snowmen and pelting each other with snowballs. The thought made him smile. Whatever Reeta learned from Bonnie, she was free now. She could build a life – he would make sure she did. He lit a cigarette and looked up at the building, wondering what was going on inside.

Seven

A young Latina girl opened the door with a nervous, questioning smile.

'I'm here to see Mrs Chandola,' Reeta said.

It took a moment for the girl to respond and when she did Reeta saw it was because she struggled with English. Reeta repeated it in the Spanish that Gloria had painstakingly taught her.

The girl smiled in relief at the language shift. '*Lo siento, ella no está aquí.*' *I'm sorry, she's not here.*

Reeta didn't believe her. She stuck her foot in the door gap and shouldered her way in, the startled young maid jumping back with a yelp. Reeta found herself in a short hallway with a round table at the centre supporting a giant vase overflowing with dramatic lilies. Gold striped wallpaper led her down the hallway into the plush living room, the girl following her with increasingly louder protests, grabbing at her arm, pleading with her to leave. The wide French windows were open, blowing a cold breeze into the apartment, and a figure wearing black slacks and cashmere jumper was smoking a cigarette from a twisted mouth.

She turned at the commotion, one side of her temple permanently fallen in above her eye, her skin as shiny and puckered as Reeta's own. She saw Reeta and her hand stopped on its arc toward her mouth, the glowing embers of the cigarette an orange pinpoint in the grey day.

'I heard you'd been released,' she said with a scratchy voice. Her eyes flicked to the girl behind Reeta. 'Constance, take the rest of the day off.' When the girl didn't move, she rolled her eyes and snapped, 'Leave! Go. Home. Now.'

Constance hesitated before seemingly comprehending, and the two women stared into each other's mangled faces in silence while the maid gathered her things and fled the apartment.

'So,' Bonnie said, taking another drag of her cigarette with a forced casual air. 'Come to finish the job?' Her mouth smirked and her eyes narrowed with menace.

Reeta walked forward, passing the threshold of the French doors onto the balcony, a thick stone wall with built-in benches and planters all around them. The cold penetrated quickly through her thin sweatshirt, but Reeta barely noticed her shivering limbs.

'I probably should,' she hissed. 'You stole seventeen years of my life.'

Bonnie frowned, as much as she could. '*I* stole *your* life?' She cackled a harsh laugh at the thought.

'Come on, *Reeta*.' She flung away the name she'd become accustomed to as her own. It was dirty and tainted and she didn't want it any more. The more she stared at this stranger before her, the more she knew the moniker must belong to her. 'There's no one else around. Just little old me. You can admit it.'

'Admit *what* exactly?' The mocking tone had gone now, replaced with an earnest severity.

'That they got it wrong. *I'm* Bonnie Powell. When we pulled off the road and fought, I hit you with the hammer

333

in self-defence. I put you in the trunk. I... I was driving off to find help, not take you to Cuba.' The mouth of the woman opposite her gaped just a touch, but the rest of her face was unreadable. 'They got it all wrong; they just assumed I was the one because I was driving the car.' She had to pause to collect herself as short, sharp breaths threatened to overtake her speech. 'I couldn't remember anything – couldn't dispute them – I had no choice but to accept it—' She broke off and shook her head, tears spilling down her face. 'You must have thought you'd gotten so lucky, waking up free and innocent. A new name, a whole *life* available for the taking. *My* life.'

Bonnie coughed in disbelief. 'Are you *fucking serious*?' She remained oddly collected, unnervingly still. 'You think *I'm* the sadistic bitch that killed all those girls?' Her voice was not quite a whisper, but it was not loud; it was not irate in its defence.

'You cut off everyone. Your parents, your friends. You knew they'd catch you out.' With shaking hands, Reeta retrieved her trump card from the pocket of her sweatpants. She held the photograph out in front of her and said with a shaking voice, 'And *you* hold onto your memories from Pine Ranch.'

Eight

Bonnie stared at the photograph. She blinked a couple of times before making an awkward, limping movement forward.

'How?' she asked, her voice faltering for the first time, her head cocked to one side in questioning. Suddenly she exhaled in comprehension and looked back to Reeta. 'Your friend,' she said. 'The journalist. She took it?'

'You met Carol, that day, didn't you? That's why she was in New York.'

'She came here to interview me. Or under the pretence of interviewing me, but it seems she came to rob me instead.' Bonnie nodded down at the photo. 'I knew she was close to you. I've read her articles. So, I was curious.' She looked around her palatial home. 'The surroundings might be a bit nicer, but I'm as trapped here as I was at Pine Ranch.'

Reeta inhaled sharply.

'This *is* you?' she asked, nodding down to the photo.

'Of course it's me,' Bonnie said. 'That's why I have it. It's of me; it belongs to me. I'm tired of my life belonging to other people.'

'So you *are* Reeta?'

Bonnie gave a deep sigh then and closed her eyes, turning her face into the cool breeze of the morning.

'Can you pass me my cane?' she said, nodding to the cane that was leaning up against the patio furniture.

Uncertainly, Reeta obliged. Bonnie moved with the same uneven *shuffle-thunk* as she had done in the courtroom, and it took an unnervingly long time for her to make it inside. Reeta stood dead still and watched as she approached the sideboard and wrenched open one of the drawers, retrieving a wooden box from within. It occurred to Reeta, perhaps too late, that Bonnie might be fetching a weapon – a gun or knife. But Reeta found she couldn't move. All she wanted was to know.

Bonnie walked back at the same painfully slow pace and handed Reeta the box.

'What your friend didn't do when she was rooting through my possessions,' she said, 'is root hard enough.'

Reeta looked down at the box and felt her uncertainty solidify. She flipped down the clasp and tipped open the hinged lid. Inside were some folded papers, which Reeta picked up, revealing more photographs underneath.

The very first one Reeta saw sent a shockwave through her.

A landscape picture of a large plantation home and a lawn of wildflowers out front. And standing in the middle of the long porch steps – two young, blonde girls.

Bonnie watched her take it in. And then she started to speak.

Florida II

'It *is* you, isn't it?' Bonnie asked, her words slurring slightly from the beer. Big Jerry's still pulsed behind them, the stoned crew still holding forth on the doorstep.

Bonnie had been trying to push it away. Trying to stop the memories from bubbling up as she'd left the blonde girl to go back inside to dance. She was just a hippy weirdo, she'd told herself. But when she'd walked out the bar to take herself home, she'd seen Gideon's old station wagon pulled up on the side of the road.

'I thought you'd recognise me straight away,' Reeta said. She was, as ever, unreadable.

Bonnie shook her head. 'I don't understand. How, *how?* There was a fire – I saw it on the news. They said there were no survivors.'

Reeta's eyes shone with glee and she reached out to grab at Bonnie's forearms, pinching them tight. 'God's miracle,' she whispered. 'I survived so I could come back for you. The angels of Pine Ranch.'

Bonnie pushed her away, shaking her head. 'No,' she said, her throat thick. 'No. I don't *ever* want to hear that again.' But it was too late. Her childhood was soaring in front of her.

She'd been only four when her parents had heard of Jeb's mission and driven them from their home near Dallas to the compound of Pine Ranch. There had been only

337

one other child back then, exactly her age and with the same bright blonde hair, freckled tanned face and dark hazel brown eyes.

'My angels of Pine Ranch,' Jeb would say, cupping their chins in his broad, rugged hands. 'God brought you to us, Leah. An identical angel to work with our Reeta.'

It had taken eight years of hardship and abuse before her parents had lost their blinkers. Whatever faith they'd had in the Lord had been stripped away by their increasingly maniacal leader. He'd removed the radio and telephone for no reason, claiming them not worthy of such luxury. He demanded families split up, and Leah and Reeta were moved from their mothers' bedsides to be the first residents of the draughty, flimsy dormitories her father had been forced to build. Rations became unreliable and hunger became the norm.

And Jeb's wives started to be chosen younger and younger.

'We must leave.' Her mother had woken her and Reeta up one night when they were twelve. Her voice had been barely a breath and she'd signalled with a finger to her lips that silence was imperative. The girls had climbed groggily from their beds, not understanding what was being asked of them. Leah's mother led them across the waterlogged grass, their bare feet slipping in the mud of the lawn, and down toward the edge of the wood, where Abra came running to greet them.

'Paul has the car waiting on the other side of the wood,' Leah's mother told her. 'He picked it up from Terry this morning when he was meant to be out fixing the guttering at the Wheton farm. We've got to go quickly.'

Abra had looked at them, her eyes wide and terrified in her tiny head. She reached out an arm and pulled Reeta back toward her, gripping the young girl tightly to her body.

'Abra, please, we must go!'

'No,' Abra said, voice trembling. 'No. We are pious. We are dedicated to Jeb. Our plans were sinful. They were the devil. No. We mustn't go.'

Leah's mother had not waited to argue. Leah's arm was yanked back and then she was running. Her blonde hair whipping through the branches, only one last look back at the sister who'd wailed in anguish as they'd fled.

The grown Reeta who stood before her now was indeed one of Jeb's children. Determination oozed out of every pore, dedication to that man.

'But we are the angels!' Reeta snapped. '*We* were the last pure perfection of Jeb's mission. We needed to start again. I tried so hard to find other angels – other angels for Jeb, but they weren't worthy,' she spat and her top lip flickered into a snarl. 'They weren't pure or true. But then I understood – my failures had taught me that *you* are the only one worthy. I knew that I needed to find *you* – my sister, Jeb's angel.' Her voice softened as she gazed at her. 'And now I've found you – the *real*, true you. We *can* start again.'

Debbie stumbled out of the bar then and called to Bonnie. 'Do you want some weed?'

Bonnie shook her head frantically, desperate to keep her past from tainting her future.

'Come with me,' Reeta implored.

'Fine, fine, whatever,' Bonnie said, reaching for the car door. 'You can give me a ride home.'

It soon became clear that Reeta intended to do no such thing.

'Jeb *is* your home,' she told her, over and over again, babbling about Cuba, about their new ark. She wouldn't listen to Bonnie's reason. She wouldn't listen when Bonnie told her she was free now. She could live whatever life she pleased; Pine Ranch was done – gone forever.

'We will rebuild!' Reeta screeched, the speed of the car ramping up.

'Reeta, please,' Bonnie begged, but she wasn't listening. Bonnie had no choice. She leaned over the central console and pulled at the steering wheel, turning the car into the field on the side of the road. Luckily Reeta plunged her foot onto the brake pedal and, after a winded moment, they were still.

Bonnie got out of the car.

'I'm walking home,' she said.

'You can't.' Reeta got out too. 'Not now I've found you.'

Bonnie stopped walking, a frown on her face as she turned back toward Reeta. 'How *did* you find me?'

'I called your parents.' Bonnie spluttered, and Reeta explained. 'I called your parents and pretended to be an old friend from camp. I've met enough college girls over the last six months; I've picked up enough details to make it convincing.' Her face turned hard at the memory of the phone call. 'They are such traitors,' she spat. 'But they are fools and they told me you were here at college. I've been here two weeks, just waiting to see you.'

'How did you know where my parents are?' A cold chill was beginning to creep through Bonnie now.

Reeta's eyes brightened and she smiled. 'Jeb.' She returned to the car and opened the trunk, gesturing to an old military backpack. 'He left me the trail to find you.'

Bonnie frowned and moved toward the trunk, her hands flipping open the flap of the backpack. Inside was a stack of papers, some of Caleb's old photos underneath. She unfolded the first few pages and saw letters from Zechariah to Jeb, reporting on Bonnie's family over the years. The most recent was from earlier last year, informing Jeb that soon Leah would be attending college, although he did not know where.

'He was keeping tabs on us?' she whispered.

'He was always watching over you.' Reeta moved closer, the smile audible in her words. 'Always protecting you.'

Bonnie staggered back; she felt ill.

'No,' she said, 'no, no. We thought we'd got away. But he was *watching* us. The whole time? He's sick, he's sick. He's sick in the head, Reeta!' She turned to her old friend and screamed in desperation. Sure that if she could just shout it loudly enough, something might rattle Reeta's senses free. 'You can't go back to him! You could be free! He's evil, Reeta, he's *evil!*'

But Reeta wasn't listening. Her face was contorted, and she was bending into the trunk to retrieve something.

The next thing Bonnie knew, she was in hospital

'What happened?' she croaked, blinking into the bright lights.

'You were in a car crash,' a soft voice said to her right. She tilted her head agonisingly to see a young man in a blue police uniform. 'But you're safe now.'

She swallowed thickly and blinked around the room, the fuzziness settling into focus on an old brown backpack on the chair next to her bed.

'Don't worry,' the young officer said with a smile. 'I made sure that came with you in the ambulance. You were

341

clutching it to yourself, wouldn't let it go. Pretty adamant you wouldn't leave it.'

She'd blinked, trying to recollect. It was all a blur. 'I don't remember.'

'Well, you've been in and out of consciousness, the docs say that's normal.' He paused awkwardly and Bonnie could tell pastoral care was not this guy's strong suit. 'So, you got a big term paper in that bag or something?' He nodded to the chair. 'I had to have a quick glance inside,' he held up his hands apologetically, 'just doing my job. You got a lot of pages of notes in there.' He smiled again. 'Don't worry I didn't read them, my sister's always tellin' me you *don't go reading a woman's stuff.*' He chuckled to himself. 'Now you get some more rest. I'm on duty here 'til midday. But don't worry – you're safe now.'

Nine

Reeta was floored.

'The police didn't even look through your backpack?' In light of everything Bonnie had just told her, she recognised this was a small thing to fixate on. But she'd been so used to her entire life being pawed over, her memories prodded and toyed with, that it didn't seem fair that Bonnie had got away with such privacy.

Bonnie gave half a shrug. 'The first guy on the scene was an idiot. Just some local beat cop. He didn't have any idea who we were, and I guess by the time the agents turned up he was too embarrassed to tell them there was another backpack that could be considered evidence.'

Reeta stared at Bonnie for a long, silent beat. Only one tiny flicker of hope licked into her mind, one last grasp that maybe this woman was lying.

'But your parents,' she said quietly. 'You cut them off. So they wouldn't recognise you.'

'Oh, they recognised me all right,' Bonnie said. 'And they recognised you. And they knew at once what had happened. And do you know what they wanted to do? They wanted to run again. They wanted me to flee whatever life I've been trying so desperately to build so I can forget the horror of the place *they* took me to. *They* took me to Pine Ranch, and they barely saved me in time.'

Bonnie looked her up and down. 'Have you been told you might have a child out there?'

The words were harsh, bitter and Reeta remembered with a lurch what Valerie had told her.

'My father heard Jeb telling Zechariah that as soon as our bloods came we would be the next to carry his seed.' She sneered at the phrasing as she said it. 'That was why we escaped. So no, I didn't want to run again. My parents are pathetic and weak, and all they wanted was for us to escape to some other bland town. But I wanted to see you pay for what you'd done to me. What, I later found out, you'd done to others too. I couldn't face my parents any more – every decision they'd ever made had failed to keep me safe.

'My friends I didn't want to see flourish when I couldn't. It was petty and jealous, I know, but I just *couldn't*. But Henry...' She exhaled, a plume of warm, smoky breath floating up into the sky. 'Henry met me at the worst time of my life. The lowest ebb I will ever reach, and he offered to keep me safe. And he has. He's given me all this, even when I can give him *nothing* but a mangled body and my undying loyalty.'

Reeta felt Bonnie scrutinising her for a moment before she spoke again.

'All I wanted that night was just to go for a drink. Just a drink, like a normal college girl. Have a dance with some friends, maybe get stoned. Just live a normal life, because I knew how precious that is. And because of *you*' – she jabbed her finger again – 'a girl I once considered a sister' – her voice broke over the word – 'I woke up like, like this.' She pointed, panting, to her screwed-up face. 'Do you know I had to relearn how to read and write? *That's* what your hammer blow did to me. I *still* have to have physiotherapy to keep me walking. Do you have any idea of the shame of being in your twenties and thirties with a fucking cane?' She shook her head and Reeta could see tears blister her eyes, but she knew Bonnie had too much pride to shed them in front of her.

There was silence for a few moments before Reeta could reply. When she spoke, though, her voice had lost its previous conviction. 'You've had seventeen years to live your own lies, to start believing them.'

The way Bonnie looked at her then scorched her more deeply than any other wound or guilt Reeta had had to bear.

She looked at her with pity

Bonnie shook her head. 'Our faces are scarred, Reeta, but not that much.' A gust of wind billowed around her then and her expression was one of incredulity. 'How...' she said, taking an unexpected step forward, '*how* could you ever believe that was a possibility?'

Reeta didn't answer; she couldn't move. She hadn't felt so blank since that first day waking up in the hospital all those years ago. She blinked, trying to block out Bonnie, who was still questioning her, getting impatient with her silence, her voice rising and rising with frustration and fury.

'Tell me! How do you *dare* come here after all you did – all you did to me?' Bonnie's chest fell, her body stopping still. 'After everything you did to me,' she repeated in barely a whisper, shaking her head, visibly searching for what to say. 'You really thought...' She trailed off again, her eyebrows pulling together into a questioning frown as much as her scars allowed. 'How?' she repeated one final time.

Reeta stared at her, unmoving, uncomprehending. Blank and confused, as she had always been. How *could* she have believed it?

Because she'd needed to.

Ten

Willow finished his cigarette and walked to a nearby trashcan to dispose of the stub. The walk warmed his limbs and it felt good to move in the brisk cold air. He returned to his car and paced up and down, still unable to face sitting back down inside the vehicle he'd spent the better part of three days in.

He turned back to the building and looked up, squinting into the low winter sun.

And then he knew.

Reeta would never see snow.

And he wished he'd taken her for pancakes first.

Eleven

Reeta remained on the balcony as the chilled wind ran through her. Her head hung as she looked at her hands poking out from beneath baggy sleeves. Reeta ran her eyes formulaically up and down each finger and thumb, zigzagged across each palm, looped around to the freckled, wrinkly back and swooped down toward each nail bed.

These hands still told a story.

They told the same story they always had, but she just hadn't wanted to read it.

She thought of Carol. Of how much she'd sacrificed, how she must have died thinking there could be hope for Reeta Doe. Reeta stumbled to one side; she felt faint and allowed her feet to take her clumsily toward the thick barricade surrounding the balcony. Her hands fell forward onto the stone, her palms smarting against the cold, and she breathed in deep, wretched breaths of air that froze her windpipe on its way down. Her vision blurred with tears staring down onto the thick grey slabs pockmarked with pigeon shit. She blinked them away, adjusting her gaze to the street below. Willow was down there, only a speck from this distance, but she could see him pacing up and down by the car. He was probably having a smoke. What exactly could she tell him? That there had been no mistake. That he'd been right to hate her as much as he had. That his conscience was clear.

She couldn't face it all over again. The awful shame, the hope ripped away, the truth about who she was.

And she knew there was no other option.

There was no way through for Reeta Doe. Only one way out.

She knew what had to be done as her legs stepped mechanically onto the inbuilt bench, deliberate, methodical movements that she felt ricochet through her.

She was vaguely aware of a question from Bonnie behind her, a question that soared into a scream as Reeta climbed onto the very edge of the penthouse balcony. She closed her eyes and raised her arms out to the side, catching the satisfying cold of the wind whipping her hair across her twisted face.

'Reeta, what are you doing?' pummelled into her ears, but it was too late.

Nothing but air cradled her limbs.

True freedom, at last, for the final few moments of the life of Reeta Doe.

Epilogue

The police had cleared out a few hours ago.

Her statement had been taken with the same repeated thoroughness as the last time Bonnie had had cause to talk to the police. But there was not much for them to do now, except clear up the body and set up a cordon to hold back the press.

Bonnie had been surprised to see the FBI agent again after all these years. He'd been the one to call the police, while she was still standing shell-shocked on the balcony. He'd seen Reeta jump of her own free will – this time, there was no question about what had happened.

Henry had rushed home from the office as soon as she'd called, and now he was making her hot tea in the kitchen. His role as her protector and saviour ever more reinforced.

She sat on the couch and steadied her breath – deep, comforting gulps of air. Grief rolled through her, rising and falling in a confused mash of rage and mourning.

In her hand she held the photograph Reeta had brought back.

Her thumb rubbed softly over Brother Jeb's face. She closed her eyes for just a moment and saw wildflowers and prairie, heard childhood laughter and felt the certainty of the Word as warm as the sun on her skin. She got to her feet and stowed the photograph safely back in the box where it belonged.

Acknowledgements

I was always very private about my writing life, it was just a personal project I kept to myself – so my first thanks really has to be my agent Clare at The Liverpool Literary Agency for taking me on and giving me a reason to celebrate my writing and bring those closest to me in on my secret ambition. Thank you for believing in Reeta's story and for supporting me in telling it the way I wanted to. On this note, too, my editor Louise for all your insight on whipping it into shape – you made this novice a professional. Thanks to Curtis Brown Creative for accepting me on your three-month novel writing course, which set the first draft of Reeta up to be something so much more than anything else I'd written. Extra special thanks to Silvester, Kerry and Grace for all your time and insight since the course finished. Finally, but most importantly – my friends and family. Katie, Steph and Shaz – you read this first and I couldn't be more grateful for your feedback, Zoom book clubs and insane level of cheerleading. You've been by my side for 26 years for a reason and I couldn't love you more. Hannah, Steve, Theo, Ruby, Tim and Sarah for just being genuinely the most proud and supportive family. Mum and Dad, there is no one else to whom this book could be dedicated – you've believed in every ambition I've ever had and your love has never failed – I truly know how lucky I am. And lastly Dave and Butter for putting up with me and always making me smile even if I don't want to. Thank you for making me (as a wise woman Charlotte York once said) happy every day.

My dream wouldn't have happened without any of you.